Sweet FA

'This is *First Wives* territory, no ... ...ping, changing and making a stand very much at its centre. It ... ...arious in parts, but thought-provoking and emotional in others.'
The Bookseller.

'C...ham's uproarious tale of a group of women who refuse to come second best to the beautiful ga... a sassy, modern tale of revenge!'
C...*mopolitan.*

...le of four women being driven mad by their partners' obsession with football ...heir revenge in a variety of ways is irresistible.'

...n Curham tells the tale in a funny, often moving and sharply accurate style, weaving ...g... e ... judices (both male and female) into an entertaining read.'
Bolt... ...News.

...ys Relapse

...h ...e cover that this was a chick-lit novel, but it is so much more than that. ...th to the characters and the love story between Jed and Caitlin. Curham has ...ialogue, even in the various regional dialects she reproduces so apparently ...e evocation of the period and the observation of teenage girls is perfect and ...ng this book was a sheer delight. Get ready for whatever this splendid and ...author comes up with next.
...*in...dard.*

'A deli... ...vel, very assured, extremely funny, well observed and ultimately genuinely movi... ...g to a climactic and rewarding ending. Compelling characters, distinctly drawn.'
Con... ...ns.

Th... ...tealers

'A ve... ...l written comedy with a touch of tragedy. Entertaining and thought-provoking. Rea... ...g this book is like spending a cosy evening with your best friend.'
Co...m... ... Book of the Month.

'... ...about a group of film buffs who come together to recreate their favourite movie ...wi... themselves in the starring roles. Set around the unique Pirate Videos Shop this is ...lity for the film world. Perfect blend of comedy and poignancy.
...or.*

Finding The Plot

a novel

Siobhan Curham

authorHOUSE®

AuthorHouse™ UK Ltd.
500 Avebury Boulevard
Central Milton Keynes, MK9 2BE
www.authorhouse.co.uk
Phone: 08001974150

First published by AuthorHouse   9/5/2007

ISBN: 978-1-4343-2769-7 (sc)

Printed in the United States of America
Bloomington, Indiana

This book is printed on acid-free paper.

For Steve O'Toole
—for helping me 'find my own plot,' and making it such a fun one.

For Curly Martin at Achievement Specialists
- a life coaching genius whose course changed my life.

And for Jack, as always.

Acknowledgements

I would like to say a huge THANK-YOU to all the people who have given me so much encouragement and support in getting this book into print – 'going it alone' has never felt so un-lonely! Mikey, Anne, Bea, Luke and Alice. Steve O'Toole, Tina McKenzie, Ginny and Jim Annison, Cassandra, Charlotte Baldwin, Stuart Berry, Wally Robson, Darren Deeks, Julia Buckley, Phil Lawder, Anjan Saha, Patti Linders, Frances Low, Liz O'Keefe, Debbie and Chris Tutton, Victoria Connelly, Judy Chilcote. A huge thanks to all of the members of the writing workshops I run for making Tuesday and Wednesday nights so enjoyable – Sonya Weiss, Larry Dainty, Margaret Hibbert, Sue Hubberstey, Ron Balsdon, Kehryse Johnson, Kaye Seeley, Jan Silverman, James Lee, Matt Snoding, Pete Haynes, Beren Reid and Jai to name but a few. Rita, Ian, Nadine, Jennie, Suzanne and all the other 'Finding the Plotters.' Thank you to all of the readers who have emailed me from around the world with such lovely messages about my books – it means so much to get such positive feedback. A huge thank-you to Dale Arndell and Steve Porter at Harrow Council and Liz McMillan, Claire Harris and Eileen Smyth at Hillingdon for your continued support. A big 'wassup!' to my cousin Sam in Detroit – my US sales manager - and all of my American family. And to my very dear friend and brilliant artist Paul Molyneaux for making sense of my ramblings and ridiculous sketches. To my 'favourite ex-husband' Colin Phillips and a massive thank-you as always to our wonderful son Jack, for being such an inspiration and playing on your play station whilst I got the final draft finished! And lastly I would like to thank my very good friend and life coach extraordinaire Lexie Bebbington for all of her expert guidance whilst I was writing this book, particularly for telling me to 'get messy' with it! I hope you all enjoy the result...

"Show me the face you wore before you were born."

Buddhist saying.

chapter One

"Life is a bountiful journey and one of the finest gift it blesses us with is gratitude." Megan Rowe, 'Help Yourself to Happiness.'

Something had changed and yet nothing had changed. Megan was still curled on top of her tall double bed. The bank of patchwork cushions were still propped against the brass bedpost. The bedroom was still steeped in darkness, save the silvery finger of moonlight poking through the crack in the curtains and pooling out across the polished beech floor. All around her the house still slept. The cooling pipes sighed as they contracted, the eaves creaked and moaned. And across the landing in his musky, parent-free enclave, Laurence still no doubt dreamt of cricketing glory. But something had changed. In the brief second it had taken for Megan to wake up and watch the alarm clock on the bedside cabinet flick from 2.59 to 3.00am there had been a seismic shift. Not in the deserted expanse of Nightingale Avenue; out there the cold wind continued to whistle through the elm trees and the neighbourhood cats continued to prowl like flitting shadows. But as Megan had watched those burning red digits flick into their new order, so too a new order had clicked into place in her mind. *No more,* a voice was saying in her head, tight and measured and white-hot with rage. *No more.*

Megan reached over to the bedside cabinet and turned on the stained glass lamp, causing the white quilt to be bathed in a reflected

1

mosaic of orange and red and blue. She looked at the leather bound journal beside her.

'My Bountiful Journal of Joy.'

Megan read the golden script curling its way across the label on the cover and shuddered. Shifting into a cross-legged position she opened the book and turned to the first thick, creamy page ~ *'Let the quality of the journal you choose reflect the quality of the life you lead'* ~ who had she been trying to kid?

'Five Things That Have Brought Me Joy Today,' her ornate script declared.

1. Going back to bed this morning, after Gerry had left for the theatre and Laurence had sloped off to cricket, to feast on warm pain au chocolat and frothy cappuccino and lose myself in Margaret Atwood's latest novel (until the window cleaner made a surprise appearance at the window, causing me to almost asphyxiate on a mouthful of pastry – hmm, possibly more humiliating than joyful?)

2. Having a healthy teenage son – at least I assume from the huge amounts of food he consumes and the occasional grunted communication he offers that he is still alive and enjoying reasonably good health.

3. Being healthy in my late thirties, as I approach forty, as I approach middle age and all the health problems that will inevitably follow.

4. Having a marriage that offers me plenty of personal space. Space to pursue my own career, space to be myself, space on the sofa on a Saturday night when the bastard hasn't come home yet again.

Needless to say she'd never got to number five. Unable to find a 'joyful' event from her day that didn't somehow end up with a miserable or humiliating twist, she had flung it to one side and fallen into a dejected, tear-stained sleep.

Megan took the gold nibbed fountain pen ~ *'Let the richness of the ink reflect the depth of love now coursing through your veins'* ~ from her dressing gown pocket and sliced through the entry with a thick dark line. 'One Thing That Has Brought Me Abject Misery for the Past Fifteen Years of My Life,' she wrote underneath. 'GERRY RADCLIFFE.'

She slammed the journal shut and examined the photo she had stuck on the cover ~ *'Let the picture you choose symbolise your own personal vision of joy'* ~ Megan had chosen a holiday snap from ten years before. It was taken after Gerry had been offered the job of directing a controversial new American play at The Royal Court following almost a year out of work. It had been his 'big break' – the first of many as it transpired – and they had decided to celebrate with a cottage holiday in Devon before rehearsals began. When Megan had been rooting through the family photo albums earlier, buzzing from the cappuccino and Gerry's false promises of dinner, a movie and an 'early night,' it had seemed the perfect choice, the three of them stood, windswept and tanned, arms wrapped around each other, a tight little unit against the wild Dartmoor backdrop. Hadn't such a family portrait always been her personal vision of joy? But now as she studied the picture in the coloured glow of the bed-side lamp the tell-tale flaws in the vision were all too apparent. The way Gerry's eyes were straying off longingly to the left, to the rambling eighteenth century inn just out of shot. And the clenched jaw propping up Megan's rictus grin as she contemplated yet another afternoon spent trying to amuse their restless four year old son Laurence whilst her husband bonded with yet another inn-keeper over yet another flagon of 'authentic' local cider. It was like a scene from the *Most Haunted*

TV show – 'Now if you look carefully at this freeze frame of Derek at the entrance to the Hampton Court maze you can just make out the headless shadow of Anne Boleyn over by the hotdog stand.' Only in Megan's case it was the spectre of a doomed marriage that hung, mist-like over the moor.

Megan glanced at the clock radio on the bedside table. 3:05 the display flashed in dazzling red, like a neon sign advertising her sham of a marriage. She closed her eyes tightly and hugged her knees to her chest. But it was too late, now the neon sign was scrolling like a ticker tape across her mind. *3:05 . . . AND HE STILL ISN'T HOME, YOU KNOW WHAT THAT MEANS DON'T YOU?* Megan sighed and opened her eyes. Of course she knew what it meant. After almost fifteen years of marriage she knew only too well that if Gerry wasn't back before twelve there was the distinct possibility he wouldn't be home at all that night. But it didn't matter anymore because something had changed. The moment she had woken up and found herself curled on top of her bed surrounded by a cluster of cold sodden tissues and that wretched journal she knew something was different. And as she watched the clock flick its way deeper into the night a strange sense of detachment descended upon her. All of the hot angry tears of earlier, the congealed dinner scraped into the bin, the tired, pathetic excuses, *rehearsals will have run over, he'll be home any moment, there's no way he'll be having a drink, no way he'll be with another woman,* all seemed to belong to another world, another lifetime.

Megan got off the bed and began pacing about the room. The question was, what was she to do now? As if searching for inspiration she walked over to the oak chest of drawers squatting in the gloom by the window and turned on the radio housed between her collection of Buddhas and Gerry's Award for Best New Director.

'Let's have a little music shall we?' an oily voice seeped through the speakers, as if answering her plea. It was Maurice Drew, medallion festooned king of pirate radio back in the seventies, now balding, cardiganed host of the twilight zone show on Loose Talk FM. 'Here's that lovely little lady Alanis Morissette with 'Isn't it Ironic?'

As Alanis began warbling about the terrible irony of insects found floating in one's chardonnay and no smoking signs when you're dying for a cigarette Megan walked back across the room and came to a halt by the door, her heart pounding. Should she leave right now? But where would she go to at this time of night and what about Laurence? Fear began clawing at the edges of her mind. What if Laurence didn't want to come with her? This was his home. Gerry was his dad, however neglectful and selfish he could be. But no – those old excuses belonged with the others – back in her old life. Megan looked up and, catching an unexpected glimpse of herself in the mirror beside the door, she was forced to do a double take. The woman staring back seemed so unfamiliar, so haunted, it looked like the framed portrait of someone else. But who? Megan walked over to the mirror and instinctively reached out and touched the gnarled wooden frame. When her grandmother had given her the mirror back when she was a child, she had told her that the ivy wreath framing the oval glass had been carved from the tallest, strongest tree in the Forest of Serendipity. Megan had chewed on the end of her plait and reached out and stroked the wood in wonder. She had had no idea what serendipity meant but just the very sound of it was magical. Se – ren – dip- i – ty – she had let the word ripple through her mind like rain drops falling on a pool. Se – ren – dip – i – ty.

'It means achieving something wonderful quite by accident,' her grandmother had explained, although to the ten year old Megan this hadn't really made things any clearer at all. Back then the word accident was always associated with something terrible, like the crash of an ornament breaking or the sting of TCP. 'All you have to do is look into the mirror and think of the thing you want the most,' her grandma had continued with a faraway look in her milky brown eyes, 'And then let Serendipity weave her spell.'

Megan looked into the mirror at the woman gazing back at her and sighed. Who was this person she barely recognised? With her hooded, swollen eyes and dark straggly wisps of hair.

'And isn't it ironic…' Alanis taunted from the radio.

It was hugely ironic really, when she thought back to the fresh faced, gleaming eyed young woman who had looked into that same mirror some fifteen years before and whispered Gerry's name. Because it had worked. Serendipity had weaved her magic and he had proposed to her that very same night.

'I'm the king of the castle!' he'd yelled, clambering on to the railing of Westminster Bridge, the Houses of Parliament glowing like the golden palace from a fairytale behind them. He'd been drunk of course, they both had. 'Be my queen?' he'd implored, his eyes widening like deep pools inviting her to plunge right on in. And she'd laughed, how she'd laughed, at the craziness of it all.

'You're insane,' she'd replied, before nodding wildly.

And then he'd whirled her round and round on the bridge, until the lights of Westminster merged into a golden blur and somewhere in the background cars honked and music and laughter drifted up from a passing ferry boat and for a moment it felt as if the whole of London was celebrating with them. And she'd pulled him to her, begging him to slow down. And she'd breathed in the heady mix of cigarettes and red wine and spicy aftershave and she'd loved it, she'd loved him. And at that moment, high on adrenalin and alcohol and youth she'd truly believed that the whole world belonged to them

– that they *were* king and queen of the castle tinging the sky gold behind them. And nothing or nobody would ever harm them.

Megan looked at her reflection once again. And now here she was, fifteen years later, miserable and wrung out, unsure of who she was or of where she was supposed to be. Unsure of anything apart from the fact that finally, after years of hurt and disappointment, a new voice was saying *no more.* A shiver of excitement ran up her spine as she moved in closer to the mirror. 'I just want to be me,' she whispered to the woman in the mirror. 'I just want to live the life I'm supposed to.' The woman looking back at her began to smile.

Then from outside she heard the unmistakeable rattle of a black cab pulling to a halt. Megan stood rooted to the spot. What should she do?

'And isn't it ironic,' Alanis continued to warble. Megan strode over to the radio and switched it off. Oh yes, her whole life was a case study in irony, but not for much longer. She just had to buy herself a little time. Time to figure out what to do. One thing was for sure she couldn't bear to have to face Gerry now. To be bombarded by drunken apologies and excuses yet again. Grabbing the journal and tissues from the bed she raced across the darkened landing into her study and curled up under the quilted throw on the sofa.

And as she lay there motionless in the dark, listening to the squeaking of the cab door opening and closing and the unsteady thud of footsteps coming up the path; staggering up the path, she didn't feel the customary anxiety or nausea. As she heard the clinking and scraping of Gerry trying to get his key in the lock and the slam and stumble as he finally made his way through the front door and into the hall she felt pulses of nervous energy prickling at her skin. This would be the very last time she heard the crashing and cursing as he ricocheted pinball-like up the stairs and the Hammer Horror style creaking as he careered across the landing before steadying himself on the table outside Laurence's room ready to launch himself at their bedroom door. Megan clenched her fists and waited.

Crash! Across the landing she heard their bedroom door fly open and Gerry stagger into the room.

'Meg?' she heard him murmur. 'Meg?' Although Gerry's voice was muffled and distant she could still make out the boozy slur, she could practically smell it. 'Where are you?'

Her heart pounded as she heard him stagger back across the landing and come careering into the study.

'Meg, are you awake?'

Of course I'm awake you bastard, she thought, but bit down hard on her lip to prevent herself saying it.

'I'm sorry, Meg darling. Sorry I'm late - auditions over ran – loads of people to see - I love you – I really do – I'm sorry. Oh shit.'

Megan remained motionless as she listened to him stumble back on to the landing and over to the bathroom. Taking a deep breath, she edged her way out from under the throw and raised herself on to her elbow. Gerry had turned the landing light on and it fell in a piercing shaft across the room. She looked at the framed certificates glinting mockingly on the wall.

Once again the words of Alanis Morissette echoed through her mind. For wasn't it ironic that she, the woman who had once believed in magic mirrors and dream endings should have ended up in such a living nightmare? That she, Megan Rowe, renowned life coach with a wall of certificates to prove it, and author of the best-selling 'Help Yourself to Happiness' had for years been trapped in a seemingly bottomless well of misery. And wasn't it ironic that as her husband sprawled over the toilet retching and spewing the poison that had eaten away at the heart of their marriage for so long, she, the creator of 'The Bountiful Journal of Joy' no less, should be considered an authority on positive living. And that as her life as she knew it appeared to be crashing to an end, in less than twenty-four hours she would be broadcasting live to London, advising people how to live life to the full.

chapter Two

"Trust is the gateway to love. Without trust
we remain forever on the outside."
Megan Rowe, 'Help Yourself to Happiness.'

Beneath the sleeping streets of West London, grimy service trains rattled through the deserted labyrinth of the Underground, transporting teams of dusty faced workers to repair the damage of the day before. And gliding above them, fleets of cabs transported the flotsam and jetsam of the capital's club-land home to welcoming beds or angry spouses in a steady stream of arcing headlights. And way, way above them, in her turreted flat beside the Hammersmith flyover, Natalie Taylor Cassidy placed a snowy white Marlborough Light between her rosebud lips and inhaled deeply.

God, how she hated Alanis Morisette, the talentless, whingy cow with her stringy hair and miserable self-pitying lyrics. Natalie pulled the belt on her satin robe tighter and hoisted herself on to the breakfast bar. It wasn't fair. Why should Morisette get all the breaks – the multi-million dollar record deals, the fame and adoration, her music played on radio stations across the globe – and yet still be so damned moody? Ungrateful bitch. Natalie took another long drag on her cigarette and gazed out of the window at the glinting lights from the Hammersmith flyover, snaking past the flats below like a giant concrete cobra. When she was famous she wouldn't be miserable. No way. Not even when she was being hassled by the paparazzi or stalked by psychos or anything. She would take it all in good grace and accept it as part and parcel of being a celebrity. Natalie sighed and bit down on her bottom lip. When she was famous…

'That was Alanis Morisette with "Isn't it Ironic?" and this is Maurice Drew's Mellow Magic on Loose Talk 107.7FM.' Natalie grimaced, she hated the slimy Maurice Drew even more than she hated Alanis Morissette.

'I'll tell you what's ironic ladies and gents,' Drew's voice continued to ooze its way like treacle throughout the flat, 'The way the Government is always banging on about global warming and yet here we are in April and it's still below freezing out there. Well don't worry, I've got a great song for you all to snuggle up to, the marvellous Marvin Gaye and "Sexual Healing." So tell me, do *you* have *that* feeling?'

'Aaahh!' Natalie leapt off the breakfast bar, her wild auburn tresses like angry flames licking at her shoulders, and padded barefoot across the living room to turn off the radio. No, *she* most certainly did *not* have *that* feeling. As she turned to make her way back to the kitchen she noticed her discarded bra draped across the arm of the sofa and shuddered. Why was it that men always left you feeling so empty? They were like waiting for Christmas Day when you were a kid – so much thrill in the anticipation – but then as soon as you got your hands on the long awaited gift the thrill seemed to get crumpled up and discarded along with the wrapping. She had hoped tonight might have been different, after all the anticipation had been huge. The way he'd stared at her hair when she'd first walked into the theatre; the way he'd had to stifle a gasp when she'd shaken it loose. The way his eyes had lingered

11

upon her breasts when she'd taken off her jacket. And the intensity with which he'd gazed at her as he directed her through the final scene of the audition, as he asked her to 'feel her way beneath the surface of her character to her most intimate core.' The dust motes dancing in the beam of the solitary spotlight had been like tiny sparks of electricity charging the air between them and her heart had pounded fit to burst as he'd cupped her face with his hand and told her he was pretty sure he could see in her a young Nicole Kidman. Natalie had widened her own eyes in wonder and perfectly matched the intensity of his gaze.

'Do you really think so?' she had replied, running her tongue along her lips.

'Oh yes, given the correct guidance and direction,' From the breathless way he responded she just knew he'd been getting hard at the mere prospect.

'I don't suppose - ' she'd paused at this point to let the unspoken thought incubate for a few seconds more. 'I mean I know you must be extremely busy and God, it's not as if I've even got the part yet or anything, I'm sure you must be seeing, like loads of other girls, but -' again she let the thought hang there for a moment as she coiled a strand of her deep auburn hair around her finger. 'It's just that I really respect your work and if there was any way you could spare me some time just to help me feel my way deeper into the character, you know, like find her most intimate core I'd be eternally grateful.' At this point she'd taken a step away and clasped her hands behind her back. Once again his eyes had flitted to her breasts.

'Well yes of course. I mean, you're right, we do have a lot of other actresses to see, but you've shown a lot of potential here today, Natasha.'

'Natalie.'

'Oh God, yes. Sorry. Natalie. You must forgive me, I'm utterly hopeless with names.'

'After Natalie Wood.'

'I'm sorry?'

'I was named after Natalie Wood. She's my dad's favourite actress.'

'Oh – how lovely. Well Natalie, if you like we could pop downstairs for a drink and I could talk you through a few of the improvisation techniques I use with my actors when they're feeling their way inside a character?'

'Oh wow, are you sure? I mean, don't you have other plans?' Noticing a cloud of concern cast a shadow across his face she hurriedly continued. 'God, thank you so much. You don't know how much this means to me. I mean even if I don't get this part, to be given some personal advice from the Artistic Director of the Theatre on the Green, that's just like, amazing.'

His face broke into a broad grin – God he was easy. 'Not at all,' he'd replied, running a hand through his dark curly hair and literally puffing out his chest. 'I know how hard it can be when you're starting out in this game. I'd be delighted to be of help.'

Natalie had left the audition and skipped down the steps from the theatre and out on to the bustle of Shepherd's Bush Common almost giddy with excitement. It was as if she could see her route to fame laid out like a red carpet in front of her. If she got this part it would be a major break. Okay so it was in theatre, and a small theatre at that. But the Theatre on the Green was internationally renowned for discovering hot young talent and Gerry Radcliffe had been directing for like, ever, he must have tonnes of contacts in the film and television world as well. She inhaled deeply and looked around her – it was as if someone had sprinkled the Common with fairy dust – and instead of the usual grime and noise all she could see were the twinkle of camera bulbs, all she could hear were roars of applause and all she could taste was the champagne fizz of fame.

Natalie returned to the kitchen and poured herself a glass of water. Her mouth felt bitter and dry from too much wine. She hadn't intended on drinking quite so much but Gerry had really been going for it in the pub, ordering wine by the bottle the way she would by the glass. She gulped a mouthful of water and shivered as it traced an icy path to her stomach. That hadn't been the only way the evening hadn't gone quite according to plan. Once they'd got back to her place she'd imagined he would be ripping her clothes off the minute they walked in the door – especially since she'd practically given him a hand job on the tube home. But he had gone straight to the kitchen to open the bottle of vodka he had bought from the off license on the way. He hadn't even noticed her painting, hanging on the wall right in front of him as his eyes had skimmed the room for some glasses. Even the most lust-glazed men she had brought back had commented on her painting, pausing midway through yanking on her bra strap or ramming their tongues down her throat to comment on the colours, the bold, slashing strokes, the 'like, raw rage, man,' as one fellow auditionee from a building society ad had so eloquently put it. But not Gerry. He had just helped himself to a mug from the draining board and half-filled it with vodka before stumbling his way into the living room.

'Aren't you going to help me feel my way to the *intimate* core of my role?' she had demanded, standing right in front of him as he settled on the sofa with his drink.

'Oh I don't know if you really need any more help in that department,' he'd replied with a dry little laugh.

'Oh but I do,' and with that she'd peeled her top off and started messing with the hem of her skirt. That had got his attention all right. Natalie smirked as she remembered how his mouth had fallen open and he'd let out a gasp.

'Jesus – what are - ?'

'Shhhh,' she'd whispered as she dropped to her knees in front of him and undone the buckle on his belt, 'I want to show you my technique.'

Natalie shivered and pulled her robe tight around her. It was as if the flush of anticipation, the promise of fame, the flashing light-bulbs and the roar of the crowd had all stumbled off apologetically along with Gerry into the back of that cab and been swallowed up by the darkness. She reached into the kitchen cupboard for her sleeping pills and took a couple from the bottle. Still, all was not lost. He might have slunk off practically the second he had come, but he had promised her a call-up for the final auditions as he staggered shame-faced out of the door.

chapter Three

*"If variety is the spice of life then
spice up your diet with some new and flavoursome recipes."*
Megan Rowe, 'Help Yourself to Happiness.'

Cheddar loved Sundays. Ever since he was a kid, at least up until the Strike and his dad had been laid off and Sundays had become a day of tension-laced silence, it had always been the day for his most favourite things. Sundays you got to laze around the house without having to be ill. Sundays you got big fat newspapers packed with all kinds of extra sections and supplements that could pin you to the couch for hours. Sundays you got special Sunday style programmes on the telly – a sports fest in the afternoon, followed by hours of sleepy dramas in the evening. But best of all on Sundays you got roasties.

Cheddar took the pot of boiling potatoes from the stove and drained the steaming water into the sink. Within seconds his tiny kitchen had been transformed into a Turkish steam bath causing Cheddar to fumble blindly for the rickety window catch. A blast of cold air and the roar from the flyover swept into the room. As soon as the steam had cleared Cheddar closed the window. Sundays were meant to be warm whatever the weather, that was another thing he loved about them; the snugness. Whistling 'Easy Like Sunday Morning' he replaced the lid on the saucepan and gave it a good hard shake. Every roast potato aficionado worth his salt knew that you had to give the spuds a right good bashing before you stuck them in the oven – it was the secret to the perfect golden crunch. After checking the potatoes were suitably scuffed and battered he removed the tray of hot oil from the oven and tipped them in. The oil sizzled and spat as the potatoes cascaded down.

'There you go my beauties,' Cheddar coaxed as he basted the snowy potatoes with the golden oil before covering them with a generous sprinkling of dried rosemary. 'Mmmm.' The smell of hot olive oil and herbs never failed to trigger a sprinkler type devise in his saliva glands. He returned the tray to the oven, where a small chicken was already crackling away, and looked at the clock. It was quarter past two. Perfect. Dinner would be ready by three, just in time for the big match. There was still half an hour before he had to put the veggies on which allowed just enough time to update his blog.

Taking a can of beer from the Romanian manufactured fridge (it had arrived without an icebox door but with a screwdriver and the instruction manual for a tractor) he repaired to his bedroom and switched on the PC. The curtains were still drawn, they had been since Cheddar had moved into the flat almost a year ago, but that was the way he liked it. Not that he was some kind of freakish creature of the night or anything – it was just that the darker the room the less apparent the complete and utter mess it had become. As Cheddar surveyed the mountainous outline of the crumpled duvets – it had been so damned cold that winter he had had to purchase an extra one – and the leaning towers of pizza cartons, teetering stacks of books, magazines, papers and scatterings of wrappers he wondered what his mam would have to say if she could see his new abode.

'Bloody 'ell son, who've you shacked up with? Stig of the bleedin' Dump?'

He rubbed his shaven head and grinned. She would have had a field day in here, would his mam, clad in that pink nylon housecoat thing and armed with her feather duster and a can of Pledge. Not that he was a slob or anything – the rest of the flat was relatively tidy, for a bloke, like, but after the split with Denise it was as if his bedroom had become an arena for his rebellion, his own small way of finally being able to stick two fingers up at her obsession with neatness. He shuddered and took a swig of beer as he thought of the bedroom they had shared, a monstrous shrine to all things pink with its frills upon frills and those bloody cushions on the bed which he swore she must have arranged every morning with a spirit level, just to get the right amount of jauntiness into the angle. God forbid he should actually recline upon one of them and risk knocking it slightly out of line. No, every night they had to be systematically transferred into a neat pile on the floor. Well at least in this bedroom he could do whatever the hell he wanted and recline upon whatever the hell he wanted and leave as many 'sweaty tidemarks' as he damned well pleased.

Letting out a grunt of satisfaction Cheddar sat down at what he believed to still be his desk beneath a year's worth of junk mail and signed on to his weblog.

User name: Joe Bailey. Password: kingcheese.

Every Sunday he wrote a weekly horoscope as well as his usual blog, 'The Extra Mature Confessions of a Cheese Ranger.' Not that he were some kind of star-gazing, weirdy-beardy kind of bloke or anything. In keeping with the rest of his blog, his horoscopes were entirely tongue-in-cheek. He sat forward in his chair, trying to ignore the way his expanding paunch was now nudging the desk and furrowed his brow in concentration. Aries, sign of the ram and that anally retentive, control freak of an ex-girlfriend of his.

'Oh dear this looks like being a tough week for you old goats,' he typed, 'as the firey planet Mars will be forming a rare alignment with Uranus, I'd recommend you avoid curry houses and invest in a packet of Imodium pronto. The full moon on Thursday makes this an ideal time to reflect upon the harm you may have caused others over recent months – like shagging your boyfriend's so-called best mate behind his back and then having the cheek to bin all of his Led Zepplin albums when he moved out – when he had told you he would be coming back to get them as soon as he'd got himself sorted with a place and had somewhere to store them. But oh no – you had them out of their faster than you had your drawers down didn't you? Must have really bugged you the way they messed up the lounge for all those years, clashing horribly with all that magnolia.'

'Bloody hell!' Cheddar highlighted the horoscope and hit delete. What was up with him? Denise was a complete cow, he was way better off without her, so why was he still getting so bitter and angry? He leaned back into his chair and sighed. It wasn't what she had done to him, though God knows that was bad enough, but it was the after effects he really hated. What she had made him become. He glanced over to his messed up bed and shuddered. How was a bloke ever supposed to recover from that kind of betrayal? How was he ever expected to regain his confidence and sense of trust? A thunderous roar from the depths if his stomach wrenched Cheddar from his gloom. Pushing back on the desk he got to his feet and turned to leave the room. He'd do the horoscopes a little later, when he had a Sunday roast inside him and had watched the game. He didn't have to get to the radio station till seven – that was the great thing about producing the Help Yourself to Happiness phone-in – it required very little effort, just a suitably happy-clappy playlist and making sure Megan didn't waffle on into the news or ad breaks. It was the sole reason he'd agreed to work on a Sunday, that and the secret hope that somehow Miss Wonder Coach could imbue him with the elixir of happiness that had somehow manage to evade him for the thirty years he had been on the planet. Not that Cheddar was the kind of bloke who was into all that self-help mumbo jumbo or anything.

chapter Four

*"No matter how far you run you will never escape
your own loneliness until you face it head on."*
Megan Rowe, 'Help Yourself to Happiness.'

'See the trouble with you yanks is you got no idea about what goes on in the rest of the world.' The bartender fixed Danny with a red-eyed stare as he busied himself drying a pint glass. Up close his face was mottled red and purple, a complex web of alcohol inflamed veins. 'I mean before 9/11 kicked off old Bush had never even been abroad. I couldn't Adam and Eve it when I found out – here's the leader of the free world, the President of the United States having to go and buy a bleeding atlas to find out where Afghanistan was. Scuse my French.'

What the hell? Danny frowned. In the two hours he'd been in The Prince Albert his conversation with the bartender had gone from moderately confusing to downright dumb-founding. What the hell was the guy going on about with the Adam and Eve references and asking him to excuse his French? And what exactly was a 'bleeding' atlas? Danny pictured George Bush poring over a map of the world, blood oozing from the edge of the page. Still the bartender did have a point with the whole geography issue - hadn't he read in horror only the day before that Britney Spears was refusing to go on tour in Japan because 'those African folks eat nothing but raw fish.' However, Danny could hardly be tarred with the same brush. For a brief moment he thought about taking his battered passport from the back pocket of his jeans and showing the guy some of the stamps, but then he would have even more explaining to do. Like why a dumb-ass yank such as himself had been to countries such as Bosnia, Palestine and Iraq amongst many others. And that would only lead to more confusion with the usual awestruck, but none the less probing questions. Questions he didn't want to answer, not even to himself. Questions like *why?* Danny took a gulp from his pint and wished he'd just pretended to be a Canadian. Then he could have enjoyed a quiet Sunday evening drink as planned, with the worst he'd have to explain being Celine Dion's crimes against harmony, rather than George Bush's crimes against humanity.

'I hear you,' he said with a sheepish grin, half raising his glass to the bartender. The bartender nodded smugly and began stacking his freshly dried glasses on a shelf above the bar. As he stretched up so too did his t-shirt and an expanse of pale hairy belly rolled into sight. Danny shifted on his stool and turned to look at the taut little blonde with whom he'd been trading surreptitious glances since he'd arrived. Within a second she'd shot a look back along the beer splashed bar, running her tanned fingers through her mane of hair and laughing animatedly at her friend. A kaleidoscope of images unfolded in Danny's mind; entwining limbs, discarded clothes, tousled hair, bare skin; all merging and parting in a breathless haze. He looked back down at the dregs of his drink and the momentary thrill of anticipation dissolved like the foamy suds sliding down the inside of the glass. He'd come to Britain to make a change, to get away from the loneliness of the past. He'd come here to find something, something he thought he had lost for good. Something he thought had died all those years ago in that rundown gas station with its unforgiving strip light and dusty floor. Something he now knew he would never find waiting for him at the bottom of a glass or glancing provocatively at him across a smoke-filled bar. He still wasn't exactly sure how or when he would find it but Faria had given him hope. In one solitary moment she had managed to ignite a spark somewhere deep within him. And that spark had been enough to fire him up and transport him to this latest destination on his journey, this latest stamp on his passport. London, England. Danny downed the lukewarm remains of his drink and got to his feet.

'See you around,' he called over to the bartender before making his way out of the bar without taking a backward glance.

chapter Five

*"It is only once you consult your own inner compass of wisdom
and love that you can hope to find your own true path."*
Megan Rowe, 'Help Yourself to Happiness.'

Megan pulled up the collar of her coat against the cold. A biting
wind was driving its way down Nightingale Avenue causing the line
of normally sentry-like elm trees to stoop and sway in the darkness.
Above her rain-swollen clouds scudded across the charcoal sky and
all around she could hear the rattle of dustbin lids and rustle of leaves
over the distant hum of Chiswick High Road. She couldn't bear
the thought of going to work, but then again she couldn't bear the
thought of being at home either, with a deeply contrite Gerry oozing
apologies and stale alcohol fumes in between visits to the bathroom.
He had slept for most of the day, his snores rumbling through the
house like distant thunder, echoing the anger building within her.
And while he had filled the house with his snores and the bitter smell
of wine-laced sweat Megan had paced from room to room, her rage
building with every thunderous roar. How dare he do this to her
yet again. How dare he lie to her and disrespect her and then sleep
oblivious for hours on end. And yet she didn't want him to wake up
either. The time for talking and soul-searching and apologies and
false promises was well and truly over. They belonged with all of
her own excuses and false hopes back in a previous lifetime. As she

had moved about the house propelled by cold rage it had felt like returning home from holidays as a child, such was the detachment with which she now viewed everything. But rather than returning, she knew she was preparing to leave. The kitchen seemed so much larger and colder, with its out-sized oven and endless granite counters. The living room now a strange, unfamiliar shade of green, harsher somehow. The plants in the conservatory an overgrown jungle, the bathroom too full of clutter. Even her study had seemed foreign and unwelcoming, surely all of those books and folders didn't belong to her? As she had sat at her desk trying desperately to formulate some sort of plan all she could hear were Gerry's damned snores and the accompanying roar from within her own head. *No more. No more.*

She could still hear it now as she marched along Nightingale Avenue, bracing herself against the cold. *No more.* A glowing light streaming from a house to her right caught her eye and she instinctively slowed down to take a look through the large sash window. It was like viewing a live advertisement for family health insurance as Megan took in the harmonious scene being played out inside. Mum and dad sat at either end of a colossal sofa with dad gently rubbing mum's feet and a cherub-like infant played contentedly on the floor. The room positively glowed with warmth, with its terracotta walls and scarlet cushion covers and throws, all illuminated by an array of strategically placed gold lamps and spotlighting. Why couldn't they close their damned curtains? It was as if they were inviting people to gaze in on them in envy. Look at us, and all we have, they seemed to be saying as they flung their velvety drapes open to the world. Bet you wish you were in here, don't you? Instead of out there battling your way through the cold. Megan felt a sudden overwhelming urge to hurl a brick through the window and shatter their perfect little family portrait. Lowering her head again she continued stomping towards the High Road. It wasn't fair. Wasn't that exactly what she had dreamt of for herself and Gerry and Laurence when they had moved to the Avenue five years ago? That same happy family scene? Hadn't she dreamt of the three of them cocooned in their lovely new home against the harshness outside? Because it was all going to be so different wasn't it? Moving to their Edwardian house with its lofty gables and majestic, snow-white façade. It was going to be a brand new start, with Gerry being appointed Artistic Director of The Theatre on the Green and supposedly giving up drinking for good and her celebrating her five figure book deal. Perhaps they could get to be king and queen of the castle after all? Perhaps they were going to be a success? Because Nightingale Avenue was the sort of place successful people lived. No need for net curtains here, as the inhabitants curled on their downy sofas like the cats who'd got the Marks and Spencers' golden-topped cream. But Megan had had blinds fitted right from the start, as if she knew somewhere deep down it was too good to be true. That despite the promises and the talk and the declarations of love she would soon need to shut the world out again – as she sat alone and weeping on the sofa.

Good grief, she really needed to shake this foul mood. How on earth would she be fit to go on air in this kind of state? How could she possibly help anyone help themselves to happiness when all she felt was abject misery? She thought back to the last caller from the previous Sunday's show, a husky voiced woman with a delicate Scottish burr. 'I just can't seem to find a man?' she had moaned. 'In all other areas of my life I'm fine, I have a great job, a lovely wee home, money in the bank, but I can't seem to meet any decent men.' At the time Megan had automatically adopted her standard coaching technique. *How do you think finding a man will make you feel? In what ways, if any do you think you prevent yourself from meeting a man?*

Why don't you believe you're attractive? Was there a time in your life when you did feel happy with the way you looked? How do you think you could recapture that feeling? How do you think you could go about meeting new people? Then she had set the woman some exercises in visualisation and confidence building and her producer Cheddar had somewhat cheesily played out with Roy Orbison's 'Pretty Woman.' If the same woman called in tonight Megan would probably cackle manically before chastising her for being so naïve. Of course you can't find a decent man – they simply don't exist. They're all selfish pigs who are full of false promises and bring nothing but pain, she could imagine herself ranting before holding up a post-it note to Cheddar demanding he play 'Only the Lonely.'

This was no good at all. Megan had to get a grip. She rounded the corner on to the High Road where a steady stream of traffic hissed and spat its way past her in the gauzy rain and desperately wracked her brains for a suitably uplifting quote. *Where there's light there's hope*, her inner voice of coaching reason piped up helpfully, *this too shall pass.* At that moment a number 27 bus zoomed past her, spraying her with the entire contents of a pond-sized muddy puddle.

'Oh for God's sake!' Megan cried, gazing down at her splattered jeans in despair. How was a woman supposed to be positive and hopeful, not to mention 'joyful' in the face of such fierce provocation? Megan punched the pedestrian button at the crossing. WAIT, the display flashed back at her abruptly – no 'please' or 'if it's not too much trouble' – just WAIT. Wait for what? Another bus to come along and soak her? Laurence to escape to university or cricketing stardom (whichever took him first) leaving her with no distractions or excuses left for her sham of a marriage? Well sorry but she wasn't prepared to WAIT any more. Hadn't she wasted enough of her life waiting? And what exactly did she have to show for it?

Megan stepped on to the crossing and began marching across the road. From somewhere behind her she heard the screech of brakes and the scream of a horn.

'Stupid cow, you wanna look where you're going!'

Megan glanced back over her shoulder and saw a man hanging out of the window of his van. His eyes were close set and steely and his ferrety face was contorted with anger. For the first time that day she started to smile.

Yes, you're right, she thought to herself, half nodding, I do.

chapter six

"Home is where the heart is. Ask yourself today – where is my heart?"
Megan Rowe, 'Help Yourself to Happiness.'

'Big Issue mate?'

Danny glanced down at the man sat huddled in the doorway of Hammersmith Station and instinctively his throat tightened. There was something about the way his translucent skin glowed bluish white in the neon light and the way his cheekbones jutted over his sunken jaw that brought back a plethora of unwelcome memories. Danny shivered and dug deep into the pocket of his battered leather jacket for some change.

'There you go buddy,' he muttered thrusting all of his change at the young man in some kind of desperate bid to buy himself back some peace of mind. From beneath a shock of lank greasy hair, the young man looked up at him in surprise – the miserable weather had obviously been having a dire effect on takings.

'Cheers, mate,' he said, extending a pale bony hand to take the money.

As Danny noticed the bruises and scabs adorning the man's knuckles he once again felt his throat constrict and the acid burn of bile at the back of his mouth. There was something all too familiar about this drained husk of a man, gazing up at him through glassy eyes, but without the comfort of his camera to hide behind all Danny wanted was to get the hell out of there. 'No problem,' he replied before carrying on his way, pulling up his collar against the cold.

'Hold on mate, you've forgot your magazine,' he heard the man calling after him over the hum of the traffic, but Danny quickened his pace and pretended not to hear. He knew he should go back there and find out if the guy had some place warm to sleep that night, even offer him the comfort of the plastic-covered, foam spewing couch in his 'penthouse' apartment, but he just couldn't bring himself to do it. It was bad enough being confronted by such an apparition, the prospect of bringing it home with him was unthinkable.

Home. As Danny made his way across the Broadway and underneath the huge rumbling flyover he let the word roll around his mind as if he were rolling a baseball in his palm, preparing to make a killer pitch. It had been a mighty long time since he'd had a proper home – or even wanted one for that matter. Of course he'd always had places to live, places to eat, wash and try to sleep, but usually they'd been beige-washed cells in concrete blocks of hotels, or glass strewn floors in blown out buildings, or a few square feet of spare floor space in other peoples' homes, but never his own. Not that he'd cared really. After the things he'd seen in his years as a war photographer it was as if the concept of home had ceased to really matter – just as love had ceased to matter. For many years now, all that had really mattered was the shot, the angle, the light. Until Faria and Nasir and what had happened in Baghdad. And how that had somehow propelled him to London.

Danny turned the corner on to Queen Caroline Street. On his left a crowd of people were queuing outside The Apollo Theatre, all stamping their feet and shivering in unison, like a gigantic, freezing cold centipede. The huge posters and neon signs informed him that they were waiting to see a bald-headed comedian who *Time Out* magazine had apparently deemed 'uproariously funny – a one man laughter fest.' Perhaps Danny should join them – God knows he could do with a laugh after his recent encounter with the homeless guy. But he was meeting Michael for breakfast the following morning so he ought to at least try and get some sleep. As he continued past the red-bricked turrets of Neptune Mansions he was practically floored by a tiny young woman with a shock of auburn hair hurtling out of the entrance.

'Hey – where's the fire?' he called as she barged past him, her hair fanning out behind her like a cloak.

'Whatever,' she called back in clipped tones, not even bothering to look at him.

Jeez these Brits could be uptight. Still she did have a nice pair of legs, Danny consoled himself as he watched her race off ahead of him, her mini skirt bouncing jauntily in the wind.

As Danny reached the sign for the Queen Caroline Estate he couldn't help a giving a wry grin. The regal sounding name was way wide of the mark, a bit like the bombed out Saddam Hussein Drive. He wasn't too sure who Queen Caroline was (one of Henry the Eighth's unfortunate spouses perhaps?) but he was pretty sure she would never have had to reside in the anaemic looking tower looming up in front of him, with its clambering tendrils of graffiti and garbage strewn driveway. Danny let himself in through the main door and took the stairs two at a time, trying hard not to breathe in the scent of stale piss. As he reached the fourth floor he felt his legs start to stiffen, still tender from the run he had taken along the river the previous night in a desperate search for sleep. It was funny, his body had never used to seize up on him, no matter what he had inflicted upon it, but now, as he found himself sliding down the all too steep slope to forty, he was starting to experience twinges and creaks in places he hadn't even been aware of before.

Finally reaching the ninth floor Danny made his way to the furthermost door, leant against the wall and caught his breath. The smell of stale cooking oil hung heavy in the air and the corridor echoed with canned laughter from his neighbour's television. Overhead the neon light flickered and spluttered, threatening to plunge him into complete darkness at any moment and making it extremely difficult to identify the correct key, but finally he managed to open the shabby door and let himself in. Home sweet home, he thought with another wry smile as he turned on the light and cast his eyes around the living room. Living room – huh – who said Americans couldn't do irony, Danny thought, as he took in the peeling wall-paper with its cancerous shadows of damp, the threadbare carpet and the bobbly curtains, each hanging on by just a couple of hooks. This was no *living* room – this was a place to - Danny shivered and ran a hand through his sandy hair. What was with him tonight? There'd been many occasions when he'd stayed in far less salubrious places than this and never batted an eyelid. Why should it bother him now? Suddenly an image of the polished wooden floors from his childhood home in Austin flashed into his mind, the brightly coloured woven rugs pushed to one side and he and his kid brother Marty playing racing cars down the hall.

'Faster, Dan-Dan, faster!' Marty was hollering as, breathless and panting, Danny pushed him on his butt across the finish line.

Danny walked over to the window and took in the view – the one redeeming feature of his soulless residence. Spread out below him like a jewelled quilt, the lights of London winked against the black velvet seam of the river. Danny felt the old restlessness pulsing and twitching within him but he knew he couldn't succumb. No matter how badly he wanted to race from his soulless tower and lose himself in the darkness below he knew he had to stop running. That was his whole reason for coming here in the first place.

Going into the formica lined cube laughingly described as a kitchen, he made himself a cup of instant coffee - how he longed for a cup of sweet chai from the café on Al Rasheed Street - and headed to the bedroom. If he were meeting Michael in the morning he really ought to have made some sort of start on his writing. Like the rest of the apartment, the bedroom was icy cold, so Danny pulled the paper-thin quilt from the bed and draped it around his shoulders before taking a seat at the table by the window. The view from the bedroom was far less distracting, being of the adjacent tenements and communal concrete courtyard, so Danny looked straight down at the table. In front of him were his trusty, if a little battered, radio, an A4 pad, open to the still untouched first page, a pen, the remains of the previous night's now greying coffee and his last pack of duty free Marlborough's. His last pack of smokes full stop – hopefully. He lit a cigarette, inhaled deeply and picked up his pen. Where to begin?

'It all began,' he wrote, 'with a Leica M6 rangefinder and a one way ticket to Split, Croatia.' Danny sat back in his chair and let out a sigh.

'Faster, Dan-Dan, faster,' Marty's words echoed through his mind. Danny's hand began to shake. Suddenly he wanted to rip the pad into tiny pieces and fling it out into the cold night air. He was no writer, he was a photographer. What had Michael been thinking, encouraging him to write his story? What had *he* been thinking, deciding to do it in the first place? But if he didn't do it – then what? He tore the first page from the pad, scrunched it into a ball and threw it on to the floor.

'It all began,' he wrote again, 'in a stucco fronted house just outside of Austin, Texas. A brightly painted, single storey building that always smelt of cornbread baking or incense burning, with wind-chimes ringing out on the porch and kids' toys covering the yard. A happy place where safety enveloped you with a smile or the simple calling of a pet name. A place of music, laughter, adventure and make-believe. A home.

Chapter Seven

"Only you can allow others to make you feel like a victim. Although we can never control the actions of others, we always have full control over our own reactions." Megan Rowe, 'Help Yourself to Happiness.'

'That was "Time" by Pink Floyd and this is Megan Rowe, welcoming you to Help Yourself to Happiness on Loose Talk 107.7FM.' Megan paused to take a deep breath. Despite having hosted her weekly show for almost two months now she still felt a surge of apprehension every time she clamped the huge headphones over her ears and switched the presenter mic on. *Just pretend you're talking to a friend,* Cheddar had instructed on her induction course, *keep it informal and chatty and remember to smile, the listeners can always hear you smile.* This would have all been fine and dandy if she hadn't already read the framed press cuttings lining the glass-walled reception downstairs. *'LOOSE TALK VOTED NATION'S BEST INDEPENDENT STATION FOR THIRD YEAR RUNNING,' 'RATINGS DOUBLE AT UK'S NEWEST TALK STATION,' 'LOOSE TALK CLEAN UP AT SONY AWARDS.'* Oddly enough, pretending she was talking to 5.2 million friends was not the most reassuring of prospects, however close they might have been. Megan often wondered if her new found friends could also 'hear' a terrified rictus grin. Mind you it was hard not to smile with Cheddar around, what with his ridiculous rants on life and his wry Yorkshire humour. His pointed choice of 'Time' for the first song of the show hadn't been lost on her as she'd hurtled into the studio with just seconds to go before going on air. When she'd got to Stamford Brook station buoyed up from her pedestrian crossing altercation and the revelation that she no longer had to WAIT for anything ever again if she just started looking where she was going, a whiny voiced London Underground announcer had promptly burst her bubble proclaiming signal failures and lengthy delays. The fact that she'd had no time for the usual pre-show preparation with the production team had done little to sooth her nerves.

Megan pulled her chair closer to the mic, glanced at the laminated intro cue pinned to the notice board and began reading it out loud. 'Do you feel as if you're stuck in a rut? Is your work life balance way out of line? Do you hate your job? Are you looking for love but just can't seem to find the right partner for you?' Megan paused for a second to take a sip from her water. Once again she was struck by a strange detached sensation; her own voice coming back at her through her headphones sounded horribly cheesy and fake, like one of those ads for lonely hearts. *Does everyone you know have a partner? Does no-one seem to understand you? Do you lie alone in bed at night staring blankly at your tear-stained copy of 'How to Make Them Love and Never Leave?'* Through the glass partition in front of her Cheddar began miming speaking actions with his hands, either that or he was doing the Birdie dance, with Cheddar anything was possible.

'Dead air, dead air,' he began squawking at her through the headphones.

Megan nodded earnestly. In the world of radio it seemed there was no greater sin than the sound of silence or the dreaded *dead air*. She took a deep breath and tried to get focused. 'Perhaps you feel you've reached a crossroads in your life but you aren't quite sure which way to go?' she offered. 'Or you know which way to go but for some reason aren't able to take that crucial first step?' *Or you've chosen your path in life only to find it's a big fat dead end street to Nowheresville,* a voice inside her head added and although it was laden with sarcasm she was sure it wasn't Cheddar this time.

'Dead air, dead air,' Cheddar barked again.

Megan gulped and clenched her fists. 'Well if so, don't worry because help is at hand. All you need to do is give me a call on 0800 107107 and I'll give you a free life coaching session live on air to show you how *you* can help *yourself* to happiness.' Megan tried to brush a few errant strands of hair from her face and inadvertently sent her headphones sliding down the back of her head. 'Oh damn!' And now she was cursing live on air – to her 5.2 million new friends and frowning and grimacing to boot, could they 'hear' that too, she wondered. How on earth was she going to get through tonight's show without losing it altogether?

'Get a grip lass - caller on line one,' she heard Cheddar's voice squeaking from the headphones now hooked around her neck. Quickly she hoisted them back up.

'Sorry about that, ladies and gents,' *ladies and gents? Where did that come from? Could she possibly sound any cheesier?* 'Had a bit of an accident with the headphones. You'd think I'd be used to them by now wouldn't you?' *Get a grip!* Her inner voice of coaching reason shrieked. *Remember your core values, your coaching vision, to transform peoples' lives with the power of positivity.*

'Chuffin' hell can you please just say summat,' Cheddar bellowed, practically deafening her.

'Yes okay,' she snapped back, 'I mean,' *deep breath, deep breath,* 'Yes, okay I believe we have a caller on the line.' Megan looked at the computer screen in front of her in desperation. *Deep breath, deep breath.* 'Mary from Ipswich, how can I help you?' Megan pressed the button for line one and the adjacent red light turned green.

Silence.

'Mary, are you there?'

On the other side of the glass partition Cheddar threw his huge arms up and clasped his shaven head in despair.

'Mary? How can I help you?'

'I'm scared.' The voice was little more than a squeak.

Megan sat up straight and leant closer to the microphone. 'Sorry Mary, could you speak a little louder?'

'I'm scared,' the voice came again, a little stronger this time.

'You're scared?' Megan turned the volume up slightly on the telephone line. 'Could you tell me what you're scared of?'

'My husband.'

Megan's heart sank as she looked at the computer screen again, the box that usually housed a breakdown of the caller's background details and the nature of their call was completely blank - all she had was her name and location. How had this happened? She was never supposed to go into a call completely blind. Megan looked to Cheddar for some kind of help but he was busy dunking what looked uncannily like a roast potato into a jar of mayonnaise.

'Okay Mary, I wonder if you could help me here. Could you give me some details regarding your current situation? You say you're married, do you have any children?'

'I think – I think he's going to take my baby away from me.'

'You have a baby?'

'Yes – well no – I mean he's almost five years old now, but he's still my baby, you know?'

Megan thought of Laurence, now a gangling six foot fourteen year old, all foreign adult smells and affected swagger, but still able to provoke in her that fierce umbilical tug of love at the drop of a back to front baseball cap. 'Yes, I do know,' she replied softly. 'So why do you think your husband is going to take your son away from you?'

'Because he says I'm not a fit mother. He says I'm unstable. But I'm not. I am a good mother. I love my son – he's my whole life. It's just my husband – he's so good at twisting things – he makes me end up doubting everything, even myself.'

Instantly Megan's own concerns melted away, along with Cheddar, her cumbersome headphones and the rest of the studio. All that was left was Mary and her whisper of a voice reaching out to her through the ether, and the palpable presence of fear. Megan knew she mustn't; she couldn't mess up.

'Okay Mary, I want you to think back to a time in your life when you did feel sure about yourself and who you were.'

There was a long pause, but without looking Megan held her hand up to Cheddar to let it go. Silences were a vital part of the coaching process, dead air or no.

'Okay,' Mary finally replied.

'Would you mind telling me when it was and what you were doing?'

'It was about ten years ago – before I met *him*. I was teaching.'

'Right – and what age group were you teaching?'

'Juniors – seven to eleven year olds.'

'And how did you get on with your pupils?'

'Very well – they were such a nice age, old enough to do as they were told and young enough to still want to learn, you know?' Mary's voice began to grow slightly stronger.

'Yes.' Again Megan thought of Laurence and how he had always returned from junior school enthusing about his latest science project or the latest exciting discovery from his maths class. He had waxed lyrical about the joys of long division for weeks. Since he had been at high school though it was hard to get more than a mumble out of him unless you asked about the cricket team. 'Do you have any particular memories from that time, Mary, that make you feel especially proud or happy?'

There was a short pause before Mary's slightly hesitant reply. 'Well there was the Year Four Christmas play.'

'Go on,' Megan encouraged.

'We did our own version of "A Christmas Tale." The kids worked so hard on it and it was such a success. The parents loved it.'

Megan leant back in her chair and adjusted her headphones. Cheddar had been right – it was possible to hear a person smile, from the sudden lift in Mary's voice she seemed to be beaming.

'Okay Mary, I just want you to take a few minutes to relive that experience. Shut your eyes and remember back to being in that school hall. You're watching those kids performing their hearts out in front of all of their parents. How did it make you feel?'

There was another pause before Mary tentatively replied. 'Proud – I was so proud for the kids. That they were doing so well.'

'But how did you feel in yourself? About yourself?'

Another long pause. 'Well proud too I suppose, although I wasn't the one up there performing, it was the kids.'

'Yes, but you were the one in charge, you were the one who brought the whole thing together. Perhaps you could give me some more details about what your role in the project entailed?' Megan felt a shiver of excitement run up her spine – this was what she loved about coaching – the way you could guide your client to the realisation that all of the answers lay within themselves, strength, confidence, pride, love, all buried like treasure beneath a blanket of doubt and fear.

'Well I wrote the script,' Mary replied, 'And directed it obviously. And organised the costumes and devised the dance routines.

'So you wrote it, directed it, organised the costumes and devised the dance routines.' Megan couldn't help smiling. 'Of course you should feel proud of yourself. So tell me, what qualities do you think you needed to pull the whole thing off?'

'Well, I guess one of the main things was patience.' Mary gave a little laugh.

'Yes?'

'You know what kids are like and some of them had an awful lot of lines to learn and there were others who you know, had certain behavioural problems, attention problems, but I decided to take a risk and let them have proper parts rather than just banging a tambourine in the background or something. I thought the responsibility would do them good, but of course it could be a bit wearing when they messed around in rehearsals.'

'But you had the patience to see it through and not give their parts to other, better behaved kids?' Bit by bit the treasure was being revealed, now all Megan had to do was get Mary to see it for herself.

'Yes.'

'So what other qualities does that show other than patience?' Megan held her breath and waited. Please, please let Mary see it.

'Er – compassion?'

'Yes of course – compassion. Anything else? What other qualities did you demonstrate, not just with the play but as a teacher generally?'

'Intelligence?'

'Yes, of course. Intelligence. Anything else?'

'Commitment,' Mary replied surely. 'I was so committed to my kids. I really wanted the best for them – not just with the play, but with everything. And I worked hard. And I was creative. I always tried to make the lessons as fun as possible.'

Megan felt all of the tension of the weekend dissolve away. She had guided Mary to the treasure chest, now all she had to do was give her the key. 'That's great. Now do you have a piece of paper and pen handy, Mary?'

'Yes.'

'I'd like you to write the following words down.'

'Okay.'

'Proud. Patient. Compassionate. Intelligent. Committed. Hard worker. Creative. Fun. Okay have you written them down?'

'Yes.'

'Good. Now I want to set you a little assignment. I want you to get a piece of card and I want you to write all of those words in large capital letters around the edge of the card and in the centre I want you to stick a photo of yourself taken while you were a teacher and you felt happy and sure of yourself and I want you to use this card to remind you of all the wonderful qualities you possess. This really is a fantastic exercise because -'

'I can't,' Mary interrupted.

'But this is what's going to help you to overcome your doubts and fears and make you realise that you are a good and loving mother.'

'You don't understand. I don't have any photos from that time. He made me destroy them all.'

'What?'

'My husband,' Mary's voice had dropped back to a whisper, 'He made me destroy them all he said -' her voice trailed off into a stifled sob.

Megan's heart sank, but she knew she absolutely must not give up. 'Right then,' she continued in a resolutely upbeat tone. 'I want you to look through some magazines until you find a picture of someone who represents your idea of happiness. So it could be someone who looks like you or it could just be someone who radiates confidence and joy – the idea being that it will help to give you a focus; something to aspire to.' All of a sudden the picture from Megan's blasted Bountiful Journal of Joy popped into her head, but she shoved it to one side. She couldn't mess this call up. She had to help Mary. 'Is there a film star or celebrity you particularly admire? Perhaps you could use a picture of them?'

'I can't – if my husband finds it he'll make my life hell. He'll use it as another example of me going mad.'

Megan's new found inner glow erupted into a flush of frustration. 'But you aren't going mad, you're just trying to rebuild your confidence. You're an intelligent, compassionate, creative woman. You're clearly wonderful with children and I'm sure you're an excellent mum. It sounds to me as if your husband is the one with the problems.' Damn! Now she had just broken one of the primary laws of coaching and live on air to boot – it was a cardinal sin to pass a negative judgement upon a client or anyone they may talk about.

'I have to go,' Mary's voice was now shrill with panic.

Shit, Megan had to do something, she couldn't lose her, not now when she had been so close. She felt like a doctor desperately trying to revive a dying patient.

'Listen Mary, please don't hang up, promise me you'll stay on the line and give the assistant producer your details. I know I can help you. I'll call you back or if you prefer you can call me privately, just ask the producer for my number, okay? Mary?'

'Okay.'

Megan sighed with relief as she flicked line one back over to the switchboard. 'Well that was Mary calling from Ipswich and I'd like to thank her for the courage she displayed in calling the show tonight.' Megan adjusted her headphones. The palms of her hands felt suddenly clammy and she wiped them on her jeans. 'Unfortunately self-doubt and loss of confidence are problems I see all too often as a life coach, but thankfully these are things that can be rectified. I think it was obvious to everyone listening to that call that Mary has all the qualities needed to turn her life around. She is compassionate and hard working and intelligent, but sometimes it's all too easy to let fear take over and we forget what a lot we have to be proud of. To paraphrase Eleanor Roosevelt, only we can allow ourselves to feel inferior or inadequate. We don't have to be victims, we all have the power to control our own destinies,' Megan glanced at her screen and saw she had another caller waiting but she needed to make sure Mary had left her details. 'If you'd like to talk about any of the issues raised during Mary's call or if you'd like some life coaching on an area of your own life you're feeling unhappy with, please give me a call on 0800 107 107. But right now I think we'll take a short break for some music.' Megan checked the screen for the next song on Cheddar's playlist. 'Here's Labi Siffri with "Something Inside So Strong."' Perfect! Megan pressed play and slid up the volume control for the CD. The timer told her she had three minutes and twenty seven seconds before the track finished. Hastily removing her headphones she got up and went next door.

'Bloody hell, that were intense,' Cheddar commented as she entered the studio. As usual it smelt of an oddly homely blend of food and men's deodorant. 'Poor lass, her husband sounds like a right bastard.'

'I know, did you get her number?' Megan asked, examining Cheddar's desk for the tell-tale post-it note, but all she could see was food. Tonight's buffet consisted of a Tupperware box of roast potatoes, a jar of Hellmans and a half eaten packet of chocolate digestives.

Cheddar shrugged and took a couple of biscuits from the pack. 'I don't know, you'll have to ask her nibs,' he nodded towards the phone room next door. 'And be careful for Christ's sake, she's in a vile mood.'

Megan walked through to the phone room, her heart pounding, please, please, let Mary have left her number or taken hers at least.

'Did you get it – that last caller's number? I asked her to stay on the line.'

'What?' Natalie looked up from the switchboard, her telephone headset barely visible through her mane of auburn hair and her mouth pursed in a tight rosebud of a pout. 'Oh her – no – she must have hung up. The line went dead as soon as you finished the call.'

'But I asked her to stay on the line, I asked her to give you her details,' Megan felt a surge of panic rise up inside of her. Natalie fixed her with an icy stare.

'Well maybe she just didn't want to,' she replied before turning back to the switchboard to answer a call, her cold little voice suddenly sweetness and light. 'Good evening, Loose Talk 107.7 how can I help you?'

chapter Eight

"Anger and jealousy are as poisonous as cancer – the only cure is to radiate them with love."
Megan Rowe, 'Help Yourself to Happiness.'

'I'd like to speak to the life coach please.' Danny gripped the mobile phone and fought to keep the anger from his voice.

'Yes of course,' the girl at the other end of the line twittered. She sounded like a junior version of the show's host – sickly sweet with pseudo positivity and an eagerness to please. All wide-eyed and glistening teeth Danny bet, like a Mormon on E. At first he'd liked Megan Rowe's voice, there had been something almost hypnotic about its honey like softness, and it had proved the perfect antidote to the severe case of writer's block that had struck him after only one paragraph. But it was when she started her sermon about people not having to be victims a red mist had descended upon him, causing his previous frustrations with his writing to pale into insignificance.

'Can I just take some personal details, please,' the girl trilled.

'Sure.' Cradling his mobile between his shoulder and ear, Danny took a cigarette from the pack on his desk and lit it.

'Can I have your name please?'

Danny paused. 'Yes, it's Michael. Michael Buckingham.' What the hell, he was sure Mikey wouldn't mind.

'And your age please?'

'Thirty-seven.'

'And where are you calling from please?' Jeez, had he got through to a human being at all? She was beginning to sound scarily like one of those voice activated answer services.

'London.' He didn't bother telling her he was just down the road. It would have been different if his call was going to be of a more positive nature, then it would have made for a nice little anecdote – that he had only been in Hammersmith a couple of weeks and when he'd discovered the glass fronted radio station at the end of his road and tuned in out of curiosity, Loose Talk FM had subsequently become his sole companion. Heck he would have even given his real name. But that was before he had discovered 'Help Yourself to Happiness,' and like discovering your head-banging biker friend is a closet Martha Stewart fan, the companionship had suddenly soured.

'And what would you like to talk about with our life coach tonight, Danny?'

Hmm, now this was a tricky one. He could hardly be honest or he'd never get put through. 'I'd like to talk about the previous caller – Mary.' He held his breath and waited for further questioning but none came.

'Okay, if you'd just like to hold the line, please, there's one caller before you and then you'll be through to Ms Rowe.'

Natalie finished typing Michael Buckingham's details into the screen and sighed. God she hated this bloody job. Who the hell did Megan think she was talking to her like that? Demanding to know why she hadn't taken that stupid woman's number as if she were just some pathetic little gofer with nothing better to do. Why the hell should she take people's numbers for that arrogant bitch? The truth was when the call had come back to her she had simply cut it off. Oh she knew she was meant to say thank you very much for calling and good-bye and all that crap but for God's sake, she had new calls coming in, how was she supposed to know that Megan had asked the caller to leave her details? Was it her fault that Megan obviously wasn't good enough to sort out the caller's problems live on air? Was it Natalie's job to take private coaching bookings for Megan? She really didn't think so. Stupid, useless cow. Waltzing into the studio late, as if she owned the place, with her long wispy hair and her tight jeans, why couldn't the woman dress her age? She had to be like, at least forty. Natalie saw line three start flashing. Fuck it – she was on a break. She reached under the desk for her bag, pulled out her manicure set and began filing her nails. God, she could not wait until she got her big acting break and she could stop doing this ridiculous job. She had thought coming to Loose Talk would have been an improvement upon waitressing – especially as the station was owned by Jimmy Levine, one of the legendary rock wild men of the sixties. She had imagined it would have been teeming with rock stars and other media types – and it was during the more controversial shows hosted by the shock jocks. But rather than get to be a researcher or assistant producer for one of them she had been saddled with answering the phones on 'Help Yourself to Happiness' and helping compile the traffic updates for the weekly drive-time show. Even working on the reception desk would have been better than this. Shut away in this stupid little box of a room answering pointless calls from a bunch of losers. How was she ever going to be discovered here?

'What the 'eck's this – a chuffin' beauty parlour?'

Natalie jumped and turned to see Cheddar standing in the doorway. Stupid, fat twat. She put her nail file down on the desk and looked up at him through widened eyes.

'Oh sorry, Cheddar, I snagged a nail on the switchboard, I was just trying to smooth it down.'

'Yes well perhaps you might like to answer a telephone in between polishing your ear lobes and plaiting your eyebrows – this is a phone-in show after all. Fat lot of good it is getting people to call in if no bugger's going to answer, eh?'

Natalie forced out a girly giggle. 'No I suppose not. Sorry. Won't happen again.'

'Good –well don't just sit there, get line three.'

Natalie watched incandescent as Cheddar went back into the studio. Gormless, northern pig. Who the hell did he think he was ordering her around? All he was was some two-bit late night radio producer. When she was famous she wouldn't give the likes of him the time of day. And he thought he was so funny too, with his quips about plaiting her eyebrows and polishing her ear lobes. And calling himself Cheddar instead of his real name, what was all that about? Probably something to do with eating all the cheese judging by the size of his gut. Well he'd be sorry, because she knew something about Cheddar, something she was sure he wouldn't want anyone else finding out and one day, when the time was right, she'd get her own back. Yes, then he'd be sorry. Natalie pulled her chair up to her desk and hit the button for line three.

'Good evening, Help Yourself to Happiness, how can I help you?' she trilled.

Chapter Nine

"When all is said and done, it is not enough to
read self-help books or recite affirmations.
In order to be truly happy you have to 'walk the talk.'"
Megan Rowe, 'Help Yourself to Happiness.'

'Thank-you Beth and good luck with the marathon training. Do let me know how you get on won't you.' Megan flicked line two back over to the switchboard and leant back in her chair. That second call hadn't been nearly as difficult, perhaps the show wasn't going to be quite such an endurance test after all? She checked her screen. 'Okay next up we've got Michael from London on the line. Good evening Michael, you're through to Megan Rowe on Loose Talk 107.7, how can I help you?'

'Yeah, hi, I'd like to talk about your earlier caller, Mary.' His voice was gravelly and he spoke with a deep American drawl.

'Yes of course, what would you like to say about her?' Megan's heart lifted, with any luck Mary would still be listening and this new caller would have something positive and encouraging to say.

'Well actually it was more about you and what you said to her.'

'Oh – okay.'

'I don't mean to be disrespectful here but I just don't think what you said is true.'

Megan's heart sank. 'What do you mean?' She looked through the glass partition at Cheddar, thankfully for once he wasn't eating and he gave her a thumbs up sign and a nod of encouragement.

'All that stuff about people not having to be victims and everyone having control over their own destinies – I'm sorry but I think it's a complete load of B.S.'

Through the glass Cheddar was shrugging at her questioningly, wanting to know if she wanted to cut the call. Megan shook her head.

'Would you care to expand on that, Michael?'

'Sure. See in my experience people have very little control over what life throws at them. I mean, how can you say to a woman who's just lost her husband in a car bombing that she has complete control over her destiny? How can you tell her that the fact she woke up that morning a wife and went to bed that night a widow was within her control? How can you tell her she needn't be a victim? Of course she's a victim.'

'Well obviously in certain cases - ' Megan began to respond, but the caller cut back in, his voice becoming increasingly agitated.

'And giving your pat Eleanor Roosevelt quote about no-one making you feel inferior without your consent. I'm sure your caller Mary didn't give her consent for her husband to be such an arsehole – I'm sure when they stood at that altar and made their wedding vows she didn't agree to him bullying her and making her life hell, for richer for poorer, in sickness and in health.'

'Yes but don't you see - '

'Oh I see all right. I see when people are being ripped off.'

'I beg your pardon,' Megan felt the back of her neck begin to burn and prickles of cold sweat erupting on the palms of her hands. Her huge headphones seemed to be clamping tighter and tighter upon her throbbing temples, like a giant nutcracker bearing down upon a walnut. Please, please, don't let this be happening, she silently implored – not tonight of all nights.

'Well don't you think it's kind of obscene that you *life coaches* – whatever the hell that means - should be cashing in on other people's weaknesses? Pretending that the secret to true happiness takes nothing more than a game of cut and paste with a bit of cardboard and a photo. You've got to be kidding, right? I mean what you've got going on here – it's like that yarn about the Emperor's new clothes.'

The studio walls seemed to be folding in on her, signs telling her to switch her mobile off and to remember to smile and not to smoke, all looming disproportionately large, like cartoon skyscrapers. Megan fought to keep her voice level. 'What do you mean?'

'Well you guys making money out of vulnerable folk by feeding them a complete load of – look I'm sorry but asking that woman to stick a picture on a piece of card – that's hardly going to save her from her arsehole husband, is it? What next – are you going to get us all to sing a rousing chorus of "Don't Worry, Be Happy"?'

Through the partition Cheddar was now making sawing motions with his finger against his throat but Megan shook her head furiously. If she cut this caller off it would be like admitting defeat, admitting that everything she believed in, everything she had worked so hard at for all these years was a complete and utter sham. It wasn't – it couldn't be. She took a deep breath before replying.

'Actually that exercise with the photograph and the card would have been a crucial first step in Mary regaining her own sense of self.'

'Listen to me – I've been - '

'No – you listen to me.' Megan interrupted, 'You've had your say, now let me have mine.'

Through her headphones she heard Cheddar whisper, 'You have his gonads for garters, lass!' and she gave him a grateful half-smile through the glass partition before continuing. 'When I said earlier that we all have the power to control our own destinies I meant that the one thing we all have control over are our own actions. Of course we can't control the way other people behave towards us, or terrible events such as car bombings or -'

'Damned right,' the man interrupted.

'But we can control how we react. And we really don't have to react like victims,' Megan clenched her hands into fists, she was not going to be beaten by this stupid, arrogant American, this argument was too important. 'All we need to do is overcome our fear or self doubt. I think Mary took a very important step tonight simply by phoning this show – that isn't the action of a victim, that's the action of a woman who is determined to regain control of her destiny.' God, Megan hoped Mary was still listening. 'And you might mock my "cut and paste" game, as you put it, but that exercise is actually an extremely effective way of reminding people who they really are and who they have the potential to be. Personally I think everyone should do it.' On the other side of the partition Cheddar was punching the air and wiggling his over-sized backside in what appeared to be some kind of bizarre victory dance. Megan paused to catch her breath. There was silence from the other end of the line. 'Michael, are you still there?'

'Yeah, I'm here.' His voice was different now, gentler, lower.

Slightly encouraged by this change Megan continued. 'I'm sorry if I sounded pat when I quoted Eleanor Roosevelt before, but I can assure you I take my life coaching extremely seriously and I passionately believe in what I say. In coaching we have a saying -'

'What – another one?'

Megan felt her cheeks begin to flush but she carried on, 'Yes – it's that in order to be a good coach you have to walk the talk.'

'Right.'

'And that's how I know my advice to be true, because I . . .' suddenly and completely unexpectedly she lost her flow.

'You practise what you preach?'

'Yes,' the lack of conviction in Megan's voice seemed to linger in her headphones long after the word had been uttered.

'Well hey – I'm very happy for you. If only life were so simple for the rest of us mere mortals.' Although Michael's voice was gentler, Megan could still detect an undercurrent of derision and she suddenly felt ashamed. How could she say she practised what she preached? How many times had her own husband made her feel pitiful and scared? Not that he'd ever abused her in the way Mary's had, but hadn't his behaviour led to her questioning her own identity? Hadn't his constant selfishness and neglect ebbed away at her confidence over the years, so that all she did was sulk and feel sorry for herself? As she'd looked into her Grandma's mirror the previous night hadn't she been forced to ask for help in finding herself again? But she had been the one to keep her family together all these years, 'my very own rock of Gibraltar,' Gerry had called her when he had been going to AA meetings and struggling to stay on the wagon. And she had been a devoted mother to Lawrence hadn't she? Always making sure her work fitted in around his needs, trying her hardest to shield him from the fallout from Gerry's drinking – those weren't the actions of a victim. Were they?

'Somehow I think it'll take a little more than a game of cut and paste to rid the world of evil though,' the American man continued, his husky voice now much quieter.

Instinctively Megan's curiosity was aroused. 'Would you like to tell me about your own situation, Michael? Perhaps I can help you in some way?'

'Oh no you don't,' he was laughing now, but it was a tight laugh, forced and unnatural.

'Are you sure?'

'Oh yes, ma'am. Believe me it would take more than a *life coach* to sort my shit out.'

Megan sat back in her chair and inhaled deeply. The walls of the studio had shifted back into their normal position, as if they too were able to breathe again. 'All right, but just remember – the answer always comes from within.'

'I'm sorry?'

'To whatever your problem – the answer always comes from within yourself.'

'Right – well thanks for that, coach. I'll bear that in mind.'

Megan chose to ignore the obvious sarcasm in his voice. 'You're welcome – and thank you for calling the show.' She flicked the line back over to the switchboard.

'Ad break, ad break,' Cheddar squawked in her ear.

Only too happy to oblige, Megan switched on to automatic pilot. 'You're listening to Megan Rowe and 'Help Yourself to Happiness' on Loose Talk 107.7FM. More of your calls in a minute but first it's time for a short break.' As the adverts began she turned off her mic and sat staring into her lap.

The answer always comes from within, her own words echoed back at her. For so long she had lived life plagued by insecurity and uncertainty, as she struggled to maintain her sham of a marriage, but now, like the first crocus of Spring, an answer began spearing its way fresh and clean into her mind.

chapter Ten

*"Do not allow others' interpretations of you to become your reality.
Know yourself and know your truth."*
Megan Rowe, 'Help Yourself to Happiness.'

Cheddar looked at the sheet of card on the desk in front of him. Well actually the sheet of card balanced on the grease splattered pizza box, on top of the old issue of the Hammersmith Enquirer on the desk in front of him. STUPID, NAÏVE, DISLOYAL, he had written in capital letters around the edge. Hmmm – this wasn't exactly going according to plan. He was pretty sure Megan had meant people to come up with slightly more positive qualities for her 'cut and paste game.' He turned the card over and tried again. What were the more positive qualities he had displayed when moving down to London from Yorkshire at the tender age of eighteen? He chewed on the end of his pen. Perhaps he should go and grab himself a bite to eat first? There was the remnants of last night's post-show kebab in the fridge – probably go down a treat livened up with a bit of ketchup. But no, he thought with a frown, he really wanted to do this. Last night's call from the American guy had really got him thinking. Normally he would have been in the yank's corner any day of the week. Much as he liked Megan and believed her to be entirely genuine – he had quite frequently seen her wiping a tear from her eye following some of the more emotional calls and she was always willing to go that extra mile, regularly staying on to phone people back and make sure they were okay – he couldn't help feeling a tad cynical about this life coaching business. Listening to people's problems and then giving them advice, well wasn't that what your mates were for – with the added bonus that they did it for free? However he had admired the way Megan had argued her case against the American and he had to admit he didn't think any of his mates down at the Prince Albert or the Rock Forum would have suggested cutting and pasting. If he ever summoned the courage to pore his heart out to that bunch of reprobates, tell them how he really felt, how often he lay awake at night wondering *is this it* over and over again as he stared at the peeling flakes of paint on the ceiling, they'd probably tell him to stop being such a sad twat and go and get the ales in. Anyway, what was so wrong with paying for friendly advice? These days you had to pay for pretty much everything else. Cheddar glanced over at his bed and shifted uncomfortably in his seat. If it made you feel better - a little less helpless – well it had to be a good thing – right?

BRAVE. Cheddar wrote in bold capitals at the top of the page. It had been brave to move to London on his own at eighteen, just as much as it may have seemed stupid. God knows he'd been scared enough as he'd heaved his bulging rucksack on to that train at Doncaster, his heart pounding louder than a Metallica base line and his palms sweating. He'd felt as if his bowels were going to open and deposit the entire contents of his stomach all over that scratchy chequered seat as he checked and double checked his ticket was still in his pocket, certain the inspector would throw him off for something. Being too young, being too scared, being a traitor – perhaps his dad had phoned the station and warned them? But no the weasel faced inspector had simply taken a bite from the ticket with his hole punch thing and trundled off down the carriage. But even that hadn't done much to calm his nerves. He remembered the steward clattering down the aisle a little later with his trolley - *'Snacks and hot drinks for the journey? Anything for you, young man?* - he hadn't been able to eat a single thing. Or bring himself to reply, merely shaking his head in terror before disappearing back behind his copy of the NME. Of course back then he never had much time for eating anyway – a right skinny little runt he was, back then. All long hair and lanky limbs, 'the streak of piss,' his dad had called him. He'd have a right laugh now, his old man, if he could see how he'd turned out. Right chip off the old block, with his beer belly and balding head. Cheddar shuddered and looked back at the word BRAVE. He had been brave though, back then, despite how he'd ended up. He'd got on that train and stayed on it, past Peterborough and York and Milton Keynes. Fighting the urge to jump off every time and head back home to comfort his mam and go into that back room – with its fug of stale cigarette smoke and stale dreams - and sling his bag down at his dad's feet and say, 'All right, dad, you win.' But he hadn't. He'd stayed on until Kings Cross and then at King's Cross he'd got off and headed out into the noise and the mayhem, all the time telling himself, don't look back son, just keep going. That took guts that did. That took courage.

And then he'd found himself a bedsit. In a shabby four-storey townhouse in a place called Willesden Green, that hadn't been very green at all if truth be told, but he'd found it, all by himself. The streak of piss, traitor from Doncaster. Used most of his guitar money to pay a month's deposit and a month's rent and found himself a home. What had that taken? Cheddar chewed so hard on the end of his biro a sliver of plastic came off in his mouth. Enterprise, yeah that's what it had taken. ENTERPRISE he liked the sound of that one. He wrote it down next to BRAVE. Shit he was starting to sound a bit like Richard Branson, who'd have thought it eh? Cheddar couldn't help grinning. And then of course he'd had to find work. An eighteen year old lad all alone in the big city, but within a week he'd sorted himself out with a job in one of the plethora of local fried chicken restaurants – not exactly Branson-esque but it was a start and it showed he was capable. Hmm – Cheddar pondered for a moment – capable wasn't exactly the kind of word he wanted to be associated with, it sounded a little too boy scoutish for his liking. STREET SMART that was more like it. And God knows he'd had to be street smart working the late night shift in the Tennessee Chicken Shack on Walm Lane – you got one too few wings or drumsticks in a bargain bucket in that place and it was likely to be your head frying tonight. It hadn't taken him long to get the hell out of there and get a job in radio either, that had shown drive hadn't it? The way he had started off in hospital radio, putting up with that twat of a would-be presenter who had made Jimmy Young look cutting edge. Listening to hours of endless mother-in-law gags just to get that invaluable producing experience. Cheddar added DRIVE and PATIENCE to the edge of his piece of card. Yes, patience – that was a quality he seemed to have in abundance when he thought about it – a memory of Denise flashed into his mind. It was when she was giving one of her many lectures about how dirty clothes do not belong on the floor and was he aware of the invention of the laundry basket? Cheddar turned from his desk to survey the carnage covering his bedroom floor, abandoned jeans and jumpers strewn everywhere like headless corpses. He remembered the weekend Denise had gone away on some SAS style outward-bound course in advanced team building and he had taken great pleasure in leaving dirty underwear on her pillow and armchair all weekend. GREAT SENSE OF HUMOUR he added to the card. Yes, he definitely had a great sense of humour, look at how many hits his weblog was getting and the comments people were leaving.

'Love the blog – has me in stitches every day. You are undoubtedly the king cheese,' a regular visitor calling themselves Bambi from Rhyl had posted today, the latest in a series of complementary messages. And that seemed to be fairly typical feedback from his spoof cheesy commentary on life. Could he venture as far as to say he was talented? Cheddar, paused, pen poised.

'You're a good for nothing waste of space, that' s what you are,' his father had spat at him, the day before he had left, the very last words he had uttered to him in fact as Cheddar had never returned, not even when his father had died the previous summer. Cheddar swallowed hard, as if trying to gulp down the reflux of sorrow and guilt this fact brought up. He thought of the last words Denise had said when he'd been standing in front of her in the doorway, rucksack heavy on his back, tears pricking his eyes, demanding to know why. 'I don't know Cheddar, it's just that you're not really, well, you're not the most dynamic of people are you? I mean what do you really aspire to? What have you ever really achieved?'

Cheddar put his pen down and took another look around his bedroom. It suddenly seemed to morph from a symbol of one man's valiant stand against domineering woman to the stinking fleapit of a teenage boy. He sighed and looked back at the card. BRAVE, ENTERPRISING, STREET SMART, DRIVE, PATIENCE, GREAT SENSE OF HUMOUR. He was all of those things – as well as being stupid and naïve and disloyal. And sod Denise and his dad, he was talented as well. He was a sought after radio producer. Hadn't Dave McNoughton, whose show he produced on weekday nights, asked for him personally? Wasn't his weblog getting hundreds of hits a week? Wasn't that an achievement? Cheddar picked up his pen and wrote TALENTED and ACHIEVER in huge capitals and then underlined them. The border of the card was completely full, now all he needed a photo. What was it Megan had said to that caller? A photo from a time when you felt happy and sure of yourself. Suddenly Cheddar knew exactly which picture it should be. It had been taken the night he had gone to see Page and Plant play at Wembley Arena, the closest he had got to seeing his heroes Led Zepplin live in concert, and although it was when they were going through their weird Morroccan inspired phase, oh the great ball-tingling joy he had felt when they played Stairway to Heaven at the end. And as the guitar solo had reached its crescendo and the crowd had gone mental he had felt like the happiest bloke alive. He had only been in London a couple of months, but he had done it, he had escaped and he had felt so completely and utterly free as he lost himself in the music. And it was at that precise moment his mate Jimbo had taken a photo of him with one of those disposable cameras and captured the moment forever. A blur of wispy dark hair and a huge open grin as he head-banged along to the beat. That was it. That was the picture he needed because that was the person he really wanted to be – that brave, enterprising, street smart, patient, funny, talented, soft lad. The question was, where the heck was it?

Cheddar looked at his bedroom and sighed. 'Time for a bit of a tidy up, son,' he said. But first things first, better finish that kebab.

chapter Eleven

"Wishes are like fairy dust we sprinkle out into the ether.
They are the source of life's magic."
Megan Rowe, 'Help Yourself to Happiness.'

Edith Jarman Literary Agency
19 Gloucester Place
London
W12 7AJ

Friday 3rd March

Dear Megan,

As you can see from the enclosed offer letter from Brondheim Publishing House in Finland, international demand for 'Help Yourself to Happiness' is still going strong – a fantastic achievement I'm sure you'll agree some four years after initial publication. But unfortunately Mercury Books are starting to get a little impatient re the delivery of 'Help Yourself to Happiness in Business.' I had Elinor Bellingham-Smythe on the phone again this morning wanting to know how far you had got with it and if I had any idea when the manuscript would be ready. I know you've been exceptionally busy with your coaching and media commitments but do you have any idea when the book is likely to be finished – it is now six months after your *extended* deadline? Sorry to be a pain, Megan but even if we had a draft to send her it would go some way to keeping them happy.

Looking forward to speaking with you soon – perhaps we could do lunch in Charlotte Street, my treat?

Warmest Regards,

Edith.

Megan looked at the letter from her agent and sighed. The truth was her long-awaited follow up book was still little further than the synopsis stage. 'Help Yourself to Happiness in Business' – at this precise moment in time it was hard for Megan to think of anything less inspiring – 'Help Yourself to Happiness in Colonic Irrigation' perhaps? She flicked absently through her diary for a possible day to meet Edith and saw with horror that she had a guest speaker booking scheduled for a computer software sales conference in Brighton that Wednesday. Oh well, perhaps it would be just the thing to kick start her second book. It was hard to believe that a whole four years had passed since publication of the first – a whole five years since she'd written it – high on the discovery of life coaching after years feeling somehow not quite fulfilled as a psychotherapist. Back then it had really felt as if she'd found her calling as she'd hammered out page after page of positive, life affirming exercises, anecdotes and case studies, but now?

Megan got up from the desk surveyed her cluttered study. The stacks of folders from numerous seminars and courses, the notice board crammed with leaflets and flyers from said seminars and courses, the piles of readers' correspondence still waiting to be answered, the pine shelves lining the entire room, laden with an eclectic mix of coaching manuals, women's fiction, self help tomes on just about every malaise known to man and there on the lowest shelf, faded and slightly tattered, an assortment of Laurence's favourite childhood books she couldn't quite bring herself to throw away. She picked one out now – "The Trouble With Jack" a beautifully illustrated tale of a naughty younger brother who sabotages his sister's birthday party.

Megan sat down on the saggy corduroy sofa beside the window and began absently flicking through the pages. She chuckled as she remembered Laurence's expression of both horror and excitement as Jack tried to find his sister's unopened birthday presents, teetering on a tower of cushions in front of the wardrobe before crashing to the floor, where his irate mother found him in a crumpled, tearful heap.

'What would you do if I did that, mum?' Laurence had asked, his dark eyes, Gerry's eyes, wide with curiosity.

'I'd make you walk the plank into a shark infested ocean, land-lubber,' Megan had cackled in her best Long John Silver impression. Playing pirates had been another favourite pastime of theirs.

Megan gazed at the picture book in awe. It must have been at least nine years since she'd last read it to Lawrence. She felt a pang of remorse as she remembered his hot little head and the way it used to fit so perfectly into the crook of her arm as she would read him story after story. Especially on a day like today. She glanced up at the window, tightened the belt on her chunky woollen cardigan and shivered. Outside the April sky remained a great unyielding sheet of white, fractured only by the spindly boughs of a wind battered elm tree flailing in the window. It seemed hard to believe that that same sweet little boy had morphed into the sullen teenager who now stalked the house, mumbling begrudging greetings before retreating to his fusty cavern of a room. Megan cringed as she recalled her feeble attempt at small talk over that morning's breakfast.

'They said it might get a little warmer, later in the week,' she had offered, as she poured him an orange juice. Gerry had thankfully left early for the theatre and it had just been her and Laurence seated at the scrubbed pine kitchen table. She had briefly toyed with the idea of telling him what had happened. But what exactly could she tell him other than something had changed, finished, died? That she could no longer live the lie that her marriage had become. And how could she drop that particular bombshell whilst she still had no other details or reassurances to offer. But still, what on earth had she been thinking talking about the weather? What fourteen year old boy is going to be interested in discussing meteorological matters with his mum? Perhaps she should have talked about the *well phat* DJ who was said to be joining Loose Talk to host a Friday night *Garage Trance Fusion* show? Whatever the hell that was. Random images of car mechanics wandering around the studios in a daze filled her mind, before she thought back to Laurence and his grunted response.

'Is it all right if I stay at Joe's tonight?' he had muttered as he got up to leave.

Megan felt her heart sink as she watched him take his plate and glass over to the draining board. His school shirt was hanging out at the back and his trousers were baggy and low. Everything about him seemed to scream out *I don't give a shit.* It took all of her strength not to rush over and smooth his ruffled hair, tuck in his shirt, hoist up his trousers and kiss him on the forehead.

'Yes, okay,' she had forced herself to chirrup, 'But make sure you get your homework done.'

'Yes, mum,' he'd said with such a fervent sigh she felt certain if she'd been standing she would have been blown over by the resultant breeze.

Megan put down the book and glanced back over to her desk. Her eyes fell upon the brightly coloured patchwork of affirmation cards she had pinned to the wall behind it.

> *My work is deeply fulfilling and will*
> *lead me to even greater rewards.*
> *Everything I touch is a success as I*
> *move into the winners' enclosure.*
> *My life is a mirror – the people in*
> *my life are really mirrors of me.*

Megan clenched her fists. Outside a branch lashed at the window, scraping down the pane like nails on a blackboard. That bastard was not a mirror of her, no way. Not unless it was one of those hideously distorting mirrors you get in fairgrounds that make you look grossly squat and overweight or ridiculously gangly and gaunt. Gerry was selfish and absent and a liar and she...

Once again Megan thought of her grandmother's mirror and the wish she had made in it on Saturday night. Who was she exactly? What had she become? And then she thought of the wish she had made in it all those years previously as she'd got ready for her date with Gerry. How could she have wished all this upon herself? Where had it all gone wrong? She looked at the affirmation cards again. *Everything I touch is a success as I move into the winners' enclosure.* What a crock of shit. How could she possibly believe that? Yes, her book and her career had been a resounding success, but her marriage had been an abject failure almost from day one. And even worse she had compounded the failure by being too stupid or gutless to leave. She got up and walked over to the desk and slowly and methodically began pulling down the cards. Was this all her life had really been – a house of cards with no real foundations at all? Had the American guy from last night's show been right? Was coaching all a big sham? The twenty first century version of The Emperor's New Clothes? And if so, what did that make her, the author of the internationally best-selling 'Help Yourself to Happiness?' The tailor who had fooled an entire court? Megan sat down at her desk and twisted her long hair into a loose plait. The screen-saver on her computer flickered haltingly across the screen in front of her - *Walk the Talk.*

Walk the talk. Walk. Walk. Walk. Megan got up and left the room. She crossed the chilly wooden floored landing and into her bedroom. The bed was still unmade, the duvet kicked back from where Gerry had been sleeping, still smooth on her side. She'd slept in her study again when she'd got home from the radio station the night before, with a cushion over her head to block out Gerry's snores. Megan went over to the huge oak wardrobe at the far side of the room and opened the door. She pulled down an armful of clothes and slung them on to the bed. Then she went over to the closet in the corner and pulled her over-night case from the top shelf. It would do for now. She stuffed her clothes into the case and then went into the en-suite bathroom and grabbed wildly at bottles and tubes, which she then slung on top of the clothes. Then she went back into her study for 'The Trouble With Jack' and squeezed it down the side of the now crammed case. Before zipping it she walked over to her grandmother's mirror and looked into it once again. This time the woman looking back had lost her haunted expression. Although she was still slightly pale and her plaited hair slightly unkempt, her eyes were no longer swollen and hooded and the large green irises glinted like jade. Once again the woman smiled and this time Megan caught a fleeting glimpse of familiarity in the dimples breaking out on her cheeks. 'They're your laughter marks,' her grandmother had explained one day when Megan had asked about the strange little hollows on her face in a school photo. 'They're very special you know. They're the sign of a happy, fun-loving spirit.'

Megan reached out and took the mirror from the wall. She'd show Gerry. And she'd show that American caller and she'd show anyone else who doubted her. She wasn't going to be a victim. She was going to take control of her life. She was going to walk the talk. She was going to walk.

Chapter Twelve

"Truth brings release. Be truthful to yourself today."
Megan Rowe, 'Help Yourself to Happiness.'

'So, my good fellow, how is it hanging?'

Danny placed his espresso down on the shiny cafe table, looked across at Michael and grinned. Man it was good to see him - the bizarre combination of Michael's clipped upper crust voice and swinging sixties colloquialisms never failed to crack him up.

'It's hanging just fine, dude. Just fine.' Danny took off his jacket and slung it over the back of the huge leather armchair before sitting down.

'Groovy. Now tell me - ' Michael sat down in the armchair opposite him and leant forward expectantly, his snowy white hair gleaming against his still tanned skin, 'How is the book coming along?'

The *book?* Jeez – he had to be kidding, right? Danny took a large sip from his espresso – he had a feeling this conversation was going to require a major caffeine injection.

'The book – hmm. Well, that's not so groovy, Mikey. I mean the *first paragraph*, well that's coming along just fine, but the book. . .'

'Ah – I see.' Michael leant back and fixed his piercing blue eyes upon him. 'You're not going to back out now, are you? After everything we talked about. After what happened with Faria and - '

'No,' Danny interrupted, feeling a sudden flush of blood to his face. 'Of course not. I'm just finding it a little difficult you know. Getting started. Hell, Mikey, I'm a photographer, not a writer, you know that. You're the words man. Maybe - ' he paused to take another large sip of his espresso, 'I don't know, maybe I could just tell you the stuff, you know about the people in my pictures and you could write it for me? We could be partners again like the good old days. You could be my ghost writer.'

Michael frowned and tore a corner off his croissant, uncharacteristically aggressively, Danny couldn't help noting. 'No way hosé. They're your pictures. It has to be you who tells the story behind them, in your own voice. Give yourself a chance man. Hang loose.'

Danny gave a wry smile. Hanging loose in Hammersmith – it had a certain ring to it – perhaps it could be the working title for his paragraph. 'I am trying. I've been sitting in that damned apartment night after night pen poised but for some reason nothing's coming. It's as if I've got some kind of mental block. Hell, maybe I am a writer after all – I always thought you guys made up writers' block as an excuse to go and get wasted. Now I know it's for real.'

Michael gave a theatrical shudder. 'I'm not surprised you're blocked, stuck up in that hell-hole in Hammersmith. It must be like looking down on Dante's Inferno. I really don't know why you insisted on picking such an un-salubrious part of town when you know full well you're more than welcome to stay with Marjorie and me here in Hampstead. Just think how much more inspiring it would be to look out upon the Heath whilst you scribe. I tell you man, once spring finally arrives you couldn't want for a more mellow setting.'

Danny instantly tensed as he thought of his first two days in London a guest in Michael and Marjorie's floral fiesta of a spare room. 'I really appreciate the offer, Mikey but I told you, I don't like to impose.'

'Impose,' Michael snorted, 'Don't be such a buffoon! Of course you wouldn't be imposing, why, you're, you're like a brother to me. After what happened – you know.' He leant forward and touched Danny on the arm.

Danny nodded, but he couldn't help squirming at Michael's sudden emotional outpouring and instinctively pulled his arm away. Yes they had worked together for a British broadsheet during the second Gulf war, and yes they had been through some harrowing times, but brothers? Sometimes it was hard for him to comprehend how a brush with death could have such a profound effect upon other people. Having stalked death or been stalked by death – sometimes it was impossible to tell the difference – for so long now he had become immune to the strange emotional side effects it could bring out in others. When the car bomb had gone off that humid January day in Baghdad it had initially seemed like business as usual to Danny. Leaping and prowling about behind his lens. Clicking and crouching, crouching and clicking as he captured the latest collage of gore. Until he had come upon Michael and their Iraqi translator Nasir of course. Danny shuddered as he recalled seeing Michael's blood splattered face looking up at him through the view-finder.

'I think, he's dead,' Michael had gasped, looking down at the limp body cradled in his arms. Danny hadn't taken a picture since.

'Are you okay?' Michael asked, leaning forwards.

'Sure.' Danny sat back in his chair, to avoid any further awkward embrace. He reached into his pocket for his cigarettes, and realised his hands were trembling. 'I hear what you're saying and please don't think I don't appreciate it, but it's probably best if I do this thing alone – no distractions. And man, Marjorie's cooking is one hell of a distraction.' He made a somewhat feeble attempt at a laugh before continuing. 'I mean if this story's going to come it's going to come from inside me isn't it? It won't make any difference where I am.'

The answer always comes from within.

Jeez, now he was being haunted by that darned life coach. Danny signalled to the bored looking waitress, playing absently with her shiny black hair behind the counter.

'Excuse me ma'am, could I get another espresso, please?' he called over to her.

She nodded and smiled, her long oval face instantly creasing into life. Something about the crinkles fanning the corners of her eyes reminded him of Faria. Ghosts, ghosts everywhere. Danny lit his cigarette and inhaled deeply.

'I know what you're saying, brother, but still, Grottsville Towers in deepest darkest Hammersmith is hardly the most pleasant of settings to pen a masterpiece is it?' Michael said with a concerned frown.

'Well it sure as hell beats Sniper's Alley or the Palestine Hotel,' Danny replied with a grin, 'And less of the masterpiece if you don't mind - I'm under enough pressure as it is.'

'Well you know what's best, I suppose,' Michael conceded, taking a consolatory bite from his croissant.

Oh if only, thought Danny. If only.

Two hours later and Danny was back in his freezing cold apartment, hunched over his desk. Outside the wind whipped and howled around the top of the tower block, completely drowning out the usual distant rumble from the flyover. Danny twirled his pen between his fingers like a miniature cheerleader's baton – a feat he was becoming worryingly skilled in he couldn't help noting. He couldn't do this. He couldn't fucking do it. It was too hard, too painful. But if he didn't – what then? He thought of Faria. Of when he had held her that awful January night. When he had cradled her, the way Michael had cradled Nasir. The way she had sobbed low guttural sobs until his chest had become slick with sweat and tears. 'Why? Why? Why?' she had moaned, a plea that had seemed to echo throughout the dusty streets and alleyways of all Iraq since the invasion.

That had been the point of writing this book hadn't it – to tell people like Faria's stories. To try to tell other people what was going on in the dusty, blood splattered corners of the world – to tell the personal stories behind his photographs – in the hope that someone might hear their plea. He looked down at the last line he had written about his childhood home in Austin.

'A place of music, laughter, adventure and make-believe. A home.'

Danny stared out of the window – nothing but white, like the rest of the page. And then, suddenly words began dropping like rain into his head.

'One of my earliest recollections of home is of sitting out in the back yard, early one summer's evening, listening to the rattling whir of the cicadas and watching mesmerised as way, way above me brilliant white trails formed out of nowhere in the clear blue sky. I guess I must have only been about six, so I had no idea what was making this random pattern and was fascinated as the thin white lines laced across the sky and then slowly spread into wispy trails of cloud. Perhaps God had a neat set of cloud crayons he was testing out? Or maybe he had one of those funny piping bags like mom used to write messages on our birthday cakes and he was icing the sky with clouds? But surely someone as wise as God would have something more impressive to pipe on to the sky than a series of random lines? GOD RULES or SATAN SUCKS perhaps? I waited and watched for some kind of profound heavenly message but to

no avail. Heck, now I knew what my Aunt Cherrie was going on about all those nights she'd sit on the porch swing with mom, shaking her head and whispering 'God sure does move in mysterious ways.' It wasn't till my father came out to find where I'd got to that I discovered the truth.

'Why has God iced a big white cross in the sky, pops?' I asked, pointing heavenwards.

Pops stared at me real hard for a moment before following my gaze upwards and then let out the almightiest roar of laughter you ever heard. 'That ain't icing, son, that's airplanes. The white stuff's the exhaust, same stuff that comes out the back of my truck.'

'Airplanes?' I was dumb-founded. 'But I can't see no airplanes.'

'That's because they're so high, but trust me they're up there. Icing! Ha.' And with that he trundled back up to the house, his chequered shirt tied loosely round his waist and his broad back glowing red brown in the setting sun.

Well this revelation had two profound effects upon me. Firstly I couldn't believe there were actually human beings all the way up there – man they were practically in outer space! Boy how I wished I was up there with them, blazing my own trail around the world, like Superman and Flash Gordon rolled into one. I decided right there and then that as soon as I could I was going to get myself a paper round and start saving for a ticket. But this was swiftly followed by the rather morbid fixation that one day those white lines were bound to meet head on and the sky would be lit up with an explosion bigger than any Fourth of July shin-dig. I shuddered in a state of perverse childish glee as I pictured bits of body and plane wreckage showering down all over the yard. (Kind of ironic with hindsight and certainly brings to mind the saying, be careful what you wish for). For the rest of that evening I watched with baited breath as those snowy white lines crissed and crossed, waiting for that fatal moment of impact when I could run into the house and save my family from the *impending doom. But then the bright blue sky began to pale and one by one the lines faded and stars lit up like golden landing lights to guide the planes through the burgeoning darkness.'*

Danny paused and absently chewed on the end of his pen. Where the hell had that come from? But he was finally on a roll and couldn't afford to stop just yet.

'Back then, where it all began, it was all going to be about saving lives not goading death. I was going to be a superhero. But the truth is – I'm no hero, quite the opposite in fact. However, I have been lucky enough to meet many heroes and heroines along the way. At first I thought I could tell their stories in pictures – a picture speaks a thousand words as they say – but unfortunately this hasn't proved to be the case. In fact all my photographs appear to have done is won me a heap of pointless awards and misdirected praise – a notion that to me is both perverse and utterly wrong. And so it seems I need to turn to words in order to set the record straight. In this book you will hear the words behind the pictures and learn the truth about me too. That unlike the subjects of my photographs, I am not 'brave,' 'heroic,' 'remarkable' or any of the other entirely inappropriate labels that have been applied to me in the past – that in actual fact I am just. . .

He was just what? Danny tightened his grip on the pen.

'a coward.'

As soon as he wrote the word he felt something in him begin to shift and the completely unfamiliar but undoubted sensation of relief.

Chapter Thirteen

"Beauty is in the eye of the beholder.
Every morning behold yourself and affirm,
'I am beautiful.'"
Megan Rowe, 'Help Yourself to Happiness.'

'Natalie, darling, it's Claudia.'

Natalie hit the pause button on the DVD player and wiped the sweat from her brow. She had been half way through a step aerobics routine hosted by an ex-reality TV 'star' from hell with about one brain cell and even less personality – so to get a phone call at all was a welcome interruption and to get a call from her agent – well, that was like, super cool. Having an agent meant she was at least half way there – half way to fame and fortune and finally being recognised.

'Claudia, darling – have you heard something? Have they called about the second audition?' Natalie perched on the arm of the leather sofa, adjusted the strap of her lycra crop top and waited for Claudia to give her the date. On the screen in front of her the vacuous reality TV 'star' remained frozen, mid squat-thrust, her overly made-up eyes bulging like a toad's. One thing was for sure, when Natalie was famous there was no way she was bringing out a keep fit DVD – that was for losers – reality TV nonentities and middle-aged TV presenters with eating disorders. The only DVDs she'd be appearing in would be blockbuster films co-starring –

'I'm afraid it isn't good news, darling. You haven't been called back. Gerry Radcliffe was extremely apologetic when he rang – and I think the fact that he rang personally speaks volumes darling, I mean normally they don't bother phoning at all if you don't get past the first audition as you know, but for the artistic director to call, well, that's praise indeed! He made a big point of saying how promising he thought you were, but unfortunately the casting director wanted someone with a little more experience and in the end he had to agree with her, but he did assure me it was nothing to do with. . .'

Blah, blah, blah. Claudia's words began merging into one long, pathetic sloaney, drone, interspersed with 'darling' and 'fabulous' at regular intervals. Natalie was sick of hearing it by now – but this time was even worse. This time it was really personal. The bastard. After everything she had done. Natalie looked down at the sofa, at the space beside her where Gerry had sat only a few nights previously, clutching on to his mug of vodka whilst she had almost gagged trying to suck some life back into his pathetic limp cock. He had promised her. He had promised she would be called back. The lying, using, bastard. 'You remind me of a young Nicole Kidman,' he had said. Wanker.

'So I really think you ought to see this as being rather encouraging, darling,' Claudia continued.

Yeah right.

'And don't worry, I've just put you up for a fabulous advert for a skin care product -'

'What kind of skin care product?'

'Well it's a dermatological lotion made by - '

'A zit remover?'

'Well yes, I suppose you could call it that although it's for a very exclusive range...'

Blah, blah, fucking, blah, fabulous, blah, exposure, blah, exquisite skin, blah. To her huge annoyance, Natalie felt tears of anger and frustration prickling at the corners of her eyes. How much longer was it going to take? She was absolutely sick and tired of having to go through this rejection over and over again. Well not this time. She wasn't going to tolerate this. She took a deep breath and clenched her fist.

'Okay, Claudia, well thanks for keeping me posted.'

'Oh you're welcome darling, and don't worry, with your fabulous look and that amazing hair, it's only a matter of time before someone snaps you up.'

And what about my acting ability? Natalie felt like screaming – *doesn't that count for anything?* She swallowed hard before replying. 'Yes I know.' All of a sudden she felt very, very tired.

She tossed her mobile on to the sofa and stared vacantly at the TV screen, at the ugly, squatting, peroxide blonde, bulgy eyed toad. God, blondes were such fakes. Bleaching the life out of their hair just to attract male attention. Well she didn't need to do that, did she? She was different - unique. Her red hair was 'amazing.' *She* was 'amazing.' 'Fucking beautiful,' wasn't that what that bastard Gerry Radcliffe had called her when she'd been all over him on the tube journey back to her flat? Well she'd show him. She wasn't some performing doll he could just play with and then discard without a care in the world. She was sick of other people trying to make her feel worthless. She was amazing, she was fabulous, she was fucking beautiful and she was going to show him.

Chapter Fourteen

"Write down the soundtrack to the happiest times of your life ... play these songs whenever you are in need of a lift."
Megan Rowe, 'Help Yourself to Happiness.'

Cheddar looked at the threadbare carpet in his bedroom and frowned. It was so worn that the remaining patches not through to the straw-coloured underlay were hard and shiny. Shiny, floral swirls in varying shades of shitty brown. Chuffin' hell – the floor had looked better when it resembled a jumble sale massacre. He looked over at the single bed with its double duvets pulled right up to the pillows, revealing not a trace of the hideous bobbly orange sheet beneath them. What they did reveal however, now they were stretched out to their full glory, was a huge, unsightly tea stain. At least Cheddar knew it was tea, but to the untrained eye, well, it looked suspiciously like the bed's occupant could be suffering from some kind of incontinence. Perhaps he ought to whip the covers off and take a trip to the laundrette? Steady on, son, he thought to himself, one step at a time. It had taken him all of Monday to get the room tidy. He'd got through practically a roll of bin-liners transporting the mountains of crap down the back-stairs to the wheelie bin. And when his own wheelie bin had reached capacity he'd had to dump the rest in the industrial sized bin belonging to the *El Paso* Mexican restaurant downstairs.

'You have body in there, innit?' Rajesh, the Asian and therefore woefully pseudo, Mexican owner had enquired when he'd caught him red-handed, hoisting a sackful of *Hammersmith Enquirers* into the bin. Cheddar had nearly had a heart attack when he'd spun round to see his poncho-clad accuser standing in the battered doorway of the restaurant kitchen. He looked like a miniature Asian version of Clint Eastwood about to cause mayhem in a Western saloon.

'Flippin' heck, Raj, you made me jump,' he'd replied. 'Just having a bit of a clear out, that's all. Hope you don't mind – me own bin's chocker.'

Raj had adjusted his sombrero and smiled. 'No, no, you go ahead. We put leftovers in the chilli, innit, no need for bin, eh?' And with that he threw back his pointy little head and emitted one of his trademark cackles, causing his sombrero to almost take off in the wind.

'Yeah, right,' Cheddar replied, not entirely convinced he was joking.

'Tell you what, compadre, why don't you take a break, come in and have some chimi-changas, innit? Nice plate of nachos, extra cheese.'

Cheddar looked at Rajesh mournfully. Was he deliberately trying to lead him astray? He looked back at the wheelie bin, which already contained the entire contents of his fridge – at least two pounds of assorted cheeses, a variety of king-sized chocolate bars, three slices of leftover pizza and a family sized tub of neapolitan ice-cream. When Cheddar had finally located the photo of him going crazy at the Page and Plant concert it hadn't just been the sight of his headful of shoulder length hair that had freaked him out. It was as if over the past twelve years his hair loss had been directly linked to his weight gain. As if his body had adopted some kind of compensatory insulation process – half a stone of fat gained for every handful of hair lost. But whatever the reason Cheddar hadn't liked what he'd seen. And as he'd stuck the photo to the centre of the piece of card and studied that exuberant, lithe-limbed young man, framed by the words BRAVE, ENTERPRISING, STREET SMART, DRIVE, PATIENCE, GOOD SENSE OF HUMOUR, TALENTED, ACHIEVER, he knew his room wasn't the only thing in need of a makeover. 'Fridge pickers wear big knickers' his mam had always repeated ad nauseum before finally succumbing and whipping the frying pan out for a couple of rounds of bacon sarnies. Well this lad wasn't for big knickers anymore, oh no. And so, along with his bedroom, the fridge had been stripped bare.

'Sorry, mate,' Cheddar replied, shaking his head dolefully at Raj. 'Some other time, eh.'

'Okay, hombre – I get back inside now,' Raj nodded towards the restaurant kitchen, 'Freeze our bollocks off out here, innit?'

'Yeah – too right. You get back inside,' Cheddar had replied before returning to the relative warmth of his own flat.

Now Cheddar looked down at the sheet of card lying on his eerily bare desk. That had taken real willpower that had, turning down a pile of fried parcels of beef and a plate of cheese-smothered chips. He wondered if he could squeeze willpower onto the card. He picked up his pen and printed the word in small capitals between DRIVE and PATIENCE. So now what?

The trouble was, Megan hadn't said. That poor lass Mary had hung up before Megan had a chance to say what you ought to do with your piece of card once you've made it. Frame it? Stick it on wall? He looked at the bedroom walls and their peeling paper embossed with a hideous sunflower design that at some point back in the 1970s someone quite obviously out of their head on a mind-bending LSD trip had deemed a cracking good match for the monstrous carpet.

He got up and went over to a particularly loose piece beside the window and gave it a tug, to his surprise the entire sheet started to come off in his hands. Wahey! Cheddar gently pulled until he had loosened the paper right the way to the top and then gave it a tug. Opening the curtains to shed a bit more light on the matter he moved on to the next sheet and the next until he had managed to strip an entire wall. It wasn't until he'd worked his way half way round the room in a mad stripping frenzy that he paused to take stock of the situation. Once again the carpet was no longer visible and neither was most of the bed – this time they were covered in balls and shreds of tatty paper.

'Chuffin' hell!' Cheddar sat back down at his desk. What the heck had he done that for? Just when he'd finally restored some semblance of order to the place as well. Down below him in the restaurant he heard the distant clank of metal and the moth-watering image of a wrought iron platter piled high with sizzling fajitas popped into his mind. His stomach emitted a growl of discontent. Cheddar looked at his watch. It was five o'clock. He had an hour before he had to be at work on the Dave McNoughton show, just time for a swift one at The Prince Albert. After all there was bugger all to eat in the flat and if he didn't go for a pint he had the horrible feeling he might have to resort to rummaging through the bin to retrieve a chunk of cheese.

*

'A pint of London Pride please.' Danny held his breath and waited for the bartender to make some smart-ass remark.

'Certainly, sir, coming right up.'

Jeez – it had to be his lucky night.

'Of course you know the Pride doesn't come chilled?' The bartender called over his shoulder as he reached for a glass, revealing a dark ring of sweat lurking in his armpit. Not like your *Budweiser*. Nah, this is a proper beer, a man's beer, only drunk at room temperature. Of course I could put some ice in it for you if you want.' His bloodshot face erupted into a broken toothed grin.

Danny sighed. No prizes for guessing where the tooth had gone. Perhaps he should just turn around and walk straight back out again, back to the apartment to resume writing, before he ended up giving this joker an even higher orthodontic bill.

'Ey up, Ray, being the landlord with the least again are we?'

Danny turned to see a large shaven headed man standing behind him. He spoke in a strange accent, which he figured to be rural and was wearing a thick winter coat and rubbing the cold from his chubby hands.

'You take no notice of him,' the man continued, this time to Danny. 'He's like this with all his customers. First time I came in here he told me to bugger off back home to me ferrets – I'm from up North you see.'

Danny nodded and smiled, although he really didn't see the connection between ferrets and "oop North" at all. 'No problem,' he said, handing the bartender a five pound note and taking his pint. He turned and looked around the rest of the pub but all of the tables were occupied, mainly by self important looking men in suits and scarily focused looking women in heels – commuters stopping off for a quick one on the way to the station no doubt. Not for the first time Danny felt baffled by the notion that the majority of the population seemed to lead their lives in such an ordered fashion, with even the consumption of alcohol having allocated time slots. For as long as he could remember, routine had seemed so stifling to him, and pointless, but now he almost envied these people as he observed the ties being loosened, the pinned back hair quite literally being let down, as the first trace of alcohol melted them from one world into another. As if the pub were a decompression chamber preparing them for home.

Danny turned back to the bar, took off his jacket and hoisted himself on to a stool. The large shaven headed man had already sat down on the one next to him and was playing with a beer mat as he waited to be served.

'There you go sir,' The barman said, placing a frothy headed pint on the bar and handing Danny his change. 'Usual is it, Cheddar?'

'What do you reckon?' the man replied. 'Chuffin' hell it's brass monkeys out there – what the hell's happened to Spring, eh?'

'Tell me about it,' Danny agreed, assuming the man to be talking about the cold, albeit in some kind of bizarre animal code – and what the hell kind of name was Cheddar? Man these Brits were eccentric.

'You American then?' Cheddar asked, before looking over to the barman. 'Here, Ray, get us a packet of pork scratchings and bag of nuts, please mate, I'm Hank Marvin.'

Cheddar? Hank Marvin? What the hell was this guy on? And what the hell were pork scratchings? Danny tried to erradicate the image of a flea-infested hog from his mind before replying. 'Yep, 'fraid so.' He took a swig from his pint and prepared for the onslaught.

'Whereabouts?'

'Huh?'

'In America – whereabouts are you from?'

'Oh – Austin, Texas.'

The man – Cheddar, Hank Marvin, whoever - turned around beaming. 'Wahey! Stevie Ray Vaughn country.'

Danny returned his smile, perhaps he wasn't such a freak after all. 'That's right. You a fan?'

'Are you kidding me? Of course I am. The way he made that guitar wail on 'Pride and Joy'. The man were a genius.'

One hour, two warm frothy pints later and Cheddar and Danny were deeply involved in an impassioned debate over whether Stevie Ray Vaughn would have gone on to become even greater than Hendrix had his life not been so tragically cut short.

'It still makes me shiver thinking about it,' Cheddar said, his voice dropping to a whisper, 'The way it happened, like.'

'I know.' Danny drew hard on his cigarette. Stevie Ray Vaughn's death had been his JFK – he would never forget the morning when he woke up to the news. His mom crying at the breakfast table, his dad slumped on the porch step, for the first time ever completely speechless.

'Victim of a fatal helicopter smash, no survivors,' Radio Austin had informed them over and over again. Danny remembered going back to his bedroom and playing the album 'In Step' at top volume – shock and fear and rage coursing through his veins. And then the tears coursing down his face. Funny really, that he should have been able to cry back then, at the loss of someone he never even knew and yet –

'The way he asked his brother Jimmie if he could have his place, on the chopper like,' Cheddar said, interrupting his thoughts. 'That's the bit that really freaks me out – the way that life – or death – can be so bloody random. That by taking his brother's place on the helicopter he ended up saving his life.'

Danny felt a familiar tightening in his chest. 'Of course you could argue that by Jimmie giving him his seat he ended up signing Stevie's death warrant.'

Cheddar scratched his head. 'I hadn't ever thought of it like that before.'

Both men sat in silence for a moment, staring into their pints.

'Here, laughing boys. How about this then.' Ray, who had been listening to them whilst filling the dishwasher with dirty glasses, came over to where they were sat. 'Did you hear the story about when his drummer heard the news and went rushing over to your man's hotel room?'

Cheddar and Danny looked at him expectantly.

'Well, obviously the room was empty but the clock radio was on and it was only playing 'Peaceful, Easy Feeling' by the Eagles, weren't it?'

'And?' Cheddar enquired.

'Well that's how he knew it was true, when he heard that line in it, the one about hearing a voice in your ear saying I may never see you again.'

'Chuffin' hell!' Cheddar shook his head.

'Makes you think, don't it?' Ray said sagely before sticking his hand up his t-shirt and scratching his huge hairy belly.

Danny shuddered. He didn't want to think about Vaughn's death even more than he didn't want to see Ray's pale flabby gut. 'Can I get you another?' he offered pointing to Cheddar's almost empty glass.

Cheddar looked down at his glass and then over at the clock behind the bar. 'Shit – is that the time?' He hoisted himself off his stool and started fumbling on the floor for his coat. 'I'd better get off mate. I was due in work twenty minutes ago. It's been great meeting you though. A real life resident of Austin, Texas, here in the Prince Albert, Hammersmith, who'd have thought it eh?' Cheddar pulled on his heavy winter coat. 'Always wanted to go there you know; pay my respects to the main man. How long are you in town for? Just passing through are you?'

Danny looked up at him and shook his head. 'No I'm here for a while yet, for work, renting a place up the road.'

Cheddar's face broke into a grin. 'Nice one. So I might catch you down here again then? I'm in here most nights – for my sins,' and he shot a pointed glance in Ray's direction.

'Don't give me none of that *for my sins* bullshit,' Ray instantly shot back at him. 'You love it in here. Where else would you get a decent pint of Pride, and a pack of pork scratchings and still have change from a fifty pound note, eh?'

Danny laughed. 'I guess he has got a point, this place is starting to feel like a regular home from home and I've only been here twice.'

'Here, he's not bad is he, for a septic?' Ray said to Cheddar, gesturing at Danny.

'A septic?' Danny enquired.

'Septic tank,' Cheddar offered by way of explanation.

'Yank!' Ray hollered, addressing Danny as if he were a kid with ultra special needs.

'Oh – I see.' Danny shook his head and chuckled. The sad thing was, the past hour had been the best time he'd had since arriving in London - bizarre colloquialisms, strange, gristly snacks and insults included.

'Tell you what I'll do, I'll look out that 'Couldn't Stand the Weather' CD burn a copy for you if you like. I'll leave it behind the bar with Ray,' Cheddar said, removing a woolly hat from his coat pocket and placing it on his shaven head.

Danny's eyes lit up. 'Are you sure?'

'Yeah – no problem, might help you feel more at home, having a bit of Stevie Ray to play. Right I'd better shoot. Nice chatting with you Danny. Hopefully I'll see you again.'

Danny got to his feet and shook Cheddar's hand. 'Yeah, sure – and thanks, thanks a lot.'

As Cheddar left the pub and Ray moved down the bar to serve a customer Danny sat down and took a gulp of his warm, rich beer, 'Peaceful, Easy Feeling,' echoing through his mind.

Chapter Fifteen

"When we rely upon others to make us feel loved
we leave ourselves wide open to pain and self-hatred."
Megan Rowe, 'Help Yourself to Happiness.'

Megan took a sip from her hot sweet tea and smiled. Outside a driving wind and foaming brown waves lashed at a deserted Brighton beach, but enclosed above it all in the pine walled deck of a seafront café she was snug and warm. The smell of frying bacon wafted up from the kitchen below and a medley of musical soundtracks played softly in the background, interrupted every now and then by the screeching of a seagull swooping past.

It was Tuesday morning. Megan had been so desperate to get away from Nightingale Avenue; away from Gerry, she had come down to Brighton the night before - a day early for the sales conference at which she was guest speaking. Upon arriving at the station she'd wandered aimlessly, almost trance-like, through the streets and Lanes until she'd found herself a B&B in a Georgian terrace just past the Pavilion. Despite the cardboard stiff sheets and scratchy blanket, for the first time in two days she had plummeted into a deep, dreamless sleep. So deep that she'd missed breakfast and had to come out in search of some. Instinctively she had been drawn to the seafront – away from the crowds of irate Brightonians wrestling with umbrellas, buggies and shopping, as they negotiated the rain-slicked streets. She needed space to think, to breathe, away from other people. And the Smugglers Den Café had proved the perfect place, tucked into the sea wall; with an ocean of wide-open space stretching out in front of her.

Megan heard a creak from the pine stepladder behind her and turned to see the owner of the café emerging through the entrance in the floor carrying a huge round tray.

'Here you go, madam,' he said, setting the tray down on the table in front of her and wiping his large weather beaten hands on his gingham apron. 'Eggs scrambled, bacon crispy, tomatoes grilled, just as you ordered.'

'Thank you very much – it looks delicious.' Megan could feel herself literally salivating as she looked at the palette of colour laid out before her, a white-flecked cloud of pale yellow eggs, gilt-edged rashers of bacon, shiny brown sausages and bright red tomatoes erupting with juice.

One by one the restaurant owner set the remaining contents of the tray before her, a fresh pot of tea, a rack of toast, various sauces and a crisp unread newspaper. Apparently Megan had been his only customer of the morning and seemingly overcome with gratitude he was pulling out all the stops.

'There you go,' he said, producing a chequered napkin with a flourish – for one awful moment Megan thought he was going to tuck it into her collar as a bib, but thankfully he placed it beside her plate. 'Music isn't too loud for you is it?'

'No, not at all. It's nice – cheery.'

They both paused to listen to the chorus of 'The Sun'll Come Out Tomorrow,' before he turned to her with a look of abject despair. 'God I bloody well hope it does – this long winter has been terrible for trade.'

'Yes, it has been awful hasn't it,' Megan replied, but as the café owner went back downstairs she realised she was actually quite enjoying the raw drama the elements were playing out in front of her. It seemed to match how she was feeling inside – a sudden and quite overwhelming need for devastation. Having spent much of the winter feeling battered down by the elements now she longed for the same storm that was raging outside to come tearing through her life and scatter it far and wide. It didn't really seem to matter where all the pieces landed, just as long as it wasn't back in the same place. It was this same devil-may-care attitude that had prompted her phone call to Gerry upon arriving at the guest-house the night before.

'What do you mean, you've left me?' he had spluttered.

'Exactly that,' she'd replied cool as a cucumber, cool with years of pent up hatred and hurt. 'I've left you – I've left home.'

'But – but – but – what about Laurence?' Ah yes, weakness number one in Megan Rowe's top ten weaknesses, but she was prepared for it this time.

'Laurence is staying the night at Joe's. I'll call him tomorrow and tell him I've had to come down for the conference a day early. Then when I get back on Wednesday night, I'll explain what's going on.'

'What conference?'

'The IT Sales Conference in Brighton – I'm their guest speaker. I told you about it last week, they want me to – oh forget it. Just do me a favour and make sure you're home for Laurence on Tuesday night, not out with some tart or drunk in a gutter somewhere.'

There was a pause – no doubt it would have been marked 'indignant' in one of Gerry's scripts - before he responded. 'I told you Meg – the auditions ran over on Saturday night and then the casting director and I couldn't agree on who to call back. A tad too much wine got consumed I admit, but I've said I'm sorry a thousand times and I really don't need to be put on a guilt trip right now - '

At this point Megan had pressed the button marked NO on her mobile, the one with the little red handset with a line slashed through it. Oh if only it were that easy to terminate a marriage. She gazed out of the window at the raging sea and imagined a registry office somewhere housing a great big button marked DIVORCE with an accompanying picture of a wedding ring slashed through with a bright red line. How much easier would the next chapter of her life be if all she had to do was press a button and avoid all the inevitable haggling and solicitors and upheaval that was set to follow. After all meeting Gerry; getting into all of this mess, had seemed so effortless. She had just looked into a mirror and wished for him – *I'm so sick of being on my own* – she could remember crying into her mirror the day before he'd bounded into her life – *I want to meet a man*. Oh if only her Grandmother had warned her about the small print that comes with a mirror of serendipity; to be bloody careful what you wish for.

He had seemed so perfect, so exciting, that night she had first met him, with his tales of touring theatre companies and fringe festivals and other Bohemian folklore. Megan had gone to see a play in the Old Red Lion in Islington with a couple of friends from Uni, a rather ludicrously violent farce if she remembered correctly. When Gerry had approached her in the bar afterwards and she'd learned that he was the director, well, she couldn't have failed to be impressed. With his long tousled hair and his ruffle necked shirt and the passion with which he spoke about his love for the theatre, it was impossible not to be swept up by it all. It was all such a world away from her years of study and almost military style planning as she carved out her carefully plotted career path. And being ten years older than her he had seemed so worldly, so experienced in the wilder things in life.

Although the writing had been on the wall from the start – the bottles of wine he consumed that first night, then the copious amounts of vodka they got through back at his flat – she had been blinded, but by what exactly?

Megan sat motionless, bacon-laden fork poised in front of her mouth. Had it been love? At the time she had felt certain it was. She had never felt so strongly about a man before. Admittedly by the age of twenty-one she hadn't exactly had that many relationships, but that was more out of choice rather than design. Until Gerry, no-one had come close to capturing her heart. But then perhaps she'd never given them a chance, having been so focused on getting her degree and qualifying as a psychotherapist? Was it really pure coincidence she'd only started feeling lonely once she'd graduated?

Megan put the bacon in her mouth and savoured the salty taste. There were so many unanswered questions all of a sudden. She couldn't help thinking of a metaphor she often used in coaching where she would get her clients to compare their lives to a tapestry, with themselves as the needle. All too often we can get bogged down in the messy business of the lives we are weaving, she would say, and it's only when we're able to look back with the benefit of hindsight we see the beautiful and rich tapestry our life has formed. Hmmm. Megan chewed on the crispy bacon. Beautiful and rich certainly weren't adjectives she'd use to describe her disaster of a marriage. It was as if hindsight had brought her out on the wrong side of the tapestry and all she could see were a mass of tatty, fraying ends.

She thought back to the heady days of their courtship – how strange and old fashioned that word sounded, Laurence would have been mortified. And really with the benefit of hindsight, courtship was completely inappropriate for her first few months with Gerry. They were messy days really, she could see that now, messy days of exuberant highs – hours spent in bed, drinking and making love, going to rehearsals and watching in awe as Gerry tenderly coaxed the very best from the lamest scripts and weakest actors. But then there were the devastating lows. The absences, not just when he was off in rep in deepest darkest Derbyshire but when he would vanish for days without a word of explanation leaving her bound to her phone on the off chance he'd call. Megan cringed as she remembered one particularly desperate, tear sodden Sunday morning where she'd actually rung BT to test her line for incoming calls such was her desperation to hear from him. Would they have lasted much longer than a year if he hadn't proposed to her out of the blue? Once again she thought of her Grandmother's mirror and winced. *Make Gerry love me* she had whispered as she'd applied that final coat of lipstick. Had she really wished that upon herself? When he'd gone and proposed she'd been overjoyed – not only did he love her but he wanted to spend the rest of his life with her too. How lucky could she be? And how wrong had she been to doubt him.

Megan put down her knife and fork and watched as a seagull descended upon a bin outside and began pilfering for scraps. She felt a shiver run down her spine. Is that what she'd been doing all those years ago – taking whatever she could get? Kidding herself that she and Gerry were king and queen of the castle when all along she was just a lowly serf? But then she had fallen pregnant with Laurence and her judgement had become even more clouded, rampant hormones leaving her even more blinded to the continuing absences and the drink. The difference being that by then she was blinded by need rather than love. The need to keep her family together at all costs.

Megan took her phone from her coat pocket and texted Laurence.

Have had 2 come 2 conference a day early, will be back Weds PM.
Love Mum.

She put the phone back in her pocket and took a large swig of
tea. The café was starting to feel oppressively hot and the music,
now 'Singing in the Rain,' gave her the sudden desire to be outside.
Hopefully the bracing sea air would give her some much needed
clarity.

After paying her bill and leaving the owner a large tip, along with
her sincerest hopes that the weather and subsequently trade, would
start to pick up, she crunched her way over the shiny wet pebbles
towards the sea. The beach was completely deserted and the sea a
frothy brown cauldron. It was perfect. As she began walking and the
wind whipped her face she felt her thoughts begin to fall into place. It
hadn't been love that had drawn her to Gerry, an element of infatuation
certainly, but underlying it all a deep-rooted and somewhat perverse
need. It was textbook stuff really. Once again Megan was hit with a
pang of irony, after all, hadn't she written the bloody textbook, or at
least one of the millions in existence – child of absent father seeks
out replacement figure so that she may torture herself with years and
years of repeated abandonment and neglect in the vain hope that one
day he will commit to her. One day he will love her and then she can
love herself.

A huge wave crashed on to the ridge of stones beside her, spraying
her with salty water. Megan turned to face the sea and smiled. She
wanted to shout 'bring it on!' like those ludicrous American wrestlers
Laurence used to love watching on Sky. For the first time in years
she didn't feel afraid. Like the wind and the ocean she too wanted to
roar. She looked down at the beach for a pebble to hurl into the water
and to her surprise saw a tiny yellow flower lying there all alone,
glowing like a sunbeam amidst all the brown. She bent down to pick

it up. It was like a sign, a glimmer of hope, that beauty was always possible even in one's darkest hour. The beauty in strength perhaps? She would have to write about this in her Journal of Joy. From inside her pocket she felt her phone vibrate; she had a text message.

It was from Laurence. Megan clicked on READ:

'WHATEVER,' it read.

chapter sixteen

"Revenge may be sweet but it leaves a bitter after taste."
Megan Rowe, 'Help Yourself to Happiness.'

The Theatre on the Green was tucked away in a corner of Shepherd's Bush Common, next door to the far more impressive if a little tatty, Empire Ballroom and upstairs from a pub.

How apt, thought Natalie as she stood just across the road, on the edge of the common, her flame red hair tucked into the collar of her cape style coat, and a green velvet cap pulled right down to shield her face from the drizzly rain. She wondered if the sad wino Gerry Radcliffe made it a pre-requisite of taking an artistic directorship post that the theatre concerned must be within pissing distance of a licensed bar. The Theatre on the Green was a pretty pathetic attempt at a theatre anyway, now she came to think of it. If it weren't for the narrow neon lettering TOTG running down the side of the building you wouldn't even know it was there. The stage was about the size of her kitchen and the capacity was only ninety something. Why it should have such a good reputation was beyond her. The place was a dump – nothing like the majestic playhouses lining Shaftsbury Avenue, with their twinkling signs boasting stellar casts. She didn't know why she'd got so hung up on getting the part now. After all it was the world of film she was really interested in. Theatre was only meant to have been a stepping-stone into that world. It was the fact that she had ended up feeling as if she'd been stepped on that had really pissed her off. And made her come down to confront the arsehole Gerry Radcliffe. She wasn't going to be stepped on, not by anyone. She dug her hands deep into her pockets and clenched her fists as her heart began to pound. Now was not the time to be hit by an attack of nerves. She took a deep breath and continued her wait.

All around her buses heaved and gasped their way around the clogged up one-way system, their windows black with grime. Sometimes she really hated London with its noise and pollution and dirt. But even in its worst moments it wasn't as bad as that horrible small minded, Stepford style village she came from. Natalie grimaced as an image of her parents' manor house entered her mind, with its picture postcard grey stone walls, complete with its obligatory overcoat of ivy and family of green wellies clustered around the WELCOME mat. Welcome - huh that was a laugh – because she'd certainly never been made to feel welcome had she? Well London was home to her now, Neptune Mansions, so why should she care? Suddenly the door to theatre opened and Natalie saw two figures coming out. One was a woman in a large floppy hat and a floor length coat – probably that bitch of a casting director, but the other was definitely Gerry Radcliffe, she could tell from his long wavy hair. Just who did he think he was trying to kid with the feeble Mr Darcy look? She watched as they both indulged in the ritual double air kiss over each other's shoulders – *mwah, mwah* – phoney wankers - before the woman strode off towards the Uxbridge Road. Gerry paused for a moment and glanced about furtively before diving into the pub. Quelle surprise!

Natalie's mouth budded into a tight little smile and she darted across the road, weaving through the crawling traffic and over to the pub. It was one of those tatty plastic Paddy affairs – all gaudy shamrocks and guinness ads, with the closest thing to the craic being the powder smoked by dirty little weasel types in the O'Toilets out back. Natalie swallowed hard and pulled open the heavy brass handled door. You can do this, she thought to herself, you're fabulous, you can do anything you want. Instantly she was hit by a wall of hot smoky air and the roar of rock music. Instinctively and almost wistfully she thought of the Cherry Tree back in the Cotswolds, where the only thing that roared was the large open fire and no-one was a stranger. Yes, but hadn't they been good at making her feel an outsider, after the 'scandal' broke, with their sideways whispers and accusing stares. They hadn't been all-welcoming country folk then had they? Narrow-minded arseholes. Natalie pursed her lips and sighed. Well this was her home now – the whole of London - and she was in full control. She was fabulous, she was amazing, she was 'fucking beautiful' and she was going to show that bastard Radcliffe that no-one trod all over her and got away with it. Not any more.

Natalie edged her way through the throngs of people - the usual bargain bucket mix of weary commuters, wide-eyed druggies, grimy builders and of course the odd map wielding tourist. God, London was cool. You wouldn't get this in The Cherry Tree - that was strictly one man and his inbred dog territory. As she neared the large shamrock festooned bar she spotted Gerry standing at the far end with his back to her. Natalie made her way up behind him until she was so close she could smell his rancid aftershave. She took a deep breath and clenched her fists in her pockets as hard as she could.

'Surprise!' she cried in his ear.

Gerry spun round and for a second he showed no recognition whatsoever, his eyes wide and face completely blank. Gormless tosser.

Natalie undid her cape, removed her cap and let her auburn hair cascade down over her shoulders.

'Natasha?'

Natasha? A flash of anger and pain coursed through her body. He couldn't even remember her name. How could she have been so bloody naïve? How could she have possibly believed he would keep his word? Natalie stood motionless as she watched Gerry's expression mutate. It was like watching the sped up footage of a flower unfurl, bloom and die as it went through an entire spectrum of emotions, from recognition to delight to shock then concern and finally crumpling into something uncannily close to shame. She also noticed that the whites of his eyes were stained bloodshot pink and his chin was shiny with a silvery stubble, as if a slug had deposited its trail all over it. In the glow of the spotlight on Saturday Gerry had looked dashing and distinguished but now he just looked washed up and old. Finally Natalie forced herself to speak.

'It's Natalie actually.'

'Oh yes, yes of course. You must excuse me I'm utterly -'

'I know,' Natalie interrupted, 'hopeless with names.'

'Yes – I – what are you doing here?' Gerry took a step away from her, his back pressing into the bar. 'I mean obviously it's lovely to see you but – I called your agent this morning. Did she get in touch with you?'

'Yes, yes she did and you see I'm a little confused.' Come on, you can do it, Natalie urged herself, don't let him get away with it.

'Ah,' Gerry looked down at his feet and began chewing on the corner of his thumbnail. The squirming, cowardly bastard.

'It's just that I could have sworn on Saturday night when I was sucking you off,' Natalie deliberately raised her voice, causing the two tightly clad gay men standing next to Gerry to turn and raise their eyebrows, 'You said I would definitely be called back for a second audition. In fact if I remember correctly you even told me the part was in the bag. Just a formality, you said, had my name written all over it.'

If cringing were an Olympic sport Gerry looked worthy of a triple Gold. 'I'm so sorry,' he muttered, red-faced, fishing in his pocket for his wallet. 'Let me buy you a drink and try to explain.'

Blatantly ignoring him, Natalie continued with her coolly executed delivery, she was on a roll now and seeing him squirm was really firing her up, her heart was throbbing like the engine of a juggernaut. 'I mean it's such a cliché isn't it? The old casting couch routine. And you even had the nerve to use my couch! Come to think of it you made a bit of a pig's ear of the whole thing really didn't you?'

'What do you mean?' Gerry's voice was barely audible. The two men next to him were now making no effort to disguise their glee at the unexpected floor-show unfurling before them.

'Well, you come back to my place, you use *my* couch, you tell me I've got the part when I don't even get called back for a second audition and – it took you about an hour to get it up.' Cue more raised eyebrows and cough covered titters from the men next to them.

'I've had enough of this.' Gerry thrust his wallet back into his pocket and jostled past her, heading for the door.

'Where do you think you're going?' Natalie cried.

'That's right, petal, you give him hell,' one of the men at the bar hissed as she began following Gerry outside. By the time she'd made her way out of the crowded pub he was half way down the road, staring anxiously into the traffic, obviously looking for a getaway bus or taxi. Natalie broke into a run, he mustn't escape, it mustn't end like this. 'Wait,' she called as she managed to catch up and grab on to the sleeve of his jacket.

Gerry stopped and turned, beneath his silvery stubble his face had taken on a matching grey pallor. 'Listen, I'm really, truly sorry about what's happened and I know I've acted appallingly, but I can't explain if you're going to berate me in public. Although of course you're perfectly justified to be furious with me.' He added, running his hand through his dishevelled hair as if desperately trying to calm himself down.

Natalie was momentarily stumped – Gerry seriously looked as if he were about to start blubbing, an outcome she hadn't considered at all when she'd been rehearsing this scene in her mind earlier on. Back then, when she'd been pacing about her flat blurting out random lines and standing in front of her wardrobe mirror pulling varying degrees of indignant expressions, she had imagined him either getting all defensive or attempting to charm her once again. Not for a moment had she thought he would have appeared so – well feeble.

'Go on then,' she said, softening her voice slightly.

'What?' He was biting his lip now and blinking a little too often. Oh good God, how embarrassing. He was going to start crying right in the middle of Shepherd's Bush Common, a grown man; an *old* man for Christ's sake. Then what would she do? She couldn't help feeling a stab of concern though. Could she have got him all wrong?

'You promise you won't shout?' He implored.

'I promise.' She watched as he shuffled from side to side, studying his feet, completely unable to meet her gaze.

'Well what happened on Saturday night – I truly don't make a habit of that kind of thing. You know, the whole casting couch scenario. I mean you're absolutely right, it is such a cliché, not to mention morally and professionally wrong. It's just that – well you are,' he paused and looked up the road towards the bank on the corner as if for inspiration, 'You are exceptionally beautiful.'

Natalie felt a little burst of satisfaction erupt in her heart. 'Yes,' she said, her voice little more than a whisper.

'I guess once I'd had a few too many it must have loosened my resolve. You were extremely hard to resist.'

'Hmm, but what about the promises – the second audition, the part?' She wasn't going to let the grovelling bastard get away with it that easily.

'I wanted you, God I wanted you for it, but the casting director had very strong ideas about the type of actress she saw in the role and then there was the question of your lack of experience and this is a very demanding part, even for an experienced actress.'

'But you're the Artistic Director, you're the boss. Couldn't you over rule her?'

Finally Gerry managed to meet her gaze and he stared into her eyes intently, sympathetically. 'I'm afraid it doesn't quite work like that.'

Natalie smarted – the patronising git. 'Oh I see how it works all right,' she replied sourly.

Gerry shook his head. 'No, you see it's so important to work as a team in theatre and at the end of the day that's why I hire a casting director – for her expert opinion – I can't then turn around and undermine her.'

'I see – but it's perfectly fine to undermine your actors?'

'God no, not at all. I always have huge respect for my actors.'

'Really?'

Gerry sighed. 'I'm not doing a very good job of this am I?'

Natalie looked down at the floor, trying to figure out her next move. Was he trying to bullshit her or did he mean what he said? 'No, not exactly.'

Gerry looked at his watch. 'Look I really have to get off now, but perhaps -'

'Oh don't tell me – another actress to *audition?*'

'No – not at all. I've got to get back for my son he's -'

'Your son?' Natalie's head shot up and she fixed him with an accusatory stare. 'So you're married?'

'Yes – no – well to be honest I don't know.'

'You don't know,' Natalie's voice began to rise, 'How the hell can you not know if you're married?'

Gerry took a deep breath before replying, his voice suddenly bitter and tight. 'Well apparently my wife has left me, although I only found out about it this morning.'

Natalie shook her head and gave a dry little laugh. 'God you really are a walking book of clichés aren't you? Don't tell me – she doesn't understand you?'

Gerry frowned. 'Oh I'd say she understands me only too well – or at least she *thinks* she does. But then again my wife thinks she understands everyone.'

Natalie stared at him for a moment. Although this scenario wasn't going at all how she'd planned it, she couldn't help feeling it was actually turning out rather better than she could have imagined. Perhaps all was not lost after all. She took a deep breath and widened her eyes, gazing up at him through the rain. 'I'm sorry,' she said.

'What?' Gerry's mouth fell open in surprise.

'I'm sorry – for being so hot-headed. It's the price you pay I guess,' and she gave her red hair a coquettish flick.

Gerry nodded and smiled cautiously.

'It's just that I was so angry and hurt and I felt I'd been used,' she looked down and began fingering the hem of her cape. 'I felt so stupid.' Cue lip quiver and desperate gaze towards the theatre.

'Oh no, oh no you mustn't. You're not stupid at all. I'm the stupid one,' Gerry replied, reaching out to touch her gingerly on the arm.

Ain't that the truth, Natalie thought as she stared up at him hopefully. 'I just so wanted that part and when you said all those lovely things about me being like a young Nicole Kidman and how you were going to help me to explore the character, I was so excited. I feel so passionately about the theatre you see and I really thought this might have been my lucky break.'

'Oh God, now I feel dreadful.' Gerry rummaged in his pocket and produced a grossly tatty piece of tissue. 'Please don't cry. Look I meant every word I said. What happened with the part was extremely unfortunate but I could still help you, if you want. I mean I'd still love to give you advice and perhaps I could even help you to get a part elsewhere, in another theatre. But I promise, no strings attached, no, you know, casting couch involved.'

'Really?' Natalie took the manky tissue from his hand and tried not to grimace as she dabbed at her eyes with it. The last thing she needed was to pick up some kind of putrid eye infection, especially with a potential skincare commercial in the pipe line.

'Yes of course.' Gerry clasped her shoulder and stared down at her. 'I really do feel utterly dreadful about the whole thing – it's the least I could do. I tell you what – why don't you stop by the theatre tomorrow. We've got a read through going on in the afternoon but perhaps if you came by about seven. I could wait behind for you and we could do some improvisation work?'

'Are you sure?' Natalie asked, handing back his tissue.

'Sure I'm sure,' Gerry replied, raising an arm to hail a cab. As the rain speckled taxi pulled up alongside them he leant over to the passenger door to speak to the driver, lowering his voice but not quite enough. 'Nightingale Avenue, Chiswick please.' Then he turned back to Natalie. 'See you tomorrow at seven then, and don't worry, I'll make it up to you, I promise.'

Oh yes, thought Natalie, smiling demurely as she watched him get into the cab, you'll make it up to me all right.

Chapter Seventeen

"True confidence doesn't need to shout or make a noise.
True confidence comes from a place of inner peace."
Megan Rowe, 'Help Yourself to Happiness.'

As Megan gripped the beech wood podium in the Hastings Suite of the Central Brighton Conference Centre with the same desperation as a drowning woman clinging to a life buoy she felt an eerie sense of déjà vu. Only in this instance she knew exactly when and where she had experienced this floundering feeling before. It had been eighteen years ago – half a lifetime ago - when as a first year student at Manchester University she had been sat on the sticky floor of the Student Union bar, clinging to the leg of a bar stool for dear life. Back then of course she had looked like an entirely different person, clad in carefully ripped jeans and customised Doc Martens rather than an immaculately tailored trouser suit and delicate kitten heels. Her hair had been different too, braided with rainbow strands of ribbon rather than scraped back into a migraine inducing pony tail. It had been lunch time and as usual half the University seemed to have converged upon the bar to drink warm, flat coke out of plastic cups, eat limp rolls out of cellophane wrapping and watch *Neighbours* on the huge TV screen suspended from the ceiling. Of course 'watching *Neighbours*' had really been more about watching the braying floor-show going on beneath, as the students all competed to out do each other in ironic laughs and witticisms. Hooting at the wooden Australian actors, shrieking obscenities in response to the corny lines. Normally Megan joined in; laughing and shrieking with the best of them in her newly acquired crystal cut vowels. And normally it had felt good to be part of this fresh-faced, middle class throng, no longer encumbered by her own, somewhat different, family background. At university nobody was really bothered about her personal history, they were all far too interested in mapping out their own futures. However on this one particular day and for no apparent reason, Megan felt a sudden hollow rush of overwhelming solitude. Similar to an out of body experience she had become painfully aware of her former self sat in the midst of the braying mob, and instead of a standard issue student all she could see was a crooked toothed, freckle faced school girl. The girl with the imaginary friends. The girl with no father. The girl with the tea-leaf reading grandmother and the mum who spent half of her life in bed. The girl who had never been asked for a slow dance at school discos, no matter how many advice columns she pored over in *Photo Love* magazine. And she had wanted to cry. Although at the time she couldn't understand why she should suddenly feel so lost and alone, surrounded by her lovely new friends all exuding effortless confidence like expensive cologne, now it was all too clear – she didn't belong. Just as here in Brighton, in front of a braying mob of cloyingly scented and sharp suited sales people, she didn't belong.

Megan took a deep breath and urged herself to get a grip. Her speech, although slightly stilted and rushed had gone down reasonably well, now she just had the role play to get through and she could be out of there. Just as she had back in that student union bar she had to snap herself back into the moment and get on with it.

'Okay,' she said, removing her suit jacket and placing it on the chair behind her, 'I need a volunteer to help me demonstrate the Core Values exercise in a role play.'

'Go on Deano!' Someone yelled from the front of the auditorium. Megan squinted but the spotlights beaming down on her were too bright for her to be able to make out a face.

'Yes go on Deano!' a cry went up around the room.

Megan watched the silhouette of a man get to his feet and began making his way to the stage. Although his bulky frame feigned reluctance as soon as he reached the pool of light by the steps she could tell from his cocky grin he was all too eager to take centre stage. Megan felt an intense and instinctive wave of dislike rush through her and immediately tried to suppress it. *You should always have respect for another person's model of the world and accept that their current behaviour is the best choice available to them,* her inner voice of coaching reason urged as she watched him stride on to the stage, punching the air and whooping. Good grief, the man was a complete twat.

'Hello there,' Megan chirruped falsely, holding out her hand as she walked over to greet him.

Deano went to shake her hand but at the last minute withdrew his huge paw and thumbed his nose instead. 'Aha!' he cried and for some bizarre reason the audience fell about laughing.

'Ho ho – I obviously have the office joker,' Megan responded through teeth so gritted they felt as if they might be forced back into her jaws. 'Well thank you for volunteering – Deano is it?'

'That's right – at your service, ma'am,' he replied directing a knowing wink to the audience.

'Okay Deano, if you'd like to take a seat.' Megan gestured at the two seats set up at the front of the stage. Oh how she longed to whip his chair away at the very last minute and see him collapse on to his oversized arse. Instead she took a deep breath, sat down opposite him and turned to address the audience. 'As I said in my speech, this exercise is a crucial tool, not only in life or business coaching but in a sales environment too. By ascertaining your clients' core values you will be able to tailor your pitch accordingly and thereby greatly enhance your chances of success. Okay Deano, I'd like you to begin by telling me your top eight values in life.'

Deano looked at her blankly.

'Shagging,' someone yelled from the crowd.

Deano smirked and shrugged his rugby player sized shoulders. 'What do you mean by values?' he asked.

'Doh!' someone else yelled, perfectly echoing Megan's thoughts.

'What is it that you really value in your life?' she replied in what she hoped was a suitably patient tone.

Deano scratched his gel-peaked head. 'Well wedge, obviously.'

Megan looked at him questioningly.

'Money,' he explained, prompting a rapturous cheer from the audience. 'Yeah money. I'd say that's definitely my number one.'

'Okay and why money?'

Deano looked at her as if she were insane. 'What do you mean, why money?'

'Well what does that provide you with?' Megan turned to the audience, 'Sometimes we need to probe a client's initial answer in order to see what their true value is,' she explained.

'What does money provide me with?' Deano asked somewhat incredulously. 'Well, nice stuff, innit? Cars and clothes and booze and that.'

'And birds,' someone yelled.

'Yeah,'Deano chortled. 'Not that I have to pay for birds, mind, but having money means I can show a bird – sorry a woman, a good time, d'you know what I mean?'

Somebody in the audience wolf whistled.

'Right,' Megan swallowed hard – she wondered if a guest speaker had ever puked live on stage at the Brighton Conference Centre before. 'But what does that provide you with?'

'What, showing a woman a good time?'

Megan nodded.

'Well it means I get a shag, doesn't it?' Cue even more whistling and hollering from the audience.

Once again Megan felt the overwhelming sensation of not belonging, only this time her feelings didn't make her feel frightened or vulnerable; she didn't feel like a lost little girl – she just felt like a complete phoney. What on earth was she doing here, trying to help people like this become even more shallow and materialistic? *Don't judge a book by its cover, we are all human, let he who is without sin. . .* her inner coach urged, although for some bizarre reason it seemed to have adopted an oily cockney twang.

'Yes but what does that provide you with?' she continued, sitting forward in her seat, determined not to be beaten by this cocky imbecile.

'What does having a shag provide me with?' Deano asked, a little less sure of himself all of a sudden.

'Yes,' Megan replied, maintaining a steadfast gaze upon his now perspiring face.

'Well, it's a buzz innit?'

'And the cars and the clothes – how do they make you feel?'

'Well – they make me feel good – about myself.'

'Why?'

Deano shifted in his chair and looked down at his lap. 'Because it proves I'm a success.'

'And what does that feeling of success provide you with?' Megan held her breath, praying that no-one in the audience would pipe up with any smart arse remarks. She had him now, she was sure of it.

'Well – I suppose it provides me with security, don't it. Knowing I've got money in the bank and that I've got a good career.'

Megan nodded at him and smiled before turning to the audience. 'So do you see how important it is to probe your client's initial answers? Often their true value will be buried quite a long way beneath.' Somewhat gratifyingly she was met with a sea of nodding heads. 'Okay Deano, thanks for that, now what else do you value in life?'

Deano looked at her and smiled before turning to the audience. 'Getting pissed, innit,' he yelled to hoots of approval.

Two excruciating hours later and Megan was back in the B&B packing her case. As she slung her clothes and folders inside she felt a horrible hollow feeling eat away at her insides. All traces of the previous day's bravado on the beach were now long gone as the reality of her situation and the enormity of what lay ahead of her continued to dawn. Had her entire life been a sham? Not only her marriage, but her student days and subsequently her entire career? Had that American caller from the previous weekend's show been right? Was it all just a big ruse? What was the point in all of the excessive coaching and questioning; the courses and seminars, not to mention the font of positivity that had for so long been pumping away at the very core of her life? What was the point in all of the sayings and the quotes; the exercises and the affirmations? People always seemed to get it wrong in the end anyway. And what was the point in people like her analysing everything to death. What was that saying? *Paralysis by Analysis.* God there seemed to be a neat little sound bite for everything. Apart from how she was currently feeling – a mixture of numbness, confusion and complete and utter fear. Just like the Emperor's New Clothes, had she bought into the myth, wrapping herself in a blanket of cod philosophy and psycho-babble that actually meant nothing at all?

Megan sat down on the bed and held her head in her hands. Was there anything real about her life? As the answer to that question emerged phoenix-like from the murky depths of her mind it caused her to shiver. Laurence was the only real and tangible thing she had and yet he had become so remote over the past couple of years, she wasn't even sure if she could still claim any type of ownership. A fierce tug of longing pulled Megan up from the bed and over to the door. She only hoped she wasn't too late.

chapter Eighteen

"Today try to recapture some of the innocence from your childhood.
Paint, dance, sing, go to your local park and swing.
Take your inner child out to play."
Megan Rowe, 'Help Yourself to Happiness.'

A man's gotta do what a man's gotta do. As Danny stood in the centre of his living room pondering his latest dilemma he couldn't help remembering his father's favourite catch phrase and a smile flitted across his troubled face. He pictured Pops standing in the doorway of his childhood bedroom, *dwarfing* the doorway of his childhood bedroom with his huge frame as he rolled up his shirt sleeves to reveal a pair of giant arms fringed with golden hair. 'A *man's gotta do what a man's gotta do,*' he'd holler before striding over to break up the latest out of control wrestling bout between himself and Marty by tickling them both into submission. 'A *man's gotta do what a man's gotta do!*' Pops would roar as his huge arms set about separating their thrashing skinny limbs and he and Marty would just about raise the roof as they screamed from the excruciating mixture of pleasure and pain.

Danny pushed up the sleeves on his faded University of Texas sweatshirt and looked down at his own arms. He guessed they had to be about the same size as his father's now, with exactly the same covering of sandy hair. Who'd have thought he would have grown so big? As a kid he sure as hell could never imagine becoming a man. Sure he'd dream about it, practically all the time, especially when he was being nagged to death by some dumb-ass teacher, but he never thought it would be possible to become a colossus of a man like Pops. Still didn't really.

Danny walked over to the living room window. He turned. He walked back over to the brutally unwelcoming green vinyl covered sofa and stopped, gazing down at the battered shoebox that sat there like an unexploded landmine. All he had to do was sit down next to it and take off the lid. That wasn't so hard was it? Danny walked back over to the windowsill where he'd left his packet of cigarettes and took one out and lit it. Outside the sky remained an unforgiving blank sheet of white, he was starting to give up all hope of ever seeing the sun again. And to think only a few weeks previously he had been complaining about the heat in Iraq. Danny exhaled and looked over at the shoebox through the plume of cigarette smoke. Jeez this was ridiculous – they were only a bunch of photographs, he'd seen them a million times before, he'd taken them for Christ's sake. The problem was he hadn't looked at them since Nasir had been killed. That day and the subsequent days with Nasir's widow Faria had caused everything to change. Something had shifted, a barrier had been obliterated, leaving him raw as an open wound. But how else was he going to get these stories written if he couldn't bring himself to look at the pictures that inspired them.

Danny inhaled deeply on his cigarette and let out a low hacking cough. London certainly wasn't proving too good for his health, a cruel irony that certainly didn't pass him by. Imagine that in all his years spent stalking some of the most dangerous places on the planet he should remain relatively unscathed by the gunfire, the shelling, the mines and the bombs and yet as soon as he came to London to hole up in a garret he fell prey to regular panic attacks, chronic insomnia and some kind of sinister bronchial sounding infection. Danny glanced at his transistor radio balanced on top of the health and safety evading gas fire. Perhaps if he had a bit of background noise it would lessen the tension? He turned the radio on and to his huge relief discovered it was one of the more entertaining presenters on Loose Talk – a shock jock called Bradley Steeple who hosted the late morning show and seemed to hail from the same irreverent mould as the New York presenter Howard Stern.

'Eeeeewwwww!' Steeple was screeching in hammed up horror, 'Thanks for that Gloria. So Gloria's mum used to tell her if she bit her nails they'd end up growing back out of her legs. How about the rest of you? What lies did your parents tell you when you were growing up? Give us a ring on 0800 107 107 and let me know. Time for a bit of a musical interlude now. Here's Lynard Skinnard with their all time classic "Free Bird."'

As the guitar struck up the artificially slow intro, a tantalising precursor for the great crashing crescendo to come, Danny recalled a particularly exuberant wrestling session from his childhood. Pops had sat between him and Marty, a huge arm weighing across each of their scrawny shoulders as they both fought to regain their breath.

'Whatever happens out there, you guys remember you're brothers and brothers always what?' he had said, looking down at each of them in turn.

'Steal each others' toys,' Marty had piped up, his sky blue eyes sparkling mischievously.

'Plant worms in their little brother's bed,' Danny had retaliated with the meanest death stare he could muster, causing Marty to yelp in horror.

'They look out for each other,' Pops had replied before tousling their hair and pushing them from him. 'Because blood's thicker than water. You got that? Now who's for a soda?'

Blood. How much blood had Danny seen? Over the years. How much blood, splattered and spilled, frothy and congealed? He must have seen oceans of the stuff. And yet it had all washed away eventually hadn't it. From the bullet riddled walls and the dusty floors. Within a day or two it was always scrubbed clean away. It wasn't really thicker than water in any sense. Pops had lied. Danny knew that without a shadow of a doubt. He had the blood on his hands to prove it.

'Freebird' was cranking up a notch now, with the guitars racing the drums towards the crescendo. Danny went back over to the sofa and sat down next to the box. Raising the lid slightly he delved in, rummaging right to the very bottom without looking, as if selecting a ticket in a lucky dip. His fingers found the smooth glossy edge of a photo and he pulled it out, holding his breath. Taking a drag on his cigarette he finally managed to look down. The grinning face of a young boy looked back at him. Although the picture was black and white you could see his hair was sun bleached blonde and his skin streaked with dirt. Jesus! It had been so long since Danny had seen this photo it was almost like seeing it for the first time. And for the first time he saw something glaring up at him, something that perhaps the camera lens had managed to filter out back then, but now it was all too apparent. Fighting the urge to cram the picture back in the box Danny looked back down at it. And once again the kid beamed back at him, his grin full of knowing and something else – pride – as if he were showing off a prize winning fish. Danny looked at the kid's scrawny arms, one placed on his hip the other toting what seemed like a ridiculously large revolver. And there at his feet the bloated corpse of a Serbian soldier.

'You want to see a dead Chetnik?' Danny could practically hear the kid's voice echoing up at him through the photo. He closed his eyes and there he was, back in Sarajevo, Spring 1993. Danny had only been there a couple of days on his first official posting and, already tired of the cliquey media pack holed up in the Holiday Inn, he had gone off exploring the surrounding streets with their shelled tower blocks and burnt out cars. It was like wandering through an extremely battered Hollywood film set, with so many of the buildings now only fronts, all set against what looked like a painted mountain backdrop it seemed so incongruous with the wreckage below. As Danny had ducked into a darkened alleyway running away from the Main Street towards the mountains he had come across the kid, Marko, that was his name, sitting on an old crate, polishing his revolver on the bottom of his grubby t-shirt.

'You press?' He'd said, pointing at the camera slung around Danny's neck.

'Uh-huh,' Danny had replied, feeling somewhat embarrassed at his new occupation. Despite having only been in Sarajevo a couple of days he knew the locals preferred the title 'war tourist' to press or media. And who could blame them? But then how else would the rest of the world hear about their plight if it weren't for people like Danny reporting on what they saw. It was a begrudging alliance that never sat entirely comfortably with Danny, in all his years of war coverage, the sense that he was in some way intruding on others' heartache. But it never quite outweighed the burning need to exorcise his own pain. So when the kid had offered to show him a corpse he felt a sickening tingle in his gut. This was it. This was what he had come here for – to confront death itself. But when they arrived at the pale bloated body of the soldier, lying in the shadows of the infamous Snipers Alley, Danny had felt a strange sense of disappointment. *Is this it?* he had felt like asking the boy. And then he had realised what was missing. This wasn't Death, this strange swollen corpse, buzzing with flies in the Spring heat. This was more like Death's calling card – leaving him wrong-footed once again.

But as Danny examined the photo now, seated on his cold vinyl sofa in his cold Hammersmith apartment, he realised that Death had been there all along – he just hadn't known where to look. It was in the kid's eyes, in that dull, muted stare belying the grin beneath. This was what he would write about first – Marko's story and the death of innocence.

Chapter Nineteen

"Try losing yourself in a piece of classical music.
Let the soaring melodies lift you to a higher plane."
Megan Rowe, 'Help Yourself to Happiness.'

'Just lie back, close your eyes and relax,' Gerry coaxed as Natalie obligingly reclined across the scratchy front row seats. She bit her lip and fought the sudden urge to smirk. What the hell was the old letch going to do now? Exactly what kind of 'character building exercise' required her to get horizontal? And he'd said there weren't going to be any more casting couch moments this time! Still doing it in the front row of The Theatre on the Green, with the Artistic Director no less, did hold a certain thrill. And perhaps he might actually be able to get it up straight away this time seeing as he had no booze inside him. Natalie wriggled slightly, tilting her groin upwards and expanding her chest.

'Good,' Gerry whispered. Was it her imagination or had he also emitted the faintest of gasps? Natalie slowly licked her lips, keeping her eyes firmly closed. She heard Gerry shuffle slightly from his crouched position in the aisle beside her before he continued. 'Now I want you to picture yourself as the central character Miranda when she was about ten years old. You are standing outside her childhood home. Take a deep breath and allow the picture of that home to appear in your mind.'

Natalie inhaled deeply, further swelling her chest, before picturing a large, grey-stoned manor house – her own childhood home. Oh what the hell, it would be a lot easier than using her imagination. 'Okay, I can see it' she whispered breathlessly.

'Right, now I want you to picture the front door. What kind of condition is it in? What details do you notice?'

Natalie saw her own solid oak door studded with wrought iron nails and the huge circular knocker hanging in the middle. As a child it had seemed as sturdy and foreboding as the door to a medieval fort.

'What can Miranda hear as she stands outside the door?' Gerry asked. 'Can she hear anything from inside the house?'

Casting her mind back Natalie could hear Madame Butterfly warbling through the open window of her mother's study – and instantly recalled the associated feelings of elation and sorrow it would inspire. Her mother was home, but would be holed up for hours in her sacred space, strictly off limits to her.

'Now I want you to imagine going into Miranda's house. What do you notice when you come into the hall?'

Well that was easy. Natalie saw the antique dresser crammed with carefully arranged clusters of silver framed 'happy' family photographs, illuminated by a crystal Tiffany lamp. The creaky wooden staircase sweeping up to the gallery, the walls lined with yet more pictures, yet more lies. The round Persian rug in the centre of the hall, a woven kaleidoscope of ruby and gold. And the huge grandfather clock looming over her sternly, its heavy gold pendulum swinging from side to side like a giant wagging finger.

'And what do you hear?'

Once more Natalie heard strains of Madame Butterfly escaping from behind the firmly closed door to the left of the hall and the hollow ticking of the grandfather clock. 'Tsk, tsk,' it seemed to be saying. 'Tsk, tsk.'

'Now I want you to imagine that the entire family is at home.' Gerry continued from his position on the floor beside her. 'What type of family do you imagine Miranda coming from? What clues have you been given in the script? Who and where are they and how do they greet her as a ten year old child upon her arrival home?'

Natalie gave a dry little cough and shifted. The theatre seats were starting to feel as stiff as boards beneath her back and a feeling of claustrophobia began wrapping itself around her like a shroud. How much longer was this bloody exercise going to take? She took a deep breath and remembered her reason for coming to the theatre, she couldn't bail out now. Natalie thought back to herself as a child returning home from school. She pictured taking off her coat and hanging it straight in the hall closet, removing her shoes and lining them up with the others ranked along the floor of the closet. Then padding through to the huge kitchen at the back of the house, the stone flagging icy cold beneath her feet. On the table, as always, were a glass of milk and a plate of cookies left by Mrs Butterworth, the housekeeper.

'Think of the smells you encounter as you move from room to room greeting each family member.' Gerry urged from beside her, she could feel his breath hot on her cheek.

The kitchen always smelt of pine cleaning fluid and sometimes the faint trace of baking, but artificial pine, that is what she remembered most. Natalie pictured her childhood self slowly walking back along the hall and coming to a stop outside her mother's study. She remembered stubbing her bare toes on the over-polished wooden floor before finally summoning the courage to knock. And then the waiting, stomach churning, skin tingling as she heard the music being turned down and the clip clop of her mother's heels across the floor. And the brass door handle mysteriously turning and the door opening and lavender, the smell of lavender wafting out like a sigh. That's the smell she remembered from her mother's room. The smell she remembered from her mother, following her around like a delicate mist, clinging to her pale blonde hair and wispy satin clothes. Lavender. It still made her want to puke. Natalie couldn't understand for the life of her how it was meant to cure insomnia. Just the mere thought of lavender gave her nightmares.

'What do each of the family members say to Miranda as she greets them? Do they call her by a pet name? Are they pleased to see her?' Gerry asked, his voice gentle and low, but for some reason also horribly grating. 'What does her mother say as she arrives home?'

'Natalie, what have I told you about interrupting me when I'm working? Now run along and play.' She heard her mother say from somewhere way above her. And she remembered focusing on her mother's beautiful shoes, the delicate heels and the satin bows blurring in and out of focus as she blinked back burning tears.

Natalie gulped. This exercise was crap. Why hadn't she done what she was told and tried to conjure up a fictional world for Miranda? It would have been so much easier. How much more of this torture did Gerry have in mind? This wasn't what she'd planned on at all. She wanted to have some fun.

'Okay. I want you to go upstairs now,' the torturing bastard, Gerry continued. 'And I want you to go into Miranda's childhood bedroom. Do you think she would have had any siblings? If so how many, and where do you think she would come in the family? Does she seem like an oldest child or the baby of the family? Does she share a room?'

Natalie almost laughed out loud. The thought of sharing a bedroom with her arrogant arsehole of an elder brother Sean was a complete joke. As with her mother's study, Sean's bedroom had been a complete no-go zone to her. Not that she would have wanted to go in there anyway. Just like its tediously dull owner, it had no personality, no flair, with its rancid red and white striped wallpaper and tubular chrome furniture. Anyone would have thought the plethora of trophies and tacky rosettes crammed inside were in celebration of championship dullardness rather than horse racing.

'How does her position in the family make her feel?' Gerry continued, in his pukey syrupy voice.

Oh just great, Natalie thought bitterly. Being ignored the entire time. Having to spend hours on my own in a spooky old house with only the TV for company.

'And what is her relationship with her parents like? From what you gather about Miranda in the play and her marriage to Gareth, what type of relationship do you think she might have had with her father?'

Natalie unclenched her fists and relaxed back into the chairs.

'So what have you got to show me this time, princess?' She heard her father ask in his Southern Irish lilt. He was the one person who had made her feel wanted – if only he'd been there a little more often, not constantly over at his stables in Galway or at some stupid race meet or other. She remembered pulling on her ballet shoes, her fingers trembling as she wound the pink satin ribbon around her ankles and praying she didn't mess up her pirouette or stumble from her blocks and have to see that look of disappointment flit across his face. But how sweet the praise when she got it right – when her feet felt light as butterfly wings as they flitted across the living room floor.

'That's my girl,' he would say, waving his hands excitedly like a little leprechaun, his huge eyes twinkling like pieces of polished jade. Natalie couldn't help smiling at the recollection.

'And her mother,' Gerry cut in, 'How do you think Miranda got on with her mother as a child?'

The sensation of overwhelming disappointment swooped down upon Natalie like a freezing fog – she couldn't breathe.

'Could we stop for a moment,' she asked, lurching upright and opening her eyes.

A mixture of shock and concern washed across Gerry's face. 'Yes, of course. Are you okay? You look a little pale?'

'I'm fine,' Natalie snapped. Why couldn't he just leave her alone, with his stupid prying and prodding? And now her eyes were starting to smart. Bugger, bugger, bugger! Get a grip, she wanted to scream to herself, but seemingly her eyes were now acting completely independently from the rest of her body, pumping streams of hot tears on to her face.

'Oh no, oh God I'm so sorry,' she heard Gerry say from somewhere next to her, but she couldn't look she was so embarrassed. Then she felt him start to stroke her hair and it made her want to scream. Because she wanted so badly to let go and let him hold her and stroke her until the tears washed all the hurt and pain away, but of course she couldn't. She mustn't. And so her body remained rigid and tight, every muscle steely and coiled against his touch. Because he was only after one thing wasn't he? Just like they all were.

'I'm fine,' she muttered, pushing him away and wiping furiously at her face with the backs of her hands. Bugger, bugger, bugger, her pale hands were streaked with black - her mascara had run. What the hell did her face look like?

'Here,' Gerry handed her a tissue. It looked suspiciously like the same putrid specimen from the previous day on the Common, but this time Natalie took it gladly and wiped her eyes. 'I'm so sorry,' Gerry whispered. 'I had no idea it would be so emotional for you. You obviously tapped into something deep within Miranda's character – a sense of loss perhaps?'

Natalie nodded whilst continuing to wipe her eyes. Great, he had given her a way to bullshit her way out of this mess. 'Yes,' she muttered. 'Perhaps it's the way she is with Gareth in the play – the way she practically forces him down the aisle - I just got the overwhelming sense that she'd had a very lonely childhood.'

Gerry stared at her for a moment. Christ, did she still have mascara all over her face or something. 'Mmm,' he said thoughtfully, stroking his chin. He had obviously had a shave since she'd seen him the day before and in the low lighting of the theatre he was looking quite distinguished again. Yes, he wasn't bad at all, dimly lit and sober. An image of Natalie arriving at a premier on his arm flashed into her head.

'GERRY RADCLIFFE ESCORTS HOT NEW ACTRESS NATALIE TAYLOR-CASSIDY TO THE PREMIER OF HER LATEST MOVIE.' She could just see the headlines. They would be like Michael Douglas and Catherine Zeta Jones – people would wonder at the age gap and yet respect her maturity for choosing such an older more experienced partner. And she could always take younger, hotter lovers when away on set.

'You obviously have a great emotional depth,' Gerry said, continuing to stare at her intently, 'And that is so important for an actress, that ability to feel, to go beyond the surface of a script, to get to the very heart of a character.'

Yada, yada, yada. Natalie let out a heavy sigh. 'It really is quite draining though.' She swung her legs round so that she was facing Gerry, also allowing her skirt to ride up even higher. 'I don't suppose we could have a bit of a break could we? Nip somewhere for a drink.'

Gerry frowned. 'I was really trying to lay off the booze this week to be honest.'

Natalie stuck out her bottom lip. 'Oh – okay. I'm sorry, I shouldn't have suggested it, it's just that doing that exercise well it – oh never mind.' She dropped her head.

'What?' Gerry covered her hand with his own, dwarfing it. 'Are you sure you're okay?'

'Well, no not exactly.' Natalie took a deep breath; it was all or nothing time. She got to her feet. 'I should go, I'm sorry.' She brought the tissue back up to her eye and pretended to wipe away a tear. 'Oh God, how embarrassing.'

Gerry stood up and put his hands on her shoulders. 'What is it? Please? I feel terrible. It seems as if every time we meet I end up upsetting you.'

'Oh no – it's not you it's me,' Natalie whispered, trying desperately not to cringe. How could he fall for this bullshit? Men were just so easy to work. 'Doing the exercise, well I thought I was thinking about Miranda but it seems to have triggered some painful personal memories for me too.'

Gerry nodded sagely. 'Yes it can happen.'

'Really?'

'Oh yes. But you mustn't feel embarrassed. It just proves that you are human. And actors do tend to be extra sensitive. It's as if that side of you is over-developed. But that is what makes you so good at what you do.' He squeezed her shoulders and gazed into her eyes. 'You must never, never lose that sensitivity, Natalie. It is your gift and I believe you have a responsibility to nurture it.'

Natalie looked up at him wide-eyed. 'Are you saying – are you saying you think I have a gift?'

Gerry shook his head and let out an incredulous laugh. 'Yes of course you have a gift. You wouldn't be here if I didn't believe that.'

'Hmm.' Natalie frowned. Why the hell didn't I get a second audition then? She wanted to demand.

As if reading her mind Gerry hastily continued. 'I tell you what, why don't we go and get a bite to eat? I haven't eaten a thing all day and I really think buying you dinner is the least I could do after you know, everything that's happened.'

"GERRY RADCLIFFE AND NATALIE TAYLOR-CASSIDY DINING AT THE IVY"

Natalie smiled and got to her feet.

'That would be lovely,' she said, pulling on the hem of her skirt and tipping her head to one side. 'I'll just go and you know, freshen up.' As Gerry stood up she reached up on tiptoes and planted a delicate kiss on the corner of his mouth. 'Thank you, thank you so much,' she whispered, before sashaying off to the Ladies.

Chapter Twenty

"Get in touch with your sensual side.
Whether it be massage or candlelit baths, exploring your own or your
partner's body, make time to give yourself pleasure."
Megan Rowe, 'Help Yourself to Happiness.'

Cheddar swung his legs over the side of his rickety single bed, hoisted himself upright and began peeling the sticky condom from his rapidly deflating penis. Cock, prick, dick – funny how just about all of the names for a bloke's manhood also doubled as common insults. And yes they were all terms he could quite easily apply to himself right now as he sat there, peeling back the slimy latex and wishing that he too could shrivel up out of sight. This was what he hated the most about sex – the way it could make you feel so damned shite about yourself so quickly. From hero to zero in just a few sweaty thrusts.

'So, same time next week then, angel?' The voice that had just a few minutes before seemed husky and sensual now sounded harsh and coarse.

'No, no I don't think so.' Cheddar couldn't bring himself to turn around. If he couldn't disappear then why couldn't she? A burning wave of shame rushed through his sweaty body erupting like fire into his cheeks. Finally he managed to remove the condom and he reached over to the bedside cabinet for the box of tissues, still not turning around.

'All right. If you're sure?' She rasped. 'You know where I am anyway. You can always give us a ring.'

'Aye.' Cheddar wiped himself and gazed mournfully at the floor, at the aqua coloured rug he had purchased from Habitat that very morning to match the freshly painted walls. Everywhere looked bright and clean; way too clean for a dirty old sod like him. What on earth had he been thinking giving his room a makeover, daring to think he could even give himself a make-over, when deep down at heart he would remain the same sorry loser he'd always been. He leant forward and picked his boxer shorts off the floor. Boxer shorts – huh – you could get an entire bloody boxing ring in the buggers, they were that big. Who the hell was he kidding with his fridge full of carrots and celery and other assorted rabbit food? He was just a fat, useless, dirty slob who let people down and caused disappointment wherever he went.

'Right well, I'll get me money and be off then, shall I?'

A fat, useless, dirty slob who had to pay for sex. Cheddar opened the top drawer of the bedside cabinet and took out his wallet. What on earth had possessed him to call her when he knew full well he would end up feeling like this? Why hadn't he learnt from the first time he had seen her? He'd felt bad enough then and he hadn't even shagged her. And what made it even worse was that he was meant to have been turning over a new leaf, what with his room and his fridge and that stupid piece of card. He cringed as he thought of the life coaching exercise. Who the hell was he trying to kid? Cheddar took some notes from his wallet and lay them down on the end of the bed, as if by doing so; by not actually physically handing them to her, he could pretend he wasn't actually paying her at all. He was just placing some money on the end of his bed and she would just happen to pick it up, that was all.

He heard her move about behind him and saw her hand reach out and take the cash. Her arm was scrawny and pale, the veins on the back of her hand a blue labyrinth like rivers on a map and her blood red nails short and chipped. *I'm sorry,* he suddenly wanted to say. *I'm so, so sorry.* But he remained frozen, speechless, to the bed. As she got up and began dressing he caught a waft of her perfume. It had smelt so nice when she had first arrived. Fresh and floral and feminine. And it had made him want to hold her to him because that was what he missed the most, being able to hold a woman, to cradle that softness and that mystery in his arms and feel strong and protective and all the things a man should. It was that need that had made him call her that first disastrous time a couple of weeks previously and then again earlier that day as he had stood in his freshly decorated room and never felt more alone. But now the perfume just smelt tacky and cheap as it mingled with the other scents in the room, the sweat and the sex, and he wanted to just curl up and die with the shame of it all.

'You all right, love?' she asked as she continued to dress.

'Yes, yes I'm fine.' Cheddar replied, hastily pulling up his pants. But inside he wanted to hang his head and wail.

'Place looks nice. You been decorating?'

'Aye, just a lick of paint and a new rug.'

'Looks great – really brightened the place up.'

'Cheers.' Oh why wouldn't she just take the money and go? He heard her move towards the door. Finally! Then she stopped in her tracks.

'It's not a crime you know,' she said from just inside the doorway.

'Sorry?' He half looked up, not quite making eye contact, just aware of her silhouette, scrawny and high-heeled in the doorway.

'Sex. It's not a crime.'

'Yeah, I know.'

'And with me – it's not a crime. I am a person, a human being.'

Cheddar turned right around and looked at her properly. The first time he had seen her he had been relieved she was older, it had seemed less embarrassing somehow. He had even kidded himself she could be his very own, somewhat belated Mrs Robinson. But now, in the post-coital glare of shame, her age made her look tired and worn, rather than worldly and experienced. Her bleached hair dishevelled and straw like, her skin creased beneath the make-up, like hairline cracks in alabaster. 'Yes of course you are. I know that,' he replied.

She laughed a dry bitter little laugh. 'Yeah right. That's why you can't look at me, that's why you can't even give me the money properly. Oh don't worry, I'm used to it, used to far worse to be honest. I just wanted you to know that I do have feelings.'

Cheddar got to his feet staring at her intently and shaking his head. 'No you don't understand – it's not you, it's me. I'm ashamed of meself.'

'For sleeping with me.' She turned to go.

'No – well yes – but not because it's you. Oh chuffin' hell. I'm not doing a very good job of this am I?' Cheddar took a deep breath, Christ he was such a loser with women he could even manage to piss off a prostitute. 'It's the fact I've had to pay for it like – of course I feel ashamed.'

She let out a dry little laugh. 'And you think half the fellas down at the Palais won't be doing the exact same thing this weekend when they pick up their Saturday night shag? The only difference is they'll be paying for it in Bacardi Breezers.'

Cheddar scratched his head and chuckled. 'Hmm.' The irony was he was way too shy to approach a woman in a bar or nightclub. After what had happened with Denise what little confidence he'd had with women had completely evaporated in a haze of pain. In the end taking a card from a phone box and calling a prostitute had seemed like the easier option, the only option, barring joining a monastery.

'The fact is nothing in this life comes for free,' she continued, rooting through her patent leather handbag and pulling out a glittery pink plastic comb. 'Everything comes at a price it's just that some are more obvious than others.'

Chuffin' hell, of all the call girls he could have picked trust him to have found the Confucius of the vice world.

Cheddar sat back down on the bed. 'So how come you ended up in this game then?' he asked.

'Oh no you don't,' she replied, pulling the comb through her matted hair.

'Don't what?'

'Start doing the old "Pretty Woman" routine on me. You know, the old tell me all about yourself routine, the old, how did a sweetheart like you end up like this malarkey. I ain't no Julia Roberts you know.'

As Cheddar watched her apply a slash of bright crimson lipstick, her scraggy neck straining like a turkey's he fought the sudden urge to laugh. 'No, I guess not.'

'And you certainly ain't no Richard Gere!'

'Oi!' They both looked at each other and laughed. She put the lipstick back in her bag and clicked it shut.

'That's better. Your face was looking like a right slapped arse. We had sex. We had a shag. No one died. No-one got hurt, so get over it. Enjoy it. You're a bloke, you're doing what comes natural.'

Bloody hell, now she was sounding like the life coach of the vice world. Perhaps he could get her a slot on Megan's show?

'Better that you come and see me than be out there messing with kids or raping old ladies.'

Cheddar looked at her and didn't know whether to laugh or cry. In the end he laughed and laughed and laughed. What the hell was he doing, he thought as he bent over clutching his side. How had it come to this? But even that suddenly seemed hilariously funny. If Denise could only see him now. Cheddar thought of Denise with those weird odour-controlled white slips that she stuck inside her pants and her refusal to ever give him a blow job and the way in which she would run from the bed straight to the shower the minute they finished having sex. At the time he had felt as if it were he who had the problem. Him, the great big smelly, inconvenient lump with his outrageous demands to pollute her body, but he was a bloke for Christ's sake, he was only doing what came naturally. He wanted sex. No, he actually wanted to make love. He wasn't a kiddy fiddler or the mad psycho stalker of old ladies. All he wanted was to love and make love to a woman. To have and to hold, Christ it was even written into the wedding vows – how could it possibly be a crime? It didn't say in the wedding vows to penetrate once a month if lucky and then escort to the nearest antiseptic delousing chamber. And if *he* wanted it then surely there had to be a woman out there who wanted it too. And didn't want paying for it. For he was BRAVE, ENTERPRISING, STREET SMART and TALENTED. He had a GOOD SENSE OF HUMOUR and was PATIENT and had WILL POWER. Yes he had WILL POWER – he had gone three days now without a kebab hadn't he, so he would wait. He wouldn't pay for sex ever again because he wouldn't need to.

'Thank-you,' he said, getting up to her show her out. 'Thank you very much – for everything.'

chapter Twenty-One

"Life is too short to allow other people's issues or baggage to poison our own happiness. Who are the 'toxic' people in your life? What steps can you take to neutralise the effect they have upon you?"
Megan Rowe, 'Help Yourself to Happiness.'

By the time Megan got back from Brighton it was almost ten o'clock at night. A fat yellow moon hung low in the sky over Nightingale Avenue and as she walked past the ranks of gable fronted houses, dragging her wheeled case behind her, the only other signs of life were the neighbourhood cats, slinking shadow-like from garden to garden. The biting wind of the previous weeks had finally dropped and the elm trees stood proud and majestic once more, as if guarding the pastel washed homes glowing luminescent behind them. For the first time in months Megan actually felt warm as she approached the end of the long wide road, her skin sticky beneath her stiff suit and woollen winter coat. As her own house loomed into view she felt increasingly apprehensive. Would Gerry be in? Would he be drunk? Would he be spoiling for an argument following her phone call and announcement that she was leaving him? Perhaps he'd changed the locks in a fit of rage in the three days she'd been away? Perhaps he'd been on a drunken wrecking spree, smashing up her belongings and throwing her clothes all over the front garden? And what about Laurence? How would he be? What would Gerry have told him?

What if he'd told Laurence she didn't love either of them, that she had left, had abandoned them both? Perhaps that's why Laurence's text message, 'WHATEVER,' had been so abrupt – oh God, what had she done?

Megan was in such a state of near hysteria as she turned into her garden path she was actually shocked by the scene of apparent tranquillity that greeted her. There were no hand-daubed signs reading 'BAD MOTHERS AND ERRANT WIVES KEEP OUT!' No smashed windows or crumpled beer cans lining the path, no bras and pants draping the elm tree. Instead the house was steeped in darkness, as if it were fast asleep, the reflection of the moon illuminating the stained glass panel on the front door like a night light, scarlet, blue and gold. As Megan stopped to get her keys from her handbag she noticed the huge azalea bush to her right had finally burst into bloom, great splashes of pink adorning every branch. And it made her want to cry, this amazing display of beauty and life because it was all so tragically late. Taking a deep breath she put her key in the lock and to her huge relief the heavy door swung open. Hoisting her case over the threshold she stepped into the hall and turned on the brass standard lamp in the corner. Apart from the pile of junk mail on the floor the hall was exactly as she had left it. The wooden floor still scuffed in all the same places, the green rug still hiding the worst of them right in the centre. The house smelt a little musty though. A trapped fug of male deodorant and fried food.

Megan went through to the kitchen. Dirty dishes lined the granite counter next to the sink and a frying pan coated with a snowy layer of congealed fat sat on top of the huge stove. She felt a pang of guilt as she saw an empty box of pop tarts lying on the scrubbed pine table. The remnants of Laurence's breakfast no doubt. She wondered where he was. The house was deathly quiet. He was probably in his room. She hoped he was in his room, not staying at a friends. She automatically glanced at the notice-board beside the fridge, but there were no scrawled messages saying *'gone to Joe's'* or *'staying the night at Bjorn's.'* No, the only note that remained was one she had written herself, back on Saturday, back in her old life when she still had a happy family and home (or at least the illusion of one) *'pick up holiday brochures.'* Megan sighed. Leaving her case in the hall she climbed the wide wooden staircase, automatically avoiding the creaky step at the top. Upstairs everything was dark and eerily quiet. As she stood in the centre of the wide landing she looked through the open door to the main bedroom – the master bedroom - no longer her bedroom. Her heart skipped a beat as she saw the silhouette of a lump on the bed – was it Gerry? But closer inspection revealed it to be the duvet bunched up in a heap. Her study and the bathroom were also empty, the only door that was closed was Laurence's. Megan looked at the crack beneath for a tell-tale glimmer of light or the blue neon flicker from his television, but it was completely black. Was he home? Please let him be home. She tiptoed across the landing and took hold of the door handle. Shouldn't she knock first? But what if he were asleep and she woke him? Megan stood rooted to the spot for a moment, thinking back to the days when Laurence was a baby and his bedroom door had never been closed. Back then she had been able to walk in whenever she wanted and scoop him gurgling and milky from his cot, and hold him to her, but now . . .

Megan shook her head and sighed. This is what she hated most about getting older, the sense that time was slipping through her hands like sand and the harder she tried to grasp on to things the faster they seemed to escape. For so long she had been blissfully unaware of the passage of time, blissfully submerged in the game of life, buried up to her neck in its endless challenges and dramas. If only she could recapture that lack of awareness. She knocked softly on Laurence's door. There was no sound from inside the room. An awful thought suddenly entered Megan's mind, causing her skin to prickle with both anger and fear. What if Gerry had taken him on some kind of father son male bonding expedition to the local pub designed to prove that they didn't need her anyway? What if the bastard was getting Laurence drunk? Megan pushed the door open and stepped into the room. Her eyes scanned the darkness, squinting to make out the darkened silhouettes. The cricket bat leaning against the desk piled high with text books and folders. The jumbles of clothes dotted across the floor leading over to the bed in the corner. And in the bed? Megan tiptoed further into the room and stood staring at the mounded duvet. After what seemed an eternity she saw it shift slightly and as she watched the gentle rise and fall and listened to the rhythmic hum of Laurence's breathing she was once again sent hurtling back in time. To when Laurence was a tiny baby and the heart-stopping moments she had stood by his Moses basket or cot, listening desperately for that little puff of breath or the tell-tale murmur that would let her know he was still alive. Let her know that the precious gift so suddenly and unexpectedly bestowed upon her had not been cruelly snatched from her grasp. For months after his birth Megan had been plagued by the certain fear she would lose Laurence; all those nights when Gerry had been away touring or out drinking and she had been left quite literally holding the baby. In those dark months when she had felt plagued by loneliness and loss; Laurence had been the one tangible presence in her life, and yet he was so fragile, with his doll-like fingers and toes and his seemingly paper thin scalp. Looking back now it seemed incredible he had actually made it to the ripe old age of fourteen. And yet something seemed to have gone amiss along the way. Although she hadn't lost him physically, somewhere along the line, on some emotional level, a yawning chasm had opened up between them.

Megan crept over to the foot of the bed and dared herself to sit down. When Laurence had been younger she had often done this, come into his room before going to bed and sat gazing upon his sleeping form; sometimes leaning over to stroke his tousled hair and inhale the scent of his hot little head. God, how she had loved that smell. Instinctively now she shuffled further up the bed and leant over. Only the very top of Laurence's head was visible, his spiky chestnut hair shiny with the remnants of gel. She knew if she smelt it now it would smell of 'Arabian Nights' or 'Midnight Musk' or some other foreign, manly scent, for that's what he was now – a man – or at least very much a man in waiting. One thing was for sure, he was no longer her baby.

A warm fat tear erupted out of the corner of her eye and rolled down her face. Damn it, damn it, damn it, she had vowed she wasn't going to cry tonight. She was going to be strong and determined and do what she had to do – whatever that was. But there was something about seeing Laurence so unguarded for the first time in recent memory that seemed to be triggering a groundswell of grief and regret. Did she really have nothing to show for all the years of trying? Was she left with nothing but memories of a closeness with her son? She put her head in her hands as her body coursed with silent guttural sobs.

'Mum?' Laurence's voice was confused and thick with sleep. 'Mum, what are you doing?'

Megan hastily leant back and wiped her face. 'I'm sorry I -' but it was no good. The wave of grief that had engulfed her was too overwhelming and although she knew she ought to get to her feet and leave the room she remained fixed to the bed, tears streaming down her face.

'Mum – are you all right?' Laurence hoisted himself upright and switched on his bedside lamp, causing Megan to cringe and turn away.

'Yes, I'm fine. Oh Laurence, I'm so sorry.'

'What's the matter?' Now Laurence's voice was soft and concerned, with not a trace of the usual hard, sarcastic edge.

'Nothing. I – have you spoken to your dad – since I've been away?'

Laurence snorted, his usual air of defiance back in a flash. 'No, not really. Why, should I?'

'He has been here though, hasn't he?' Megan experienced a sudden surge of alarm. What if Gerry had stormed off after her phone call and left Laurence on his own for two days?

'Yeah, he was here last night. Didn't talk to him though. And he left a message on my phone today saying he was going to be home late because he was caught up in a rehearsal. Why?'

'Something's happened.' A wave of nausea rose up and burnt at the back of Megan's throat. How was she going to say this? How was she going to tell him? The one thing she had vowed she would never, ever say to any child of hers. The one curse from her own past she had vowed she would never pass on.

'Oh yeah?' As if knowing something awful was about to happen, all of Laurence's barriers of bravado slid back in place. He sunk back down the bed, pulling the duvet up under his chin, staring at the wall.

'Your dad and I -' Megan sighed. This was unbearable but the alternative; staying another second with Gerry, was even worse. 'I'm leaving your dad,' she said quietly, then held her breath.

There was a long silence during which Laurence didn't move a muscle, then finally he muttered, 'Congratulations,' and rolled over, pulling the duvet over his head.

'Congratulations?' Megan repeated, feebly. 'What do you mean, congratulations?'

'CON-GRAT-U-LATIONS,' he said again, slowly, as if spelling it out.

'Laurence?' Megan shifted back up the bed and gingerly placed a hand on his shoulder. He shook it off violently.

'Can I get some sleep now please?' He muttered, from beneath the duvet.

'Don't you want to talk about it?' Megan asked.

She was greeted with a tight little laugh.

'Laurence please,' she implored, once again placing her hand on his shoulder.

This time he sat bolt upright and swiped her arm away with his own. In the muted glow of the bedside lamp his cheeks looked hollow and sunken and his dark eyes were glinting with rage.

'What?' he spat. 'What do you want me to say? You're finally leaving the drunken bastard. Well, nice one mum. Have a good life. Don't forget to send me a postcard.'

'Laurence!'

'What?'

Now she could see tears springing into *his* eyes despite his rage.

'What do you mean, send you a postcard? I'm not leaving you – not if you don't want me to.'

'Oh no – why not?'

'What do you mean why not?'

'Well why would you want me hanging around, getting in the way of your new life.'

'You wouldn't get in the way. What are you talking about?'

'Oh come on mum, get real.'

'What?'

'Of course I get in the way – with both of you and your precious work. I don't know why you bothered having me, neither of you give a shit.'

'That's not true Laurence, of course we do. But we have to work.'

'Why?'

'Well to pay the mortgage on this place.' Megan felt she needed a moment to catch her breath, Laurence's attack had left her feeling completely winded.

He let out a sarcastic snort, 'Yeah and to pay his bar bill.'

Once again Megan felt utterly bewildered. All the way home from Brighton she had been steeling herself for Laurence to say he wanted to stay with his father, not launching into an attack on him.

'I don't know what you mean,' she offered lamely.

'Bullshit!' Megan winced as Laurence hugged his knees to his chest and fixed her with a teary stare. 'Of course you know what I mean. He's an alky, a piss-head. That's why you're leaving him and you're leaving me with him. Cheers, mum.' Laurence began trembling as he hugged his knees tighter, angry tears spurting on to his face.

Megan gently placed a hand on his and shook her head. 'No I'm not, of course I'm not. I wasn't sure what you'd want to do – this is your home, he's your father, I didn't think -' she couldn't bring herself to say it – that deep down she feared he wouldn't want to come with her, that he'd rather stay with Gerry than live with an annoyance of a mother who liked talking about the weather and didn't understand the rules of cricket. She took a deep breath in an attempt to steady herself before continuing. 'I'd love it if you came with me. There's no way I'd leave you somewhere you don't want to be. I'd never want to leave you, but I have to leave him, I can't go on living with the – well with the drinking. But it isn't because he's a bad person, Laurence. You have to know that, your dad is a good person and he loves us both very much but –'

'Bullshit!' Laurence half shouted, half sobbed. 'Why do you always do this?'

'Do what?'

'Always look on the positive side of everything and put up with so much crap? He doesn't love us. He never has. He's a selfish bastard.'

Megan's mouth was so dry she felt it might crack if she tried to speak or even swallow. She had had no idea Laurence felt like this. She thought she'd protected him from the side effects of Gerry's drinking, with her endless excuses and covering up – *your dad's got another migraine, he's come down with a stomach bug, he's had to go to a late night rehearsal.* And reserving her occasional angry outbursts for when Laurence was at school or out with friends so that all traces of smashed crockery or tear stains could be wiped clean before his return. How could Laurence have known all along? He couldn't have known – not the full extent of the problems.

Megan looked over at the wall where the shadows from Laurence's cricketing cups loomed like rounded cartoon figures with their hands on their hips. *Come on,* they seemed to be saying, *get on with it.* 'Your dad's an alcoholic, Laurence. Do you understand what that means?' Cautiously she turned back to face him. Laurence stared at her angrily.

'Of course I understand what that means. He's a piss-head, mum. He's an embarrassment. Why do you think I never ask you to any of my cricket matches? Because I'm terrified he'll turn up drunk. Like he did that time for my Year Five sports day.'

Megan shuddered as she remembered Gerry running on to the track during the fancy dress race, whooping and cheering as he helped himself to a feather boa from the dressing up box. It had only been eleven o'clock in the morning but he had been up all night drinking wine and had insisted on coming with her. 'I want to cheer my boy on,' he'd slurred, 'I want to see him race.' But when they'd got there he'd ensured that all eyes were upon him. Megan cringed as she thought of Laurence standing frozen on the track as his father staggered past him and his classmates fell around laughing. She hadn't talked to Gerry for weeks afterwards.

'I thought you'd forgotten about that,' she whispered, turning away from him again.

Laurence snorted. 'Yeah right – like I'm gonna forget that.'

'Is that really why you don't invite us to any of your cricket matches?'

'Er, *yeah*.' Laurence's voice was laden with sarcasm.

'But I thought it was just your age, that none of you wanted your parents there.' Megan glanced at him hopefully. 'Why didn't you ask me? I'd love to see you play.'

Laurence sighed and wiped his face. 'Because you're such a wimp, mum. I knew if I asked you and he got wind of it and for some bizarre reason actually wanted to come too you wouldn't be able to say no. Why didn't you ever stand up to him, mum? Why didn't you kick him out like you tell people to do in your book?'

'You've read my book?' Yet again Megan felt floored by Laurence's latest revelation. For months, possibly even years now they'd had so little communication and now it was all coming in a rush of angry bursts and none of it was remotely what she had expected.

'Yeah,' Laurence's reply was gruff and bashful. 'Who hasn't?' he recovered bitterly. 'That's what I don't get, mum. How can you write a book and go on the radio talking about happiness when in real life you -' he stopped abruptly as if aware he had gone too far.

'In real life I what?' Megan felt compelled to ask although she knew she didn't want to hear his reply.

'In real life you're so sad.'

There it was – the ultimate teenage insult – levelled at her by her own son. She was sad. Sad and pathetic. It was official. Could things possibly get any worse?

'I hear you, you know,' Laurence continued, his voice now barely audible.

'Really,' Megan felt numb, she didn't want to know any more.

'At night time, when he hasn't come home.'

Megan gulped and clenched her fists.

'I hear you crying.'

Megan looked at Laurence and saw that all of his earlier rage had now left his eyes. There was a long pause and then Laurence took hold of her hand.

'I don't want you to be sad, mum.'

'Oh Laurence.'

And then she was holding him, rocking gently in the glow of the bedside lamp. Both of them crying and clinging on tighter and tighter as if catching up on lost time or clinging on to fleeting time she couldn't be sure. And as she wrapped her arms around his back and felt his own arms wiry and strong around hers she buried her face in the nape of his neck and inhaled. And beneath the spicy aroma of gel or deodorant or aftershave she could just make out that old familiar scent. The smell of her son, the smell of her baby, the smell of pure and unconditional love.

chapter Twenty-Two

"Fill a photo album with pictures from key positive moments in your life. Use this book to chart your own personal development and see how you have grown, not just physically but emotionally too."
Megan Rowe, 'Help Yourself to Happiness.'

Danny sat back in his chair, rubbed his eyes and looked out of the bedroom window. A huge moon was suspended between the two tower blocks opposite. In the hours he had been writing it had slowly swung into view, like a giant golden pocket watch and now it held him in a hypnotic trance, as the strain of the previous hours work began to ebb away. Although he only had a few pages to show for his efforts he knew they were worthy. He had taken his time over the words, allowing sentences to seep from his mind and out through his pen on to the crisp white sheet. After so much initial struggle the words seemed to flow quite effortlessly now; as if Marko's story had already been written and was just waiting to be transcribed. Danny had begun by writing about the Chetnik corpse but swiftly moved on to talk about Marko and the tales he told, tales of brutality and destruction no kid should ever have to hear let alone experience. But it was the contrasting flashes of innocence Danny had ended up focusing on. The way Marko and his gang of street urchins would play 'jacks' with empty bullet shells on the floors of the looted flats they called home. The way they would tease each other mercilessly between over-exaggerated tokes on shared cigarettes. The way they would hoot and holler at the sound of a fart and yet seem oblivious to the sudden crackle of machine gun fire. That was the real tragedy of the story, the real sense of loss his photo revealed.

Danny looked at the photo again now, lying on his desk bathed in a pool of pale moon light. What had happened to Marko, he wondered. Had he survived the war? He thought of the way Marko and his buddies had played their own version of 'chicken' across Sniper's Alley – shrieking giggled insults as they darted and wove their way across the four lanes, bullets pinging around their feet, like a scene from a cartoon – and he shuddered. Somehow he didn't think so.

Danny picked up his pack of cigarettes and lit one. He and his friends back in Austin had used to play chicken, on the rail track that bordered the Jackson farm. Ethan Jackson had been his best friend all through school, a sturdy athletic type with a mean pitch and a kick-ass Spiderman comic collection. One particularly hot summer back in the late seventies when they had been about ten years old, they had taken to hanging out in the bottom field of the Jackson's farm, taking refuge in the shade of the sycamores and plotting their future lives. Their future heart-stopping adventures. Fired up by the swash-buckling dreams of daring deeds and saving the planet from intergalactic doom, dodging the inter-state Amtrak as it thundered past on its way to Dallas had seemed like small fry for this gang of future super heroes, cheered on by an awestruck Marty. Of course they had always left plenty of time to get across before the huge silver train had gone screaming past. And they weren't dodging gun fire either. But man it had been scary.

Danny scratched his head. Why were kids so intent on terrorising themselves when there was so much horror awaiting them when they grew up? Then he remembered the time that same summer when he was meant to have been minding Marty, but Ethan had called him about a bunch of hot looking older chicks who were sunbathing in their underwear down by the lake. Tingling with an excitement he couldn't yet quite comprehend, he had grabbed his dad's binoculars and given Marty the slip. When he had gotten home and Marty was missing there had been all hell to pay. His mom had gone crazy, hollering all manner of horrific threats, not least being 'wait till your father gets home.' Danny remembered how his heart had been hammering fit to burst as he had torn around the neighbourhood on his bike, all burning thoughts of bras and panties and bronzed midriffs vanished from his mind and replaced by an ice cold fear. He had eventually found Marty on the train track, standing gazing down the line.

'What are you doing?' he'd yelled, a mixture of anger and relief now reverberating through his rib cage.

'Waiting to play the train game, Dan-Dan,' his brother had replied and Danny had felt sick with the awful realisation. That just as Marty had copied his haircut and the clothes he wore and the way he walked (an embarrassing John Wayne type swagger if memory served him) he was about to copy the deadly game he had watched him play that summer with Ethan and the gang. Danny had grabbed him by his scrawny shoulders and shaken him hard.

'You mustn't ever, ever come down here alone again, you hear me,' he'd shouted. And then Marty had started to cry.

'I didn't know where you was,' he'd sniffed, his tanned face streaky with dirt.

And Danny had pulled him close and wrapped his arms around him, overcome by a mixture of anger and frustration but most of all love. 'Don't worry, I won't leave you again. Just don't tell pops, you hear.'

'I won't,' Marty sniffed – and he'd kept his word. They both had until …

Danny sighed, exhaling a thick column of cigarette smoke. Why was it everything kept coming back to the same starting point? Impulsively he reached across to the battered shoebox of photographs that now sat on his rickety single bed and tipped the contents on to the scratchy woollen blanket. There it was – his life spread out like a patchwork quilt of nameless, haunted faces and tortured, twisted bodies. It was his job to weave them all together with words, but he realised that until he located the common thread running between them all, his job would be impossible. Danny sat down on the edge of the bed and began rooting through the pictures, hands trembling. And then there it was – the centre piece of the quilt, the one photograph he hadn't taken. He remembered his mom on the steps of the porch, her hair loosely tied in its usual strawberry gold braids, a light dusting of freckles on her button nose and wide cheek bones. 'Say cheese, please, Louise,' she giggled as she held her big black box of a camera up to her face.

'Cheese, please, Louise!' Marty and he had screamed before the glass cube on top had exploded in a blinding light.

Danny took a long draw on his cigarette before picking up the faded black and white snap shot, his fingers tracing the softness of the scuffed edges. Thinking of his mom like that reminded him of what had made him fall in love with photography all those years ago, when he was still a boy. The magical notion that you could capture a moment in time forever. That you could somehow swallow it up into the camera and it would be yours to keep forever more. And back then, like his mom, it had been the beauty and the fun he had wanted to capture not the carnage. He looked down at the picture in his hands, at that moment captured in time forever more, he and Marty on the porch swing, arms slung around each other's shoulders, dazzling broad grins splitting their tanned faces from ear to ear. And eyes wide open for the camera, wide open with innocence.

chapter Twenty-Three

"Make time to be with your loved one. Special time, sacred time. Crack open a bottle, talk and sing and dance. Make love. Don't allow the pressures of modern living to force you apart."
Megan Rowe, 'Help Yourself to Happiness.'

'Maybe it's because I'm a Londoner,' Gerry sang as he skipped in and out of the line of concrete bollards in front of the Apollo. Overhead cars thundered along the flyover and somewhere in the distance a siren wailed. Natalie couldn't help laughing. Gerry Radcliffe might be a lying bastard but there was no denying he was also a lot of fun.

'That I love London so,' she joined in, in her best Eliza Dolittle as she skipped along in his trail.

Gerry turned and smiled before leaping on top of one of the bollards. 'And maybe it's because I'm a Londoner,' he continued, holding his arms out to her, his wavy hair tumbling wildly about his chiselled jaw.

'That I think of her, wherever I go,' Natalie replied, skipping towards him and finishing with a pirouette at his feet.

Gerry stepped down from the bollard and took her hands in his. 'I think you're amazing,' he said, his face suddenly serious and his eyes wide and intense.

'Really?' Natalie's pulse began to race. 'Why?'

'What do you mean, why?' Gerry looked at her as if she were mad. 'Look at you, you're beautiful, talented, you have the most amazing presence.'

'Really?' *More, more, more*, Natalie wanted to scream.

'Of course, really.' Gerry cupped her face in his hands and leant forward and kissed her on the tip of her nose.

Natalie gazed up at him her heart pounding. In the orange glow of the street lights his eyes were as dark as the night sky, as endless and deep too.

'I'm sorry,' he said, taking a small step back. 'I shouldn't have done that, it's just that I've had such a nice night. I haven't had so much fun in ages and – well – you really are something special you know.'

Natalie smiled – yes she was, she was special, if Gerry could see it then why couldn't everyone? 'It has been a lovely night hasn't it,' she said, looking off wistfully towards the arched entrance to Neptune Mansions. 'Seems a shame for it to come to an end really.'

'What are you suggesting Miss Taylor-Cassidy?'

NATALIE TAYLOR-CASSIDY AND TOP DIRECTOR GERRY RADCLIFFE IN NIGHT OF PASSION SHOCKER!

Natalie smiled coyly. 'Well I thought maybe you might like to come in for a coffee – or something stronger?' Gerry's earlier resolution to keep off the booze seemed to have evaporated as soon as he clamped eyes on the leather bound wine list in the restaurant. But this time he had drunk at a far more measured pace and had subsequently been a lot of fun, regaling her with endless tales about his life in the theatre and anecdotes about other, more famous colleagues. Natalie had listened spellbound, basking in the golden glow of association, however tenuous.

'Hmm,' Gerry said, glancing from side to side as if trying to make up his mind.

Natalie felt anger begin spearing at her insides. Who did he think he was – playing hard to get? He was old enough to be her dad for Christ's sake. He was hardly going to get a better offer than her. Perhaps he needed reminding of that fact. She stepped in close so that her breasts just brushed against his chest and gazed up at him through lowered eyes. 'I didn't mean, you know – it's just that I've had so much fun tonight and well, this hasn't exactly been the best week for me.'

Gerry nodded emphatically, 'You and me both,' he said. 'What the hell. Come on then, lead me hither.' He took her by the hand. 'I shouldn't really be hanging about out here anyway,' and he glanced about the concourse furtively. 'My wife, or rather, soon to be ex-wife works here you know.'

Natalie followed his gaze over to the curved, pillared front of the Apollo. 'What – in the theatre?' she asked, a thrill of excitement fizzing up her spine.

'Oh no,' Gerry shook his head, frowning. 'She isn't in the business. She works a bit further down the road, at the radio station.'

'You're kidding.' Natalie stopped in her tracks and stared up at him. 'What does she do?'

'Hosts a show,' Gerry replied flatly. 'Nothing major, only a once a week gig. She's a guest presenter – radio isn't her main line of work.'

Natalie felt a strange mixture of nausea and elation churning together in the pit of her stomach. 'So what is her main line of work?'

Gerry replied with a bitter little laugh. 'She fixes people. Makes them happy. Helps them see the error of their ways and leads them to great and unimaginable success.'

Natalie remained frozen to the spot, staring at him questioningly. Gerry turned away.

'Come on then, lets get that *coffee*. I don't suppose you've got any scotch have you? I make a mean Irish coffee.'

Natalie shook her head. 'No, but I still have that vodka you bought the other night.'

'Excellent! We can have Russian coffee instead – as a tribute to Checkov.' Gerry grabbed her by the hand and started leading her towards the flats.

'What do you mean, she fixes people?' Natalie hardly dared entertain the idea now looming in her head. Could it be? No – the chances were ridiculously remote. She didn't even know if Megan was even married. In the two months she'd been working at Loose Talk she'd hardly said a word about her personal life. Just that she lived in Chiswick – *Nightingale Avenue, Chiswick* – Natalie suddenly remembered Gerry's instructions to the cab driver the day before. And that she had a son – *I've got to get back for my son*. Bloody, shitting hell!

'She fixes people; she helps to make them whole, gets them to unleash the wondrous being within and all that crap. She's a life coach,' he replied, quickening his step.

Fuck! Natalie couldn't believe it. Gerry was married to that sanctimonious witch? This was incredible. This was like Christmas, birthday and Easter all rolled into one. But wait – she had to play it cool. She mustn't let on that she knew Megan; that could spell disaster. But she had to find out for absolute sure.

'What's her name?' Natalie asked, as casually as she could, running to keep up with Gerry's strides.

Gerry stopped in his tracks. 'Why? What difference does it make?'

'Oh none,' Natalie tilted her head to one side and gently stoked his cheek. 'You had a stray eyelash,' she lied.

Gerry softened his gaze. 'Thank you.' He grabbed hold of her hand and kissed it. 'Her name's Megan Rowe. You've probably heard of her. She wrote a book. Christ you probably even *have* the book. Most people seem to. Second only to the Bible it would appear.'

Natalie shook her head. 'To be honest I don't have an awful lot of time for that life coaching stuff,' she said with a frown. 'Load of Californian psycho babble if you ask me.'

Gerry's face broke into a broad grin instantaneously making him look years younger. 'Ahh – music to my ears,' he sighed. 'Is there no end to your wonders?'

Natalie giggled coquettishly. 'Well I don't know, you'll have to wait and see.'

*

'Bloody hell!' Gerry rolled off her, sweat streaming from his face. 'That was amazing. You were – Jesus!' And with that he lay back in a contented sigh.

Natalie forced a smile and wiped the sweat, Gerry's sweat, from her brow. She felt disgusting. Sweaty and smelly and disgusting. Once they had got into the flat Gerry had made them both a Russian coffee, or rather a mug of vodka slightly laced with a few granules of Nescafe and a dash of hot water. After that it had all been a bit if a blur. Buzzing from the caffeine and the alcohol, but most of all the earlier revelations, Natalie had set about him like a viper, her tongue licking and flicking and pressing and coaxing. And as Gerry had got harder and larger she had pulled out all of the stops. Working her way around his body like a dancer making full use of every inch of floor space, his cries and moans the perfect soundtrack. And she had felt turned on, more turned on than she ever had before, but as always more turned on by her own performance rather than anything he did. Anyway his repertoire wasn't exactly the widest ranging, but she didn't mind. She preferred it that way, with him just lying there, occasionally running his hands over her breasts or clutching on to her backside. She preferred men to just watch, loved to see the vulnerability in their gaze as she sucked and stroked and thrust away on them. Moulding and melding them, melting them with her power. But then, as always, there came the crashing moment when he came and suddenly all the power was sucked from her into him in one huge pulsating wave. And as he removed himself, sucked himself out of her, she was left feeling empty and hollow inside. An empty shell washed up on the beach, terrified of being trodden on.

Natalie looked over at Gerry lying next to her, his eyes closed, dark hair tumbling all over her crisp white pillow, one arm flung above his head. She examined the lines on his face, the jowls sagging down onto his neck, the skin on his chest slightly slack, the skin on his stomach tight over his paunch, and she felt sick. Sick, sick, sick. *Get out!* she wanted to scream. *Get out of my bed, get out of my flat. Get out! Get out! Get out!* She clenched her fists and took a deep breath. She had to get a grip. She was lying next to Megan Rowe's husband. She had just screwed Megan Rowe's husband. Miss Perfect with her stupid long hair and her holier than thou attitude. *Help Yourself to Happiness?* No I think I'll just help myself to your husband if you don't mind. Natalie smirked. Let Megan ask her to take a caller's details this week, or bitch and moan if she didn't book her a private appointment. What a sham the woman was. Acting like she had it all sussed with her crappy best-selling book and her radio show and her stupid articles. What a great role model, what a great ambassador for life coaching. A woman who couldn't even keep her own husband happy. But Natalie knew how to keep him happy, didn't she? Look at him lying there now, peaceful as a little baby. Natalie reached over and ran her fingers lightly over Gerry's balls.

'Oh!' he moaned, rolling on to his side to face her. 'Amazing,' he whispered, still not opening his eyes. *Fucking. Amazing.*

'I know,' Natalie replied, smirking in the darkness as she thought to herself, you ain't seen nothing yet.

chapter Twenty-Four

"Use song lyrics as mantras. In times of darkness listen to songs with uplifting messages to inspire and motivate you."
Megan Rowe, 'Help Yourself to Happiness.'

Cheddar stared at the computer screen in front of him. 'I Will Survive,' 'Everybody Hurts,' 'My Way,' 'Tougher Than the Rest,' 'Sisters Are Doing it For Themselves,' 'All You Need is Love,' 'Bridge Over Troubled Water,' 'I Believe I Can Fly,' as usual the playlist for Megan Rowe's show was cringingly heart-warming – oh if only he could slip in something a bit darker for a laugh – what about that Guns and Roses track 'I Used to Love Her, But I Had to Kill Her,' or 'When You're Alone You Ain't Nothing But Alone,' by Bruce Springsteen. Cheddar chuckled and looked at the clock on the studio wall. It was still only quarter to seven. Fifteen minutes until Megan and lady muck were due in for the pre-show production meeting – that's if they actually showed up on time this week. He hoped so, he really wanted to put his exercise of the week proposition to Megan. Her 'cut and paste' exercise had ended up having quite a profound effect on him in only a week – as his brightly painted bedroom and woefully empty fridge would testify. It had also, indirectly, stiffened his resolve to take the plunge into the relationship pool once more. But he knew that if he were to make the changes he really wanted in his life he needed more than a piece of card with a few words and a picture. He needed direction for a start. It was as if last week's show had provided him with a rowing boat and an oar but no compass or map.

Cheddar looked at the clock once again. Fourteen minutes to six. Oh what the heck, he may as well kill a bit of time by checking out his blog, see if he had any new comments since the last time he checked, oh, all of an hour ago.

He had titled his last blog 'Builders Uninterrupted' and had based it upon the frighteningly base exchange he had had the dubious pleasure of over-hearing the previous day. Cheddar had been giving his bedroom a second coat of paint and had the windows wide open when suddenly he had been greeted by the sound of a hefty smoker's cough, followed swiftly by a lengthy burp. Putting down his paint brush and peering discreetly out of the window he saw a couple of builders had entered the yard below – Raj had been having a bucking bronco installed in El Paso, 'good for customer moral, innit,' although Cheddar had failed to see how being thrust backwards and forwards after a plate of re-fried mince meat would be good for anyone's 'moral,' let alone digestion. Anyway the transcript of the builders' conversation as they had made use of the outside toilet and enjoyed a post-defecation cigarette had gone down extremely well on his weblog, receiving a tremendous twenty-four comments to date, but unfortunately none from the one person he wanted to hear from.

Cheddar typed in his password and waited. Agonisingly slowly the screen flicked on to his site. Flippin' heck! To his surprise and delight there were two new comments already. He swallowed before clicking on the view button. The first one was from Red Squirrel, a regular visitor to his web log and always game for a laugh.

'I really had no idea there were so many uses for the word twat,' Red Squirrel had written, 'And as for the turd curling contest, well I'm glad those guys aren't working at a restaurant near me. Keep up the good work King Cheese.' Cheddar grimaced as he remembered one of the builders returning from the outside khazi, loudly proclaiming his creation of a 'twatting great corkscrew to end all corkscrews.'

Hurriedly he scrolled down and bingo – there it was. A message posted by Bambi from Rhyl. As he clicked on view Cheddar felt a strange fluttering in his stomach but he knew it wasn't hunger, although after almost a week on a diet Bugs Bunny would die for, he felt sure he was in the first stages of starvation.

'After the week I've just had I didn't think it would be possible to find anything funny,' the message read, 'but once again you've proved me wrong, thanks so much King Cheese. Is it really biologically or grammatically possible to call someone a "twatting hairy arsed twat for brains?" Would love to take up your current special offer of a personal horoscope based on my 'plaice' of birth. According to my mum I am a fish finger with chips rising! Lol Bambi'

Lol. Cheddar sat back in his chair and stared at the screen, his heart pounding. Lol. Three little letters loaded with meaning – or not. He scratched his head, not knowing where to begin the necessary thought process now required to dissemble this latest posting. Lol. Laugh out loud or lots of – He shook his head. This was ridiculous, he was behaving like a big soppy girl. But he couldn't help himself. There was something about Bambi's postings that were different to the others, at least they certainly made him feel different, but why? Perhaps it was the name? Conjuring up images of soulful doe eyes and fragile limbs – although the real Bambi was a lad, lets not forget about that, and a deer! But Cheddar knew this Bambi were a lass. He could tell. What he couldn't tell was what the 'lol' stood for. Normally he would have said laugh out loud, no question, but put at the end of a correspondence – well. You wouldn't end a letter, lots of laughs, would you now? But on the other hand would she really sign off 'lots of love.' They'd only shared a few exchanges on a website, that hardly constituted outpourings of undying love. Cheddar shook his head and grinned ruefully. This starvation diet was obviously playing havoc with his mind. Perhaps his brain was starting to eat itself or something spooky like that. No wonder those supermodel types were always as dim as a nine-watt bulb. He looked at the Tupperware box in front of him and sighed. A distinctly unappetising pile of celery and carrot sticks lay inside. How the heck was a man supposed to be a hunter-gatherer on a diet of celery and carrot sticks? Let alone decipher the modern day hieroglyphics left on the walls of his website. He took a sip from his insipid tasting diet coke, in the vain hope that some caffeine might jolt any remaining brain cells back into life. Thankfully it seemed to work, for the fizz on his tongue was accompanied by a fizz of excitement as he realised that regardless of what the lol meant, Bambi had requested a personal horoscope.

The 'plaice of birth' offer had been in response to all of the positive feedback he'd been getting for his spoof Sunday horoscopes. He'd come up with idea whilst writing that day's predictions, asking readers to email him with details of the favourite fish dish their mother had enjoyed whilst pregnant with them. The deal was he would then write them a more detailed and personal prediction. All a complete load of bollocks but completely in keeping with the rest of his site. Not such a load of rubbish now though - now he had an excuse to get in further contact with Bambi. Cheddar re-read her comment once again. 'After the week I've just had I didn't think it would be possible to find anything funny,' and he felt a pang of concern. What had happened he wondered? Well whatever it was it was down to him to make her feel a bit better. He scratched his head and thought. Took a bite of carrot, fought the urge to hurl and thought. Took another swig of flavourless coke and clicked on reply.

'You fish fingers can be a complex lot. What with your luminous crunchy coating,' Cheddar's stomach growled loudly, this time a definite hunger pang but he valiantly continued, 'And your delicate white interior, you are not quite as tough as would at first appear. However the fact that you have chips rising would suggest that you are surrounded by supporters – just be careful none of them climb on to your shoulder or you could find yourself losing friends.' Cheddar stopped typing – that should do it. He clicked on post and sat back, stomach positively roaring. All that talk of chips was making him feel quite weak. How long had it been since he'd had a plate of chips? Only a matter of days but it felt like a lifetime. Perhaps he could nip to the café over the road? But it was too late. He heard the door open and turned to see Megan enter the studio carrying a huge holdall.

'Hi Cheddar, sorry I'm a bit late.' She plonked the holdall on to the floor and sat down at the desk next to him. Cheddar couldn't help wondering what was in the bag and if there was any way it could be edible. Perhaps she had stopped off to do some food shopping on the way to work, or maybe she'd rustled up a picnic to bring to the show? A swirling collage of sausage rolls, scotch eggs, over-filled sandwiches and gold-crusted pork pies kaleidoscoped into his mind.

'What you got in there, the kitchen sink?' He enquired in what he hoped was a nonchalant manner, completely belying the ratcheting desperation gripping his mind, not to mention his belly. Please, please let it be the kitchen cupboard at least, a voice inside his head pleaded, preferably the one you keep all the best grub in.

Megan shook her head and laughed. 'No, not exactly.' Then her smile faded and Cheddar noticed shadows of tiredness ringing her eyes. 'I'm actually in the process of moving,' she explained, looking down at her lap. 'I had to stop off at home – at my old house – on the way here to pick up some stuff.'

Cheddar didn't know whether to be curious or disappointed. He should have known it wouldn't be food. That was the trouble with working with lasses, especially ones as skinny as Megan, he didn't think he'd ever seen her eating now he came to think of it, and as for that other one, Natalie, well he wouldn't be surprised if she feasted solely on blood or men's gonads. She was right scary that one.

'Oh lovely, crudités. Do you mind if I have one?' Megan asked.

Crude what? Cheddar followed her longing gaze to his Tupperware box. Was she having a laugh? 'Yeah, be my guest,' he replied warily, watching in shock as she helped herself to a piece of carrot and actually looked as if she was enjoying it!

'I'm starving,' Megan said, 'Haven't had a chance to eat much this weekend, what with the move and everything.'

'I didn't realise you were moving, I could have given you a hand,' Cheddar replied.

'Oh don't worry, it was all a little unexpected actually.'

Cheddar noticed a cloud of concern pass across Megan's face, as she pushed a wisp of hair from her eyes. Something was definitely amiss. In the two months he'd been working with her she'd been like a weekly ray of sunshine, with her witty anecdotes and ability to see the positive in just about everything - seemingly even a crude-shite or whatever the hell they were called, Cheddar mused as he watched her tuck into a stick of celery.

'Where have you moved to?' he enquired, studying her carefully and noting that there was definitely something different about her. Her pale skin and dark hair seemed to lack their usual shine.

'Oh just a flat in Turnham Green.'

'Turnham Green, but don't you, didn't you only live down the road from there?'

'Yes.' Megan looked at him, frowning slightly as if weighing up whether or not to say something more. 'The thing is I -'

'Hi guys!' Cheddar looked over to the door to see Natalie breeze into the room. As usual she had a miniscule skirt on – a fanny pelmet his mam would have called it - with thick woollen tights and a pair of knee high boots. On any one else it would have looked saucy as hell, but on Natalie, well, there was something about her that made him shiver and definitely not in a good way. 'Everyone okay?' she asked, hanging her velvet jacket on one of the pegs behind the door and tossing her flame red mane of hair over her shoulder.

Cheddar logged out of his weblog and clicked back on to his playlist for the show. 'Well, well, well, must be my lucky night,' he said with a chuckle. 'Both of you here on time for once. Don't tell me we can actually have a production meeting?'

'Oh my God, what is he like?' Natalie said to Megan as she perched down on the seat at the end of the desk.

Cheddar frowned. In the two months she'd been working at Loose Talk he'd never seen Natalie so chirpy. Megan looked equally dumbfounded as she nodded her response.

'So how have you guys been, had a good week? 'Natalie continued.

Cheddar was about to reply but then realised she was looking straight at Megan.

'Yes, I guess so,' Megan replied cautiously, taking off her jacket to reveal a dust streaked tracksuit top. Once again Cheddar felt a twinge of concern. He had never seen Megan look so drab, still she had been moving house.

'Done anything exciting?' Natalie continued to focus on Megan as she swung from side to side in her chair, playing with the ends of her hair.

'Not really. Went down to Brighton to give a talk at a sales conference.'

'And moved house,' Cheddar reminded her.

'Oh yes.'

'Really?' Natalie practically shrieked, causing Cheddar to wince. 'Where have you moved to?'

'Nowhere far. Just Turnham Green.'

'Oh. Right.'

'Okay ladies, how about we have a meeting eh? Talk about the plan for tonight's show.'

'Plan?' Megan turned to him, a look of utter panic on her face.

Cheddar frowned. He hoped she wasn't going to object to his idea. But why the heck would she, she was a life coach for Christ's sake, he was only going to ask for a coaching exercise, he just had to make sure it didn't sound like it was for him that was all. He took a deep breath before continuing. 'Yes, well I was wondering if we could introduce a new feature.'

'Oh.' Now Megan looked downright terrified. What the heck was up with her? Yes she was moving house and yes that was stressful but it wasn't the end of the world. Cheddar wondered if she was a fish finger with chips rising too and once more his stomach growled.

'Whoops, sorry about that, ladies, not had a lot to eat today.'

'You're not on a diet are you?' Natalie piped up, her voice still sickly sweet.

Cheddar looked at her cautiously. 'Well, yes I have decided to make certain alterations to my eating habits,' he replied turning to gaze mournfully upon the Tupperware box.

'Good on you,' Megan said, finally showing a flicker of enthusiasm.

'Yeah, good on you,' Natalie echoed.

Cheddar felt his cheeks begin to burn. 'Anyway, back to the show. I was thinking it might be a good idea if you did an exercise of the week slot?'

'What do you mean?' Once again Megan seemed extremely guarded.

'Well, do you remember the exercise you set that poor lass Mary last week. The one who was married to the arsehole who got rid of all her pictures?'

Megan nodded. 'Oh yes. I don't' suppose she ever rang back did she?'

Cheddar shook his head.

'I'm really sorry about that Megan,' Natalie cut in. 'She just hung up before I had a chance to say a word.'

Megan shook her head. 'It wasn't your fault. She was obviously very distressed.'

'Anyway, that exercise you set her?' Cheddar continued.

'Oh yes, the personal affirmations card.'

'Yes, yes, that's the one. Well I thought it would be quite nice if perhaps you could do a general exercise like that every week. One that everyone could try out at home if they wanted. To make them feel a bit more positive or confident or give them a direction in life or whatever.' Cheddar held his breath and waited. Once again Megan hardly looked enthused.

'Oh yes, what a fab idea!' Natalie piped up. 'Your exercises are always so cool and inspirational. I think everyone could do with a bit of a confidence boost, eh Cheddar.'

Cheddar looked at her suspiciously. Why was it that everything that girl said seemed loaded with some kind of cryptic double meaning?

'Really?' Megan was staring at Natalie as if seeing her for the very first time.

'Oh for sure. I often try out the things you recommend at home. Don't you Cheddar?'

Cheddar's face began to burn even hotter. 'Well I –'

'And to be honest I could really do with a bit of a pick me up right now,' Natalie continued, 'Problems on the man front,' she whispered to Megan conspiratorially.

'Oh no,' Megan turned to face Natalie. 'Are you okay?'

Natalie turned away biting her lip. 'Yeah – I think so – it's just – oh God – I'm so sorry guys, I swore I wasn't going to do this. I really wanted to put a brave face on it.'

Cheddar looked up, dismayed but it was too late, his worst fears had been confirmed, she had produced a tissue from her bag and was dabbing furiously at her eyes. Oh, chuffin' stuffin' hell! There was something about lasses crying that sent him spiralling into a hopeless shuddering wreck of panic and ineptitude. He always so desperately wanted to say or do the right thing but the first sight of a mascara streaked tear and he seemed to be rendered mute if not retarded and this was no exception.

'Er, okay, er –'

Thankfully Megan stepped into the breach, instantly leaping to her feet and walking over to Natalie. 'Don't worry, it's all right. Do you want to go and get a cup of coffee or something? Do you want to have a chat?'

Natalie half raised her head in Megan's direction. 'Really, are you sure? Have we got enough time?'

Cheddar nodded and got to his feet to usher them out. 'Yes of course,' he leant forward and touched Natalie awkwardly on the arm. 'You take as long as you need.'

'Will you come with me?' Natalie asked Megan, once again dabbing furiously at her eyes.

'Sure.' Megan got to her feet and put her hand on Natalie's shoulder. 'We won't be long,' she said glancing back at Cheddar.

'No problem, no problem at all,' Cheddar relied, mournfully helping himself to a stick of celery.

chapter Twenty-Five

"Don't be afraid of making new friends.
Friendship opens us up to new experiences, viewpoints and ways of life.
It also teaches us to love and trust."
Megan Rowe, 'Help Yourself to Happiness.'

'Oh God, I'm like, so embarrassed,' Natalie said glancing at Megan in the dimly lit reflection of the Ladies toilets' mirror.

'Oh you mustn't be,' Megan replied, going into one of the cubicles to fetch Natalie a tissue. Although it was horrible to admit it, and she really didn't want to ponder the ethical implications of a life coach finding comfort in another's obvious distress, Megan couldn't help feeling slightly hopeful at this unexpected turn of events. In the two months she had been working with Natalie on the radio show she had found her extremely unapproachable and at times downright rude, perhaps in some perverse way her impromptu breakdown would provide an opportunity to finally break the ice. It was also providing a timely reminder that Megan obviously wasn't the only one with problems. *Shame on you,* her inner coach scolded. *Oh, whatever,* a more teenage sounding Megan thought in response. 'Would you like to talk about it?' she asked somewhat cautiously as she handed Natalie the tissue.

Taking it with a slightly trembling hand Natalie blew her nose and then shook her head. 'No. Yes. I don't know. Oh God I'm so sorry.

I try so hard to be strong but sometimes it all gets a bit too much.' Once again she bowed her head and dissolved into tears.

Megan gingerly placed a hand on her shoulder. 'You mustn't worry. We all go through hard times. The important thing to remember is that you're not on your own.' *Now that's more like it*, her inner coach enthused. *Love is all around. No man is an island. She ain't heavy, she's your sister.* Megan frowned, what on earth was going on in her head these days?

'Really?' Natalie turned to her, dabbing at her huge pale blue eyes.

'Of course. I mean, you can always talk to me if you need to.'

'No what I meant was – oh this is going to sound really stupid,' Natalie turned away, head bowed, thick skeins of auburn hair falling over her face.

'What?'

'Well when you said we all go through hard times. Do you have bad times too? It's just you seem so sorted. So wise. I'd give anything to be as grounded and together as you are.'

Megan wanted to laugh. If only she knew the truth. That her marriage was in meltdown and so, it would appear, was her head. 'Let's just say things aren't always as they might seem,' she replied.

'What do you mean?' Natalie asked, turning back to look at her in the mirror.

Megan sighed and glanced down at her hands, the newly bare third finger on her left hand seemed as crassly obvious as a streaker at Wimbledon. 'Well sometimes when we're going through tough times it can seem as if the rest of the world is having a huge party and we're the only one not invited, but it's never the case. Even the seemingly happiest, most sorted people have problems.'

'Wow!'

Megan looked up at Natalie's reflection, which was now gazing at her wide-eyed and shell-shocked. She really had been very wrong about her. It seemed utterly bizarre that this person she had been so quick to label arrogant and aloof should in fact have been rather intimidated by *her*. And even worse, she seemed to have been holding her up as some kind of guru. Yet again Megan was struck by the horrible irony of her situation. How many other people must also think the same? And how could she possibly tell them the truth? That it was all a big sham. She leant against the sinks and studied her own reflection. The woman looking back frowned - the dim lighting emphasising the dark half moons beneath her eyes. 'Would you like to talk about it?' she offered gently.

Natalie nodded. 'It's a relationship thing.'

Megan nodded and smiled. 'Go on.'

'Well a while ago I split up with someone and I'm finding it really hard to cope. I know this sounds pitiful but being on my own after such a long time – well it's scary.' Natalie sniffed and bit down on her lip.

Megan nodded sympathetically. 'I know.'

'Do you though?' Natalie continued. 'Do you know what it's like coming back to an empty flat and trying really hard to keep yourself busy but not being able to stop thinking about them, wondering what they're doing and who they're with. Night time's the worst.'

Megan thought of her new flat, a characterless grid of rooms, in an equally characterless block, tucked away behind Turnham Green High Street. Moving in had all been such a whirlwind; she had been so determined to get away from Gerry she had paid three months rent plus the deposit up front for the first place she had viewed and been in within two days. But throughout the maelstrom of packing and unpacking, cleaning and sorting she had been all too aware of another, more ominous storm of doubt and fear brewing in the back of her mind. She placed a hand lightly over Natalie's on the counter and fixed her gaze in the mirror. 'Believe me I do know exactly what you're going through. How long ago did you split up?'

'Oh it's been a few months now, in a way that's the worst thing, I feel I should be moving on.'

Again Megan nodded sympathetically. Now it all made sense. No wonder Natalie had been such hard work, not only was she nursing a broken heart, to make matters worse she had been under the illusion she was working with a woman who had it all sussed. Who had not only 'helped herself to happiness,' but written the book and hosted the show to prove it.

'Would you like to go for a coffee some time?' Megan asked. 'We could have a proper chat? I could even give you some coaching if you like?'

Natalie pursed her lips and turned away. 'Oh I don't know. The thing is I don't have a lot of money at the moment. I don't think I could afford a coaching session –'

'Oh God I didn't mean you'd have to pay.' Megan replied, horrified. 'Of course not. It's just that obviously as a life coach I do get to see a lot of people going through relationship crises and well, there are techniques, things you can do to help you move on.' Megan looked at Natalie, she looked so fragile, just like a little doll, with her porcelain skin and her rose bud mouth. 'And as I said, if it's any small consolation I do have personal experience of what you're going through. Maybe it would do us both good to have a chat.'

Natalie's face broke into a smile. 'Really? Are you sure you're not too busy? What with your moving house and your work and everything?'

Megan frowned and shook her head. 'Of course not. I think it would be nice to get to know you a little better, we never seem to get a proper opportunity to chat when we're here.'

Natalie clasped hold of her hand, her tiny fingers icy cold. Megan instinctively wanted to rub some warmth into them the way she'd done with Laurence when he was a child and come in from playing in the snow. 'Oh thank you. Thank you so much,' Natalie said, her pale blue eyes radiating gratitude. 'You don't know how much this means to me, to finally have someone to talk to. I don't have any proper family or friends here in London. I came here after the break up, you know for a fresh start.'

'Well then we must go out.' Megan replied, smiling warmly. This was going better than she ever could have imagined. 'How about lunch tomorrow? Don't worry - my treat.'

Natalie nodded and brought the tissue back up to her eyes. 'Thank you,' she whispered, wiping away a tear.

Megan reached out and squeezed her shoulder. 'Don't mention it. Now are you going to be all right for tonight's show? I'm sure Cheddar can man the phones if you'd rather have the night off.'

'Oh no I'll be fine now.'

'Great.' Megan opened the door and then turned to let Natalie through. 'You know I'm really glad we've had this chat.'

'Oh me too,' Natalie replied. 'Me too.'

chapter Twenty-Six

"When it comes to transforming our lives, writing is one of the most powerful tools at our disposal. By writing about our dreams we can start to visualise and subsequently, actualise a happier future."
Megan Rowe, 'Help Yourself to Happiness.'

Danny gave a final, futile tug on his penis and collapsed back against the unforgiving foam pillow on his bed. It was as if his writer's block had travelled south and set up camp between his legs and none of his old stalwarts – Bo Derek emerging glistening from the ocean in the film '*10*', Cindy Jeffries unleashing her marshmallow- like breasts down by the campus lake on prom night – seemed to do the trick. Danny stared vacantly at the tired looking curtains hanging unevenly in the bedroom window, flecked with bobbles and fraying at the edges. He wondered where Cindy was now, what kind of curtains she would have hanging in her windows. Something homely and floral – he'd lay a hundred bucks on it. He tried to picture her as she would be now, almost twenty years on, still curvy and soft but with a few fine lines fanning from the corners of her eyes and mouth, as she pulled on a silky cord to open a pair of thick creamy drapes embroidered with dusky pink roses. He pictured shimmering beams of sunlight cascading on to her face, the way they'd done the morning after the prom as he'd stroked her wavy blonde hair and the sun had risen golden and majestic over the lake.

'Don't hurt me,' she had whispered, her breath warm and sweet as he pulled her to him, one hand squeezing the peachy soft flesh of her ass, the other moving up between them to cup the magnificent breasts squishing against his bare chest. He had kissed her softly on that beautiful swollen mouth of hers and on her eyelids delicate as butterfly wings and promised that, no, he would never hurt her. Another promise broken.

Danny sat up and sighed. One thing was for sure. Wherever Cindy was now and whoever she was with and whatever goddamn type of curtains she was opening, she was bound to be better off without him. He ran his hand through his hair and listened to the murmur of next door's television. Although he couldn't make out the actual words, he could hear the phoney enthusiasm of the show's host oozing through the wall, followed by the obligatory oohs and ahhs and ripples of applause from the studio audience. Jeez - how had he ended up here, in this box of a room, listening to someone else's life seeping through a paper thin wall, imagining someone else's life through their curtains and yet not living his own? That graduation summer back at the lake had seemed so full of promise. As that glistening ball of light had risen over the water, bathing Cindy and him in gold, the world had seemed like one huge overflowing treasure chest, with his major in Photographic Journalism being the map showing where X marked the spot. It was all supposed to have been so different – his life. And yet had it? Fate seemed to have thrown him such a curve ball that summer, altering the course of his life forever, but maybe it had always been predestined? Because what happened had been down to him, hadn't it? A fatal flaw in his circuitry, which would have been bound to trip him up at some point. Had he only ever been kidding himself with his dreams of swash-buckling adventures and coming home to rest on marshmallow breasts? Danny frowned. Too many questions, he needed to drown them out. He leant out of bed to the transistor radio on the rickety fake pine chest of drawers and turned it on.

'Exercise of the week slot,' a voice purred at him, smooth as honey.

Shit – it was that life coaching woman again, this was all he needed.

'Something for you all to do at home. This week's exercise is one of the first I do with a new client as it helps us both to gage where the client really wants to go, what they want to achieve and where their true values lie,' she continued.

'Yeah and what about where *your* true values lie?' Danny retorted, 'Big fat dollar signs, baby.'

'It's a written exercise,' the life coach continued.

Man, why did her voice have to be so cute though, it was soft and husky like a British version of Brigitte Bardot. Danny felt a faint twinge in his by now flaccid penis. 'No way,' he moaned, shifting uncomfortably. The day a life coach made him horny was the day he checked in for an emergency castration.

'So you'll need a pad and a pen.'

Danny automatically began to get out of bed to fetch his pad and pen from his desk and then stopped in his tracks. Darn it, the woman was obviously carrying out some kind of spooky mind control over the airwaves with her hypnotic voice and subtle commands. He'd read about this kind of thing going on in Guantanemo Bay, this power of suggestion. 'So you'll need a pad and a pen to write down a full confession for all of your heinous crimes.' Huh as if he was going to fall for that old chestnut. Danny swung his legs back into the bed and pulled the scratchy blanket back over him.

'And I want you to write, My Perfect Day at the top of the page.'

'Oh you do, do you,' Danny responded, folding his arms and staying firmly put in the bed.

'And then I want you to take some time to imagine the perfect day in your perfect life.'

'Oh please!'

'It helps if you're in a relaxed state with no distractions.'

Danny glanced around his barren room. Well apart from the fascinating optical illusion he had discovered in the stained paintwork on the ceiling – if you squinted it at it for long enough through your left eye you could see the Statue of Liberty smoking a doobie - he sure as hell had no distractions. But what was he thinking? He wasn't doing this goddamned exercise was he, so he could have all the distractions in the world. Man this woman was good, but she wasn't going to outwit him, no sir.

'Okay first of all I want you to imagine a life free from negativity or self doubt or limitation.'

Danny let out a sarcastic laugh. 'Yeah, right!'

'This is your perfect day in your perfect life so the world is your oyster, the sky's the limit. All of the things or people or situations or thoughts that usually hold you back no longer exist.'

Oh if only. Danny rolled his eyes ceiling-ward and sighed.

'First of all I want you to imagine waking up on your perfect day. What would your bedroom look like? Where would it be? Who, if anyone, would you be with?'

Danny looked at the damp-stained walls and ceiling, the bobbly curtains, the threadbare carpet and the scratchy blanket. 'Well I sure as hell wouldn't be here,' he retorted. Oh man, there she went again with her hypnotic commands dragging him under her spell. What was he thinking of, even engaging in conversation with her, or the radio or whatever?

'What kind of home would you be living in? What kind of clothes would you be wearing?' she continued.

Danny looked at his faded University of Texas sweatshirt balled up on the floor by the bed. What the hell was she implying? That top was like an old friend to him. They'd been through everything together and there wasn't a thing he didn't know about it, from every last fray and pinhole burn. It was the perfect article of clothing and that was that.

'What would you do first on your perfect day? Who would you see? If you worked what would your perfect occupation be? Who would you socialise with and where would you go? What food would you eat? How would you look?'

Danny scratched his stubbly chin and ran his hand through his tousled sandy hair. Okay, so it could probably do with a trim, but – oh what the hell was he thinking?

'How would you feel? What music would you play? Work your way right through the day and remember this is your *perfect* day, you are the author of your own destiny so don't let anything hold you back. And when you write it all down remember to use all of the senses in your description. Don't just write about what you see but what you feel, taste, smell and hear too.'

Danny sighed. As far as he was concerned all he was hearing right now was a complete load of bullshit. What was this woman on with her cut and paste games and her tales of happily ever after? Hadn't she set foot in the real world? Didn't she realise that life wasn't just some series of feel good, kindergarten games? It was a place where rules and hearts got broken all the time and no amount of cutting and pasting or fantasy writing could fix it.

'And don't worry about punctuation or grammar, just let the words flow freely through your pen or keyboard. Let go and let your dreams alight upon the page.'

'Oh please – now she really was taking the piss. Did she have no idea how hard it was to write? Had the woman never heard of writer's block?' Danny shook his head in disgust at the transistor radio.

'The most important thing is to have fun with this,' his tormentor continued. 'Writing is such a powerful tool in our own personal coaching – not only is it a channel for feelings and emotions but it is also a key way to help visualise and subsequently actualise a happier future.'

'Oh really?' Danny looked at his mobile lying on top of the chest of drawers. Could he possibly get away with ringing her again? Perhaps he could try a fake accent, Mike always used to crack up at his attempt at Irish. But no, it was bad enough he was actually talking to his radio, calling the presenter in person for a second time in two weeks had definite shades of 'Play Misty for Me' about it.

'The final stage of the Perfect Day exercise is once you've completed your written account. Then I want you to re-read it and make a list of all the things you've written about that aren't yet a part of your life.'

Aren't *yet* a part of your life. There she went again with her suggestive language – that tiny little word 'yet,' implying that of course these things were all one day going to happen, simply because they'd now been written down.

'I'm on to you lady,' Danny muttered, scowling at the radio.

'Then you need to break them down into a manageable list of goals, starting short term and increasing to the long term goals set out in your account. For instance-'

Oh man was there no let up in this drivel? 'Play some music for Christ's sake,' Danny moaned.

'You could have written that on your perfect day you -'

There was a pause.

'Yes?' Danny asked the radio.

'You -'

Again silence. Had Miss Buzzy Bee finally run out of honey? Danny stared at the radio, breath baited, the faintest trace of a grin dancing about his mouth.

'You are living in a beautiful house with wooden floors and antique furniture and gables, but currently you are living in a block of flats.' There was something different about her voice, something rushed, panicked. Danny sat motionless staring at his radio.

'So you would set moving to your dream house as the long term goal,' she carried on, her words tumbling out. 'Then work your way backwards and say to yourself, well what first step could I take towards this goal this year? It could be that you start a savings plan or seek financial advice. You could start viewing dream homes. Or perhaps you could make changes to your existing home to make it more like your perfect one – buy some new furniture or something. Or you could start keeping a scrap book about your dream home, cutting out pictures of similar types of houses and the furniture you would have. To make it more real to you.'

Danny groaned. What was it with this woman and her cutting and pasting obsession?

'Anyway, it's time to take a break now. Here's 'I Believe I Can Fly,' by R. Kelly then I'll be back to take some of your calls. You're listening to Megan Rowe and Help Yourself to Happiness on Loose Talk 107.7.'

Danny frowned. What had happened there? She had sped through the last bit with all the enthusiasm of someone reading a orbituary. Danny winced as the song cranked up a notch. He'd had more than enough happy clappy bullshit for one night. Some lousy R&B singer telling him that he believed that he could fly and touch the sky was more than he could take. He got out of bed and went over to the window. For the first time since he'd moved in it wasn't slick with damp, the pane was dry and clear and there weren't any icy blasts sneaking in under the window either. It looked like spring had finally sprung. Danny decided to go for a run. Clear his mind.

*

But rather than clear his mind, running only seemed to fill it with more questions. No matter how hard or fast his feet pounded as they tore along the bank of the River Thames he could still hear that damned Megan Rowe woman. What would your perfect day be? Who would you be with? What would you be doing?

Fuck off! He wanted to yell. Don't you get it – some of us don't deserve to have a 'perfect day.'

What would you be wearing? What would you look like? Who would you be with? How would you feel? Danny ran past a pub, a handful of drinkers were sat hunched around a table outside, making the most of the relatively warm night.

'That's what I love about you,' he heard one of them say to another as he ran past.

Love.

Danny slowed his pace and a picture of Faria entered his mind. Her dark eyes were glassy with tears and her hands were trembling. It was the day of Nasir's funeral and they had all gone back to the house, Faria, the kids, Danny and Michael.

'What will I do without him?' she had asked. And Danny had felt so useless, so impotent as he had stared at her blankly and he had hated himself. Then they had heard a terrible screaming and crashing from the living room next door and run through to find Ali, Faria's oldest son flinging his toy cars at the wall.

'I'm killing the man who killed daddy,' he shouted, his little face crumpled with rage and sorrow. 'I'm blowing up his car.'

Faria had pushed past and scooped him up in her arms. 'I love you,' she had whispered over and over again. 'I love you,' rocking him backwards and forwards until bit by bit his anger had abated and he had slumped against her and closed his eyes. Danny had watched transfixed from the doorway, feeling that he was intruding and yet unable to tear himself or his eyes away. There was something so pure and powerful in that moment. And the power seemed to be emanating from Faria herself as she held that little boy in her arms and rocked him over and over, a peaceful smile rising like a warm sun across her face. Then Danny had turned away shamed.

Danny slowed to a halt and bent over to catch his breath. What was he doing? Always running, always running away. He turned back towards Hammersmith and watched the glinting caterpillar of cars creeping over the bridge. That day he had been so moved by Faria, by the display of raw and unconditional love and the strength she had derived from it he had vowed to change. To stop running from the truth, stop courting death and write about life. But it turned out coming to London and writing the book wasn't enough. Now, finally, he knew what he had to do. The answer was both glaring and terrifying. Danny turned left on to the bridge, leant on the railings and stared down into the deep dark water of the Thames. How many dreams he wondered had been ended down there? People often said it was cowardly to kill yourself but they were talking out of their asses. Wasn't it more cowardly to live a life on the run, never facing up to your responsibilities? Pretending to be brave when all you were doing was hoping that one day the sniper's bullet or smart missile would hit home, or the car bomb would be triggered just as you walked past and you wouldn't have to make that decision.

Well not any more. There was to be no more running away, no more taunting death arms wide open. Danny looked back down at the water. A ferry boat passed by underneath, screams and shrieks echoed up at him in the dark. Danny imagined clambering up on the railings, letting himself drop off into the dark. Down, down, down. Finally letting go. But something inside of him said no. Something, or maybe some*one* wouldn't let him. Danny gripped hard on to the railings. And then he realised with a dazzling clarity what it was that he had to do. He had to find the courage to kill himself mentally rather than physically, to finally let go of the past and the old him and walk arms wide open into the future.

Chapter Twenty Seven

"When we store anger and resentment from past events, it clogs us up inside like limescale in a kettle. Start letting go of corrosive anger today and see how cleansing it can be."
Megan Rowe, 'Help Yourself to Happiness.'

Cheddar stood in the doorway of studio nine and sighed. It had been a right weird night – a right weird week, all things considered. He looked at Megan's cue cards pinned to the wall, shining in the reflection of the soft spot lighting. *DO YOU FEEL AS IF YOU'RE STUCK IN A RUT?* Yes, Cheddar thought grimly. *DO YOU HATE YOUR JOB?* No. That was something at least. He turned off the light in the presenter's half of the studio and returned to his own desk. No, he loved his job, of that he was absolutely certain. And this was one of the parts he loved the most. When everyone else had gone home and it was just him sat there in the studio, echoes of the show still ringing about the walls; the buzz from producing a live broadcast still flickering around the semi darkness like an errant fire fly. And the knowledge that further down the deserted corridor another show had begun, that he was still part of that unseen network stretching out for miles into the darkness, connecting unseen people, floating into their lives and minds like dreams. That to him was the magic of late night radio. Cheddar hated Loose Talk during the day, when the corridors were full of posey work experiences and researchers racing around with clipboards and the studios were crammed with presenters jostling for space with their transmitter-sized egos. And speakers everywhere pumped out the endless jingly jangles and the fake bon hommie that was daytime radio. Of course it could have been a lot worse. At least at Loose Talk they were slightly more cutting edge than the other national commercial stations. At least the daytime shows encouraged controversial phone-ins and the play-list was blissfully pop-free. Well it had to be with Jimmy Levine as the owner. That was another thing Cheddar loved about his job – the fact that he worked for the rock legend that was Jimmy Levine. Although truth be told he had never actually spoken to him and had only seen him once at a station Christmas party. But that had been enough. Seeing that wizened prune of a face at the far end of the restaurant, beneath the trademark bandana with its skull and cross bones motif, the same face that had stared down on him from his bedroom wall throughout his childhood years – and thinking, I work for this man, this guitar legend, Mr Twelve Bar Levine, had sent pulses of excitement resonating through his body like echoes through an amp.

Cheddar leant back in his chair. On the desk in front of him the sticks of celery and carrot sat looking decidedly limp and rubbery and even more unappetising than ever in their plastic container. Yes, it had been a weird week all right. This had to be the first Sunday in God knows how long he hadn't had a roast, for a start. But it wasn't just him who had gone a bit soft. What about the lasses? Natalie seemed to have turned from ice queen to emotional wreck over night – although he still wouldn't trust her as far as he could throw her scrawny arse - and then there was Megan. Cheddar frowned as he rammed the lid shut on his box of rabbit food. She was obviously tired from her house move but he knew there was more to it than that. For a start she hadn't mentioned anything to him about moving the previous week, or any of the previous weeks and everyone knows it takes months to plan a move. You don't just do it over night, do you, unless. Cheddar couldn't help thinking back to his last move, almost a year before. That certainly hadn't been planned, had it? No, when he had come home to Denise's that fateful night and picked up the living room phone to call his mam and heard Denise saying those things on the upstairs extension, well the double barrelled whammy of shock and pain had propelled him straight out of there hadn't it? 'You've been a very bad boy,' Denise had been saying in a strange, almost comical baby voice. And being the dimwit that he was, Cheddar had almost apologised. 'Sorry, I only wanted to call me mam,' he'd almost said. But thankfully he'd realised in time that she hadn't been talking to him at all. How could she have known he was going to pick up the phone and anyway she'd never spoken to him in that soppy, coochie-coo style voice in all their five years together. The shrill nagging bark she reserved for him was nowhere to be heard. But it was the next part that really threw him. The part when he heard a man reply. 'Oh I know babes, I know, but you ain't seen nothing yet.' Cheddar had stood there in the highly polished magnolia lounge, the receiver clamped to his ear, frozen not only by the horror of what was unfolding but also a strange sense of déjà vu. But then he realised it wasn't déjà vu at all, it was just that the man's voice was uncannily familiar and yet he couldn't quite place it in this context. On his phone, talking to his girlfriend about being such a 'naughty boy.' And then as he stood there rooted to the thick creamy shag pile listening to this man tell his girlfriend what he intended doing to her next time they met, the awful truth dawned. And yet bizarrely the first thing he thought wasn't, why is Denise talking about having sex with my mate Darren but, what the hell is Darren doing calling a lass 'babes' in that ridiculous Barry White style voice? In his heightened state of shock he'd almost wanted to laugh and shout down the phone, get a grip Daz, you sound like a right twat. But of course he hadn't. Instead, once he'd regained the use of his limbs he'd carefully replaced the phone, turned around and walked straight out. And walked. Until somehow, at some ungodly hour of the night he'd found himself at Jimbo's. Found himself drinking scotch at Jimbo's kitchen table. Found himself eventually crashing out on Jimbo's couch and staying there until somehow the pieces of a monstrous jigsaw all fell into place and he was able to get back on his feet again. No, that move hadn't been planned and hadn't taken long at all.

In a bid to suppress the eruptions of molten anger now coursing through his veins Cheddar forced himself to think back to Megan. Something bad must have happened, he was certain. She had had that same emptiness about her on tonight's show, running through the calls as if she were on some kind of coaching autopilot, saying all of the right things but with none of the usual enthusiasm and passion he found so addictive too watch. Could her own move have been triggered by a break-up? She had been about to tell him something when she'd first arrived at the studio he was sure but then Natalie had burst in and then burst into floods of tears and the opportunity had passed. Cheddar racked his brains and tried to remember what he knew of Megan's personal background. She'd definitely mentioned a husband when she first came to the station, and she frequently talked about her son, Laurence but that was all he really knew. He scratched his shaven head and frowned. Lasses eh! Never seemed to know what was going on with them. Still all was not lost. The week may have been weird but at least it had seen him making the first awkward moves out of his rut. He'd done up his bedroom and much as his diet was making him thoroughly miserable his jeans did feel a tad looser round the waist. And tomorrow he would make a start on Megan's latest exercise and write all about his 'Perfect Day'. But now. Now he would get down to the Prince Albert for last orders. A bloke deserved a pint after the kind of week he'd just had and anyway he had that Stevie Ray Vaughn CD to drop off for the yank.

The sound of laughter and chatter and clinking glasses was music to Cheddar's ears upon arriving at the pub. The sound of an over-weight, middle-aged cockney dressed in a skin-tight, white sequinned jumpsuit and murdering 'Love Me Tender' by Elvis, however, was not.

'What the hell's going on?' Cheddar asked Ray as he took up his normal position at the bar.

Ray shrugged his huge rounded shoulders as he began pouring Cheddar a pint. His alcohol-pickled face looked ruddier than ever. 'The Recclaimers pulled out at the last minute, pseudo Scottish wankers, dip shit here was all I could get.'

Both men stopped and watched for a moment as the Elvis impersonator began thrusting his hips in violent slow motion to the beat of the backing track, every thrust causing the dartboard on the wall behind him to shudder.

'Watch it mate, you'll have those hip replacements popping out of their sockets,' Ray called over before passing Cheddar his pint. 'So how's it going up at Loose Talk then? I see Brad Steeple's been booted off the breakfast show.'

Cheddar took a welcome gulp from his pint. 'Aye. Been moved to the late morning slot. I think the bosses figure that way he's got more of a chance of making it in on time from the Groucho.'

'Yeah – or from that weather bird's bed.'

Cheddar nodded and both men chuckled.

'Thank-you, thank-you so much,' the Elvis impersonator said in a woeful American accent that sounded more Teddington than Tennessee.

Cheddar turned to see the large group of people who had been sat by the door standing up and pulling their coats on to go. 'Not exactly what you'd call a crowd pleaser is he?' he commented.

Ray shook his purple head mournfully. 'Calls himself the Peckham Pelvis would you believe? You should have seen him doing "Blue Suede Shoes" earlier, I thought he was going to have a bleedin' coronary.'

'Here, mate, you couldn't do "If I Can Dream" could you?' Cheddar called across the now almost deserted pub. Elvis' anthem of hope and positivity was just what he needed to build on the momentum of the past week, and no matter how bad the Peckham Pelvis' rendition, surely he'd manage to capture some of the sentiment?

'You've got to be bleeding joking,' the Peckham Pelvis gasped, before lighting himself a cigarette. 'I'm knackered, mate.' And with that he hit a switch on his backing track machine and the famous Elvis exit music began blasting throughout the pub.

Just at that moment the door opened and Cheddar saw the American guy, Danny walk in wearing a tracksuit and sweating profusely. Although Cheddar couldn't hear him over the din he could clearly make out his mouth forming the words, 'What the hell?' as the Peckham Pelvis made a staggering circuit of the pub, arms half raised in limp celebration, fag dangling from mouth, before diving into the disabled toilets at the back.

'Elvis has left the building!' a voice boomed out, followed by a piercing screech of feedback.

'For fuck's sake,' Ray exclaimed, pulling a pint glass down from the shelf. 'All right, Septic, pint of the usual?'

'Yes sir,' Danny replied as he made his way over to the bar. 'Hey, Cheddar, what's up?'

'Wasssupp!' Ray immediately mimicked. 'We're not in some ad for that Budweiser crap you know.'

'Well I can see that,' Danny retorted, casting a smirk towards the disabled toilet, 'Clearly we have somehow time-travelled back to Graceland. Do you think it's wise to leave him on his own in there though.'

'What do you mean?' Cheddar asked, pulling out a barstool for Danny.

'Well you know what happened last time Elvis went to the toilet.' Danny frowned and shook his head mournfully.

Cheddar burst out laughing. 'Chuffin' 'ell Ray, he's got a point. And let's face it he wasn't exactly looking too bright when he went in there was he?'

Ray frowned. 'It may say disabled khazi on the door but I'll have you know that also happens to double as the back stage area and dressing room for our guest performers. I'll give him five minutes then I'll send you fellas in.' he said, plonking Danny's pint down in front of him. 'It's been bad enough watching the geezer die a painful death for the past two hours. I ain't disposing of his corpse an' all.'

'So, how have you been?' Cheddar asked, as Danny took a long drink from his pint. Judging from the sweat beading his forehead and darkening his sandy hair the lad was in need of some serious re-hydration.

'Oh you know, hanging on in there,' Danny replied, running his hand through his hair and wiping the resultant sweat on his tracksuit bottoms.

'Been running?' Cheddar asked, gesturing at the tracksuit.

'Don't be stupid,' Ray called over from where he was starting to load the dishwasher with dirty glasses. 'Yanks don't run, ever, unless it's to get to the front of the queue in McDonalds, eh Septic?'

Danny shook his head and laughed, before taking a pack of cigarettes from his tracksuit pocket and offering one to Cheddar.

'Yeah, just did a few miles along the river – I head there was a special offer on Big Macs down in Holborn,' he added to Ray. 'Smoke?'

Cheddar laughed and shook his head, He was pleased to see Danny was obviously a follower of the same kind of fitness regime as himself; everything in moderation, no need to over do it, nothing wrong with a pint now and then. He hadn't even drunk half his own beer yet but due to his ridiculous new diet he was already starting to feel pleasantly pissed. This fitness malarkey might have some advantages after all.

'Here, I've got something for you,' he said pulling the Stevie Ray Vaughan CD from his jacket pocket, 'I was going to leave it with Ray. It's the Stevie Ray Vaughan CD we talked about. I burned a copy of "Couldn't Stand the Weather" and put a few extra tracks on there too.'

Danny took the CD and smiled. It was a wide, open smile, the kind that Cheddar liked in a bloke, an honest, no bullshit kind of smile.

'Hey, that's great,' Danny said, taking the CD and studying the neatly printed list of titles on the back. 'Thanks, man, I really appreciate it.'

'So do you do much running then?' Cheddar asked, glancing furtively at Danny's toned physique. Didn't want him getting the wrong idea, but seeing Danny's lean torso and muscular arms had set him thinking. Perhaps he ought to take up running too, that way he could lose weight and still enjoy a pint and eat normal food.

'Yeah. I like it,' Danny replied. 'Helps clear my head, especially when I can't sleep. Hey this is great, you've got most of "In Step" on here too,' Danny said, looking back down at the CD.

'Yeah, well, that was always my favourite,' Cheddar replied.

'Yeah mine too.'

'Such a shame wasn't it – he had to go and -'

'Here, don't you start going on about that morbid old bollocks again,' Ray called along the bar, 'It's been bad enough having an exhumed Elvis lurching about the place all night without you pair starting.'

Cheddar looked at Danny and grinned and shrugged his shoulders.

Danny grinned back and put the CD in his pocket. 'Cheers for that. So, how've you been?'

'Yeah, not bad, mate, not bad. Been a bit of a rum old week though.'

Danny frowned. 'What do you mean? You've been on the piss?'

Cheddar looked momentarily baffled. What was Danny trying to say? Did he look like the type of bloke who spent the whole week boozing? He glanced down at his large belly and shifted uncomfortably on his seat. 'No – well I've had a couple of pints, after work like, but nothing too extreme. To tell you the truth I'm on a bit of a health kick.'

At the other end of the bar Ray let out a raucous sixty-a-day laugh. 'Bloody hell – I've heard it all now.'

'Oi, you carry on cleaning the pots, bar-keep' Cheddar shouted back.

Danny smiled. 'Good on you, man, it's just that when you said rum, I thought maybe you'd been hitting the Captain Morgan's.'

Cheddar shook his head mournfully. 'If only, mate, if only. No I meant it's been a bit of a weird week. I don't know, things have happened, unexpected things.'

'You're damn right there,' Ray interjected with another chortle. 'Here Cheddar, fancy a nice packet of tasty scratchings?'

Ignoring him, Cheddar continued, lowering his voice. 'I decided I needed to have a bit of a makeover,' he put one hand on his belly and gave it a gentle wobble. 'You know shift a bit of tonnage.'

Danny nodded. 'Tell you what – lets have a drink to new beginnings,' and he raised his glass. Cheddar laughed and clinked his own pint against Danny's before taking another welcome gulp.

'Listen I don't suppose,' Cheddar paused. 'Well you're obviously a fit bloke, you know keep yourself in trim, like. I was just wondering, well,' he lowered his voice even further, he really didn't want Ray hearing this next bit. 'Well perhaps one day you could give me a few tips on running?' Thankfully Ray continued loading the dishwasher.

'Sure. I'd be glad to.' Once more Danny treated Cheddar to a broad smile. 'I tell you what, I'm going to be taking a trip in the next few days but when I get back, I could work out some kind of fitness programme for you if you want. We could even go running together.'

Cheddar grinned. 'Aye, that would be great. So where is it you're off to? Anywhere nice?'

'No, not really, just a work trip, back to the States for a few days.' Danny stubbed out his cigarette and ground the butt down hard in the ashtray.

Cheddar sighed. 'You lucky bugger. I wish I got sent to the States for my work.'

'You're not the only one,' Ray called along the bar. 'I wish you got sent there an' all.'

'Where do you work?' Danny asked.

'Just down the road, at the radio station, Loose Talk. I'm a producer.'

Danny turned and stared at Cheddar. 'You're kidding. I live just round the corner from there. I'm renting a place on the Queen Caroline Estate. I've been listening to Loose Talk on and off since I got here. What show do you work on?'

Cheddar smiled. He couldn't help feeling a stab of pride at Danny's reaction. It felt good when people reacted like this, made him feel special, important.

'The Dave McNoughton show,' he replied, 'It's on every weeknight from seven till ten. Have you heard it?'

'Have I heard it? Man I love that show. Naughty McNoughton,' Danny chuckled and gazed into space. 'The way he talks to some of the callers, Jeez.'

'I know.' Cheddar laughed. Tact and diplomacy were hardly Dave's strongest points, on air at least. Off air he was actually a pussy cat, one of the most caring compassionate men you could wish to meet, but on air. . .

'Hey what about the other night when he told that reverend guy that religion was the root of all evil?' Danny laughed and shook his head, 'I thought the guy was going to hyperventilate he was so mad.'

Cheddar chuckled. 'Don't. I half expected him to come up to the studio and perform some kind of exorcism.'

'Wow, so you're Dave McNoughton's producer.' Once again Danny shook his head in appreciation and once again Cheddar felt a warm flush of pride.

'Yeah and he produces that bird's show, don't you mate?' Ray added, as if wanting to capitalise on Cheddar's sudden boost in status rather than completely humiliate him as before.

Cheddar nodded. 'Yeah every Sunday night. There's a show called "Help Yourself to Happiness". It's hosted by a life coach called Megan Rowe. You might have heard of her – she wrote this best-selling book a few years back?'

'Load of old bollocks if you ask me,' Ray said, '"Help Yourself to Happiness," I mean, I ask you. If only it were that easy.'

Danny shifted on his barstool, looking suddenly uncomfortable.

Cheddar frowned. This was why he didn't normally mention his work on Megan's show to other blokes, he knew it could make them quite cynical. 'It's actually a pretty good show,' he said somewhat defensively. 'The lass Megan really knows her stuff, she's great with the callers - really helps them, you know? And besides I see it as the perfect antidote to producing a week of abuse and outrage from Dave.'

Danny smiled. 'Yeah – it must be. I'll have to listen out for it when I get back. Most Sunday nights I'm out running.'

A silence descended and Cheddar couldn't help feeling a certain awkwardness had mingled in with it like wisps of cigarette smoke. But before he had time to try and work out why, a plaintiff cry rang out from the disabled toilet.

'I say, hello! Could someone give me a hand with me jumpsuit, I can't seem to get the zipper open.'

Chapter Twenty-Eight

"Take an afternoon off work and meet a friend for coffee or a trip to the cinema. Find the joy in spontaneity."
Megan Rowe, 'Help Yourself to Happiness.'

'Congratulations, Ms Taylor Cassidy on being voted the world's sexiest woman by *FHM* readers for the third year running. Tell me do you have any beauty tips for our viewers?'

Natalie adjusted her satin robe and gazed coquettishly into her dressing table mirror.

'Yes, Lorraine. I always swear by two litres of water a day and I always take my make-up off before going to bed.' Oh purlease! Natalie took a wipe from the pack in front of her and set about removing the remaining clumps of the previous night's mascara. When she was famous there was no way she was going to trot out all of that clean living bullshit other models and actresses spouted. She was going to keep it real – that would be her thing, her trademark. *NATALIE TAYLOR-CASSIDY TELLS IT LIKE IT IS.*

'Yes, Lorraine,' she repeated, wiping away at her eyes. 'Never drink water – I mean, hello, God gave us taste buds for a reason. And always keep your make-up on if you have a man staying the night. Would a tribal chief remove their war-paint mid-way through battle?'

Natalie discarded the mascara streaked wipe into her waste paper basket and looked into the mirror. She shuddered at the pallid reflection squinting back at her. There was no way she would let Gerry or any other man see her like this, she looked about twelve and her make-up stripped eyes had shrunk to the size of two forget-me-nots. And as for her hair. She grabbed a handful of it and pulled hard until her eyes watered. The early morning sun streaming through the bedroom window was as harsh and unforgiving as fluorescent, making her frizzed mass of curls radiate orange. As orange as a carrot, a carrot top, a ginga, a Duracell. Ghostly echoes of playground taunts seemed to resonate around the room. She leapt up and pulled the dark pink velvet curtains shut, returned to the dressing table and switched on the flower shaped fairy lights draped around the mirror. That was better. In the dim half-light her hair was once again auburn. Sophisticated. Flame coloured. 'Fucking amazing,' as Gerry would say.

He had ended up staying every night since the previous Wednesday and to her surprise Natalie had actually quite enjoyed having him about the place. Apart from when he'd got really drunk on Saturday night and started rambling on about that arrogant know-it-all Megan.

'How can she say she needs space? I hardly ever see her,' he'd suddenly blurted out, half way through a hideously congealed chilli from the tacky Mexican restaurant across the road. Natalie had forced a sympathetic grin and bit down hard on a tortilla chip. And then later on, when they'd been lying in bed and Natalie had leant over and stroked his hair, like she'd seen Jennifer Gray do to Patrick Swayze in *Dirty Dancing*, he'd actually started to cry. 'She's taken my boy,' he'd sobbed, 'I'm all alone.' It had taken Natalie a few seconds to figure out he was talking about his son, and even longer to get over the pang of jealousy she felt at the fact that Megan and this kid could inspire so much heartfelt emotion in Gerry. But she knew what to do – and sure enough, a few strategically placed strokes and nibbles had him moaning in a completely different way. And God it had felt good, walking into the radio studio the following evening, still smelling of Gerry and sitting down next to his arrogant, know-it-all wife, who really didn't have a clue. And how good would it feel today, when she met Megan for coffee and took her up on her offer of a life-coaching session? Oh the irony, of taking advice from that holier than thou do-gooder, and all the while knowing that her husband would be coming home from the theatre to *her* that night, leaving Megan all alone and man-less.

Natalie picked up a pot of moisturiser, a freebie after getting the part at the skin care audition on Friday, and began kneading dollops of the oily cream into her face. As a rosy glow burst into her cheeks she instantly felt transformed. She closed her eyes and inhaled the delicate scent of primrose. Yes, things were definitely looking up. Not only did she have one over on Megan, but she had an acting job, albeit a commercial, *and* she'd been asked to cover the phones for the Bradley Steeple show for a week. Now Brad Steeple was a real star. Although he'd recently been moved to the late morning slot, people still talked about his legendary breakfast show and the anarchic mix of celebrity wind-ups and outrageous phone-ins he was renowned for. He was gorgeous too, in an edgy, mean kind of way. *BUDDING ACTRESS NATALIE TAYLOR-CASSIDY WOOS TOP DJ, MAN OF THE PEOPLE BRADLEY STEEPLE.* It would be a huge buzz answering the phones on his show. Who knew what celebrity friends of his might phone in? How much cooler than the fucked up saddos who called in on a Sunday night? Natalie opened her eyes and reached for her make-up bag. This was what she had been waiting for. What she had moved to London for. Finally she was on her way. What with her artistic director lover, boyfriend, whatever, and her acting and her job in radio – oh how she'd love to see the faces of those narrow minded arseholes back in the village once they found out what she was doing with her life. One day she'd go back there, just like Catherine Zeta Jones going back to Mumbles or Bumbles or wherever the hell it was she came from in Wales. But rather than open a hospital wing or poxy village fete Natalie would only go back to gloat. *Who's laughing now?* she could imagine herself yelling from the back of her limo, waving a champagne flute in a bejewelled hand. *See, I don't need you at all,* she would shout as she was whisked past her mother looking all butter-wouldn't-melt and demure at the gateway to the house. Natalie took an eyeliner from her make-up bag and set about framing her eyes in smoky rings of kohl. She loved the feeling this gave her, this ability to transform herself from pallid little schoolgirl to wide-eyed seductress in a few expertly applied strokes. As she began smudging the eyeliner with the tip of a cotton bud to soften the effect she couldn't help thinking back to her paintings. The way she used to get a similar kick from lashing the canvas with broad streaks of colour and then working away with a selection of brushes and scrapers to get just the right effect. Smudging and blending until the image or emotion filling her mind had been transferred on to the easel in front of her, like downloading a file on a computer. Natalie sat motionless, staring at the pink plastic flowers twinkling and twining their way across the top of the mirror. Should she start painting again? Should she go into Hammersmith later and buy herself a new easel, or perhaps just a sketch pad and pencils, to ease herself back in? But it had been so long – almost a year since she had last painted; since *the* painting. And she had vowed that would be the last. A wave of nausea tore through her stomach. Natalie frowned and looked back at her reflection and saw that her eyebrows needed plucking.

*

Across West London, in Turnham Green, Megan was sat on her rented black leather sofa, staring blankly at her rented black wrought iron shelves and CD racks, silhouetted against the pristine white rented walls. It was like sitting in the middle of a giant (rented) chess board – the room was crying out for colour. Megan looked down at her black tracksuit with its white piping trim. God, it was as if she had become a chameleon; instinctively taking on the guise of her new environment. But rather than her camouflage making her feel safe, she felt as if she were somehow being swallowed up. Somewhere deep inside, her inner coach whispered something about doing a visualisation exercise in which she imagined herself being bathed in golden light and lolloping about in a magical meadow of colour, but for some reason she really couldn't be bothered. Or maybe she should do the Perfect Day exercise Cheddar had made her recommend on the show the night before. But how could she have any faith in that? For wasn't that the very same exercise she had devised and done herself before finding the house on Nightingale Avenue? Hadn't she filled an entire scrapbook with a collage of cuttings from interior design magazines in the months prior to her and Gerry finding the house? Hadn't she written in loving detail about the 'lofty gables raised like eyebrows above a pair of wide sash windows and a snowy white façade,' weeks before she'd even laid eyes on them? Hadn't she waxed lyrical about 'creaky wooden floors and a wide stair case, a stained glass panel in the front door and a sun-filled conservatory.' And how had she described her perfect kitchen? 'A huge airy room with an aga glowing away at it's heart, the source of nourishment for the whole family.' Megan grimaced. 'And a scrubbed pine table covered with a gingham cloth, a vase of freshly cut flowers at its centre, a place for laughter, contentment and bonding.' One by one, detail by excruciating detail, she'd visualised them all into existence, but just like her grandmother's Mirror of Serendipity she hadn't realised the potency of the magic she'd been dabbling with. What had she been thinking on Sunday night, broadcasting such hocus pocus to the nation without warning them in no uncertain terms to be extremely careful what they wish for?

Megan got to her feet and walked over to the gleaming double glazed living room window – no wide sash windows here. Everything was entirely characterless here in her rented box of a flat. From the pale oatmeal carpets to the white-washed walls and glossy skirting boards and sills. There were no imprints of any previous life or love or laughter within these walls. No telltale finger prints or scuffs or smells. Not even the faintest hint the flat had ever been inhabited before. It was like entering a void. But in some ways Megan didn't care. For the first time in her life she was sick and tired of trying. And the surprising thing was, it actually felt good, for once not having to bother. When she had moved in at the weekend she had brought with her only the absolute basics. This was to be a fresh start, so it felt right that she should be unencumbered by the clutter of her past. There would be no glowing aga or scrubbed pine family table in this kitchen, anyway there was barely room for the existing miniscule breakfast bar and slimline cooker. Megan pressed the lock on the spotless white handle of the window and pushed it open. The cacophony from Turnham Green High Street drifted over the roof and wafted in to the room like random musical notes on the air. A discordant mix of purring cars, tinny music and the high pitched cries of children. Megan looked down across the sunshine bathed car-park beneath her, and at the far end a Piccadilly line train raced by into town, a glinting flash of silver between the trees.

She turned back to face the barren room. It's going to be okay, she told herself. You've done the right thing, you just need a bit of time to adjust. And at least you still have Laurence. At the thought of Laurence she started to smile. Rather than be unsettled or upset, as she had feared, he had positively embraced their move. He hadn't uttered the word 'whatever' once over the entire weekend. In marked contrast he'd said 'cool,' when he'd seen how close they were to Pizza Hut, 'wicked' when he'd seen the intercom system and 'well sick' when he'd seen the power shower in the hotel-like bathroom. This last one had thrown Megan somewhat and she'd been about to agree that yes, having a bathroom with no coloured tiles or quirky toilet seat was a little disappointing, but nothing a trip to Homebase couldn't fix, until she'd taken in his wide-eyed, awestruck grin and deduced that perhaps 'sick' in teen-speak was actually a term of praise. At first she'd felt confused and even a little hurt by the enthusiasm he'd shown for the flat – had he really hated Nightingale Avenue that much – and after she'd put so much energy into conjuring it into being. But it didn't take her long to realise that a monochrome flat with a power shower in Turnham Green was the perfect abode for the young man about town he was rapidly becoming.

Megan looked about the living room and smiled with a bit more conviction. Yes, she had done the right thing. If Laurence was happy then it had to be okay, didn't it? They would have fun the two of them in their bachelor / bachelorette flat. But what about Gerry? *Sod Gerry*, a voice in her head scolded, *he had his chance, had his chances, about a million of them.* But she couldn't help wondering. In the days between getting back from Brighton and moving out she'd seen him only once, when he came back from work on Thursday evening.

'I've made an offer on a flat,' she had told him, standing on the opposite side of the kitchen table; the 'family' table, the place for 'laughter, contentment and bonding.' 'It's a rented place so hopefully I'll be out of here by the weekend.'

His response had been strangely muted. She had prepared herself for tears or apologies or even, worse case scenario, a drunken rage, but he had just stared at her for what seemed like an eternity, his dark eyes deadened, like two stagnant ponds and then he'd nodded. 'Right,' he'd said, before turning away and going upstairs to the bedroom. Megan had followed out into the hall, unable to quite believe it had been so easy as she listened to the faint murmur of his voice on the telephone and then watched as he had come back downstairs, his coat still on. 'See you then,' he'd said before walking straight back out of the front door. And she hadn't seen him since. Once again Megan felt a strange fug of numbness descend. It didn't matter where he'd gone or where he'd been since. She was way past caring. Wasn't she?

She shut the window and made her way out of the living room and along the long narrow hall, past the kitchen on the left and Laurence's bedroom and the bathroom on the right, to her own bedroom at the front end of the flat. It was a large airy room painted the palest shade of lilac, the only room with any colour in the whole place. A breeze was blowing in through the open windows causing the paper thin cream curtains to billow into the room. The noise from the High Street was louder here and instinctively Megan was drawn over to the window. Across the road a couple of young women were sitting at a table outside a café. One of them, dressed in a beautiful plum coloured woollen dress and matching beret was leaning forwards waving her hands animatedly as she regaled a story to the other. Suddenly her companion leant back in her chair and erupted with laughter. Megan felt a pang of wistfulness. The women seemed so full of life and so carefree. She crouched down, one hand propped against the glossy white windowsill and watched them intently. What were they talking about these women? Why were they not at work? What was the one in the beret saying to make the other one laugh so hard? And as she crouched there just watching and admiring the relaxed style they both exuded like expensive scent, she remembered back to when she was a child and she used to crouch at her old bedroom window, picking at the peeling paintwork and watching various big kids from the estate kissing behind the huge communal bins. There were two in particular Megan used to love, Debbie and Tommy, in her mind the Romeo and Juliet of Stanley Grove, who were by far the most frequent visitors to the rather unlikely romantic hideaway. Some nights Megan would watch them kissing and groping each other for so long her knees would seize up and her feet would go numb. But her heart would keep pounding, sending blood fizzing to the surface of her skin. How she had wished she had been Debbie back then. How she had wished she could have been the one with the shaggy perm and highlights, surrendering herself to Tommy's wiry arms, succumbing to Tommy's sneering mouth as it practically devoured her. And when they finally walked off hand in hand into the labyrinth of darkened alleyways, Megan would crawl into her cold, hard bed and lie there for hours staring at the ceiling and hugging her pillow and wondering if anyone would ever love her as much as Tommy loved Debbie and all the time fighting the sinking feeling that the answer had to be no.

Megan sighed and slid down into a seated position on the carpet with her back to the window. What was happening? Had she worked so hard for so many years only to come full circle? To once again have to resort to peering through a window and wish herself into someone else's life. Well, balls to that. She was thirty-six now, not ten. She had money in the bank. A career. A flat of her own, well, a rented flat of her own, in a very desirable part of West London rather than a sink estate in South London. And anyway wasn't she about to go and meet a girl friend of her own for coffee?

Megan got to her feet and looked at the piles of clothes leaning against the fitted wardrobes. When she had woken that morning she had felt a little apprehensive about meeting Natalie – what if she reverted back to her cold and aloof self? What would they find to say to each other? Wouldn't she have been better off meeting one of her coaching friends or her agent Edith? But no, Natalie was perfect. With Natalie she would be able to continue her fresh start and not have to face any awkward questions, instead she could try to help her with her own heartache. Megan strode over to her clothes, fired up with determination. She would show those women outside the coffee shop, they weren't the only ones who knew how to laugh and throw their glossy hair back and look so damned effortless. She was going to meet her brand new, extremely young friend and exude youth and energy herself, if only by association. She would wash her hair in the 'well sick' power shower and dress up in something effortlessly chic and she and Natalie would meet and talk and laugh and be the envy of all the stressed out, unhappy women trudging by. Because she was finally free, wasn't she? Finally free from all the crap and she wasn't scared at all. Oh no.

chapter Twenty-Nine

"What did you dream of becoming when you were a child? Adult life can blanch the colour from our dreams. Today make time to revisit the technicolour day- dreams of your youth."
Megan Rowe, 'Help Yourself to Happiness.'

As Danny fed his ticket through the greedy metal mouth at Hammersmith Station and hauled his rucksack through the opening gate he made himself carry out a mental checklist of all the places he had been since leaving home. He wasn't sure if it would be able to keep his burgeoning sense of fear in perspective, but it had to be worth a try. Split, Croatia had been his first port of call, back in 1992, en route to war-torn Bosnia – perhaps not the obvious destination for most twenty-two year old graduates fresh out of college. But then he hadn't been like most graduates had he, not after what had happened. He hadn't been scared either, not really, just numb. As Danny hoisted his rucksack back on to his back and walked along the white-tiled concourse for the stairs that would take him down to the Piccadilly Line he couldn't help smiling a wry smile. It was funny really when he though about it, that all through his college years, all through the drinking and the partying and the rolling into his photo-journalism lectures tousle haired and dishevelled – the dreams he had harboured, stored away in the back of his mind like precious jewels to be taken out every once in a while to hold up to the sparkling rays of youthful ambition – should have been of assignments to capture the world's excitement and beauty. Danny thought back to the hours he had spent in the bathroom as a child, sat on the cool linoleum floor, his back pressed against the door, ploughing through the pile of National Geographic Magazines lining the bottom shelf of the wicker stand by the sink. The hours he had pored over the crisp, glossy pictures, drinking in the colours as if they were the most magically refreshing sodas in the whole, entire world. Icy white mountain peaks fingering brilliant blue skies, rich, velvety forests of majestic pines and glinting gold expanses of desert-scapes. Hours he would spend, leafing through those inky smelling pages, gazing awestruck at the giant tapestry of the world unfolding before him and longing to be out there, weaving his way through it, capturing treasures of his very own.

As Danny made his way down the stairs to the platform, wincing slightly from the residue of the previous night's run stiffening the backs of his legs, his smile broadened, as he remembered the issue from June 1979, the yellow spine fraying white from age and frequent use. He could still remember the page number, 72 for the feature on an Amazonian rain tribe and in particular the picture of a group of women, their skin as shiny and dark as molasses and their breasts, their naked breasts, hanging full and low, beneath their multi-coloured strings of beads.

'What you doin' in there, Dan-Dan?' Marty would sometimes holler, hammering on the door, after he'd been in there for a while., 'Come and play racing cars.'

Danny's smile instantly faded and he looked up at the display screen suspended above the platform edge. The next Heathrow train was due in one minute. Darn it! His stomach churned. He could just turn around and head back to the flat. It wasn't too late. The ticket to

New York he had bought on line that morning had been dirt cheap being a last minute cancellation - he could just write it off and go back home and ...

And what? Sit in that cold damp room going round and round in circles, slowly spiralling out of his mind with frustration, and writer's block. Anyway, he knew better now. He knew it wasn't writer's block he'd been suffering from, it was – Danny walked a bit further up the platform, away from a jostling group of Japanese tourists – it was block full stop. He'd been suffering from it for years. The surge of determination he'd felt last night, that moment down by the river, had somehow managed to blast through the block and he couldn't go back on it now, he had to see it through. He swallowed hard. His mouth felt bitter and dry from the remnants of his breakfast of coffee and nicotine. This was it, his chance to do the courageous thing, to face up to his fear rather than keep on running. Once again he reverted to his mental checklist of all the terrifying places he had been to in the world. Bosnia, Chechnya, Palestine, Iraq, Afghanistan, Sierra Leone.

'Ladies and gentlemen, the train approaching platform two is the Piccadilly Line for Heathrow. All stations to Heathrow, platform two,' the announcer's tinny voice crackled through the air.

Zimbabwe, Somalia, Rwanda. A shudder of dread coursed through Danny's body as the train came thundering out of the tunnel towards him and he gripped on to the straps of his rucksack as if for dear life. All of those gut-wrenching, war-torn places and yet now, faced with the prospect of finally going home he was more terrified than he'd ever been.

chapter Thirty

"Honesty is not just the best policy – when it comes to our dealings with ourselves it should be the only policy."
Megan Rowe, 'Help Yourself to Happiness.'

Natalie turned past The Prince Albert and began weaving her way through the bustling hordes on King Street, her heart pounding. Could she really be about to do this? To meet Megan for coffee when only hours before she'd been screwing her husband? She swallowed hard. It wasn't her fault if their marriage was in trouble. It wasn't her fault if Miss Wonder-Coach couldn't keep Gerry satisfied. It wasn't. And besides, she'd had her fill of not feeling good enough. It felt great to be the chosen one for once, rather than the reject. As she drew level with The William Morris bar, crowded with early lunchtime drinkers, she took her mobile phone from her cavernous leather holdall and began to text:

'Have been a very bad girl, keep thinking of you inside me and – '

She paused, what would really get him going?

'Getting really wet xxx.'

With a little shiver of excitement she scrolled through her address book, found Gerry's number and pressed send. Now to find Megan. Natalie turned into the piazza on her right and made her way over to the grey concrete block of the Lyric Theatre, squatting on the end of the King's Shopping Mall. It had been her idea to meet at a theatre, the irony had been too sweet an opportunity to miss. Natalie pulled her hair from beneath her velvet jacket and shook it loose. It really was a lovely day, with the spring sun causing the newly unfurled leaves on the trees bordering the square to glisten a rich green against all the grey. She spotted Megan immediately, sitting at one of the tables outside the theatre coffee shop. Her hair looked thicker than normal and fell in loose dark curls around her shoulders. Although she was clad from head to toe in black, around her neck a striking antique style amethyst necklace glinted lilac in the sun – gaudy cow. Natalie decided to pretend not to see her and headed straight for the smoky glass door of the coffee shop.

'Natalie,' she heard Megan call in her stupid soft voice. Natalie wondered if Gerry had bought her the necklace. She forced her mouth into a surprised smile.

'Oh hi,' she cried, spinning back round. 'Sorry, I didn't notice you sat there. How are you?'

'Fine, fine,' Megan replied, getting to her feet.

God, who did she think she was, Natalie inwardly fumed, letting herself get so thin? Didn't she realise women of her age look nothing but haggard if they don't bulk out a little. Natalie looked down at her own tiny frame. Still Megan wasn't nearly as thin as her and Natalie had the bonus of being short. Men loved short women – it made them feel powerful, needed. The last thing they wanted was a beanpole like Megan beside them – and even worse a know-it-all beanpole. Gerry was living proof of that.

'Take a seat, I'll go and get you a drink,' Megan continued, grinning her stupid fake grin. Oh how Natalie would love to wipe that smirk off her face, but all in good time. 'What would you like?' Megan asked, as she pulled out a chair for Natalie to sit down.

Natalie smiled sweetly. 'A latte please. Skinny,' she replied.

*

'A skinny latte and a normal cappuccino please,' Megan asked fumbling in her bag for her purse. God, why was she so damned nervous all of a sudden? She was just meeting a friend for a coffee and a bite to eat, there was absolutely no reason to feel so apprehensive. Only there was, more than one reason in fact. For a start, Natalie could hardly be termed a friend. In the two months they'd worked together they'd only shared a few perfunctory exchanges, until the previous night. And she was so young. What on earth would they have to talk about? What if she found Megan boring, out of touch? Megan glanced outside to where Natalie was reclined back in her seat raising her glowing heart-shaped face to the sunshine – a study in effortlessness, much to the admiration of a passing couple of builders Megan noted. She took a deep breath and savoured the rich aroma of roasting coffee. Why was she being so down on herself all of a sudden? After all she was now the proud renter of a girl about town flat, cohabiting with a hip and streetwise teenager. Perhaps she should go back outside and declare Natalie's choice of coffee shop as being 'well sick?'

'You have lovely necklace.'

'I'm sorry?' Megan looked up from her panicked daze to see the waitress behind the counter gesturing at her neck.

'The necklace – it is beautiful,' she said in an Eastern European accent as thick as espresso.

'Oh.' Megan smiled and instinctively fingered one of the cube shaped amethysts. It had been her grandmother's. Her mum had given it to her on the day of the funeral. Her mum had been having a good day, ironically. She had even managed to greet every one of the many mourners personally at the door of the church, and made all of the sandwiches for the wake. Megan frowned – she hadn't called her mother for nearly two weeks now, kept putting it off, not wanting to tell her the news. But she knew she couldn't put it off forever.

'It make you look like a princess,' the waitress continued, passing her a tray.

'Thank you,' Megan replied. 'Thank you very much,' and she clutched the amethyst tightly. *Are you there, Grandma,* she whispered inside her mind, amidst all the chatter and clatter of the cafe. *Are you still with me?*

*

Back outside Natalie shifted in her seat and peeped through her lowered eyelids to make sure she was still receiving admiring glances from any passers-by. She had taken her coat off and pulled down her tightly fitted cropped jumper so that the lacy trim of her black bra was clearly visible. She thought back to the previous night when she had got all kitted out for Gerry, stockings, suspenders, boned corset, the works.

'God, the black against your pale skin looks incredible,' he had gasped as she had shimmied up and down the pole at the end of the breakfast bar.

Natalie had run her hand over her breasts and then down lower and lower.

'Jesus Christ!' he had gasped, reaching over to the counter for the bottle of wine. 'Absolutely incredible.'

And as he had poured himself another huge glass she had sashayed over to him and began shimmying up and down against his body.

'Am I the best fuck you've ever had?' she'd purred in his ear, causing him to splutter the blood red wine all down the front of his shirt.

'Oh yes,' he'd replied, looking at her and shaking his head in disbelief.

'Better than your wife?'

He'd looked away then, over the top of her head. And a silence fell.

Undeterred Natalie had moved a hand very slowly up the inside of his thigh, stopping just short of his crotch. 'Well, am I?'

Gerry had sighed a long sigh before looking back down at her. 'Could we go into the other room?' he asked.

'Why what's wrong?' her hand remained frozen at the top of his thigh.

'Nothing – it's just that picture.' He gestured to her painting on the far kitchen wall. 'The eyes. The way they seem to be staring straight into me. It's a bit unsettling. Sorry.'

Natalie felt her throat instinctively begin to constrict, but fighting the urge to run from the room she took the glass of wine from his hand and took a large gulp instead. 'Come on then,' she said, trying not to gasp from the burning at the back of her mouth as she led him into the lounge. And once they had got in there it had all been okay again. As she had clambered on to him and run her fingers through his hair and as she had watched him watching her, gazing at the tops of her stockings and the curved crest of her corset. As she had ridden him harder and harder and faster and faster it hadn't taken long for him to tell her how he felt.

'Am I the best?' she had asked again as she felt every muscle in his body tense ready to come.

'Yes,' he had cried. 'Oh God, yes.'

'Better than your wife?'

'Yes. Yes. Yes.'

*

'Here you go, one skinny latte.' Megan placed the tray down on the table and took her seat opposite Natalie. Seeing Natalie appear so happy and relaxed in the sunshine made her own tension start to melt away.

Natalie opened her eyes, sat up and smiled. 'Oh thank-you, Megan. And thank you so much for suggesting this, it really means a lot, you know.'

'Don't be silly,' Megan replied. 'It was horrible seeing you so upset yesterday, I just wanted to help.'

Immediately Natalie's face clouded over. 'It has been a tough few months,' she murmured, looking off wistfully across the square. 'Especially when . . .'

'When what?' Megan asked.

'When everywhere you look there seem to be couples enjoying themselves like those two over there.'

Megan followed her gaze to a couple standing by the fountain. The man was stroking the woman's hair and looking at her with such intensity it felt almost indecent to watch. Megan looked away. 'Sometimes I think our brains are trained to seek out the things we really don't want to see. I remember a friend of mine once saying that after she had a miscarriage practically every woman she encountered seemed to be pregnant.'

Natalie gave a strange pained expression before forcing a smile. 'Yes. Anyway don't let me go on about my crap. I don't want to put you on a downer too.'

Megan smiled ruefully. 'Honestly you really don't have to worry about me. As I said to you last night, I do understand what you're going through.'

'Do you?' The intensity in Natalie's stare was almost scary.

'Yes of course I do,' Megan replied. She smiled gingerly at Natalie before continuing softly. 'You really aren't alone, you know.'

Natalie wriggled forwards in her chair, still staring at her. 'But you're happily married aren't you? I mean I read the cover of your book and it said you were married with a son.'

Megan took a deep breath. This was it, a new beginning, a new start, time to tell the truth, and what better person to tell it to than her hopefully brand new friend. 'Actually my husband and I have just separated.'

'Oh my God!' Natalie's hand shot to her open mouth in horror. 'I'm so sorry. I had no idea. And there was me last night going on about my crap and all the time - oh you poor thing.'

Megan smiled. 'It's okay. It had been on the cards for a while to be honest.'

'So what happened? When did it happen?' Natalie clapped her tiny hand to her mouth again. 'Oh God, what am I like? I can't believe I'm being so nosy. It's just that – well –'

A loud beep came from Natalie's bag. 'Oh bugger. Sorry, I think I've got a text.' She fumbled in her bag and pulled out a wafer thin frosted pink phone. Flipping it open she clicked on a button and smiled. 'It's just a friend telling me what he wants to eat tonight. Excuse me for a second, I'll just super-fast reply and then I'll switch it off.'

Megan watched wistfully as Natalie's thumb flew over the keypad at 'super-fast' speed. Oh to have friends texting her to arrange dinner dates. Another realisation hit home. Now she and Gerry had split who could she go to dinner with? All of her friends were happily married and ensconced in family life – the thought of taking part in the dinner party circuit on her own made her shudder. And yet the thought of plunging herself back into the white-knuckle ride of the dating game was even worse. She felt caught adrift between two worlds and realised that it wasn't her new flat that was a void – it was her entire life.

Natalie clicked her phone shut and returned it to her bag. 'I am so sorry. Now where were we? Oh yes I was being a nosy cow,' she leant forward and fixed Megan with her penetrating stare. 'But really, would you like to talk?'

Megan looked at Natalie, at her huge pale blue eyes. Perhaps it would help to talk to her. Perhaps the fact that she was a virtual stranger and completely objective would help her get some sense of perspective on things. And perhaps by doing so it would help Megan chart a way out of her void and maybe even make it easier for Natalie to unburden her own troubles. She fingered her necklace and took a deep breath.

'I guess we just grew apart really. – or maybe we never had anything much in common in the first place. I don't know.'

Natalie nodded encouragingly.

'You see we hadn't been together all that long when I fell pregnant, but at the time I was sure I loved him, so it somehow felt all right.'

'So who ended it?'

'I did.' Megan felt a caffeine-like buzz of excitement course through her. It felt good to say it; to acknowledge out loud that finally she had found the strength to walk away.

Natalie nodded and looked away.

'Do you want to talk about your own – situation?' Megan asked gently.

'Not really.' The old, shuttered off Natalie seemed to have returned. Megan's heart sank. The whole point of meeting up had been to help Natalie not upset her. 'Are you sure?'

Natalie nodded.

'So how are you finding it working at Loose Talk? You started about the same time as me didn't you?'

Natalie nodded. 'Why did you end it?'

'Oh. Well - ' Megan took a sip from her cappuccino to buy herself some time. What should she say? Should she be honest? She hardly knew Natalie. 'Well as I said, we grew apart, over the years. And it just got to the point where we didn't seem to have anything in common any more.'

'Right,' Natalie continued to stare at her, her own drink still untouched. 'But still, after all that time together, it seems such a drastic step, to just leave.'

Megan frowned and stared out across the square, at the shoppers and office workers weaving their busy, determined paths.

'I mean, I think you're very brave to like, take such a big step,' Natalie continued.

Megan looked up and smiled. 'Thank you. Yes it did take a lot of soul searching. And it was – is - pretty scary to be honest, but I knew it was something I had to do.'

'Wow.' Natalie looked at her shaking her head.

Megan was starting to feel slightly unnerved now, coming under such scrutiny. 'Anyway, enough about me. Last night you said you hadn't been in London all that long. How are you finding it?'

'Oh okay, I guess.'

'I know it can be a little unfriendly,' Megan gestured at the swarming hordes in King's Square. 'Everyone's so busy.'

Natalie gave a tight little smile. 'Oh don't worry, I like that. I love the energy. It's way better than where I used to live.'

'Oh, where was that?'

'The Cotswolds. You know the saying sleepy village?'

Megan nodded.

'Well mine was more comatose.'

Megan laughed. 'It's funny, as someone who's lived in London all my life I always imagine rural life to be idyllic – all that fresh air and open space and peace and quiet.'

Natalie gave a wry smile. 'Hmm. You can have too much peace and quiet though. Anyway I had to get away – for career as well as personal reasons.'

Megan nodded. 'So would you like a career in radio then?'

'Oh God no!' Natalie leant forward placing her tiny hands on the table. 'No, I'm an actress really. I just do the radio work to fill in between acting jobs.'

Megan fought the instinctive urge to groan. This was just typical. Her new friend was an actress. *Now, now,* her inner coach scolded, *they might not all be insecure, attention craving brats. Remember we all have the potential to be wonderful, well-rounded people and that includes actors.* Megan frowned. Oh no it doesn't, she thought bitterly, recollecting the hundreds of high maintenance acting types she had encountered over her years with Gerry. *Now turn that frown upside down,* her coach scolded and Megan hastily forced a grin.

'An actress – how exciting,' she trilled, before taking a large gulp from her cappuccino.

Natalie smiled back shyly – oh well that was something at least, Megan consoled herself. 'So tell me about your work. What kind of acting do you do?' Megan braced herself.

'Well I'm just starting out really. I only graduated last year.'

'Oh. Where from?'

Natalie took a sip from her latte and licked her pale pink lips. 'New York Academy for the Performing Arts.'

'Really? Wow!' Megan couldn't help feeling begrudgingly impressed. 'Isn't that where Brando and De Niro studied?'

Natalie nodded and looked down into her lap. 'I don't really like to talk about it though. That's why I've never mentioned it at the radio station. I'd hate for you and Cheddar to think I was bragging or anything.'

'Oh God no, we wouldn't think that,' Megan smiled warmly – how wonderfully bizarre – an actress who didn't like to brag, perhaps there could be hope for their friendship after all. 'You should be very proud of yourself. I've heard great things about the New York Academy.'

'Oh really. Do you know anyone in the acting profession then?'

Shit. Megan grimaced. She really didn't want to have to talk about Gerry again. This was meant to be a fresh start after all. 'No, not really,' she replied. *Remember your core values – honesty, integrity* – her inner coach shrieked. Megan shook her head. 'Not anymore.'

Chapter Thirty-One

"Walking is great exercise for the mind as well as the body... like the ripples of raindrops on a pond, allow your thoughts to become lulled by the steady rhythm of your footsteps."
Megan Rowe, 'Help Yourself to Happiness.'

Cheddar looked at the dirty yellow front of the El Paso Mexicana restaurant and frowned. The S in Paso had come loose and was dangling wearily on one side, as if weighed down by its huge bloated curve, which seemed extremely apt somehow. The restaurant owner, Raj had had a stencil of a cartoon cowboy riding a bucking bronco stuck in the window, advertising the electronic version now installed in the middle of the restaurant to 'improve customer moral, innit.' However the overall effect was not doing an awful lot for Cheddar's moral or morale as he stood there holding his bag of 'organic, pre-washed and ready to eat' rabbit food from Tesco Metro. As far as he was concerned he couldn't imagine ever being 'ready to eat' five different varieties of lettuce, no matter what weird and wonderful colours and textures they came in. So rather than go home and accept that he lived above a complete and utter shit-hole and force feed himself pre-washed plant-life he decided to go for a walk. Turning back on to Queen Caroline Street, he stared up at the green turreted Neptune Mansions, which seemed positively regal compared to his abode. It was as if they were the palace on the hill towering snootily over the peasant-like parade of shops. To his right, under the flyover, Hammersmith was buzzing in the sunshine, but having just fought his way through the bustling Broadway Centre he had no desire to plunge back into the throng. So instead he turned left and began making his way along Queen Caroline Street towards the river.

'Queen Caroline Street W6' the sign read. W6. It still made him smile, the fact that he was now a Londoner, albeit an immigrant from Doncaster. He had achieved one childhood dream at least. Cheddar remembered back to when he was little, and it had been taken for granted he would follow his father and grandfather and seemingly all the fathers and grandfathers before them into the coal industry or 'down pit' as they would have said. But then the Strike came and everything changed. Cheddar felt the usual churn of apprehension in his stomach as he remembered back. He had only been eight at the time of the Miners' Strike of 1984, but it had been such a life-changing event it had etched itself on his psyche like one of the stickers they all used to wear proclaiming 'Coal Not Dole' or Victory to the Miners.' Bright yellow they were, those stickers. Bright yellow with thick bold black print as if emphasising the determination and power they had felt. He remembered his dad, back then, before it all went wrong. How powerful he'd seemed. Watching him sat around the kitchen table with the other lads from pit – Bill Watson and Jimmy and Jock, talking about flying pickets. Cheddar had wished he could have been a big man like them and gone on a flying picket too. It had all seemed like such an adventure. Cheddar had lain in bed at night picturing his dad and his pals sprouting wings out of the backs of their heavy duty donkey jackets and flying off all over the country like superman, and he wondered if somehow he could attach himself to his dad without him realising it, stowing away in one of his huge pockets or summat. But then it had all gone wrong.

Despite the warm spring sunshine Cheddar couldn't help shivering as he continued along Queen Caroline Street and thought back to that cold winter, when suddenly everything seemed to run out and 'no son, not while strike's on,' seemed to become the answer to his every question. He remembered the winter coat he'd got from the Miners' Welfare – a horrible green thing with a bright orange trim that his mam told him had been donated from 'some kind little lad down South.' And he'd thought why? I don't want some other lad's coat. I want a new one from C&A like I get every year. But of course he hadn't dared say owt because he didn't want his dad to smash another plate. Because if he smashed another plate then they might have to go to the Welfare to get more plates and they might be green with bright orange trim too. Cheddar gave a wry smile as he remembered how he half imagined everything 'down South' being green and orange and horrible. Yes he'd come to quite hate 'down South' back then, because not only did they have horrible clothes but that was where that woman lived. The woman with the witchy voice who lived at number ten and hated the miners. The woman who sent all of those horrible police men into his village to chase people over walls and into houses. They were nothing like the police he was used to. Nothing like Auntie Sylv's husband Bob who used to come to their school and tell them all about stranger danger and crossing roads. These police men weren't humans anyway. Cheddar knew that. He wasn't sure which planet they were from but they spoke dead weird and wanted to kill them all with their truncheons and their horses.

Cheddar glanced over to his right as he went past the Queen Caroline Estate. The belated Spring sunshine had brought out a gang of kids, sprawled all over the wall like ivy. 'Here, Dermot, give us a light,' one of them called, in exactly the same kind of voice the alien police had used when they'd been shouting stuff like 'cheers for the overtime' and waving wads of money at his dad. Cheddar sighed. He wondered what his new mate Danny made of his London residence and whether he'd left for his business trip yet. Then he realised he didn't even know what it was he did for a living. By the time they'd got Elvis out of his jumpsuit and into his equally offensive 'civilian wear' of a red satin shirt, skin-tight jeans and stained, blue suede shoes, Ray had called time and Cheddar had made his excuses and snuck off down King Street for a kebab. Well, man cannot live on rabbit food alone and the beer had not only prompted a killer craving for a super-size portion of fat and salt but had also obliterated his will power.

'Pathetic, weak-willed streak of piss.' His dad's words, raspy and slurred echoed through his mind. Cheddar swallowed and clutched on tighter to his Tescos carrier bag. 'Traitor.' As he reached Crisp Street Cheddar glanced to his left where the Riverbank Studios housing Loose Talk sat, its coffee stained glass front glinting in the sunshine. Compared to the Estate opposite it looked positively futuristic. Cheddar smiled a tight little grin. He worked there, he reminded himself. He, Cheddar Bailey, worked in that impressive looking building in London W6. He worked in that impressive looking building in London W6 for the rock legend Jimmy Levine, at a cutting edge new radio station, producing one of the most popular phone-in shows in Britain, working with Dave McNoughton no less. So stick that in your scraggy old roll up and smoke it, dad, he thought. Cheddar paused – should he pop into the station, grab a coffee or some poncey herbal tea in the canteen and see who was about? Or should he nip into the café opposite and people watch for a while. No, the smell of bacon frying would be way too tempting and after last night's kebab, a fry-up would herald a fatal decline into his old ways. Gritting his teeth Cheddar carried on walking to the end of the road and the narrow alleyway that led to the river.

As soon as he got to the river he felt himself begin to relax, as if the sudden expanse of space in front of him allowed his fears and anxieties to disperse a little. His dad's voice began to drift off, merging into the hum of traffic steadily making its way over Hammersmith Bridge. He wasn't a sell out coming to London. What the hell was there for him up in Doncaster anyway? The pits had all closed and anyway once he'd got into his teenage years he'd realised the last thing he wanted to do was follow in the footsteps of his dad. Sitting in a smoky room coughing up phlegm and blood and spitting out words as bitter as bile. No, he'd wanted to see the world, he'd wanted to escape and he had. Cheddar looked up at the sky and way overhead a plane glinted in the pale blue sky, like a silver bird. Again he thought of Danny. He reminded him a little of a cop. Not the alien kind that had terrorised him as a kid and not the Dixon of Dock Green kind who had visited his school either. No, more like the edgy Mel Gibson from Lethal Weapon kind. The ones who live life on the edge, and whose traumatic past mean they're only one bourbon away from falling over into the dark side. Cheddar shook his head and let out a chuckle – just because the guy had an American accent and looked a bit rugged it didn't mean he was some kind of lone desperado. Still there was something solitary about him. But there was something solid about him too; a genuineness in his smile. And his promise to help Cheddar with a fitness plan on his return from the States had been really sound. Cheddar smiled as he turned to the right and began walking along the river path. He would walk into Chiswick, maybe stop along the way for a nibble on a carrot. Maybe. And start thinking about Megan's exercise of the week. Just what was his Perfect Day?

chapter Thirty-Two

"Make a collage of the types of clothes and accessories you would wear in your perfect world. Use this as the template for your makeover. Let your style be an expression of the beauty, originality and creativity that is you."
Megan Rowe, 'Help Yourself to Happiness.'

Megan pulled the top over her head and shimmied her arms through the sleeves. As the delicate chiffon folds skimmed over her, goose bumps pin-pricked her skin. She pulled the top down and looked nervously in the mirror. The boutique Natalie had taken her to was one she'd never been to before, tucked away down a side road off Kings Street. The kind where clothes were displayed like works of art upon polished wooden podiums and individual pieces of jewellery hung glinting from ornate silver frames in the soft spotlighting. And the clothes themselves were certainly not the kind she would normally try. Normally every season she would shop on the high street to stock up on the latest staples, her wardrobe a smart yet unadventurous collection of tailored trousers in varying shades of greys and black, co-ordinated fitted tops and the latest cut of jeans. There was nothing like the top she was now wearing, a beautiful emerald green kaftan embroidered in swirling patterns of gold. Megan turned slowly from side to side, examining herself sternly in the long mirror. It was so colourful, so ethnic, so not her. She put her hands on her hips and frowned. But why, why was it not her? She looked at the golden weave and the way it shone under the spotlighting. She looked at the way the emerald green set off her dark hair and made her eyes seem brighter, greener somehow, and she began to smile. When she had seen the top displayed on a mannequin at the far corner of the shop she had been instantly drawn to it. And if she had seen it on a model or celebrity in a magazine she would certainly have given it an admiring glance, so why the hell wasn't it 'her?' Megan tossed her hair over her shoulder and smoothed her hands down over the delicate chiffon folds and suddenly she was cast back to her childhood days and the hours of joy she had had experimenting with her dressing up box (a battered cardboard box crammed with her mother and grandmother's cast offs, a wonderful jumble of silks and satins and lace). She hadn't always dressed conservatively, had she? As a child she had loved to experiment, demanding to go shopping in her grandma's old fur hat and one of her mother's old silk nighties on a regular basis. And then as a teenager she had made the most of her minimal clothes allowance by scouring jumble sales and charity shops for hidden treasures she could easily excavate with a quick spin on her Grandma's sewing machine. It was only once she had gone to university and then qualified as a psycho-therapist that she had begun dressing to blend in rather than stand out.

Megan smiled as she looked over her shoulder for a rear view. She would certainly stand out wearing this top, it was gorgeous, and teamed with a pair of faded jeans and some beaded flip-flops it would be perfect.

'How are you getting on in there?' She heard Natalie call through the door of her changing cubicle.

'Fine,' she replied, opening the door with a flourish. Natalie was standing barefoot in a turquoise kimono style mini dress. 'Oh Natalie, you look beautiful. The colour really suits you.' Megan paused and gestured to her kaftan, 'So, what do you think of the top?'

'Oh.' A tight little frown etched itself into Natalie's brow.

'What?'

'It's just -' Natalie broke off and looked away, as if embarrassed.

Megan felt a claw of dread clamp hold of her stomach. Did she look ridiculous? Is that what it was? And Natalie couldn't find the words to tell her.

'Well – it's a bit Robin Hood, don't you think?' Natalie finally replied.

'Robin Hood?'

'Yes, you know, the old green tunic. All you need are a pair of woolly tights and a bow and arrow and you'd be well away. Still never mind.' She smiled sweetly at Megan, as if in sympathy. ' So what do you think of this dress?'

'It's lovely. Really lovely. Goes really well with your hair.' Megan fought to keep her disappointment from her voice. How on earth could she have contemplated buying a top that made her look like one of Sherwood's finest? She clearly had no fashion sense whatsoever.

'Oh thanks. I just wish I could afford it.' Natalie looked down at the floor, dejected.

Megan sighed. There was no point in both of them being disappointed, after all the purpose of the shopping trip was supposed to have been to lift their spirits, a 'retail therapy fix' Natalie had called it as she had grabbed her hand and led her from the café. 'Don't worry, I'll get it for you.'

'What?' Natalie's gaze shot up to meet her own, her pale blue eyes sparkling with hope.

'I'll get it. To say thank you for today.'

'Thank you, but what for?'

'For coming for a coffee, bringing me here. It's been really nice to get out and about, it's been ages since I've had a girly day like this.'

'Really?' Natalie stared up at her wide-eyed like a child. 'But I can't accept it, it's too much.'

Megan laughed and placed a hand on her thin pale arm, it was icy cold. 'I insist. Now let me get out of this tunic before I get rounded up by the Sheriff of Nottingham and I'll meet you back by the cash desk.'

Natalie clasped hold of her hand and stared at her intently. 'Thank you so, so much. Tell you what. Next time lets go for a night on the town. We can have a proper girls' night out.'

Megan smiled. A girls' night out, who would have thought it? The disappointment about the top began to fade away as she contemplated this latest development. Suddenly the pieces of her new life began to fall into place and the vision of a youthful version of herself began to appear. A version who went out with younger people on a whirl of shopping trips, coffees and nights out. No more sitting alone and weeping on the sofa for her. Perhaps leaving Gerry hadn't caused her to enter a void after all. Perhaps she had fallen Alice-like into some kind of bizarre black hole that was taking her back to a time before they'd ever met, to find out who she really was, and who she should have become. Megan went back into her cubicle and pulled the kaftan over her head. All she had to do was let go and enjoy the ride.

Chapter Thirty-Three

"The best thing about The Perfect Day exercise is that you quite literally get to be author of your own destiny. So don't hold back, let all of your hopes and dreams flow through your pen and out on to the page."
Megan Rowe, 'Help Yourself to Happiness.'

Cheddar sat down at the table outside The Crown and turned his face up to the sun. Although it wasn't quite tanning weather there was a definite warmth to the sun's rays that had been absent for many months. He took a sip of his freshly squeezed orange juice - which incidentally, and quite outrageously to his mind, cost exactly the same as a pint of Pride – and thought. What would his perfect day consist of? If asked previously and perhaps by one of his mates down at the Prince Albert or the Rock Forum he would have come up with some elaborate yarn involving waking up in a huge bed scattered with a mixture of peanuts and pork scratchings, being serenaded by the lasses from the 'Addicted to Love' video and jamming with Jimmy Hendrix on 'All Along the Watchtower.' But not anymore. Things had changed in the past week and although he couldn't begin to explain the whys and the wherefores of what had prompted such a shake up in his life, he knew he had to keep the momentum going – it was *essential* he kept the momentum going - if he were to ever escape his current rut. So, what would be his real perfect day?

Cheddar took another sip from his orange juice and felt the little segments of flesh burst like sherbet upon his tongue. He had to begrudgingly admit that this, along with the sunshine gently toasting his skin, was quite a refreshing experience and he inhaled deeply. The air smelt warm and sweet with the newly budding promise of spring. Megan had said to start the description of your perfect day with waking up – he knew because he'd been making surreptitious notes on the back of his schedule for tonight's Dave McNoughton show, which he pulled from his jeans pocket now. So where would he be, what would his bedroom look like, who would he be with, upon waking on his perfect day? Mournfully Cheddar bade a mental farewell to the sea of scratchings and the leggy stunners from the Robert Palmer video and thought. Well he certainly wouldn't be in a single bed on his own above El Paso with a slumping S that's for sure! He looked down to the grassy riverbank where two student types were slouched on their sides, rucksacks cast adrift as they gazed down to the glistening brown water.

'I said give me the tobacco,' the girl called out, rolling onto her stomach and playfully grappling with her male friend. As she wrestled with him her pale blonde braided hair fell like a beaded curtain across her face.

Cheddar thought of Bambi from Rhyl and wondered what colour hair she had. He hoped that whatever the colour it was in some way slightly wild like this girl's. Anything but the severe helmet-like bob favoured by Denise. And she would be kind too – his perfect lass. Cheddar closed his eyes and smiled. Yes she would be kind and sweet and scatty and fun. But most of all she would be glad to be with him. When he awoke on his perfect day, he would open his eyes and she would be lying there right next to him, smiling sleepily, hair tousled but not caring, and she would cup his face in her hands and kiss him on the lips. And her kiss would taste as sugary and sweet as candy floss and he would wrap his arms around her and feel happy and strong – and needed. He would be needed and loved. Cheddar sighed, opened his eyes and took another sip from his orange juice. It was good stuff this juice, he was starting to feel a definite buzz – must be experiencing some kind of vitamin C overdose or summat.

So what next on his perfect day? Where would he be? Cheddar looked further along the river towards Chiswick and thought of the neat squares of grey-stone cottages set just off the river, usually around an oak-beamed pub. Little tree-lined enclaves walled off from the surrounding noise and grime. It was nice down here by the river, peaceful and calm. Perhaps he would be in a cottage actually on the banks of the Thames? What the hell, it was his perfect day after all, he could be anywhere he wanted to be. Cheddar closed his eyes again and suddenly a white-washed cottage materialised in his mind, with ivy creeping up the walls and a long rambling garden leading down to the river, and kids. Where the hell had they come from? Cheddar frowned slightly but no – he could definitely see a couple of nippers running about in the long grass, all chubby and rosy cheeked. 'Daddy, daddy,' they were calling, and when Cheddar imagined himself walking down the garden towards them they came flying into his arms. He could practically smell their hot little scalps and their golden curls as he imagined hugging them to him.

Denise had never wanted babies – 'if I'd wanted to shovel shit all day I'd have gone to work in a zoo,' she used to say. And Cheddar had always gone along with her in his usual bumbling, amiable way, not really fussed one way or the other, always too busy trying to make sure he didn't piss her off – keeping the toilet seat down, making sure he didn't knock anything over or stain owt. But now – away from Denise and in the realms of his perfect imaginary kingdom the prospect didn't seem that horrific at all. In fact it seemed downright appealing. He could build a tree house, play hide and seek, have a valid excuse to act like a complete buffoon if he had children. And just think of the love he'd be able to give them. All the things he'd learnt not to do from his old man. Cheddar couldn't help a wry chuckle at this and he opened his eyes and raised his glass. 'Here's to you dad' he thought as he took another drink.

So he knew where he'd be living and who he'd be living with, Cheddar looked back down at his scrawled notes. But what kind of clothes would he be wearing? He glanced at his jeans and faded Sex Pistols t-shirt, the first things that had come to hand that morning. What would he be wearing? Hmm, that was a toughie. The truth was he didn't really give clothes much thought. He was a bloke for Christ's sake, as long as it fitted and kept him warm or cool, whichever was required, he didn't much care what it looked like. He never had. Actually that wasn't strictly true. There had been that phase back when he was about thirteen and he'd experimented with the gothic look, investing his hard-earned paper round money in a pair of black ball crushing trousers and a huge metal crucifix. His mam had screamed when he'd emerged from his bedroom looking like a cross between Iggy Popp and Morticia Adams. 'Jesus Christ, son, Halloween isn't for another three months, what are you trying to do to me?' she'd gasped, clutching her latest Mills and Boon romance to her chest. And his dad, well he hadn't had to say anything; his withering stare and shake of the head had said it all really. Cheddar sighed. Perhaps he should just overlook this particular detail of the exercise? But what if this were a crucial detail? Too much was at stake to risk blowing it. Although he didn't quite understand how all of this imagining was going to help him sort his life out, as with the cut and paste exercise he somehow felt sure it would, and that was all he needed to know right now. So what would he be wearing on his perfect day? What kind of look did he like on a bloke? Cheddar shifted uncomfortably on the bench seat. This kind of thinking was straying into rather uncomfortable territory. But then he thought of Jimmy Levine and what he had been wearing at the Loose Talk Christmas party. The scarlet kaftan over faded blue jeans, and the black cowboy boots, intricately carved with curling designs - Cheddar had made sure he'd got a good look when he'd walked by him on his way to the toilet. He thought he'd give the bandana a miss, but the rest of the ensemble was pretty cool. But could he, Cheddar Bailey really get away with wearing the clothes of an ageing rock God? He closed his eyes and once more pictured himself in the garden of his perfect home, messing around with the kids, clad in a kaftan and cowboy boots and he immediately grimaced at the thought. It was all right for Jimmy 'Snake-hips' Levine, but on his bulky physique the kaftan stretched and strained over his paunch. But hang on a minute, this was his perfect day, so on his perfect day he would be slim too. Cheddar smiled as the image of himself morphed down into the wiry physique of a rock God. Now he looked good in his garb and what's more he was able to keep up with the kids as they tore around the garden laughing and shrieking.

Grinning, Cheddar looked back at his notes, what would your perfect occupation be? Well that was easy and the best part was he was already doing it. He looked at the next note. Who would you socialise with and what would you do? What would he do? The old him would have automatically said 'go down the pub, see my mates down the Rock Forum,' because that was what blokes did for fun, wasn't it? They went down the pub, had a craic with the lads. But now he wasn't so sure. Was this really what he wanted to do for the rest of his days? An image of Ray's purple leering face loomed into his mind and he shuddered. What would he do if he could do anything? He gazed down at the murky river, rays of sunlight were jumping like silver fishes on the brown surface. And then it came to him in a flash. He would cook. On his perfect day, the perfect way to socialise with friends would be to cook for them. Yes, he would invite friends over and while they all milled about in his rambling home, admiring his record collection, playing with his lovely kids, being charmed by his beautiful free-spirited, tousle-haired wife he would be holed up in the kitchen preparing a veritable feast. Radio playing in the background, glass of merlot on the counter, the smell olive oil and herbs flooding the hot air. And then when it was all ready he would yell out 'grub's up' to roars of delight from his friends and family and they would all sit down around the huge wooden table, overlooking the back garden. And his wife would have lit loads of those little candle things and they would be twinkling away like stars. And they would all sit and eat and talk, really talk for hours. Until dusk melted into night and then Cheddar would scoop up the sleepy-eyed kids, one in each arm; one in each *muscular* arm, and deposit them up to bed. Then he would return to his wife's side. And the table would be littered with empty wine bottles and all the other remnants of a cracking good night and laughter would echo around the room, like music. And he would feel so happy and warm, and every now and then he would look at his wife, his perfect girl and she would look at him and he would be knocked sideways by a wave of love all over again. And then, when their guests finally took themselves off into the night totally sated from the wine and the food they would look at each other, he and his wife, and he would say, 'Shall we do the dishes?' and she would look at him and smirk incredulously and say, 'Dishes, schmishes!' and take him by the hand and lead him up to bed.

Chuffing hell! Cheddar opened his eyes and placed his hands on the wooden pub table, as if to ground himself.

'Everything all right?' A girl's voice chirped from over his shoulder. Cheddar turned to see a barmaid standing behind him holding a cloth and a stack of clean ashtrays. Her face was shiny and round, with two huge blue eyes set above a pair of the rosiest cheeks. She reminded him of an apple. Cheddar's stomach growled.

'Yeah everything's sound,' he replied with a broad grin. 'Everything's perfect.'

Chapter Thirty-Four

"Sooner or later, whether you like it or not, all of the things you are running from will catch you up."
Megan Rowe, 'Help Yourself to Happiness.'

Thursday night was blues night in The Speakeasy, and this particular Thursday night, according to the dusty chalkboard outside, patrons were going to be treated to the sultry tones of Big Bill Walters. Situated on Lafayette Street, just north of Chinatown, The Speakeasy was Danny's favourite bar in the whole of New York. A narrow, dimly lit joint, lined with sepia prints from the prohibition era, it was the type of place you imagined people still said, 'here's looking at you kid,' and smoked snowy white cigarettes from gilt edged cases. It also somehow managed to remain relatively tourist-free. Danny watched from his stool as the barman, a heavy set New Yorker called Anthony, dealt out a line of crisp clean cardboard mats on the gleaming mahogany bar. He smiled as he thought back to the beer soaked bar in the Prince Albert and the purple-faced, white-bellied landlord, Ray. It all felt a world away now, hard to believe he'd been sat at that very bar, batting off abuse from Ray only a few days previously.

'You wanna refill?' Anthony called up the bar to him, over the melodic twang of the double bass from the band playing in the far corner.

Danny nodded. 'Sure.' He watched as Anthony picked up the bottle of Jack Daniels and made his way over to him, clinked the bottle to his glass and sloshed the golden liquid over the ice. 'Cheers.' He gave the barman a ten dollar bill and sighed. Usually he felt safe in a bar, no matter where it was. There was something comforting about the clink of glass, the chatter of people, the smell of the beer and the smoke, but not tonight. Tonight he felt on edge, compressed by a mixture of jetlag and fear. This time tomorrow he would be back in Austin for the first time in fourteen years, the first time since...

Danny took a sip on his drink. Over in the corner Big Bill Walters began a heartfelt rendition of 'Summertime,' his voice as soft and thick as freshly picked cotton. Danny turned to watch, but as he stared at the elderly black man singing the blues in his saggy pin-striped suit and battered pork pie hat, his mind was miles away, two thousand miles to be precise, slap bang in the middle of Texas. What would his parents say when they saw him after all this time? What would he say to them? Danny frowned. What was he doing? Why had he come here? What had gotten into him since he'd arrived in England, since he'd started writing that darned book? But Danny knew deep down that the rot had set in long before all of that. He stared down into his drink and shook the glass from side to side causing the melting ice cubes to dance. It was meeting Michael that had summoned the beginning of the end, he realised that now. Previously Danny had worked for American papers and had been teamed up with current affairs correspondents who were working on a constant deadline for blood and gore. And ironically well anaesthetised by his own pain, Danny had been only too willing to oblige. However, at the start of the second Gulf war he had been hired to work for a left of centre British broadsheet, to work with their prize-winning war correspondent, Michael Buckingham. Michael and Danny had hit it off from the moment they met in the dusty lobby of The Palestine hotel in Baghdad, where most of the press and media were holed up during the war. Unlike most of the hyped up, war hardened hacks he had worked with before, Michael was a gentleman in every sense of the word. Not for him the crushingly insensitive, battle weary sense of humour so common amongst his fellow war correspondents. He was unfailingly polite to everyone he encountered, with a cheery smile and bizarre sixties colloquialism for all. Michael was solely interested in reporting the human angle of the war story, delving beneath the surface gore for the real people whose lives had been shattered by the conflict. Within a couple of weeks of working with Michael Danny felt his attitude to his own work beginning to change. The corpses he photographed were no longer just spent shells, they were people with families and histories and stories to tell. And what's more their stories needed to be told. As Danny spent hours with Michael chasing through the dusty back streets of Baghdad, dodging the US tanks and Iraqi henchmen in search of the story behind the picture, he felt the first germ of the idea for his book. That one day, if he ever made it out of that desert hell-hole he would go back over all of his best known pictures and tell their story too.

Unlike the other correspondents Michael wasn't a fan of travelling with the ex-SAS types many of the papers were hiring as bodyguards, believing that he wouldn't win over the locals' trust with a shaven headed henchman in tow. Consequently Danny and Michael had employed the services of a local man, Nasir as their driver and translator. Nasir was a Shia Muslim, a tiny live wire of a man with olive skin and bushy jet black hair and a passion for gossip which made him a fantastic source of stories and leads. Within a few short weeks and after a few too many narrow escapes from the gun-toting gangs who were starting to fill the void left by Saddam, Danny felt as if he'd known this funny little squirrel of a man most of his life. Every morning Nasir would arrive at their seventh floor room laden with flat bread and a flask of sweet Iraqi chai announcing, 'I breeng breakfast, meester Danny and meester Michael,' and the three of them would sit on the stained mattresses on the floor and exchange stories about their lives. For Danny these would always be tales from different war zones, but for Michael and Nasir the stories were always of family and home. When Nasir invited them for lunch in his tiny home in a tatty suburb of Baghdad Danny felt as if he already knew his wife Faria and son Ali, he'd been regaled with so many stories about them.

An image of Faria crying filled Danny's mind and he slowly turned away from the band and back to the bar. It was seeing what Nasir and Faria had in the midst of all the death and destruction and abject poverty that had finally broken through Danny's wall of pain. The abundance of love and laughter captured between those shabby whitewashed walls, like helium in a balloon elevating them all higher, had resonated somewhere deep within and reminded him of childhood days back in his parents' home. But what would his parents' home be like now – all these years later? Surely the love and the laughter were long gone? Danny remembered that first day he'd gone to Nasir's and how they'd all sat cross-legged on the floor around a steaming dish of spicy chicken and rice sprinkled with plump sultanas. And how Nasir's three year old son Ali had clambered all over his father's back like a monkey, giggling and chattering in Arabic as they feasted on the delicious food. Danny gazed down into his lap as he remembered the pair of them so full of life. Why had Nasir had to die? It seemed so unfair. That fateful morning when they had gone to interview and photograph men queuing to join the new Iraqi police force, why had it been Nasir who had been standing right by the car. Why had he been the one to have his brains blasted all over the pavement when he had a loving wife and son at home? Why hadn't it been Danny who had no-one? But it wasn't witnessing the death of his friend that had finally broken down Danny's wall of pain, it had been seeing his widow Faria afterwards and the way she had radiated love instead of anger and bitterness. Smiling gently as she talked about Nasir and reassuring them that it wasn't their fault and hugging and stroking Ali until his tears dried up. And for the first time in years Danny had felt drawn to this light rather than wanting to run away.

Danny frowned as he put down his drink and leant his elbows on the bar. Was that what he had come back here for? To retrace his steps back to that fateful day of his own and make a different choice? To follow Faria's example? He was so tired now he could hardly see straight. In the background he heard a ripple of applause as the band's set came to an end and he felt someone brush past him on the way to the rest room. In just a few hours he would be boarding a plane back home and although the prospect still filled him with dread at least it meant an end to all of the running.

chapter Thirty-Five

"Sometimes it's very hard to ignore our fears. But for the sake of your own happiness and the happiness of those around you, do not become a mouth-piece for fear."
Megan Rowe, 'Help Yourself to Happiness.'

'So who is it supposed to be?' Gerry put his rinsed glass on the draining board and gestured to Natalie's painting hanging on the kitchen wall. The sweeping arc of headlights from the Friday night rush hour were causing the crimson and black slashes of paint to glow in a strange, pulsating effect.

From behind him, Natalie, wearing her new dress, the dress that his wife had bought her, let out a long sigh. 'I er – I don't know. Anyway, you still haven't told me what you think of my dress.'

'Hmm.' Gerry remained with his back to her, seemingly transfixed by the painting. 'It reminds me of that picture by Edvard Munch.'

'"The Scream,"' Natalie responded flatly, looking away.

'Yeah, that's the one. Only it seems more angry, what with all the red. And those eyes. So what does it mean, darling?'

'It means whatever you want it to mean,' Natalie replied, before biting hard on her lip. Why the hell couldn't he shut up about the damned painting?

'But what does it mean to you? What was going through your mind when you were painting it? It feels so intense.' Gerry finally turned to face her, his eyes full of concern.

Natalie bit on her lip and turned away. 'I told you, I don't know, I can't remember,' she replied sullenly. She felt Gerry come up behind her and gently place a hand on her back between her shoulders. She did her best not to flinch.

'Are you okay?' he asked gently.

'I'm fine.' She paused, and, for the briefest of moments felt the sudden urge to lower her guard for once and let it all pour out. All the tears and the hurt and the hollow ache she knew would never leave her till the day she died. If she told Gerry then maybe it would go some way to easing the pain. Maybe he would hold her and make her feel safe and wanted and loved. Maybe he would tell her that it wasn't her fault, that none of it was her fault and that she was a good person after all. But no, she couldn't, she mustn't. She'd make that mistake before and look where it had got her. She clenched her hands into tight little balls. 'I just – I just don't like talking about it okay.'

'Yes, of course. I'm sorry. I didn't mean to pry. Now let me get a look at that dress.'

Reluctantly Natalie turned around and stood in front of him staring down at her bare feet.

'Wow,' Gerry said, 'You look beautiful. My very own geisha girl.'

Natalie managed to force the tiniest of smiles, but still couldn't bring herself to look at him. She felt as if she had been tossed around on a stormy sea and now just the slightest movement, the slightest gesture from him would cause her to buckle.

Gerry cupped her chin with his hand and raised her face until she was looking at him. 'You look beautiful,' he repeated. 'The turquoise really goes with your hair.'

'Really?' Natalie could feel tears pricking at the corners of her eyes. Tell him, a voice in her head began to urge. Tell him everything.

'Right, well, I'd better get going,' Gerry took his hand from her face and began walking to the door.

'What?'

'I told you yesterday. I've got to meet my son. I said I'd be there at eight and it's already twenty to. Who'd have thought it eh? Me a Pizza Hut dad.'

Natalie took a few steps after him. 'But you've only just got in from the theatre. I haven't seen you all day.'

Gerry turned to face her, his dark eyes suddenly stony. 'I know and I'm sorry, but this is important. He's my son.'

'And I'm your-'

Natalie turned and looked out of the window, the silence forming like a ravine between them. Outside the cars continued to whoosh by one after another, an endless stream of glaring light. Natalie shut her eyes and gripped on to the counter. A hot tear trickled down the side of her cheek.

'Right, well, I'd better be off,' Gerry finally said.

'Oh I see. You're not going to answer me then?' Natalie wiped her face and turned and stared up at him defiantly.

'Answer what?'

'Well what am I exactly?'

Gerry looked at her for a moment, then took a step towards her and took both of her hands in his. 'You're amazing, that's what you are.'

Natalie shook her head and pushed his hands away. 'No – I mean, what is *this*? You and me? Us? What is going on here?'

Gerry sighed and Natalie was instantly reminded of her mother. *How many times have I told you Natalie, I'm working, I can't be disturbed. For goodness sake Natalie look at the mess you've made, there's paint everywhere. Oh Natalie, what have you done now?*

Gerry stuffed his hands deep into his jeans pockets. 'This really isn't the right time for this conversation, Natalie. I've got to meet Laurence. I can't be late.'

Natalie felt a terrible rage building up inside of her and it took all of her might not to scream. 'It might not be the right time for you, but what about me? I need to know and I need to know now.' She stared at him angrily.

'Well I'm sorry, but I just don't know.'

'Don't know what?'

'What this is. I've just split up with my wife, Natalie. My wife of fifteen years.'

'Your wife who dumped you after fifteen years.'

Gerry frowned and looked away. 'I'm not ready for all of this.'

'All of what?'

'This pressure. Don't you understand? Fifteen years is a long time. I can't just bounce straight into another relationship. I really like you Natalie, you're an amazing girl, but I can't make any kind of commitment to you right now.'

'Do you still love her?' Natalie held her breath, nausea welling in the pit of her stomach, pushing up into her throat.

Gerry looked at the floor, then looked at her painting and then picked up his jacket from the end of the breakfast bar. 'I have to go. I'll see you.'

'When?' Natalie grimaced as she heard the rise of panic in her voice, but she couldn't do anything to stop it.

'When what?'

'When will you see me?'

'Soon.'

'How soon? Tonight soon, next week? When?'

'In a couple of days. I promise.' He moved closer and placed his hands on her shoulders. 'Perhaps we need a bit of a breathing space.'

'Right.' Natalie could hear barriers slamming shut like bomb-proof steel in her mind. She took a huge breath and forced herself to smile sweetly. 'Have a lovely evening, then.'

Gerry looked at her gratefully. 'Thanks. You too. I'll call you. I promise.'

'Yes of course.' Natalie stood on tip-toes and kissed him lightly on the lips. 'You do what you have to do. I'm sorry if I got a little heavy. To be honest I could probably do with a night out with the girls.'

Gerry smiled. 'Great. Well you behave yourself won't you.'

Natalie looked at him and tilted her head to one side. 'Hmm,' she replied.

As soon as she heard the front door close behind him she picked up his empty glass from the draining board and flung it against the wall.

'Bastard, bastard, bastard!' she yelled as the glass shattered into tiny pieces. She slammed her fists down on the counter and looked up at her painting. 'I know,' she screamed looking directly into the hollow accusing eyes. 'I know.'

*

'Have a good time,' Megan chirruped, hoping that it sounded genuine rather than the 'but not too good a time,' that fear really wanted her to say.

'Yeah, I'll try,' came Laurence's gruff reply as he poked his head around the living room door. His chestnut hair was spiky and gleaming with gel and there was a faint flush on his chin where he had obviously attempted shaving. 'I'm telling you though if he gets pissed I'm out of there.'

Megan smiled. 'I'm sure he won't,' she reassured. 'He hasn't seen you for over a week. I'm sure he'll make an effort. He'll probably be really looking forward to it.'

'Mum,' Laurence warned, coming into the room and collecting his mobile phone from the glass coffee table. He was wearing a green hooded top and dark baggy jeans. He looked so tall and so handsome Megan couldn't help smiling as a burst of pride erupted in her heart.

'What?' she asked, innocently.

'Stop doing your "help yourself to happiness" routine,' he replied sternly, but with a cheeky half grin.

'Sorry.'

Laurence plonked himself down on the sofa next to her and a musky waft of aftershave descended upon them. 'Do you know what, I'd really love it if one day you just totally flipped out,' he said casually flinging an arm across the back of the sofa around her shoulders.

'What do you mean?' Megan hardly dared move, this was the first display of physical affection he had shown her in years.

'Well you know, if you went bad, just for a day or something. It would be well funny.'

'What, become some kind of psycho mum?'

'Yeah. If you just weren't so positive and happy and nice all the time. If you just told it as it is.' Laurence looked at his watch. 'Anyway, I'd better go. I said I'd meet him at eight and it's already ten past. And don't forget I'm going over to Joe's for a sleepover after.' He gave her shoulders a squeeze then leapt up and over to the door.

'Laurence,' Megan said with a sly grin.

'Yes?'

'Have a really crap night.'

Laurence burst out laughing. 'That's more like it. Wicked!'

'Yeah and you make sure the tight old sod pays for everything. And make sure you order everything on the menu too.'

Laurence looked at her from the doorway his heart-shaped face beaming. 'Respect, mum, man, respect.'

But as soon as he had gone, Megan felt a sense of foreboding wash over her. Now what? She looked around the empty monochrome room and sighed. It was Friday night and she was all alone. But that was a good thing surely? At least she wouldn't have to spend the evening waiting for a drunken Gerry to return. No because Gerry was out with their son. And she was all alone. Megan stared at the dormant television and her motionless reflection stared back. Perhaps she should watch a movie. Or maybe she could read a book. She could do whatever she wanted. So why did she feel so uneasy? She got up from the sofa and walked over to the phone on the windowsill. She would call her mum. It was about time. She picked up the receiver but rather than dial her mum's number she stared out blankly into the dark. Was she really ready to tell her mum? The moment she did that it would be like admitting defeat, admitting that she had failed; that as hard as she had tried she hadn't been able to lift the family curse. And what about the effect it might have on her mum, the slightest thing could often tip her over the brink, so what on earth would her news do. Outside at the far end of the deserted car-park a train whizzed by, a blaze of silvery light in the dark, no doubt transporting hordes of excited revellers into town. Megan put the handset down and sighed. She couldn't do it, she just wasn't ready to tell her. But almost as soon as she put the phone down it began ringing.

'Hello,' she said nervously as she picked it up, it couldn't be her mum, she didn't have her new number, she didn't even know she'd moved.

'Hi Megan, it's Natalie. I was wondering if you fancied going for that girls' night out?'

Chapter Thirty-Six

"Tears can be the most powerful of cleansers. Left pent up they stagnate and pollute but allowed to run free they wash away hurt and pain."
Megan Rowe, 'Help Yourself to Happiness.'

This was what Danny had been terrified of all these years, one of the major factors in his never going home. He held his breath and looked down into his lap as the taxi swung round the corner of Burton Street and Farmington and past the small red brick elementary school he and Marty had attended. Memories, memories everywhere, like ghosts leering up at him from the shadows. As the cab slowly picked up speed Danny swore he could hear the chanting of children drifting through the humid air, but as he scrambled round and stared through the grimy rear window he saw that, apart from an empty chip packet rolling across the concrete like tumbleweed, the playground was deserted

It was early Friday afternoon and as soon as the cab had left the busy interstate from the airport the streets had gotten quieter and quieter. Now, as they hummed along the back streets of his home town, a sleepy suburb of Austin, there wasn't a soul in sight. Not a soul but plenty of ghosts. Danny gulped as they pulled on to Main Street. There was the Laundromat, the sign no longer yellow as he remembered it but bright red. And there was the drug store where he and Marty had spent their pocket money every Saturday on brown paper bags of brightly coloured candy. And there was the bench Marty had fallen off and broken his wrist when they were playing Batman and Robin and there was …

Danny closed his eyes tight. Every time he tried to breathe he felt as if his chest was going to burst. It still wasn't too late. All he had to do was tell the cab driver to turn around, head straight back to the airport and he could be back in New York in a few hours, maybe even back in England in a day.

'You say you wanted Oakdale?' The cab driver barked.

Danny opened his eyes with a start and looked at the shiny sunburnt bald patch on the back of the driver's head. A string of rosary beads was bouncing wildly from the rear view mirror. 'Yeah, that's right. It's left off Jefferson Hill.'

'I know.'

Danny looked out of the window and sighed. It was too late. He had to see it through to the end, whatever that end might be. Despite the oppressive heat shimmering off the sidewalks and heating the cab as if it were a can of soup, a shiver ran up his spine. What if his mom didn't recognise him? He'd sent a couple of photos home with Christmas and birthday cards, but nothing for a long time. He looked down at his muscular legs in their scuffed jeans and the pair of strong, hairy arms resting in his lap. He guessed he looked a little different from the fresh-faced twenty-two year old who'd left here all those years ago. Danny's stomach lurched as the cab indicated left on to Oakdale.

'Just here will be great thanks,' he said. He needed to get out, breathe in some air, get his head together before he made his grand entrance.

The cab screeched to a halt sending the rosary beads into a frenzied jig. 'No problem,' the driver replied, turning to face him. 'Twenty-one dollars.'

As the cab pulled off, Danny picked up his rucksack from the edge of the curb. Well, this was it. He took a deep breath and pulled himself up to his full height. But what if they were away? Then what would he do? Danny began trudging along the sidewalk gazing down at the pavement slabs. Were they still the same slabs he and Marty had played hopscotch on, he wondered, half expecting to see the ghostly chalked outline preserved in the concrete. Once again he heard the echo of children's laughter ringing in his ears. And then there it was.

Danny gulped as his parents' house came into view. Like an old photograph it seemed to have faded with time. The pink stucco front now sun bleached to creamy white, the cornflower blue shutters now grey and peeling. The front yard that was once littered with toys and bikes was now empty save an old rolled up newspaper and a crumpled beer can. Danny stopped dead. What if his parents no longer lived there? What if they had moved? Bought a condo in Florida and retired to the sun and sea? Whenever he had sent cards home he'd never given a return address – it felt safer not giving them the option to reply, or rather, not giving them the option to *not* reply. As Danny stood there staring at the house he heard the click of a lock turning and the next thing he knew the front door had opened and a hand was pushing at the screen door. He watched transfixed as a woman came out on to the porch. She was wearing a pair of pale denim dungarees over a tie-dyed t-shirt that resembled a rainbow that had run in the wash. Her angular face was lined at the edges and her wiry red-blonde hair was tied into two loose braids.

'Mom?'

The woman stopped at the top of the porch steps and stared at him expressionless for a second before throwing her hands up in – what? Surprise? Shock? Horror? Danny couldn't tell.

'Danny?' She took a tentative step towards him. 'Is that you?'

Danny couldn't move. His legs felt like lead and his hands began trembling like a leaf.

'Danny?' She almost screamed. 'Danny?' And then she was running down the steps and over the dusty front yard to him, stopping right in front of him to stare into his face. 'Oh my God. Oh sweet Jesus! I never thought -'

As Danny looked down at her, still completely motionless, his eyes felt strange, burning hot and blurry. And then he realised why. For the first time in over fourteen years he was starting to cry.

chapter Thirty-Seven

"On down days try lifting your spirits with music. Put on a favourite tune and lose yourself in the melody and beat. By allowing your body the freedom of dance you liberate your mind too."
Megan Rowe, 'Help Yourself to Happiness.'

A gauzy rain was hanging over Ealing Broadway, forming pools of dark orange mist under the sodium streetlights. Outside Club Rendezvous a queue was forming, made up largely of mouthy teenage girls and posturing young men, Megan observed. She pulled her jacket tighter and shivered. The first part of her 'girls night out' with Natalie had gone reasonably well. They had visited a couple of wine bars along the Broadway, expensive looking places fitted with glistening wood and furnished in downy leather. Not normally the type of place Megan would go to, but tonight she had embraced the change, sinking into her huge leather armchair as if trying on a new shoe for size. Trying to figure out, as she sipped on her drink and gazed about her, if this new life was the right fit. Were swanky winebars with her new young friend to be the norm from now on? Was this where she really belonged? Was this who she really was? After sharing a bottle of Merlot in the first bar and a jug of margarita in the second Megan still wasn't sure, but quite frankly she no longer cared. As the music merged into one continuous pulsating soundtrack and the lights became increasingly bright she felt as if she were riding a magical golden carousel and she didn't want it to stop. Ever. So when Natalie had suggested going on to a club, Megan had jumped at the idea. But now the combination of the cold damp air and the shrieks from the teenage girls in front of them was the equivalent of screeching to a halt and being flung into an icy tank of water. Megan started to frown, but as if reading her mind, Natalie grabbed hold of her hands.

'Don't worry, we'll be inside soon and it is going to be *so* cool,' she enthused, her auburn hair fanning out around her face like an aura. 'I can't wait to hit that dance floor.'

Megan felt another fuzzy pang of apprehension. No doubt with her drama school training, Natalie would be like one of the *Kids From Fame* or *Footloose*. But perhaps she would teach her some moves. Megan couldn't help giggling as she imagined Natalie and her doing the scissor splits in the middle of the dance floor while everyone else gathered around clapping in awe and admiration.

'What's funny?' Natalie asked.

'Oh nothing, I was just thinking of a dance routine.'

'Right. So do you think this dress looks okay then?' Natalie did a half twirl, allowing her cape like coat to fall open and expose her tiny kimono style dress. She had teamed it with a pair of shimmery tights and matching turquoise satin stilettos.

Megan looked at her and attempted to rally her mouth into a smile, every muscle in her body felt worn and slack. She had already told Natalie about a million times the dress looked more than okay, what was up with her? 'Yes, it looks lovely,' she said, 'Luverly, jubberly.' Oh God, she was drunk. The cold air had gone some way to making her more alert, but only to the fact that she was completely and utterly inebriated. Megan looked about her defiantly. Who the hell cared? She was in a queue for a nightclub for Christ's sake, if a person couldn't be drunk here then where the hell could they be? 'Here! Here!' she agreed with herself.

'What?' Natalie was giving her one of her stares now. God what was with those stares, they were seriously unsettling.

'What, what?' Megan replied and immediately started giggling again. *Get a grip*, her inner coach slurred from somewhere far, far away; the bottom of a bottle probably. Oh what the hell. So she was pissed, so what? It felt good actually. No, better than good, it felt – Megan searched through her alcohol-addled brain for a suitable adjective – it felt wicked. Yes that was it – it felt wicked, being drunk and abandoned and not giving a damn. She thought of Laurence and what he had said to her earlier about telling it like it is or keeping it real or whatever. What would he think if he could see her now, standing in a queue for a hip happening club, surrounded by half of his class mates by the looks of them. Megan felt a slight twinge of longing as she thought of Laurence out there somewhere in the dark, with Gerry, or with his friend Joe. Without her.

'Here, what?' Natalie said.

'Here what, what?' Megan repeated dumbly. This was great. Laurence had been right. It was fantastic not having to worry about saying the right thing for once. It was as if a cloud of lethargy had descended upon her brain, the way the rainy haze had descended upon the Broadway and washed all of the stress away.

'All right ladies, in you go,' a gruff voice barked from somewhere above.

Megan squinted upwards in the darkness and saw a great wall of a man towering above her. He was clad in a dark suit and dark glasses and had some kind of earpiece clamped to the side of his head. A bouncer. If your names not down you're not coming in. Once again Megan erupted into a splutter of laughter. 'Thank you officer,' she stuttered before being firmly guided into the foyer of the club by Natalie. Once inside she felt a little more human again as the warm air wrapped itself around her, a blanket of perfume and cigarette smoke. Megan took a deep breath and followed Natalie as she handed her coat to the gum-chewing infant behind the cloakroom counter.

'Come on, let's find a pair of suckers to buy us a drink,' Natalie said, smoothing down her dress and fluffing up her hair before gesturing to a set of leather padded doors. From behind the doors Megan could hear a muffled bassline, pounding like a heart about to burst.

*

Natalie scanned the bar, the drum beat from the music causing her entire body to throb. She felt consumed by a sudden burning need, pulsating through her in time with the music. She would show Gerry. She would show every sad bastard who took her for granted. At the end of the bar she spotted a heavy-set man of about thirty. His dark hair was slicked back and he was wearing a black satin shirt over a pair of well fitting jeans. He would do. She turned to Megan who was looking completely off her face, sad cow, and gestured to her to follow. Still, being out with someone so much older did have its bonuses even if she couldn't hold her drink. At least Natalie would get all the attention from the guys – they might even think she was out with her mother! Oh that would be an absolute classic. Natalie wove her way through the crowd and sidled up behind the man. He was holding a twenty-pound note aloft, waiting to be served. Perfect. Natalie nudged up against him, as if she had been jostled.

'Oh sorry,' she yelled over the music, as the man turned to look at her. 'It's rammed in here, isn't it?'

The man looked down at her and smiled. 'Yes, yes it is,' he yelled back.

'I was wondering if you could do me a huge favour,' Natalie said breathlessly, standing on tip-toe, bringing her just about level with his broad shoulder.

The man looked at her, his eyes quickly flitting from her face to her breasts and back again. Natalie pressed herself against him and the edges of his mouth began to curl into a smile. 'Well that depends,' he said, turning towards her and placing a hand on the small of her back.

'On what?' Natalie replied, gazing up at him through lowered eyelashes a la Princess Diana.

'On what it is you want and what you can do for me in return.'

Natalie grinned. This was going to be easy. She'd show Gerry who was boss. How dare he treat her like some stupid little girl with a crush. She was a woman and she was hot. He was lucky she was even giving him the time of day let alone a place in her bed. And to think she had nearly confided in him. Nearly told him everything.

'Natalie.' She felt Megan tugging at her elbow and chose to ignore her. What was wrong with her, the stupid cow, couldn't she see what she was doing. She carried on gazing up at the man with doe eyes.

'Well what I want is for you to order my friend and I a drink - I *so* can't be bothered to wait another hour, and don't worry, there's plenty I can do in return,' she let her hand brush lightly against the man's thigh.

'Natalie.'

Oh for God's sake, what the hell was Megan's problem? Natalie turned to her, glowering. Megan's normally immaculate make-up had smudged forming smoky rings beneath her eyes and her wispy hair looked wild and unkempt, giving her the appearance of an ageing rock chick. Or Alice Cooper in drag, Natalie thought with a smirk. 'What? What is it?' she said. Megan attempted to say something but a cheesy eighties anthem had just started playing and Natalie could barely hear herself think let alone what Megan was saying. 'I'm just getting us a drink,' she said through gritted teeth, miming a drinking motion when Megan stared back at her blankly. 'A drink,' she repeated, pointing at the bar.

Megan shook her head and nodded towards the dance-floor. Oh good God, the sad cow wanted to dance. Didn't she realise how seriously uncool it was to dance this early on in the night? Only the drunken desperados, the Bacardi Breezer Brigade committed such shameful atrocities, lurching around their handbags, pretending to be engrossed in their own sad company and singing along to the song when all the while they were scanning the outskirts of the dance floor desperate for something, anything with a penis. Natalie wouldn't dream of setting foot on the dance floor until well into the evening, when the dance floor was busy and the guys had all assembled in packs at their vantage points. Then she would take to the floor with a vengeance, make her entrance in style, dancing the stilettos off all the silly Traceys and Sharons and making sure all male eyes were on her as she snaked and writhed her way around. Natalie shook her head firmly at Megan and turned back to the man. 'So, what do you say?' she asked giving him a cheeky wink. She figured he liked cheeky, he looked like some kind of manager, with his firm set jaw and broad shoulders. Yes, he probably loved his women petite and cheeky just like her. But then she could be whoever he wanted her to be. Didn't Gerry realise that, didn't he realise what he was risking losing? She, Natalie was every bloke's wet dream, because she could morph into whoever they desired.

The man looked down at her and smiled. 'I say, what are you drinking?' he said, bending down so his face was level with hers. His breath smelt of beer and cigarettes and the faintest trace of garlic.

'Oh fabulous,' Natalie gushed, smiling back at him and once more allowing her hand to brush against him, only this time up the inside of his thigh. 'I'll have a Cosmopolitan and my friend will have -' She turned to ask Megan what she wanted but Megan had disappeared.

*

As soon as Megan reached the small oval dance floor her heart sank. The only other people dancing were a group of rather dirty looking young women, the kind who wore bare legs and boob tubes in the middle of winter and displayed tattoos and sovereign rings like badges of honour. Still, at least the dance floor wasn't completely empty, at least she would be able to dance without standing out like a sore thumb, wouldn't she? The deejay was playing one of Megan's favourite songs from the eighties and as soon as she heard the opening chords she felt compelled to dance, just as she had all those years ago in the student union bar. Holding on to the brass railing, Megan carefully made her way down the small set of illuminated stairs to the dance floor. So what if she didn't have a dance partner, she didn't need one, she didn't need anyone anymore. She was free. A free agent. A free spirit. Young free and single. Free. Oh yes. There was no stopping her now. Oh no. She gingerly stepped on to the polished floor, closed her eyes and let her feet find their way into the rhythm of the song. Then, feeling slightly emboldened and with the drum beat surging up through her toes and vibrating through her rib cage she danced her way over to the centre of the floor and started to allow her body and her arms to take up the beat. Yes, this was what it was all about. She'd already lost herself in the alcohol, now she was losing herself in the rhythm and it felt great. Yeah man, she though to herself. This is what life's all about, it's all about the music. When it really comes down to it, what else really matters? It was like Abba once said, or was it the Bee Gees? Thank you for the music. Yes music was cool.

It was the best. In fact if she had her way, all people would do all day was dance and sing and lose themselves in the rhythm. Megan danced faster and faster, letting her arms and legs go wherever the music dictated. She was the rhythm, she was the beat, she *was* music. She was lying flat on the floor.

Megan rubbed her eyes and stared around her, baffled. How the hell did she end up down here? And why were those scary looking women staring at her?

'Are you all right, love?' One of them was now saying, leering in on her so close Megan could see every one of her amalgam-capped teeth.

'Yes, yes, I'm fine,' she muttered, putting her hands down on the sticky floor beside her and trying to push herself up. Once again the entire dance floor seemed to capsize, sending Megan reeling over to one side. Somewhere way above her she heard some women saying something about 'one too many' and 'poor love,' before she felt the firm grip of a man or gorilla, she wasn't sure which, pulling her to her feet.

'Come on darling,' I think you ought to be going home,' the man, obviously a bouncer from his dark suited attire, said.

'But my - ' But Megan couldn't find the right words and before she knew what was happening she was back out through the leather padded doors and being bundled out of the foyer, much to the obvious interest of the queue of people still snaking in. It was only when she was back out on the Broadway, standing shivering in the orangey mist that she realised what had happened. She had been thrown out of a club. She Megan Rowe, internationally best selling author and renowned life coach, not to mention national radio presenter, had been thrown out of a nightclub for being drunk and disorderly. She didn't know whether to laugh or cry. Never in all of her wildest dreams had she imagined that in leaving Gerry she would morph into him. Megan sighed. What on earth was happening to her? What had she done? Her head was starting to pound and she felt cold and sick. All she wanted was to be at home, wrapped up in her duck down quilt, tucked up in bed.

'Do you want a cab love?'

She looked up and saw a man leaning out of the window of a taxi. He was about sixty with a round ruddy face and a welcoming grin. He looked like everyone's favourite granddad and seemed just the person to take her home.

'Yes, yes please,' she said, getting into the back of the cab and fumbling with the seatbelt. 'Nightingale Avenue, Chiswick please,' she murmured before slumping against the side of the door and closing her eyes.

chapter Thirty-Eight

"Sometimes we forget the simple things we are blessed with every day. Sunshine, good food, the smell of freshly brewed coffee. Today make a note of all the blessings you would normally take for granted."
Megan Rowe, 'Help Yourself to Happiness.'

'I can't believe – I never thought –' Danny's mother leant against the kitchen sink and wiped her tear-streaked face with the back of her hand. Despite the creases lining her eyes and mouth she looked like a frightened little girl in her dungarees and braids. Behind her the sun glared through the wide kitchen window presenting an over-exposed snapshot of the back yard, smaller and scruffier than Danny remembered it. 'I didn't think I was going to see you again,' she muttered.

Danny wiped his own face and stepped further into the room. There was the old pine dresser, still housing the same set of blue and white china plates that never got used and the monstrous china egg holder in the shape of a constipated looking hen. Danny scanned the rest of the room. There were the olive green cupboard fronts with the same old scuffs and grazes. There was the cork notice-board crammed with leaflets and notes and oh God, the pictures he and Marty had drawn of the Easter Bunny. Danny gulped and looked away. And there was the huge pine table, dead centre, now covered in a green tablecloth rather than red. He remembered the sliding drawer in the middle of the table where his mother kept the place mats and how he and Marty would ram each other with it when their parents weren't looking. Danny shook his head and looked back at his mother.

'I'm sorry,' he whispered.

She looked at him for a second and then hastily turned and opened one of the cupboards beside the sink. It was the cupboard she used to store her pans in, Danny remembered but now he could see it was lined with packets of food.

'Coffee?' she asked softly.

Danny nodded and watched as she put a clean filter in the coffee pot and tipped the dark brown coffee grounds on top. Her hands were bigger than he remembered, swollen, and the backs were covered in a labyrinth of raised veins. They were also shaking.

'So why – how long – what made you - ?' She broke off and turned to stare out of the window. Outside the sun was so bright it was practically white, bouncing off the bleached grass and rusting garden furniture.

Danny placed his rucksack by the door and sat down at the table. 'I've been so busy,' he began, lamely.

Still staring out of the window he saw his mother visibly wince. What was he doing? Why had he bothered coming back if he wasn't going to be honest? But how could he? How could he begin to tell the truth?'

Over on the counter the coffee percolator began spluttering into life and the first wafts of the roast beans drifted across the room.

His mother spun around and walked over to the huge fridge. 'You must be starving. Let me fix you some food.'

'No mom, you really don't have to - ' but before he could say any more she had laid a dish in front of him and then another and another.

'There you go – potato salad, apple coleslaw and some pork barbecue. I made it last night. Oh and here,' she fetched a small basket from the side and removed the chequered cloth covering it. 'Corn muffins.'

Danny stared down at the sweet–smelling mounds as yellow as buttercups. 'Thank you.'

'Uh-huh. Oh son!' She stood in front of him wringing her hands. 'Let me get a good look at you.'

Danny looked up at her and smiled. 'I've missed you mom.'

She looked at him for a second and then turned and walked back over to the window. 'I've been so worried about you – what with the war and all.' She turned back. 'I guess you've been in Iraq?'

He nodded. 'Uh-huh. Till pretty recently, but I've been in London for the past few weeks.'

'London, England?' His mom's eyes widened and she thrust her hands into the pockets of her dungarees. 'Have you seen the Queen?'

'Mom!'

She gave an apologetic little smile. She was still beautiful, her face still a perfectly crafted heart shape and her button nose still dusted with freckles. Danny felt a pang of something so strong it was as if he had been winded. She began walking back over to him and pulled a chair out from under the table. 'Sorry, son. So why London? Are you covering a story there?'

'Kind of.' Danny looked away. 'I'm trying to write a book.'

'A book?' His mom sat down opposite him. 'What kind of book?'

'About my pictures.'

'Oh – I see.'

'I'm finding it pretty tough though so I'm not sure if anything will come of it. Anyhow what about you? What are you doing these days? You still at the library?'

His mom sighed. 'Yes. They've got me driving the van these days. Delivering books to the old folks. I don't mind though. It's nice to get out and about. Don't think I've ever drunk so much iced tea in my life though, every house I call at they insist I have a drink with them before I go.' She fell silent before getting back to her feet. 'Oh my gosh, I didn't fix you a drink. Let me get you a drink. You want some iced water before your coffee?'

Danny nodded. 'Yes, please, that would be nice. So how's pops?' He held his breath as he waited for her answer. He saw his mother visibly flinch before opening the fridge.

'Oh he's fine. Still on the trucks. Only does one job a week now though. Those long drives were starting to take it out of him.'

Danny nodded.

'So are you married? Got any kids?' She asked with a formality that made Danny wince as she brought a jug of iced water over to the table and poured him a glass.

He shook his head vigorously. 'No.'

His mom sighed. 'I wondered sometimes you know, if I had any grand children out there.' She went back over to the coffee pot and fiddled with the handle.

Danny stared down into his lap, ashamed. He was responsible for this – for his mother being a virtual stranger, for keeping her at way longer than arms length for all these years. While he'd been away it had been all too easy to focus on his own pain, but now, as he watched her darting about the kitchen like an anxious sparrow he was all too aware of the pain he'd caused her.

'My job – it isn't really conducive to a wife and kids,' he offered feebly.

She turned back to face him. 'No, I guess not. But don't you -' she left the question hanging there, only half asked.

But Danny knew all too well what she wanted to say. Don't you miss having a partner, don't you long for the patter of tiny feet? And don't you wish you had somewhere you could call home? He thought back to the many times he had de-camped to Asia in between assignments. When a bellyful of destruction and gore had sent him hot-tailing it to a beach to blitz his mind on magic mushrooms and pot – rinsing away all the blood in a psychedelic power shower – and how he would inevitably end up entwined with some long limbed woman with golden skin and hair smelling of trapped sunshine. And how he would temporarily lose himself in the heat of the moment only for alarm bells to be triggered at the first mention of 'so where do we go from here?' Or, 'what next?' Or even worse, 'I love you.' And those fateful words would always prompt the same response. Books and passport slung in rucksack on top of balled up clothes retrieved from beach hut floor. A hasty phone call to a paper or news agency and next stop the airport for a one way ticket to the next war zone.

'I guess I'm not really cut out for that whole marriage and kids thing,' he finally uttered in attempt at jaunty but failing miserably. 'Well not just yet anyhow.'

His mother nodded sadly and looked away. 'So what made you come back now?' she asked quietly and then she stared at him in concern. 'You're not sick or anything are you?'

Danny shook his head. 'God, no. It's nothing like that, mom. I just wanted to see you guys.'

His mom turned back to the spluttering coffee pot and turned it off. 'It's been fourteen years, Danny. Fourteen years.' She fetched two mugs from the cupboard and began pouring the coffee. Danny's nose was flooded with the aroma. But rather than feel comforted he felt sick.

'I know – I'm so -'

The sound of the screen door slamming echoed through the house causing them both to jump. Danny clenched his hands together as he heard the footsteps thudding along the hall.

'Hi honey, I'm home.'

Danny couldn't help smiling as he heard his father calling out the same greeting that used to send the three of them into a frenzy of excitement whenever he returned from one of his road trips. He turned to face the door just as his dad walked into the room.

'Hi pops,' he said with a tentative grin.

His dad stood frozen in the doorway and, as with everything it seemed, he appeared a smaller and somehow faded version of himself, his sandy hair now almost white, his once broad shoulders slightly stooped. Danny waited as his dad stared at him, then looked questioningly at his mother and then back to him again.

'How you doing?' Danny said, getting to his feet.

His dad continued to stare at him for what seemed like an eternity, before turning on his heel and striding back down the passageway.

'Get out of my house.' He said as he went, in a voice compressed with what seemed like white-hot rage, 'And don't ever come back.'

chapter Thirty-Nine

"A happy marriage has to be built upon friendship and trust. It is this bedrock that sees you through the darker days, this knowledge that there is someone who will be there for you whatever happens."
Megan Rowe, 'Help Yourself to Happiness.'

'What's going on? Meg is that you?' Gerry's voice echoed through the darkened hallway. Megan put her keys back in her handbag and lurched through the front door, reaching out instinctively to steady herself on the hall table.

'Meg?' She heard Gerry call again. He sounded anxious and far away. Far, far away. What was she doing? Why was she here? She'd asked the cab driver to take her home. She hadn't meant here. This wasn't her home. Not any more. Why hadn't he taken her to Turnham Green? Oh how her head hurt. She heard a click and suddenly the hall was bathed in light. Megan squinted upwards. Gerry was hunched at the top of the stairs, his wavy hair messy from sleep, holding his dressing gown around him, the blue and green striped dressing gown she'd got him last Christmas.

'What the hell are you doing?' he asked, crossly, and then softer, 'Are you okay?'

Megan started to laugh. She didn't know why and she knew it probably wasn't the right thing to do, but then that seemed to be the story of her life didn't it? Not knowing the right thing to do. She looked down at her feet, her black boots were scuffed and dirty. How had that happened?

'I don't know what to do,' she heard herself say in a tiny voice. 'Nothing seems right any more.'

Then she heard the stairs creaking, that old familiar creaking, as Gerry came down towards her and the next thing she knew she felt his arm around her back and she was being guided into the kitchen. Don't turn the light on, she wanted to say, as they shuffled into the room. She didn't want to see the epicentre of her old home; the place for 'laughter, contentment and bonding' she had conjured into existence, now that it was no longer hers. She turned to face Gerry.

'Don't,' she whispered as he leant across to turn on the light. 'Please.'

They stood there for a moment, motionless in the half-light from the hallway. They were so close Megan could feel him breathing, feel the rise and fall of his chest through the velvety towelling of his dressing gown. How many times had she lain in the dark watching that same chest rise and fall, listening to his rumbling snores and wanted so badly to fling her arms around him and bury her face into him and pretend that everything was just fine. But she never had. Something had always held her back. Self preservation; the knowledge that no matter how hard she wished, he would never be able to give her what she wanted.

'Oh Gerry,' she said. And then his arms were round her and she felt him kissing the top of her head.

'I've missed you,' she heard him whisper. 'I've missed you so much.'

It was like standing on top of a precipice, as she leant into him and let his body take her weight and she closed her eyes. The darkness was warm and inviting. Just let go, a voice seemed to be urging her, let go and stop fighting. But now the darkness became deeper and she felt herself falling, spinning, out of control. 'Oh God, Gerry, I'm going to be sick.'

*

'Well I suppose that's what you call karma,' Gerry said with a chortle as he wiped at the corners of Megan's mouth with a damp face flannel.

Megan shook her head and looked away. 'What do you mean?'

'Well, what goes around comes around. How many times have you had to clean up after I've been sick?'

Megan couldn't help laughing. 'What, so you reckon that was some kind of cosmic vomit?'

'Well yeah, don't you think?' Gerry put the flannel back on the edge of the bath and leant over and flushed the toilet.

'I'm sorry about the dressing gown.'

Gerry smiled and looked down at his bare chest. 'Oh don't worry – call it divine retribution. Do you want a glass of water or a cup of tea or something?'

Megan shook her head and perched on the edge of the bath. 'No, not just yet, I'm still feeling a little wobbly to be honest.'

Gerry closed the lid of the toilet and sat down opposite her. 'How much had you had to drink – not that I'm trying to keep tabs on you or anything.'

'No because that really would be the pot calling the kettle rat-arsed.' They both laughed. Megan felt her stomach heave and grimaced. 'Half a bottle of wine and a jug of margarita,' she replied.

Gerry nodded, looking suitably impressed. 'Where did you go?'

Megan looked at him suspiciously but he wasn't looking accusing, more amused. 'Oh just out to Ealing with a friend from the radio station.'

'Right.'

Megan looked down at the faded bathmat on the floor. She remembered when she had bought it from a little shop in Bournemouth and the border of seashells had been vivid coral and green. Now she could barely make out their colours in the pale moonlight. 'This is so weird,' she said, finally breaking the silence.

'I know,' Gerry replied.

'How was your meal with Laurence?'

'Okay,' Gerry turned to look at the frosted glass window, dappled in silvery raindrops. 'It was nice seeing him again, nice having a chance to talk. Not that he said all that much, he seemed to be on some kind of sponsored eat-athon.'

Megan smiled, remembering her earlier instruction to Laurence to eat everything on the menu. It seemed like a lifetime ago now, her drunken haze seemed to have obliterated all concept of time.

'I hear you have a "well wicked" flat,' Gerry added with a bemused look.

Megan laughed, 'Yes, he does seem to like it, did he tell you about the -'

'Come home, Meg.'

'What?' She looked at him and her stomach gave another lurch.

'Come home. You and Laurence. Please.' Gerry got up from the toilet and crouched down on the floor in front of her. 'Look, I know I've messed up big time and I know I've got to sort myself out, with the drinking and everything, but I promise you this time it will be different. I never thought you would leave me before. I guess I took you for granted and for that I am truly sorry. But now I know differently. Now I know I can't mess you about anymore. And I won't I promise. I want you back, Meg. I want both of you back. I don't want to be without you. You're my queen remember? You're my rock.'

Megan sighed. 'Oh I don't know, I -'

'I've been miserable without you Meg, absolutely wretched. Please?' He put his hands on her knees and gazed up at her imploringly. Megan shivered. An icy draft seemed to be coursing through the bathroom and chilling her to the bone.

'I can't think about this now, Gerry. I'm tired and I'm not feeling well.' She saw a tear forge a shiny path along his cheek. 'Oh please, don't cry.' Now she felt tears forming in her own eyes. How easy would it be to just fall into his arms and pretend like the past two weeks hadn't happened? How easy to just slot back into her old life and make everything all right again – be the perfect coach with the perfect life and not have to justify herself to anyone. Except it wasn't. It wasn't perfect and never had been, and how then could she justify going back to Gerry to herself? She shivered again. Gerry stood up and took the huge bath towel off the back of the door and wrapped it around her. It smelt of his deodrant.

'I've been a complete and utter arsehole, Meg,' he said, pulling the towel tight around her, his face suddenly more sombre than she'd ever seen before. 'You wouldn't believe what a prat I've been. The thing is -' he turned and looked away. 'The thing is, when you left I was really pissed off. I was almost glad you'd gone.' He stared down into his lap, his dark hair falling about his face, 'I know I haven't been the easiest person to live with but neither have you, you know.'

Megan's pulse began to quicken. 'What do you mean?'

Gerry sighed. 'Well being married to the guru on perfect living, the queen of happiness, it can be quite taxing you know.'

'What?'

Gerry looked up at her, his tear-filled eyes imploring, 'Oh look please don't take this the wrong way. I'm not trying to criticise you, it's just that I never felt I could quite match up. I felt that you had this idealised view of marriage and I never quite made the grade. And I think that's what made me act so selfishly.'

'So you're saying it's my fault?'

'No – I'm saying I was an idiot. I was frightened and insecure. I used to dread it every time you went off to one of those coaching conferences, I was convinced you'd run off with some kind of Mr Motivator type.'

'But you were the one who stayed out nights and got drunk all the time.'

'Yes, because I guess I wanted to get in there first.

'I see. So you did have affairs then,' Once again Megan's stomach lurched and she shuddered beneath her towel.

'No,' Gerry almost shouted. 'No I didn't. That used to drive me mad too. The way you always suspected me of cheating on you. I – I -' he broke off mid flow and sat back on his heels, staring dejectedly at the floor. 'I was never a cheat, Meg, from the day we married till – till the day you left, I promise, I never ever cheated on you.' His eyes were glossy with tears.

'But I felt so lonely.' It was all Megan could say, all she needed to say as she sat there, the edge of the bath cutting into the backs of her legs and the icy air chilling her face. The catchphrase from her marriage, or was it the epitaph? She stood up and the towel tumbled to the floor. 'I ought to go.' As she made her way over to the door and out on to the landing she heard Gerry standing up behind her.

'Please, Meg.'

She stopped dead on the landing, facing her was Laurence's room, the shelves and bed eerily empty in the moonlight. Slowly she turned and faced Gerry, standing silhouetted in the bathroom doorway, all alone. Loneliness had never been something she could have associated with Gerry before. He was always so gregarious, the life and soul of any party, always so busy, so many friends. But now standing here in the half light, in the shell of their former home, he looked quite pitiful.

'I'll think about it,' she said, before running down the stairs and out into the night.

chapter Forty

"There is nothing wrong with the so-called 'negative' emotions. Anger, pain, fear and regret only become harmful if we fail to process them. What emotions are you suppressing today? How could you go about letting them out?"
Megan Rowe, 'Help Yourself to Happiness.'

Fear and nausea combined to perform a deadly knockout blow just below Danny's ribs, causing him to gulp for air.

'Don't go, pops, please,' he yelled running out on to the porch. Over by the steps the porch swing was bouncing wildly in his dad's wake, the once polished wood splintered and faded and the ropes frayed. Taking the steps two at a time Danny followed him down on to the stubbly sun-bleached grass. 'Please,' he repeated as his dad opened the door to his truck and prepared to get in. His father stopped and turned, his tanned, leathery face wracked with fury.

'You're right,' he said, slamming the truck door shut behind him. 'Why the hell should I be the one to go?' He began walking back towards Danny, fists clenched. 'You go. Go on. Get the hell off my property.'

'But pops.'

'Don't you "but pops" me,' his dad squared up to him at the foot of the porch steps. Beneath the wrinkles and the white hair he still looked just as tough. 'Go on. Get out of here.'

'But I -'

'He's come a long way to see us, Jake. All the way from London.' They both turned at the sound of Danny's mother's voice. She was standing in the doorway, clasping her hands.

'I don't care if he's come from hell on a hand-cart, he's not welcome here. You're not welcome here,' he repeated staring straight at Danny, his clear blue eyes icy cold against his weather-beaten skin. Danny looked away, sorrow rendering him completely mute.

'But he's your son,' his mother continued.

'I don't have a son,' his father muttered, then raising his voice, 'You hear me? I don't have a son.'

Danny swallowed hard to stop himself from retching. What had he expected? That they'd welcome him back with open arms? That there would be some kind of Waltons style home-coming with a sing-along around a hog roast? He turned to go back up the porch steps.

'I'll just go get my stuff,' he muttered. 'I'm sorry, I should never - '

'Well I do,' his mother said, staring straight at his dad.

'What?' His dad looked at her, shocked.

'I do have a son,' she replied defiantly, her eyes filling with tears. 'And I don't want him to go,' she continued, her voice breaking with emotion as she walked over to the top of the porch steps and looked down at Danny. 'Please.'

Danny looked up at her and then back to his father. 'But - '

'It's been fourteen years, Jake,' his mother continued. 'Fourteen years.'

'Exactly,' his father shouted. 'And who's the one who wiped your tears and held you all those nights when you thought you'd never see him again?' Danny's father stubbed him on the shoulder with his finger, his hands were still the size of shovels. 'Have you any idea how much pain and suffering you've caused your mom all these years? Her not knowing whether you're alive or dead or whether she was ever going to lay her eyes on you again. Never phoning, never coming to visit. Just a few goddamned cards when you could be bothered to remember. And after - ' he broke off and turned away to face the deserted street. 'After everything that happened - '

'Oh Jake, don't go bringing that up now,' his mom pleaded.

His father spun back around and stared up at her angrily. 'Don't go bringing what up now?'

'You know.'

Danny looked at the floor and swallowed hard.

'Oh I see,' his father retorted. 'So I can't say how I feel. But it's all right for his nibs to waltz in here after fourteen years as if nothing happened. As if he'd just been down to the store to pick up some groceries.'

Danny looked at him nervously. 'It isn't like that.'

His dad stared at him. 'Oh isn't it. So go on then.'

'What?'

'Tell me what it's like. Why you've suddenly decided to show your face now?'

'I - '

'He's writing a book, aren't you Danny?'

Danny cringed.

'A book?' His father began shaking his head in disbelief.

'Yes.'

'About what?'

Danny kicked at the ground with the toe of his boot.

'It's about his work, isn't it, Dan? About his pictures.'

'Oh I see. About his pictures,' his father's voice was laden with sarcasm.

'Jake,' his mother chided.

'What?'

'Don't be like that.'

'Like what?' He turned to Danny with a look so bitter Danny had to turn away. 'Tell you what, maybe one day I'll write a book. Yeah I'll write a book about my so called son and what he did to this family.'

'Jake!' Danny's mother put her hand to her mouth in shock. 'Jake, don't.'

'Why the hell not?' his father yelled. 'If he wants to come crawling back to my house then why the hell can't I have my say?' He gave a bitter little laugh. 'I guess it'll be a mighty long time before I get this chance again.'

'No,' Danny's mother cried, taking a step down towards them. 'I won't have it. I won't have you drive him away. Come into the house Danny. Please.'

But Danny shook his head. 'Let him have his say, mom.'

'What? But -'

'Please?' Danny stared up at her imploringly. This was it. This was what he had been dreading and avoiding for so long. But strangely now the moment had finally arrived he didn't feel so bad, he just wanted it over. He turned back to face his father. 'Go on.'

His father stared at him for a minute, then looked away.

'Go on,' Danny repeated. 'Say it. Get it off your chest.'

A silver saloon car purred along the street and his father gazed after it blankly.

'Okay. I'll say it for you.' Behind him Danny heard his mother gasp and whisper 'No,' but he had to carry on. Perversely he almost wanted to. 'I'm a gutless piece of shit.' His mother began to sob, but nothing could stop Danny now. 'I'm a gutless piece of shit who doesn't deserve to be alive.'

His father began to walk away, towards his truck.

'Hey, pops? That's what you've been thinking all these years, isn't it? That and why did it have to be Marty? Oh don't worry. It's nothing I haven't thought myself every minute of every day of every month of every year. Go on – say it!' Danny was shouting now, he couldn't help it, the release of years of tension was like a volcano erupting inside him. He sat down on the porch steps in an attempt to calm himself. 'Every minute of every day pops, I think to myself, why did I let him go and pay for the gas? Why didn't I get it myself?' An image of the rundown gas station flickered into Danny's head. The harsh fluorescent lighting and the rusting pumps. And Bruce Springsteen playing on the crackling car stereo and Danny singing along. And him playing the older brother card and making Marty go pay, while he sang of breaking out and being 'born to run.' And then that noise. Louder than a fire cracker as it rang around the deserted forecourt cutting through the guitars and the sax and the singing. And then the scream causing Danny to freeze in the driver's seat, his hands gripping the wheel as if they'd been fossilised there. And then –

'It's okay, Danny. We don't blame you.' He heard his mother's footsteps soft on the porch steps behind him. 'It was just one of those things. How could you have known what was going to happen? How could you have done anything to stop it?'

'But that's it, you don't understand - I could.' Danny dropped his face into his hands, all of his nervous energy of before dissipating like the air from a burst balloon. He gulped, this was it, this was what he had come here to say. He took a deep breath. 'I could have gone into the shop, mom. When I heard the first shot. I could have gone in there. I might have been able to save him.' Danny's eyes began to burn and his body began to shake. 'But I froze. I - ' he swallowed again. 'I froze.' He looked up at his dad, who was standing motionless by the truck, still with his back to him. 'Do you remember pops, how you always told Marty and me that blood was thicker than water and that we should always look out for each other?' His father nodded. 'Well I let him down. I let Marty down. I just sat there like a big pussy. Until it was too late.'

'But I don't understand,' his mother said from behind him.

Danny stayed where he was, head in hands. 'Oh it's quite simple, mom. Marty had gone in to pay for the gas and I heard the shot and I just sat there. And sat there. Then I heard another shot and I saw the guy running out waving a gun about and I – I dived down on to the floor.' Danny hit the porch step he was sitting on with his fists. 'While my brother was lying in that garage bleeding to death I was cowering on the floor of the car.'

'But you were the one who called the police,' his mom said, sitting down next to him. 'You were the one who tried to revive him. All of that blood on your sweater - ' she broke off with a shudder.

'Yes but that was long after the guy had gone. I should have gone in there sooner. After the first shot. I should have run to Marty but I didn't. That's why I could hardly face you after the funeral. Why I took off first chance I got. That's why I haven't been back since. I was so ashamed. But the thing is - the thing is – I can't go on, carrying this thing around with me. I'm so sorry, mom,' he turned to look at her, tears streaming down his face. 'Pops,' he turned to his dad. 'I'm so sorry. I wish it had been me too. Marty was too good. He was too sweet to die. He was only fifteen. He would have -' His mother put her arm around his shoulders and all of a sudden every muscle and sinew in Danny's body seemed to melt to a mush. He buried his head on her shoulder. 'I'm so sorry,' he kept saying over and over again between ragged sobs.

'Shhh,' his mom whispered, her breath cool as a spring breeze on his burning, tear-streaked face. And suddenly he had plummeted back thirty years to a six year old kid with a graze on his knee and his mom was rocking him better. 'It wasn't your fault,' she said. 'It wasn't your fault.'

Danny heard his father's feet crunching over the dry grass towards them and he looked up anxiously, wiping his eyes. He wouldn't blame him if he wanted to punch the hell out of him. He stood up and prepared himself. 'I'm so sorry, pops,' he whispered, but as he looked up he saw his father's eyes were full of tears too.

Finally his father spoke. 'You did the right thing,' he muttered.

'What?'

'The son of a bitch would have shot you both. You think I wanted to lose two sons that night?'

'But - '

'But nothing. You weren't the one carrying the gun were you?'

'No but - '

'And you didn't know what you were sending Marty into.'

'No.'

'Hell, the number of times I got that kid to pay for my gas.'

Danny gulped. 'But you would have run in, wouldn't you pops? If you'd heard a shot?'

His father looked away. 'How do I know? How do any of us know what we'd do in that kind of a situation?'

Danny nodded weakly. 'I just wish I could have been more like Marty. He didn't run away. He tried to help.'

'Yes and if you had I'd be putting flowers on two graves now instead of one.' his father replied looking back at him. And as Danny looked into his watery blue eyes it was like staring down into a kaleidoscope crammed full of tumbling memories. If only he could turn back the clock, back to a time when those same eyes were twinkling with laughter as he tickled him and Marty half to death.

'Why couldn't you have told us this at the time?' his mother asked, coming up behind him and stroking his hair. 'We wouldn't have blamed you, we would never have blamed you.'

Danny turned to face her. 'But you were both so devastated and all I could think every time I looked at you was that I was responsible for this. If I hadn't made him go – if I'd gone to him sooner, maybe he wouldn't have -'

His mother shook her head and took hold of his hands. As always her hands were cool as spring water, Danny squeezed hold of them. 'But by taking off the way you did it was like losing two sons. Don't you see that?'

Danny nodded. 'I guess I was too eaten up by guilt. Maybe I wasn't seeing straight.' He looked out across the street. Over at the house opposite two young kids were arriving home from school. One of them, the taller one, was swinging his bag in large loops around his shoulder while the smaller one kicked a stone along the curb. *You wanna play racing cars, Dan-Dan*, he could almost hear the smaller one plead. Completely involuntarily he let out a cry, like the yelp of a new born calf. 'I miss him, mom. I miss him, pops,' he sobbed, his legs beginning to buckle beneath him. And then, just when he felt sure he was going to hit the deck he felt a grip like steel take hold of him.

'I know, son,' his father said gruffly, grasping him in a bear hug. 'I know.'

Chapter Forty-One

"What are your dreams trying to tell you? What messages from your subconscious do they deliver? Let yourself be guided by the inner wisdom of your night-time visions."
Megan Rowe, 'Help Yourself to Happiness.'

It was six o'clock in the morning and the Shepherd's Bush Road was deserted, apart from the occasional delivery van, racing to deposit tightly bound bundles of the latest news and scandal outside the still shuttered shops. Natalie hobbled along the rain-slicked pavement, cursing her decision to wear the high heels now slicing into the backs of her feet and cursing her decision to go back home with the man from the club, the residue of who was causing a dull ache between her legs. Why had she gone out in the first place? Why hadn't she just stayed at home? But she knew the answer to that only too well. She had had the burning need and nothing would have stopped her back then. But now, now she had to endure the come down and as she slowly picked her way around the grimy puddles it seemed to be the come down to end all come downs.

Rewind a few hours and it had all been so different. The fierce eyed attention from the guy in the club had got her so unbelievably hot, she hadn't even noticed Megan had left, let alone cared. On the dance floor and then later, in the toilets, she had shown him a few moves he wouldn't forget in a hurry. And the coke – well that had only made it even better. When he had cut a line on top of the chipped porcelain cistern she had grabbed the rolled twenty-pound note off him in a flash. It was just what she'd needed to forget all about Gerry Radcliffe, blasting him right out of her mind in a snort of magic dust. But now, now for some bizarre and completely fucked up reason, he was all she could think about. Gerry and his stupid Mr Darcy hair and his stupid big brown eyes and the way he would look at her sometimes as if she were the only woman on the planet, and the way he would ask her questions about herself, as if he really wanted to know the answers. The man from the club hadn't asked her anything, apart from, 'fancy a night-cap?' as they had staggered out at closing time. And neither had his friend, his flatmate, who had been waiting up for them when they got to his place, a top floor apartment in a new block just off Goldhawk Road. When she had first seen his friend, Natalie had felt a little apprehensive, but the pyramid of coke on the coffee table had soon put pay to that. Yes, she had actually found it all quite amusing watching them both getting off on her as she performed an impromptu striptease around the living room.

Natalie shuddered and pulled her cape tighter around her neck. Everything looked so bleak in the cold milky light, all the litter and the graffiti and the flattened fag butts drifting in the oily puddles. 'Slut.' 'Whore.' She heard the men's voices echo up the deserted street and had to cast a glance over her shoulder to make sure that the voices were really just in her head, just a memory, and they weren't actually following her. After she had done it, she had felt the usual wave of revulsion; made even worse this time by the way the men had treated her. The animal way in which they had taken it in turns to thrust away on top of her and then egg each other on. She had never been called those names before, at least not during sex, and not since leaving the village, and although at the time she had managed to block it out with her own mental diatribe about them, now she felt nothing but a horrible slow rising shame.

By the time Natalie got home to Neptune Mansions the backs of her feet had been sliced to ribbons and her turquoise satin shoes were stained with a crimson tidemark of blood. Natalie kicked the shoes off and padded into the kitchen. It was no more than she deserved, she thought as she stared down at the ragged flaps of skin hanging from her ankles, wondering if she ought to bathe them. She went over to the sink to get a glass of water. Her mouth was drier than sandpaper and it tasted vile. Then she saw the remnants of the glass she had thrown at the wall after Gerry had left the evening before. Dull jagged shards, scattered all over the floor and the work surface. Why had he had to go? If he hadn't left none of this would have happened. Perhaps it wasn't too late? Perhaps he could make it all better again? Natalie reached into her handbag for her mobile phone, hands trembling, but when she called Gerry's number his phone rang a couple of times before being diverted to voicemail. The bastard! He was avoiding her. She clenched her hands so hard she could feel her nails cutting into her palms, but for some strange reason the pain felt good. It's no more than you deserve, the voice in her head repeated and she looked up at her painting and the dark hollow eyes staring down at her.

'I know,' she cried, slamming her fists down on the counter. 'I know. But can't you see? You're way better off without me.'

*

In her rock hard rented bed with its shapeless polyester duvet, Megan was plunging deeper and deeper into an alcohol laced, sweaty dream. Unlike the pale morning light flooding her bedroom through the open curtains, the other-world of her dream was dark and shadowy. She was outside somewhere, in a windy lane lined with tall, prickly bushes and Gerry was standing a just few yards from her, at the end of the lane, but no matter how hard she called to him he couldn't seem to see her. 'Gerry, it's me,' she screamed but he continued to stare straight through her, as if she no longer existed, as if she were dead. As tears of frustration poured down her face Megan felt a tap on her shoulder and she turned to see her Grandmother.

'Grandma!' she gasped and her grandmother nodded. 'What's happening? Why can't he see me?' Her grandmother shook her head and took her by the hand. 'What is it? Am I dead?' Megan's relief at seeing her Grandma began to be replaced by a chilling fear. Was she dead? Had she become a ghost? Had her grandmother come to take her to the other side? If so where was the brilliant golden light at the end of the tunnel? Why was she in this dark passage way? Her grandmother began to lead her back up the lane away from Gerry and suddenly they were in a deep forest, columns of trees surrounding them on all sides. Megan felt the prickle of bracken beneath her feet and when she looked down she saw she was now wearing her favourite childhood nightie, a downy nylon tribute to Snow White and her seven dwarfs. Megan studied the beloved pictures dotted around the garment. There was Sleepy above the hem skimming her left knee and there was Grumpy scowling up at her from her right. And there, over her chest smiled Snow White with her glossy black hair and cheeks as rosy as apples. Megan stroked the bobbly material absently as she followed her grandmother deeper into the wood. She had forgotten all about this nightie and how much she had loved it. It was like being reunited with an old friend. Finally her grandma came to a halt in front of a huge tree, its roots reaching out like giant veiny claws upon the mossy earth. Megan craned her neck to gaze up the gnarled trunk but it was so tall she was unable to see the top. Suddenly the sound of laughter tinkled like a bell from somewhere behind the tree, causing a flurry of unseen flapping wings above. Megan peered around into the darkness. 'Who's there?' she called. Again the laughter came and then she saw a little girl, thin with straggly hair peeping around the tree at her. 'Who are you?' Megan repeated. 'What do you want?' The girl came dancing out in front of them, whirling around faster and faster. She was wearing a raggedy summer dress and had a daisy chain around her neck. But as Megan stared harder at the dancing figure she realised she wasn't a girl at all. Her thin face was lined and although she was laughing her huge green eyes were clouded with sorrow. 'Mum?' The figure stopped dancing and stared at her, startled for a moment before running off into the darkness. 'Mum, come back. Don't go. It's too dark in there. What's going on? Where are we?' she asked, turning back to her Grandma. But her Grandma just pointed triumphantly at a hollow in the trunk. Megan took a step closer and stood on tiptoes and there right in front of her, carved into a hollow in the trunk was an oval mirror. She held her breath and opened her eyes wide and –

Megan sat bolt upright in bed, fear clutching at her stomach and icy beads of sweat breaking out all over her body like dew. As fuzzy memories from the night before began merging with her dream she felt a sudden surge of dread. Was her dream a premonition? Was she about to die? What was she doing? What had she done?

chapter Forty-Two

"If life is a journey then dreams are the co-ordinates we use to chart our course. Without dreams we flail and flounder. Without dreams we become directionless."
Megan Rowe, 'Help Yourself to Happiness.'

Cheddar took a deep breath and clicked on PUBLISH POST. There, he'd done it, sent his wildest dreams whistling out into the ether and up through the broadband connections of limitless numbers of people. He hadn't planned on publishing his 'Perfect Day' on his blog, but as he'd sat down in front of his computer that Sunday morning and prepared to write his normal spoof horoscopes, nothing came. He couldn't even muster up the usual anti-Aries diatribe directed at Denise. And as he'd sat there, staring blankly at the keyboard he'd had the sudden overwhelming urge to write down his fantasy of a few days previously. Then his fingers had flown like a concert pianist's over the keyboard as all of his hopes and dreams poured from his head down through his arms. He'd included every loving detail, from the ivy clad cottage to his free-spirited, wild haired girl-friend. When he'd got to the part about the dinner party he'd had to put on a Pink Floyd CD to drown out the grumbling from his rapidly shrinking stomach, but apart from that it had been the easiest thing he'd ever written in his life. He'd even signed it in his real name, Joe Bailey, rather than his usual web alter ego The King Cheese. It was only now, now he'd actually published it that the first tiptoe-ings of doubt began creeping into his mind.

Cheddar clicked the renew button and viewed his latest blog. There it was in black and white, well blue and green actually, entitled 'If I Can Dream.' Cheddar scanned the introduction nervously;

This week the most amazing thing happened to me – I learnt how to dream. And this is going to sound dead weird, but by learning how to dream it seems I've finally woken up. For so long now I've plodded through life accepting everything that's been thrown at me. Years of me old man's bitterness and resentment, a crap relationship, an even crapper break-up, me old man dying –

Cheddar gulped and looked away from the screen. The sun was streaming in through his bedroom window and the new sea green curtains were dancing in the crisp spring breeze. Had he really written about his dad dying on his website? Admitting it to the universe when he wasn't sure he'd really admitted it to himself. It had been almost a year since emphysema had finally taken his dad, only a couple of weeks after he'd found out about Denise and Darren, and still numb from that discovery he had barely acknowledged the passing of his dad, refusing even to go back home for his funeral. Why the hell should he, he'd thought at the time, the old bastard had given him nothing but grief for years. And anyway how can you pay your last respects to someone you'd lost all respect for long ago? Cheddar remembered his mam crying and begging with him on the phone and then his sisters having a go, in their usual indomitable way; 'selfish twat' and 'stubborn bastard' were two of the more endearing terms they'd used; but it was as if his heart had been entombed in a thick marble case that no-one could pick their way through. He gulped and looked back at the screen.

I think if you get hurt enough times then eventually you just stop caring, or at least you kid yourself you do. For months now I've hid away – that might seem strange to those of you who regularly visit this site – how can I say I hide away when I publish my musings every day on the internet? But what you read on this blog, that isn't the real me, or at least it's just a tiny part, a part that's safe for me to share. I don't even publish it under me own name for Christ's sake. But today I've decided to share everything with you, my deepest dreams, the lot. Maybe I'm hoping that if I put it out there then I'm going to have to get off me arse and actually do summat about it, I don't know. Today I was going to write my usual spoof horoscopes; giving you lot a load of ridiculous instructions for the week ahead – wear yellow shoes on Tuesday to attract your sole mate, destiny sees you falling in love over a broken teapot at the jumble sale – that kind of nonsense. But now I only want to give you one instruction, whatever your star sign. And that is to listen to your dreams. And after you've listened to them, chase them, chase them like mad. And never give up, even when they leave you far behind. Because without our dreams, we become shut off, half people, trudging through life like zombies or the cast of *EastEnders*. What follows below is my own dream of my perfect day in my perfect life. I know I've got a hell of a lot of chasing to do, but it's got to be better than trudging and hiding. Hasn't it?

Cheddar sat back from his desk and swallowed hard. He couldn't quite believe that he'd written all that. It was as if he'd gone into some kind of weird trance and woken up to find he was William Shakespeare. Where the hell had it all come from? All this talk of dreams and hiding and finally waking up? Was it all the vitamins he was now consuming? Was it turning him into a lass or summat? He looked down at his chest, but if anything his man-breasts seemed to be shrinking along with his stomach. Cheddar smiled as he remembered how loose his jeans had felt that morning and how he'd gone down a whole notch on his belt. He sighed deeply. Now what? As the nervousness about publishing his dreams began to lift he felt strangely purged. It had felt good to set it all down like that, as if by seeing his dreams displayed on the screen they were now somehow legitimate. But of course they were still only words. How could he transfer those words into action? Cheddar looked across his newly debris-free desk and picked up the piece of paper with his notes from Megan's exercise. 'Break them down into a manageable list of goals,' she had said. 'Short term to long term.' Hmm. Well they were all pretty long term weren't they? Moving to a cottage, finding the woman of his dreams, having a couple of nippers. Cheddar felt a wave of dejection sweep over him. How the heck could he possibly achieve that lot? He scratched his head and then rubbed his hand absently over the bristles. His stomach gave a long languorous howl, as if in sympathy for his plight. Then Cheddar began to smile. That was it. The one thing he could do almost straight away. He could have a dinner party, invite his new friends. Yes, he could hardly see the lads from the Rock Forum being up for a four-course extravaganza, unless it involved copious amounts of King Fisher lager and buckets of vindaloo. But if he invited his new friends he could recreate the dinner party of his dreams. He could clear out the living room, buy a decent dining table. Light loads of those little candle things and cook up a storm. He could try some new recipes, there'd been a great one for lemon and garlic chicken in one of the colour supplements that morning. And he could make French onion soup for starters with cheese toasted French bread, and possibly even have some of those crude-shite things that Megan seemed so fond of. Yes, Megan would be up for a dinner party surely? She was a life coach and an author for God's sake. Dinner parties were probably as common as cleaning your teeth in those kind of circles. And it would be a great chance to get to know her a little better. And he could invite Danny too, if he was back from America. Cheddar frowned. He supposed he really ought to invite another lass, even up the numbers and all that, but who? An image of Natalie popped into his head, with her mass of flame red hair and that heart-shaped face of hers which should really look sweet, but somehow never quite managed to look anything other than evil. There was something about her that scared the hell out of Cheddar. Her knowing, haughty air seemed quite wrong in one so small and young. She was like that doll from the horror movie, *Chucky*. But who else could he ask? He didn't really know any other lasses, and at least Megan knew her, and they seemed to get on all right. Yes, he concluded with a sigh, he would invite them both at work that night.

chapter Forty-Three

"Embrace life with the energy and enthusiasm of a child."
Megan Rowe, 'Help Yourself to Happiness.'

'A dinner party?' Megan took off her jacket and slung it over the back of the chair next to Cheddar's. This was the very last thing she had expected upon arriving at work. Not only an invitation from Cheddar but an invitation to a dinner party. She looked at him cautiously. He was wearing smarter clothes than usual, a cornflower blue shirt and dark jeans and there was something else different about him but Megan couldn't quite put her finger on what.

'Yes,' Cheddar looked at his screen and began tapping his fingers on his knees. 'I just thought it would be nice for us to do summat away from this place for once.' He gestured around the dimly lit studio. 'Get to know each other a little better. And besides I do a mean roastie.'

'Roastie?' Megan looked at him questioningly.

'Yeah, you know, roast potato.' A crimson blush began working its way up Cheddar's round face. 'I was thinking of doing roast potatoes and chicken and all the trimmings and French onion soup to start and some of those crude things you like as appetisers.'

'Crude things?' Megan bit her lip to stop herself from laughing. Beads of sweat had begun erupting on Cheddar's brow.

'Yeah, you know those bits of carrot and celery and stuff. I'll get some dips as well.'

'Oh – crudités?'

'Yeah, that's the one.'

'So, er, would it just be me, then, coming to this dinner party?' She wasn't sure whether to be flattered, delighted or alarmed.

'Oh God no! I mean,' Cheddar wiped his brow with the back of his hand. 'No, I was going to ask an American friend of mine as well. And her nibs,' he gestured to the empty telephone room next door. 'If she ever gets in.'

Megan followed his gaze to the door. She'd been dreading seeing Natalie after Friday night. Her recollections from the whole experience were somewhat hazy to say the least but unfortunately she could remember the parts where she was sprawled on the dance floor and being frog-marched from the club all too vividly. When Megan had tried calling Natalie on Saturday to apologise she had been quite relieved at getting no reply but now she wished she had. It was going to be excruciating seeing her in the studio. Especially when she would then have to go through the farce of advising the nation on how to live the perfect life when her production assistant had seen her blind drunk and legless only two nights before. Still perhaps Cheddar's surprise invite might deflect the attention somewhat, soften the blow.

'I think it's a lovely idea,' she replied, smiling at Cheddar. Cheddar immediately beamed back.

'You do?'

'Yes, of course. I had no idea you were a cook. It sounds great. When were you thinking of doing it?'

'How about next Saturday? Of course I'll have to ask Danny and Natalie –'

'Ask me what?'

Megan's stomach lurched as the door opened and Natalie walked into the studio, but as soon as Megan saw her she did a double take. Natalie looked even worse than she felt. Her hair was scraped back into a severe bun and her eye make-up was so thick and dark the rest of her face looked deathly white in comparison. She looked like a tiny walking skeleton. Not helped by the fact that she was clad from head to toe in black.

'Bloody hell, you all right, lass?' Cheddar asked, frowning with concern.

Natalie fixed him with one of her stares. 'I'm fine,' she replied in a tight, little voice.

'Megan,' she said, nodding at her brusquely.

Megan swallowed hard and leant against the desk. 'Natalie, about Friday night. I am so sorry. I haven't had that much to drink for ages, I don't know what came over me.'

'Aye, aye, this sounds interesting,' Cheddar leaned back in his chair and folded his hands in his lap. 'Tell me more.'

Megan sighed and turned to face him. 'Natalie and I went out to a club on Friday night and I got a little the worse for wear and – well I got thrown out.' There, she'd said it.

Cheddar tipped his head back and let out a roar of laughter. 'You got thrown out? Chuffin' 'ell! What did you do?'

Natalie took off her coat and flung it down on the desk.

Megan gulped. 'I – well - I made a bit of a fool of myself on the dance floor.'

'No!' Cheddar looked at her, still laughing. 'Bloody hell, what were you doing that they had to throw you out? Please don't tell me it was "Agadoo."'

Megan shook her head vigorously. 'God, no. I'm not really sure what kind of dance it was to be honest but I ended up flat on my back and then I was – well I was - escorted from the premises.'

'Don't worry about it,' Natalie cut in. 'I just wish you'd let me know, that's all. I ended up getting a load of hassle off these two guys and I had no idea where you were. I really could have done with your help.'

'Oh Natalie,' Megan felt terrible. No wonder she hadn't answered her calls.

'I said don't worry about it,' Natalie replied, turning her gaze to Cheddar. 'What was it you had to ask me, Cheddar?'

'Oh, well I was thinking of having a dinner party next Saturday and I wondered if you'd like to come?' Cheddar looked down into his lap and twiddled his thumbs as he awaited Natalie's reply.

Natalie stared at him for a second, before picking up her coat and making her way over to the door to the phone room. 'Sure, why not,' she replied before leaving and closing the door behind her.

Megan looked at Cheddar and smiled sheepishly. 'Oh dear, I guess I'm in the dog house.'

'Don't worry about it, I'm sure she'll get over it,' Cheddar nodded towards the door. 'Something tells me madam can look after herself fine when it comes to men. Probably just trying to put you on a guilt trip. So come on then,' he pointed to the small space in front of the desk.

'What?' Megan asked.

'Throw us a few moves. I've got to see what was so bad it got you booted out of a nightclub.'

Megan laughed, relieved that at least Cheddar wasn't appalled by her behaviour. 'I can't. I really can't remember.'

Cheddar tutted. 'And you a top life coach and advisor to the nation.'

Megan's face fell. 'I know, I feel terrible, it's just that I'd had a bit of a bad week what with moving and everything, I suppose I just wanted to let my hair -'

'I was joking,' Cheddar interrupted. 'You are allowed to get pissed you know. I won't tell anyone. Still you'd better behave yourself at my dinner party. I'll have none of that kind of behaviour round at my gaff.'

Megan sat down in the chair next to Cheddar and smiled gratefully. 'Don't worry, I think I'll be laying off alcohol for the foreseeable future. So have you done the playlist?'

'Yep.'

'What have we got first?'

'Well it was going to be "Bridge Over Troubled Water" but maybe I ought to change it to "Red, Red Wine."'

'Oh ha ha.'

'Or "Dancing Queen?"'

'All right, all right.'

Cheddar leant back in his chair and stretched out. He'd lost weight; that was what was different about him. Megan smiled. His skin looked healthier to, less blotchy. 'So have you come up with your exercise for the week?' Cheddar asked casually.

Megan nodded. After she had sobered up on Saturday she had spent hours trying to come up with a damned exercise that she could feel any kind of enthusiasm for but to no avail. Her head had been pounding and thoughts of Gerry and what had happened the night before kept barging uninvited into her brain. But then on Sunday morning, when she had been walking along Turnham Green High Street to fetch the papers and some fresh croissants for her and Laurence's breakfast she had come up with the perfect idea.

'Yes, I've got a really good one to help people get in touch with their true selves,' she replied.

'Oh yeah?' Cheddar reached over and picked up a pad and pen from his desk. Megan looked at him curiously, surely he wasn't about to take notes?

'Yes. I'm going to ask the listeners to write about when they were children.'

Cheddar frowned and began chewing on the end of his pen. 'Why?' he asked.

'Because that should help them uncover their hidden qualities and dreams.'

'What do you mean?'

Megan looked at the clock. It was twenty to eight. Twenty minutes before she had to go on air. She really ought to go next door and attempt to make the peace with Natalie, but then on the other hand talking the exercise through with Cheddar might help her to clarify it in her head and make it easier when she came to telling the listeners. All five point two million of them. She shuddered. 'Well,' she began. 'Think how imaginative and optimistic we are as children. Ask a child what they want to be when they grow up and the sky's the limit. What did you want to be when you were a kid?' she asked.

Cheddar chewed some more on his pencil. 'A cowboy,' he replied. 'And an astronaut.'

'Right, so even the sky wasn't the limit for you.' They both laughed.

'And then there was a brief stage when I'd been off sick with chicken pox and watched *Quincy* every day for two weeks and I decided I wanted to be a forensic scientist,' Cheddar continued.

Megan laughed. 'I bet that went down well with your parents.'

'Yeah – great. Me mam put all the sharp knives into hiding for months. But I don't get it. How is what you wanted to do as a kid relevant to who you are as an adult?'

Megan sat up straight in her chair. 'Of course it's relevant. We're still the same people.' It was this thought that had prompted Megan into choosing the exercise as she had been walking back up the high street, the smell of the warm croissants drifting up her nose and the gentle hum of Sunday morning traffic buzzing in her ears. All the desperate doubts and fears from the past week had come rushing helter-skelter to one conclusion. Perhaps her dream on Saturday night had been a pointer, with her grandma and her mother and the mirror and even the Snow White nightie all being signs that she was looking for answers in the wrong place. Perhaps the key to her future was rooted in her past? Perhaps it was her childhood that held the clues as to who she really was and what she should do? Megan turned to Cheddar and smiled. 'I'm going to ask the listeners to write about a favourite childhood game of theirs. One that involved their imagination, a made up game rather than something like Monopoly. So that they can remember what it was like to have no fear of failure or any other limitations.'

Cheddar nodded. 'And then what are they supposed to do?'

Megan stared at the wall for a moment, not seeing the clock or the laminated signs or the Lose Talk logo, her head suddenly too chock full of ideas. 'Well hopefully it will make them remember who they really are, the essence of them. And hopefully,' she looked at him and smiled. 'Hopefully they can bring that person back to life again. Do you think I should get them to actually play the game as well as write about it?'

Cheddar smiled. 'Yeah. Why not. Although I think I'll pass on the cutting up dead people.'

Megan laughed. 'Yes, maybe a pretend spaceship or horse would be safer.'

Cheddar shifted in his seat, pulling it closer to the desk. 'I was wondering,' he said cautiously. 'I was wondering if you had any copies of your book on you? I know I should have read it before, but I've – well I -'

Megan smiled and felt her face begin to flush. She wasn't sure what had happened to Cheddar but she certainly liked the transformation. He was so big and blokeish and, well, Northern, she'd always felt a little apprehensive talking about coaching with him, not sure if he didn't find the whole concept, and therefore her, a complete waste of time.

'I don't have a copy on me but I could bring you one next week, to the dinner party, as a gift.'

Cheddar shook his head. 'Oh no, look I wasn't trying to be a tight wad or owt, it's just that I looked in Waterstones in the week and they'd sold out, so I though it might be quicker, easier to buy a copy off you.'

Megan shook her head. 'Don't be silly. You don't have to buy a copy. You're the producer of the show. You should have a copy. And you've been so supportive since I've started, it's the least I could do.'

Cheddar smiled. 'Well if you're sure.'

'Of course I'm sure.'

'Sound.' He looked at the clock. 'Okay, ten minutes to go. Let's see if her highness has got any calls lined up yet.'

Megan watched as Cheddar got up from his seat. What a strange turn of events. She had come to work expecting to have lost a new friend not made one. But maybe this was all part of the weirdness she seemed to have triggered by leaving Gerry. It was as if a box of fireworks had been ignited beneath her ordered life, causing sparks to fly in any and every direction. And now anything seemed possible, from getting thrown out of nightclubs to getting invites to dinner parties from six foot skinheads. A prospect she found both thrilling and terrifying in equal measure.

chapter Forty-Four

"Loss is as big a part of life as breathing. But after loss comes renewal
– a chance to grow, to learn, to start over again."
Megan Rowe, 'Help Yourself to Happiness.'

'Now you promise you'll be back for Thanksgiving?'

Danny smiled at his mom across the kitchen table. 'Of course I will. You think I want to miss one of your turkeys?'

There was an awkward silence for a moment, then his father got up and walked over to the stove. 'Never mind her turkey, what about my pancakes? You got room for one more, Dan?'

Danny nodded. 'Sure.' He looked down at the table and grinned. The green chequered tablecloth was littered with glimmering trails of maple syrup, specks of scrambled eggs and splashes of fresh orange juice. He felt about as stuffed as a Thanksgiving turkey but the offer of another of his dad's thick, buttery pancakes was too good to refuse.

'Let me get you some more coffee,' his mom said, leaning over to refill his mug.

Danny watched as she poured the thick dark liquid into the cup, her slender arm dusted with freckles and lined with bangles, glinting amber and gold.

'Thanks mom.'

Over at the stove there was a loud hiss as the batter hit the hot pan and instantly the smell of pancakes blended with the rich aroma of the coffee. Danny sat back in his chair and smiled. As the sun poured in through the kitchen window he felt awash with a contentment he hadn't felt in years. In the four days he had been home all the tension and anger and guilt that had eaten its way to his very core like a cancer seemed to have miraculously gone into remission. Washed out on a tidal wave of tears by day and then at night, when he collapsed back into his old childhood bed he had been taken by a sleep so deep and dark and dreamless he woke each morning feeling as if he had been purged. It was as if whilst his body shut down, the curse that had plagued it for so long was somehow spirited away on the night air, drifting through the drapes and out through the open window to the creaking chorus of the cicadas.

'Here you go, son,' his dad said, coming over to the table holding the griddle pan, a pink gingham tea towel slung over his huge forearm. Danny held out his plate and smiled.

'Thanks, pops.'

'Uh-huh.' His dad flipped a golden brown pancake on to the plate and went back to the stove. 'You want another one, Rosie?'

Danny's mom shook her head and patted her tiny stomach. 'No thanks, honey, I'm about fit to burst. So Danny, how long do you figure it'll take you to write this book of yours?'

Danny shrugged. 'I'm not sure.' He laughed. 'It took me about a month to write the opening paragraph so I wouldn't hold your breath.'

'But -' his mother looked away, frowning as she gazed out of the window. 'You don't think you'll be going back to the photography. To the wars.'

Danny shook his head and smiled. 'No. I think I've had my fill of blood and gore for one lifetime.'

Again an awkward silence descended upon the kitchen, broken only by a hiss of steam as his father rinsed the griddle pan under the tap.

'So, what time is your flight again?' His father asked as he sat back down at the table and took a sip from his coffee.

'A quarter to twelve. You guys really don't have to take me to the airport you know, I can easily get a cab.'

Both his parents shook their heads in unison.

'Don't be stupid,' his father said. 'Now have you fixed him some food, Rosie? You know those folks don't know how to eat properly in Europe. It's all kid sized portions and vegetarian baloney.' He shook his head and sighed.

Danny's mom nodded. 'Yes, honey.' Then she looked at Danny and smiled before getting up and opening the fridge door. 'Now I've made you a fresh tub of barbecue and two blueberry pies. Oh, and I've got a ham you can take too.'

'A ham?' Danny stared aghast as his mom removed what looked like half a pig from the fridge.

'What about a nice piece of steak?' His father turned to him, his face wracked with concern. 'I guess you haven't eaten much beef in a while, what with being in Iraq and then London.'

Danny looked at him baffled. 'They do get meat in England, pops.'

'Yes but it's all insane isn't it?'

'What?'

'All that mad cow business. Heck son, you've got to take some Texan beef back with you. No mad cows over here, no sir. You got any steak in that refrigerator Rosie?'

His mother smiled. 'Sure.'

Danny laughed and shook his head. 'And what do I tell customs when they find half a farm yard in my case?'

'Tell 'em you're bringing some decent meat with you. Some sane beef. Tell 'em man cannot live on lettuce leaves alone. Tell 'em you're an American.' His father bellowed proudly. Danny half expected him to burst into an impromptu chorus of "The Star Spangled Banner."

'Hmm,' he replied.

'So what do you think you'll do once you've finished the book?' His mom asked as she began placing tubs and boxes and foil wrapped carcasses on the table in front of him.

Danny shrugged. 'I don't know.' He looked up at her and smiled. He had never thought that far ahead. Never been able to. But now, now anything seemed possible. He felt a tingling in his belly he hadn't felt, well since he'd graduated. 'I might try and get a job for *National Geographic*,' he started to laugh, 'Heck, I might even hire myself out as a wedding photographer. One thing I do know though,' and he looked over at his dad. 'I'm going to be seeing a hell of a lot more of you guys.'

His dad looked across the table at him, his hair as luminescent as freshly fallen snow in the sunshine, and he nodded.

His mom walked around the table and stood behind him. She put her arms around his shoulders and rested her chin on the top of his head. Danny closed his eyes and inhaled her delicate, rose scented perfume. 'And you'll call us won't you?'

Danny nodded. 'Of course.'

'And email.'

His father tutted. 'What's wrong with a letter. The boy can write can't he? Jeez he's writing a book, I'm sure he can manage a letter.'

'Your dad isn't much of a fan of the internet revolution,' his mom said with a laugh as she patted Danny on the head and walked back around the table.

Danny chuckled and watched as his father snorted and got up to take the dishes over to the sink. 'Information super highway, my backside.'

'He thinks it's all a conspiracy to stop people going out,' his mom explained as she began packing Danny's food into a bag.

'Of course it is,' his father retorted. 'All that virtual reality nonsense. What the heck's wrong with real reality? Eh?'

Danny grinned and shook his head. 'Don't worry, pops. I'll write you a letter.'

'Yes, honey and he'll get a carrier pigeon to fetch it over to you. I guess he'll get it before he reaches eighty, eh Dan?' his mom said with a playful laugh.

Danny nodded. 'I guess so, depends on the racing pedigree of the pigeon.'

'All right, all right,' Danny's father began making his way over to the door. 'Just going to check the oil in the truck,' he said giving Danny's hair a playful tousle as he walked by.

Danny watched as his mom began loading up the dishwasher. 'Hey, mom, leave them, I can do that.'

'No, no, you relax son. You've got a big trip ahead of you,' and she turned to him and smiled. And the smile reminded him of something. A picture perhaps? Or maybe it was yet another childhood memory? Danny smiled back. And then he knew. It was Faria and the way she had looked at Ali that day. The day of Nasir's funeral when Ali had gone crazy throwing all the toy cars. The look she had given him, the look that had made every last particle in Danny come slamming to a stop, it was the very same look his mom was giving him now. All this time he had felt certain he hadn't deserved to be on the receiving end of such burning unconditional love. But his mom had forgiven him, hadn't she? She had listened to what had happened, what he had done that night and she had still loved him in spite of it all. And if she could forgive him, then surely he could forgive himself? Danny looked down at his lap and began fiddling with the edges of the tablecloth. Then, accosted by yet another childhood memory, he lifted it up and felt for the drawer beneath. Absently he started sliding it back and forth as he remembered the way he and Marty had slid that same drawer into each other all those years before. He closed his eyes and heard Marty's laughter echo around the kitchen. *Gotcha Dan-Dan!* He smiled and pulled the drawer out and looked inside. It was empty. No more neat piles of place mats or shrivelled up remains of unwanted food. Just some jagged etchings in the wood. He pulled the drawer out further and studied the uneven letters.

MARTY AND DAN-DAN ROCK!

Danny traced his fingertips over the grooves in the wood and smiled, his eyes filling with tears as he imagined his kid brother sitting exactly where he sat now crouched over the drawer chiselling away with his pen-knife. He thought of Marty's shock of white blonde hair and his clear blue eyes with the ever-present glint of mischief. And he thought of how kind and funny and warm his kid brother had been and how many countless possibilities had died along with him on that humid September night. All the people Marty could have loved, all the possible paths he could have taken, all the lives he could have created all trickling away along that pale linoleum out into the dusty forecourt. Then Danny thought of himself, sitting on that same floor, cradling his dying brother and he realised that it wasn't just Marty who lost his life that night. As Danny had sat there crying and screaming and watching that river of blood flow out of the door his own dreams and aspirations had all been swept away too.

'You okay, son?' His mom asked walking over to him. Behind her the dishwasher began humming into life.

Danny pushed the table drawer shut and wiped his eyes. 'Yes I -'

Hi mom sat down opposite him and took hold of his hands. 'He would have wanted you to be happy, you know.'

Danny closed his eyes and swallowed hard.

'He loved you so much. You were his big brother, his hero. He was so proud of you.'

Danny shook his head.

'We all are.'

Danny felt her squeeze his hands tighter.

'Let it go, Dan. For Marty's sake. Let it go and enjoy your life. It's what we all have to do.'

Danny looked across at his mom. Her hair hung loose around her shoulders, a glorious frizz of strawberry blonde and as she began to smile he felt a rush of love so fierce he could hardly speak. He nodded and smiled.

'Let's be a family again,' she whispered. 'Please.'

Danny nodded again.

'He's still with us you know. In our hearts and in our memories he'll always be alive.'

Danny looked around the sunlit kitchen, at the cupboards and the stove and the notice board and the table. His mom was right. Marty was everywhere. Darting around amongst the dust motes, etched into their hearts as well as the very fabric of the place. '*You're still here, aren't you?*' he asked in his head. And over the hum of the dishwasher and the sound of his father singing out in the yard he swore he heard '*You betcha Dan-Dan,*' dancing in on the breeze.

chapter Forty-Five

"We all need a home. Somewhere we feel safe and wanted and loved. My home is the epicentre of my world and absolutely crucial to my happiness," Megan Rowe, 'Help Yourself to Happiness.'

'All right, love, fancy a dance?'

Against her better judgement Megan glanced over her shoulder in the direction of the squeaky voice. From beside the doorway of Manor House station an old man was leering at her. His face was the colour and texture of corned beef, topped with tufts of greasy grey hair springing out from beneath a battered trilby hat. Slowly he extended his trembling arms towards her and shuffled a couple of dance steps in time to the pulsing drum and bass coming from a car stereo somewhere on the Seven Sisters Road.

'No thanks,' she said, forcing a hasty smile before turning right on to the bustling Green Lane.

'Never mind, maybe next time, eh?' The man called after her.

As Megan jostled her way past a crowd of people at a bus stop she fought to keep the usual feelings of dread that accompanied a visit to her mother's at bay. So she had been accosted by a drunk almost as soon as she had left the station? So the road looked even grubbier than ever despite the sunshine? So a young black woman in a hoodie was now staring at her as if she wanted to kill her? It didn't mean anything. It didn't matter. She didn't live here anymore. She was just visiting. The vision of a Monopoly board formed in Megan's mind; she was just visiting – her mother was the one who remained 'in jail.' Megan came to a halt outside the mini-market. She really ought to get a present of some kind. A hand-written sign in the window read 'Polski Zywnosc – Polish Food.' When Megan was a child most of the local shops had been run by Asians. She smiled as she remembered Mr Singh and the way he had always popped an extra couple of sweets on to the shiny silver scales as he measured out her quarter of bonbons or lemon sherberts. Now as Megan entered the shop she saw that the couple behind the counter were white and spoke with thick Polish accents. Everything was changing and moving on, not just her. Fear began prickling at her skin. Megan grabbed a bunch of rather insipid yellow chrysanthemums and took them to the counter. As the man took her money and counted out her change she searched vainly for the jars of sweets that had once lined the shelves behind him, but they were long gone, replaced by a wall of cigarettes and assorted indigestion and headache remedies. Megan took her change and made her way out of the shop. As she walked up to Woodland Grove she heard her mobile ringing from inside her bag. Stopping to take it out she saw from the display that it was Gerry. After a moment's hesitation she clicked on the answer button.

'Hello.'

'Hi Meg, it's Gerry.' His voice was soft and so, so familiar.

'Hi.' A bus roared past her and she was hit by a wave of warm air and exhaust fumes.

'I just thought I'd give you a ring, see how you were feeling after the other night.'

'Much better thanks. How about you?'

'Oh you know – muddling on.'

A lorry raced by blaring its horn at a meandering cyclist.

'Where the hell are you?' Gerry asked, 'It sounds like the M25 on a bad day.'

Megan laughed and turned into Woodland Grove. The Kings' Arms was still there on the corner, tattier than ever, it's peeling red paint faded almost pink in the morning sun. 'I'm in Finsbury Park, I've come to visit my mum.'

'Oh, I see. Well say hello to her from me.'

'Yes, yes, of course.'

'So have you had a chance to you know, have a think about things?'

Megan took a deep breath. All she seemed to be doing these days was think. It was a shame she couldn't seem to come to any conclusions. 'Yes, kind of,' she replied.

'And?'

'And what?'

'And have you decided what you're going to do?'

'Er -' Megan walked on up the road to the first block of flats. *Earmarked for regeneration* a sign proudly proclaimed above a burnt out bin. 'I don't know, it's a little difficult to talk right now. Perhaps I could call you later?'

'Why don't you come round here?'

'What?'

'Tonight. Come home and I'll cook you dinner.'

Megan sighed. Come *home*? Didn't he understand, she no longer had a home? Megan glanced across the stubbly grass slope running between the tower blocks. Despite having spent fifteen years of her life here, she couldn't even call this place home, she had been so desperate to escape from it.

'Meg?'

'Okay,' she replied, needing to get rid of him. 'Okay, I'll come by about seven.'

'Really?'

'Yes. Now I'd better go, I'm almost at my mum's.'

'Great. Okay. Well I'll see you later then.'

'Yes. See you later.'

Megan switched off her phone and came to a halt just beside her mother's block of flats. But before she went in through the cracked glass doors she turned and looked back at the grass slope. How many hours had she spent playing out on that slope? How many times had she pushed her doll's pram back and forth, chattering away to her glassy eyed, peachy plastic baby about what they were going to have for dinner and what they were going to do when daddy got home. Megan couldn't help smiling as she stared out over the grass. Somewhere in the distance she heard a door slam and the echo of footsteps along a passageway. The estate had been brand new when she and her mum and her grandma had moved there back in the early seventies. The paintwork had been bright and shiny and the freshly laid grass had been lush and green. She remembered one morning going out to discover someone from the council had been to mow the grass and it lay everywhere in thick, sweet smelling clumps. Megan had eagerly got to work, moulding the mown grass into narrow lines, marking out the foundations of a house. A small square for a kitchen and two larger ones for a living room and bedroom, all with small gaps in between for doors. She had played in her sweet-smelling grass house for hours that day, furnishing the kitchen with her doll's china tea-set and the bedroom with old towels for blanket beds. Megan sighed and looked down across the slope to where Haringey lay spread out like a model village. As with everything else the skyline had changed somewhat since her childhood, but she could still see the same office blocks and factory chimneys nestled amongst the new glass-fronted structures. 'Wave to daddy,' she used to say to her doll, waving her small plastic arm at one of the buildings in the distance. For that was where her fictional daddy worked before coming home to them in their grass house. The daddy in her childhood games always came home. Megan gulped. Had she been trying to magic the perfect family into existence way before her grandma even gave her the Mirror of Serendipity? Building houses out of grass and conjuring imaginary husbands and fathers out of thin air? But Gerry wasn't imaginary. He was real and he was her husband and Laurence's father and he wanted her to 'come home.' She could still go back. It wasn't to late. Did she really want to end up all alone and miserable after working so hard to achieve her dream? Megan turned back to the entrance of the flats. This was what her mother saw day in day out. This miserable tatty block with its boarded up windows and stubbly grass and burned out bins. No wonder she was depressed. Megan wanted to turn and run. If she went in now, if she told her mother what had happened; that her marriage had failed and she too was now on her own, would that be the end? Would she follow her down the path of doom and gloom, hiding away in her bed and popping prescription pills for the rest of her days?

'Meg?'

Megan turned to see her mother coming up the footpath behind her. 'Mum.'

Her mother was wearing her favourite green coat, a sixties swing style that Megan had bought her from a shop on Chiswick High Road. As usual she looked painfully thin, her brown doe eyes even larger than ever and her dark hair hanging in wisps over her shoulders, but she was smiling and holding out her arms. Megan breathed a sigh of relief. It was a good day. Not only was her mother up and about, but she looked really happy. She stepped forward into her embrace.

'How are you mum? You look really well.'

Her mum took a step back and continued to smile. 'I'm good thanks. I think it must be seeing the sunshine at last,' and she gestured to the pale blue sky.

Megan nodded. 'Yes, it certainly took its time coming this year didn't it? I got you these,' she handed her mother the flowers.

'Thank-you, they're lovely. I've been out, getting cakes,' her mother explained as they made their way into the entrance of the flats.

Megan swallowed and tried not to notice the sour smell of stale urine. 'Oh lovely.'

'Yes. I got iced buns. Do you remember how I used to get you iced buns every Friday after school.'

'Oh yes.'

'And you used to eat all the bun first and leave the great strip of icing till the end.'

Megan laughed. 'Yes, and one day Grandma hid my icing when I wasn't looking.'

Her mother turned to face her, her eyes wide with mock horror. 'They must have heard your screams all the way to Chelsea. Here we are then, home sweet home.'

Megan waited while her mother fetched her keys from her shabby canvas rucksack and opened the door. Inside the hallway felt cold and dark. Once again Megan felt a rush of nostalgia for Nightingale Avenue and Gerry. Is this really what she wanted - to end up cold and alone like her mum?

'How's Laurence?' Her mother asked, leading her into the small kitchen. Megan did her customary quick scan, but it looked reasonably tidy, with only a couple of dishes in the sink. Sometimes when she visited, when her mum was going through a bad patch, the counters would be lined with dirty cups and the congealed remnants of ready meals.

'He's fine,' she replied.

'Still mad on his cricket?'

Megan laughed, 'Oh yes.' She watched as her mother went over to the kettle and began filling it with water. This really was a good day. Often when she visited her mother would be in the grips of a depression so deep it would be hard to get two words from her, let alone enquiries about Laurence.

'And Gerry?'

Megan felt a rush of panic. What should she say? Should she tell her right now and risk ruining her mother's good mood? 'He's fine,' she replied. 'Sorry I haven't been around for a while but things have been a little hectic at home.'

Her mother put the kettle on, took off her coat and sat down at the small formica topped table, prompting Megan to follow suit. 'Don't worry about it. I understand.' Her mother clasped her hands together and looked off dreamily into the distance. 'I've been pretty busy too, you know.'

'Have you? Doing what?'

'I've been having a bit of a clear out.'

'Oh.'

'Yes. It was after listening to your show on Sunday actually.'

'You – you listen to my show?' Megan's face began to flush.

'Of course I do. Sometimes I forget, or I'm asleep, you know,' she looked at Megan and Megan nodded. 'But usually I put it on. Anyway, when you were talking about the exercise of the week, you know about remembering your childhood games.'

'Yes?'

'Well it made me think about the games you played as a little girl.'

'Really?' Megan was so used to thinking and worrying about her mum, she had stopped even contemplating that her mother might actually think about her.

The kettle spluttered its way to the boil and clicked off. Her mother got up and fetched two cups from the cupboard. 'Coffee?' she asked.

'Yes please,' Megan nodded. 'So what did you remember?'

'The dressing up box,' her mum replied. 'Do you remember how you used to love that fur hat of Grandma's?'

Megan laughed. 'That's funny, I was only thinking about the dressing up box the other day.'

'Well I've got it out for you.'

'What? You still have it?' Megan began to tingle with excitement.

'Yes it was in the cupboard next to the bathroom – and the dolls house.'

'My dolls house. Where?' She looked about the room eagerly.

Her mother finished making the coffees and brought them over, her eyes were wider than ever and she was smiling broadly. She looked as excited as Megan felt, like a young child. 'Come on they're in the living room. You'll never guess what else I found.'

Chapter Forty-Six

"We transmit our emotions to all around us
and they in turn to all around them.
Today radiate happiness and know that the knock-on effect will
reverberate far and wide, to places and people you won't even see."
Megan Rowe, 'Help Yourself to Happiness.'

'Chuffin' 'ell,' Cheddar grunted as he heaved one sturdy leg over the end of the see-saw. If his mam could see him now! As soon as his foot touched the other side and he sat down on the bright yellow seat his weight sent the see saw plummeting and his arse crashing to the ground. 'Chuffin' 'ell.' Cheddar gripped on to the orange handle in front of him and took another furtive glance around the park. Mercifully it was still empty. It was only a small park, tucked away behind the run down houses and tatty shops lining Hammersmith Grove. Cheddar had first happened upon it when he'd just moved to the area and been looking for an emergency pharmacist. Desperation after a particularly nasty bout of food poisoning had led him through the dark green gates between the barred up bookies and cab office, but rather than find an oasis of indigestion remedies all he'd found were a patch of unkempt grass, a net-less tennis court and a couple of token swings. And the see saw. Cheddar tightened his grip on the handle. Why the heck did it seem so small? Okay, what was it he used to yell? As if he didn't know. Cheddar took a deep breath before muttering, 'Yee ha!'

He shook his head despairingly. What the heck was he doing? And more to the point, why? Much as he liked and respected Megan he really didn't see what possible use there could be in reliving your childhood games. Not unless you had a burning desire to get carted off to the funny farm. He thought back to the days before the Strike, before his mam had had to go out to work and how she'd always taken him to the park on the way home from school. 'You be Calamity Jane,' he used to tell her, 'and I'll come and rescue you from the Red Indians.'

'Chuffin' 'ell,' his mam would sigh, before clambering to the top of the climbing frame, the tops of her pop socks showing beneath the hem of her skirt and a fag dangling from her brightly painted mouth. 'You'll have me in A and E with a hernia, soft lad.' But she always did it, always played along. Even used to scream if there weren't too many folk about. 'Help me help me, I've gone and got myself captured by those pesky Injuns.' Cheddar chuckled as he remembered his mam's attempt at a wild west accent, about as wild west as West Thurrock. He began bouncing up and down on the see saw, the sunlight beaming down on his face. He closed his eyes and began to grin. He was back in that park in Doncaster, felt Stetson tied to his head, plastic cap-gun tucked into the waist of his school trousers. Faster and faster he bounced, his legs stretching and bending to support his weight.

'Ride 'em cowboy,' he yelled, lifting up the see saw. 'We gotta git them pesky injuns.'

Cheddar nearly had a heart attack when he heard a woman coughing loudly behind him.

'Mummy, mummy, what's that funny man doing?' A child's voice enquired, much to Cheddar's complete and utter horror. He remained frozen, half squatting over the see saw, not daring to turn around.

'I don't know darling. Let's go to the other park, there are better swings.'

'Oh but mummy, I wanted to go on the see saw. I want to play with that man.'

'No darling. Come on.'

Cheddar remained motionless until the plaintive sound of the child crying and pleading had completely faded away. Letting go of the see saw he lifted his leg back over and turned around. The park was empty once more. But not for long, Cheddar thought. Not once that traumatised mother had got on her phone to the old bill, social services and the NSPCC. Cheddar strode hastily towards the park exit. What on earth had he been thinking? Attempting a rooting, tooting cowboy impression in a kiddies park. Him a grown man? But as soon as he reached the safety of the road outside he couldn't help laughing. It had been fun, pretending to be a kid for a moment. Remembering a time when imagination had made anything possible – even being able to transform his plump homely mum into a beautiful, butt-kicking, damsel in distress. And as Cheddar continued to walk along Hammersmith Grove, cars, trucks and motorbikes whizzing by in the sunshine, he finally realised what Megan had been getting at. If he was at one time capable of imagining himself as a gun toting Western hero, then why the hell couldn't he imagine himself as a healthy, trim, fun-loving father and devoted husband? Cheddar chuckled and let out a whoop, 'Yee ha!'

*

An hour later he was back at home, having bought his daily selection of rabbit food from Tesco Metro and taken out two cookery books from the library. Cheddar opened his smoothie and took a swig. The sweet blend of strawberries and banana felt like velvet on his tongue. He smiled. This healthy living malarkey was definitely getting easier. Now, he would just go on-line for a few minutes, before planning the menu for his dinner party, and check out some fitness websites for a few tips...

But once he had logged on he couldn't resist going straight to his blog. In the three days since he had published his 'Perfect Day' he had been inundated with messages, way more than he'd ever received for any single posting, and to make it even better the messages were all so touching and genuine. It was as if by opening up to his readers he had enabled them to open up too. Not only had he had people offering their encouragement and support but some of them had posted verbal snapshots of their own dreams too. Cheddar clicked on to his website. YOU HAVE 5 NEW POSTS the message at the bottom of the screen informed him. Hastily Cheddar clicked on 'read.' As before they were all extremely positive – a guy from Staffordshire telling him to 'seize the day.' Another bloke from Hove saying that his greatest dream was to own his own hair salon. Two from site regulars Meathead and Webscribe offering their congratulations and best wishes and one from a fellow blogger called Netspeak simply saying 'Respect!' But nothing from *her*.

Cheddar shook his head and took a bite from his apple. What was up with him? Why did he keep thinking about Bambi? Why was he so concerned about her reading his blog and her response? He took a moment to analyse his motives. He wasn't some scary stalker type, it wasn't as if he was fantasising about her or anything creepy like that, but he just had a feeling, that was all. From the moment she had first posted a message on his blog he had sensed a kindred spirit. There was something about the humour in her first posts that had made him think she was his type of lass. Then, when she had requested the Plaice of Birth reading and he'd been sure he'd detected a sense of sorrow between the lines it had made him concerned, the way he would be for a friend. But they weren't friends, not even really acquaintances, never even met for Christ's sake. But still – he had a feeling. Absently, Cheddar clicked on his email account and saw he had one hundred and twenty-seven new messages. He sighed. The problem with having a website was that you were susceptible to an onslaught of junk mail. He scrolled down numbly hitting delete every time he saw mention of 'jackpot winner,' crazy love meds' and 'penis extensions.' And then amongst all the promises of sexual magnificence and financial nirvana he saw an email entitled 'THANK-YOU!!' from someone called Laura Jones. Thank-you? What for? Cheddar scratched his stubbly head. He didn't even know anyone called Laura Jones. Curious, he clicked on the mail.

Dear Cheddar, he read,

I am just writing to say thank you so much for your blog on Sunday. I had been away for the weekend and so have only just read it, but I have to say it is one of the most beautiful and moving things I have read in a long time. The description of your 'Perfect Day' felt so warm and heartfelt, I can't quite believe you're not already living it, you certainly deserve to be. Recently I have been through a pretty tough time. At the end of last year I was diagnosed with breast cancer and although they caught it very quickly and I only required a lumpectomy, the treatment has been very gruelling and unfortunately I have lost my hair. I know this probably sounds really shallow, after all what's losing your hair when you could have lost your breast, or even worse your life? But I have been finding it pretty hard to deal with. However, reading your blog on Sunday made me remember just how lucky I am. I'm still alive and more importantly I am still able to dream. Last night I sat down and wrote about my own 'perfect day.' Needless to say I had a full head of flowing hair from the very first line! But it also reminded me of all the other things I want. For months now all I've focused on is beating this thing and I think in a weird way while fighting to stay alive I actually stopped living. Does that make sense? Anyway, all that is beginning to change and it's largely thanks to you. The sun is shining. Spring is finally here and the first tufts of my hair are starting to grow back. Now you've inspired me to write about my dreams I'm determined to start to live them. Your blog has been such a godsend to me, keeping me smiling through the darkest times, but now I can honestly say it has changed my life. Thank you so much and please keep up the good work,

With warmest wishes

Laura (aka Bambi) xxx

Cheddar sat back in his chair and scratched his head. Chuffin' 'ell! He didn't know whether to feel happy or heart-broken. Bambi had written to him, but Bambi had cancer. He took a swig from his smoothie and looked about his room. Sunlight was streaming in through the window and outside, above the rumble from the flyover and the clattering of dishes from El Paso below, he could hear a bird chirping. Cheddar turned back to his computer and scrolled back through her words. 'Beautiful,' 'moving,' he couldn't quite believe the adjectives being used to describe his blog. To think that he, Cheddar Bailey had been able to help someone through their darkest hours, that he had even 'changed her life,' well, it was too much to comprehend. Cheddar shook his head as he continued to stare at the screen. He, Cheddar Bailey had made a difference. To a woman he had never met – Bambi or Laura – he had actually made life a little easier for her. He gulped and turned to look upwards.

'See dad, I'm not such a waste of space after all,' he whispered, tears burning in his eyes. Blinking hard he looked back at the screen and began to smile, before clicking on reply.

chapter Forty-Seven

"When we act out of anger or fear our actions will always rebound on us."
Megan Rowe, 'Help Yourself to Happiness.'

Megan licked the last sticky traces of icing from her fingers and kneeled back on the threadbare living room carpet. Fanning out in a circle all around her were the contents of the battered cardboard dressing up box and in front of her sat her doll's house.

'I thought you got rid of all this when I went to Uni,' she said, turning to look at her mother who sat behind her cross-legged on the faded two-seater sofa.

Her mother shook her head and frowned. 'Of course I didn't.'

'But you - ' Megan broke off and turned back to examine the clothes. She picked up the black fur hat and placed it on her head. It no longer fell straight down over her eyes, but fitted perfectly.

'I what?'

Megan took a deep breath and pretended to study the seam on a pink satin glove. 'You threw out all of Grandma's stuff.'

'Do you want another bun?' Her mother's voice seemed to have cranked up an octave.

'No thanks.' Megan looked at the dolls house. She remembered the moment she had first laid eyes on it, on the toy stall at her school Christmas Bazaar. The roof had been dented and two of the windows had been missing, but she had fallen in love with it on the spot. Her mother had told her they couldn't afford it, but three weeks later, on Christmas Day, it had somehow magically appeared with the other presents under the tree, spruced up and fully furnished. Her mother had even painted a clambering rose over the door. Megan stared at the faded blotches of pink and green. Then she opened the front and peered inside. There, as if she'd never left them were her family of dolls. The two rubber children propped on chairs at the kitchen table in front of miniature plates of painted food and the china mum and dad, lying prostrate on the double bed upstairs.

'I had a bit of a play with it last night,' her mother said from behind her. 'Thought I'd get it ready for you.'

Suddenly Megan was consumed by a completely unexpected rage. How dare her mother play happy families? 'Do you remember that time I painted flowers all over your bedroom?' she asked, the words bursting from her mouth before she had time to stop them.

'Er- I don't know.'

Megan spun around, her eyes burning with the onset of angry tears. 'You must do. It was when I was about ten years old and you hadn't got out of bed for weeks.'

Her mother pulled her legs up in front of her and wrapped her arms around them tightly. 'I don't think I do.'

'Oh come on mum. I crept into your room one night and painted flowers all over the walls, the way you'd painted them on my dolls house because I thought it might cheer you up.'

Megan watched as her mother began rocking gently backwards and forwards. 'I don't know Meg, it's all a bit hazy.'

'But it didn't work, did it? Nothing worked.' Megan took the fur hat off and flung it to the floor. 'Why couldn't you have been a proper mum?' She was crying now and aware that everything she was saying was deeply unfair, God knows she'd studied depression enough to know there was nothing anyone could do or say to lift that black cloud when it descended, but still. All those years of trying to do the right thing, of being the parent rather than the child, there were so many things bottled up unsaid. 'Then dad might not have left.' There, she'd finally said it. Finally spoken the accusation that had plagued the darkest reaches of her mind for most of her life.

'I'm sorry,' her mother's voice was little more than a squeak.

'Gerry and I have split up,' Megan said flatly, turning away to shut the dolls house. She gulped to try and prevent the avalanche of tears, but to no avail. She hugged her arms to her chest and let them flood out.

'I'm so sorry,' her mother's voice was closer now and suddenly she felt her thin arms wrapping around her. Megan turned, blinded by hot, angry tears and grasped hold of her. 'I've left him, mum and I'm so scared.'

'It's okay,' she felt her mum's thin fingers stroking her hair, pushing it back from her tear-streaked face.

'Is it?' Megan blinked and looked at her and saw her eyes were full of tears too. 'It doesn't feel okay. It feels terrifying. I feel I've let Laurence down. I feel such a phoney.'

'What do you mean?' Her mother continued to stroke her hair.

'Millions of people all over the world have bought my book, millions of people listen to my show. But how do I have any right to tell them how to be happy when my own life is such a disaster? I'm like the tailor from the Emperor's new clothes' Megan covered her face with her hands and continued to sob.

Her mother looked at her, shocked. 'But your life isn't a disaster. It's amazing. You're amazing. I'm so proud of you Meggy – everything you've achieved.'

Megan stared at her. 'But you've never - ' she couldn't bring herself to say it.

'Never what?'

'You've never said.'

'Said what?'

'That you're proud of me.'

Her mother looked away and wiped her face with the back of her hand. 'I felt too ashamed.'

'What?'

'You've always been so successful. Going to university, getting a degree, becoming a psychotherapist and then this life coaching thing. I felt ashamed Meg.'

'Ashamed of me?'

'No – myself.'

Megan sat back and stared at her. 'I don't understand.'

'Look at me, Meg,' her mother gestured down at her thin body and then around the shabby living room. 'Look at my life. Do you think I feel proud of what I put you and Grandma through? I can't help it Meg, it's like living in this horrible nightmare world where someone's come along and scoured away all of the sparkle. And I get so tired and all I want to do is hide away from it all. But it doesn't mean I don't love you, or I'm not proud of you. Sometimes I even think of you as my angel.'

Megan gasped. 'What?'

'You're so positive and full of light. I can't believe I actually created someone like you. People like you bring sparkle to the world Meg, don't ever lose that.'

'But Gerry and I have split up. I'm all alone.'

Her mother shook her head. 'No you aren't.'

'What do you mean?'

'You still have Laurence don't you?'

'Yes.'

'And you still have your friends?'

'Yes.'

'And you have me – for what that's worth.'

Megan gave her a teary smile and took hold of her thin hand. It was icy cold. She wanted to rub it warm.

'And you have your work.'

Megan snorted. 'Great, conning people.'

Her mother sighed. 'Don't you understand. Going through hard times doesn't make you a sham, if anything it makes you more genuine.'

'How?'

'Because you have a deeper understanding. You've always been such a kind person, Meg, so thoughtful and caring. That's why people buy your book and listen to your radio show, because you understand what it's like to go through hard times.' Her mother began picking at a frayed hole in the carpet. 'I'm so sorry. I wish you'd had it easier. Really I do.'

Megan put her arm around her mother's bony shoulders and hugged her close. 'I know, and I'm sorry too, for saying all of that stuff. I was just lashing out, looking for someone to blame.'

Her mother looked up at her and smiled. 'I don't mind you being angry with me, Meg, but please don't be angry with yourself.'

Megan nodded.

'It wasn't all bad, was it?' Her mother asked, staring at her anxiously.

Megan looked at the dolls' house and the dressing up clothes, the source of endless hours of magic and make-believe. She looked back at her and smiled. 'No, it wasn't,' she replied. 'Not at all.'

Chapter Forty-Eight

"Who would play you in the movie of your perfect life? Who would you cast in the lead role and why? What and who do you aspire to be?"
Megan Rowe, 'Help Yourself to Happiness.'

The sunlight was beating down in blinding shafts on Shepherd's Bush Common causing Natalie to pull her velvet cap further over her eyes. Everything seemed too bright, too noisy, too dirty. From the thumping bass-lines and rumbling engines of the snarled up traffic, to the hordes of people cluttering the dusty pavements. She turned the corner and came to a halt as the Theatre on the Green slid into view. Her heart began to pound. She had to see him. It was no good. For three days now he hadn't returned her calls or texts and with every day that her phone remained silent and the inbox displayed no new tiny envelopes, a sickening dread was gestating inside her. He couldn't dump her, not now, not like this. Not after she'd let down her guard to him. Not after she'd let him in. Natalie scanned the street before weaving her way through the stationary traffic. A guy in a gleaming BMW looked at her from behind a set of designer shades and his moth curled into a lecherous grin. Piss off, Natalie thought venomously, a cold sweat erupting on her skin as she marched past the car and over to the theatre. She had no idea if Gerry was even there, but she had to do something. When she had woken up that morning she knew she couldn't face another day of waiting and wondering, another day trapped in the flat being plagued by her thoughts. Taking a deep breath she stepped up to the small wooden side door and pressed the intercom. There was no reply. Natalie stood there motionless. Now what? She knew he lived in Chiswick, in a road called Nightingale Avenue, she could remember that from when he had got into the cab, another time he had been trying to get away from her. Natalie's face began to burn. How could she have been so stupid? She slammed her fist against the intercom, leaving it there for a good few seconds. What if she went to Nightingale Avenue and tried every house until she found him? What if –

'Hello.'

Natalie jumped as the woman's voice crackled out of the intercom.

'Hello, can I help you?'

Natalie composed herself and moved her face close to the speaker.

'Yes, I'm here to see Gerry Radcliffe,' she shouted over the roar of the traffic. She clenched her fists tightly as she ran through her story in her head – here for an audition, been sent by my agency, can I just come in and see him anyway. But to her surprise she didn't need it. After a couple of seconds silence the door buzzed open.

Natalie climbed the steep narrow steps to the theatre, her heart in her mouth. This was it, there was no backing out now. Should she appear angry or upset? Or should she go for the sympathy vote and pretend something terrible had happened?

'Natalie. What are you doing here?'

Natalie looked up to see Gerry at the top of the stairs. It was too dark to make out the expression on his face, but the tone of his voice was one of shock.

328

'Why aren't you returning my calls?' Natalie asked as she reached the top of the stairs. Gerry was wearing a pair of faded jeans and a white linen shirt, untucked. His hair hung in dark curls nudging the top of the collar. He looked as he had done on the day of her audition, rugged and dashing, his cheekbones chiselled by the shadows of the half-light.

'Something's happened. I needed to talk to you.' Natalie bit her lip as she gazed up at him. Distraught, that was the way to play it. She turned away and brushed her eye as if wiping away a tear. From inside the theatre she could hear voices ringing out. Rehearsals. No doubt for the play she was meant to have been cast in.

'Look, come with me. Come back stage for a minute. I need to talk to you too.'

Natalie felt a surge of relief as Gerry took her by the hand and began leading her down the narrow passageway that led backstage. Once she had him alone she knew she would win him back. When she told him how she'd had her drink spiked and been taken to a flat and attacked. Then he'd be sorry he hadn't returned her calls. Then he'd be sorry he'd gone to see his stupid son on Friday night instead of staying with her.

Gerry opened the door to one of the dressing rooms and turned on the light. Natalie glanced about as she followed him in. One day this would be her very own dressing room. When he cast her in the lead role for his next production. That would be her mirror surrounded by golden lights. Those would be her beige-streaked, crumpled up make-up wipes. That would be her chair; that would be her costume rail.

'Sit down,' Gerry said, pointing to one of the chairs.

Natalie sat but Gerry remained standing by the door, staring down at his thumbs as he brought them together and clasped his hands. Right, she would have to work fast, get straight to the point; burst into tears. But before she could do anything he spoke.

'There's something I need to tell you.' He looked at the door, then back at his hands. 'You see, my wife and I, well.' He stopped again, sighed and finally met her expressionless gaze. 'We're making another go of it.'

'What?' Natalie gripped on to the edge of the chair.

'I'm so sorry. I feel utterly dreadful. After everything that happened after the audition I know how this must look. But if it's any consolation, I really did have powerful feelings for you. If we had met in another lifetime well who's to say, but -'

'You're making another go of it?' Natalie stared at him.

'Yes.'

'But you said it was over. You said she'd left you. You said I was -'

'I know,' Gerry interrupted, 'And at the time I truly believed it was over, but she came to see me on Friday night -'

'What?'

'My wife. She came to see me on Friday night and -'

'What time on Friday night?'

'What time?' He looked at her for a moment, puzzled. 'Oh no. I know what you're thinking, but I honestly had no idea. When I left your place I was going to see my son, I promise, but then she turned up back at home later on. Much later on and – well we had a long talk and -' he tailed off.

Natalie continued to stare at him, darts of red hot anger causing sparks to appear before her eyes. 'You decided to make another go of it?'

Gerry looked down at the floor. 'Yes.'

'I see.' Natalie looked about the room as if for inspiration. What should she do? She had been prepared for him to give her the cold shoulder, for excuses like age difference, needing some space, needing more time, but this? Getting back together with that smug arrogant bitch. The bitch who had left her on Friday night, left her to be used and abused by two coke heads, and all the while she had been getting back together with Gerry. Gerry who had only left her flat a few hours earlier. The pair of them reminiscing about past times, no doubt having reunion sex while she had been - Natalie gagged and brought her hand to her mouth.

'Are you okay?' Gerry asked, taking a step towards her.

'I'm fine.' Natalie got to her feet. No wonder the bitch had barely said two words to her in the studio on Sunday night after her crawly-arsed apology. She had no use for her any more, did she? Not now she was getting back together with her arsehole husband. And to think she had even taken Megan shopping, taken her under her wing. This was how she was rewarded. Well they deserved each other, the pair of users. Natalie made a dash for the door.

'Natalie! Are you all right? Natalie?' Gerry called as she barged past him back to the stairs. She had to get out of there, get some fresh air.

'What do you care?' she yelled, almost stumbling in her haste to get down the stairs. 'You selfish bastard.'

chapter Forty-Nine

"Try to imagine your emotions as colours and as you drop down into a deeper meditative state, work your way slowly and surely through the spectrum until you reach the brilliant gold of love and release."
Megan Rowe, 'Help Yourself to Happiness."

The sun was setting as Megan made her way along Nightingale Avenue painting the sky a glorious spectrum of burnished red, deep violet and vivid blue, all reflected on the gleaming fronts of the houses lining the street. As Megan took in the large sash windows glinting gold beneath their brow-like gables and the brightly painted doors, many of them framed with clambering wall flowers, she was reminded of her dolls' house. She wondered what kind of dream world she would create if she were to play with it now. Would there be a mum and dad upstairs in bed and two children down in the kitchen as her mother had constructed, or would the little wooden dad be out at the pretend pub and the mum be all alone and crying drawn-on tears? As Megan saw her own house come into view she wondered why there were no doll's flats. Brightly painted small apartments for single mum dolls and their kids. She smiled as she pictured opening up the front and peering inside. She would have the little rubber son sat on a chair eating miniature plastic pizza but what about the mum? Megan stopped at the gate. The mum would be dancing on the rickety wooden table, a broad painted smile lighting up her face.

Grinning, she walked up to the front door and knocked loudly. The stained glass panel was a riot of colour in the setting sun. Everything suddenly seemed beautiful and right.

'You didn't have to knock,' Gerry said, opening the door with a flourish. He was wearing a navy apron over his shirt and jeans and was smiling broadly. 'Come in.'

As Megan stepped inside, the rich aroma of tomatoes and basil came rushing out from the kitchen to greet her. Gerry shut the door behind her and led her down the hall.

'How was your mum?'

Megan couldn't help giving a wry smile, he really was trying to impress. 'Great, happier than I've seen her in a long time.'

'Good. Good. Here, let me take your coat.' Gerry stopped and turned in the kitchen doorway, grinning at her and holding out his hands expectantly. Megan looked at him. Her first love, the father of her child, her husband of fifteen years.

'I can't,' she whispered.

Gerry's face froze. 'Can't what?'

'I can't stay. Can't come back. Can't be married to you any more. It's over.'

Gerry looked at her for a second before turning and walking slowly into the kitchen. 'But I thought -'

Megan stood in the doorway. A large saucepan was bubbling away on the stove and mellow jazz was drifting from the radio, the music and the aroma forming a perfect symphony in the air. The pine table had been laid with two place settings and a copy of 'The Twelve Steps' lay on the side. She felt a pang of complete and utter sorrow.

'But I've cooked. And I've been to AA again.' Gerry pointed to the book. 'I mean it Meg. I'll do it this time, I promise. I don't want to lose you. You and Laurence. I'm – I'm scared.'

Megan walked into the room and took hold of his hands. Gerry looked away towards the cooker, distraught. Fingers of steam began pushing out from beneath the saucepan lid.

'You'll be fine Gerry. You haven't lost Laurence. He's a little angry that's all. Just give it some time.'

'But you. What am I going to do without you?' As he looked at her imploringly his dark eyes filling with tears. 'You're my – you're my – my everything.'

Megan reached a hand to his face and gently stroked his cheek, tracing the contours slowly as if trying to commit them to memory. 'I'm sorry, Gerry. I tried. All these years. I tried so hard, But - ' She swallowed hard to prevent herself from crying. 'You know it too, if you're honest with yourself. It's been over for ages.'

Gerry turned away, his shoulders convulsing with deep, silent sobs.

'I just didn't want to give up. I don't want to let go,' he whispered, turning back to her, his face slick with tears.

Megan looked at him and nodded, her own eyes filling. 'Me too.'

They stood there for a moment, in the kitchen, the pan bubbling, the jazz playing, just staring at the floor. Then Gerry took a step towards her and wrapped his arms around her tightly. 'I don't want to let go,' he whispered again, into her hair, before inhaling deeply.

Megan nodded, shaking with silent tears. 'I know. But I just can't take any more of the pain - and the loneliness. I've been so lonely, Gerry. So lonely.'

She disentangled herself from his arms and wiped the tears from her face. 'Good-bye.'

Trying to ignore his low, gasping sobs she turned and walked into the hall and through the front door. Once outside the fresh air felt cool as spring water on her face. She stopped for a second, took a deep breath. The sun had set and the sky was turning a dark plummy blue. Slowly and slightly unsteadily, Megan began making her way back up Nightingale Avenue and as she did so part of her was crying out for Gerry and their home and the safety of the familiar, but another part seemed to be fluttering like a butterfly around her heart. And as its eager wings flapped faster and faster it spoke of freedom and hope after so many years of hurt. Megan stopped beneath a streetlight and stared up at the sky. The first stars were beginning to appear, pale pinpricks of silver in the deep blue. And there, in the inky twilight she took a deep breath and imagined releasing that butterfly, finally letting it fly free. And as she continued to stare upwards she could almost see the gossamer wings, glowing amber in the fading light as they soared higher and higher into the velvety night.

chapter Fifty

"What was your favourite fairy story as a kid?
What was it about the hero or heroine that you could identify with?
What parts did you wish for your own life?
Megan Rowe, 'Help Yourself to Happiness.'

As Natalie wearily emerged up the final set of steps from the Hammersmith underpass Neptune Mansions loomed into view. She laughed out loud, a brittle little laugh, as she thought back to the day her mum had brought her here, six months previously, and how she'd actually thought the red bricked building with its wrought iron balconies and aqua green turrets looked like something out of a fairytale. Oh it was that all right, Natalie thought to herself with a frown, but rather than being the fairy tale castle where Prince Charming married Cinderella it was more like the tower from Rapunzel. Yes, ever since she had been installed in her top floor flat, directly beneath one of the turrets, she had been like the poor beautiful Rapunzel locked up in the tower by the evil witch. The evil witch that was her mother. Natalie stomped across the concourse and out from the darkened shadow of the flyover, studiously avoiding the Apollo Theatre to her left and the bollards where Gerry had serenaded her only a couple of weeks before. How could she have ever thought he would be the one to rescue her? Her knight in shining armour? She shook her head in disgust. Just as she reached the entrance to the flats and began keying in the entry code for the door she heard someone shout.

'Natalie.'

Shit, it was that lard-arse Cheddar, the last person she wanted to see. Pretending not to hear him Natalie hurried into the foyer. Luckily a lift was waiting and she rushed in and hit the button for the sixth floor.

Moments later the lift juddered to a halt and Natalie got out and made her away across the carpeted landing to her front door. As soon as she opened it she was hit by the stale mix of perfume, wine and cigarette smoke. Since she had got back from the radio station on Sunday night she had lost herself in a fug of alcohol, nicotine and depression as she waited vainly for the phone to ring. For Gerry to ring. But not any more. Natalie marched into the kitchen, where the marble counter was littered with dirty wine glasses, ringed with the crimson residue of countless bottles of merlot. She had never really liked red wine before Gerry, but now it was all she wanted to drink, loving the burning sensation it caused at the back of her throat and the way it warmed her empty stomach.

After Natalie had left The Theatre on the Green, Gerry's words ringing in her ears and sickening dread clawing at her stomach, she had staggered, zombie-like to Shepherds Bush station and boarded a train into town. She couldn't remember getting out at Oxford Circus or how long she'd spent roaming around the gargantuan Top Shop in a trance. Fingering random clothes, picking up random shoes, allowing the throbbing beat from the super sonic stereo system to send her deeper under. Finally, when tiredness began to wear its way through the numbness she somehow got on the escalator and allowed it to carry her back out into the real world. Losing herself in the crowd she had traipsed along Regent Street, head down, charting an unsteady course through the hordes of tourists and business people and laden down shoppers to board a train at Piccadilly Circus and come back home.

It was only now as she stood in her cold, stale-smelling kitchen that reality began to take hold. Natalie stared at the shards of glass still littering the counter. Gerry had dumped her, just like that. The way a child might dispose of a plaything once they had grown bored of it, once something better came along. Natalie thought of Megan and her stupid skinny body and her nasty stringy hair and the way she seemed to think she had all the answers. The smug arrogant bitch. And what a liar. Telling Natalie her marriage was over when clearly it wasn't. Telling her they had 'grown apart.' Obviously not that far apart. Natalie grimaced. And to think she had trusted Megan, taken her into her confidence, taken her for coffee, taken her shopping, taken her for a girls' night out. And all the while she was planning on crawling back to Gerry. What a bitch. If only Gerry knew what a two-faced liar he was married to. Maybe then he wouldn't be so quick to get back together with her.

Natalie picked up one of the empty wine bottles lining the draining board and lifted it to her lips. There was about a mouthful left. Natalie downed it in one. Then she put the bottle back down and opened the cupboard where the spirits were housed. Most of Gerry's vodka was gone too, but there was enough for about one decent sized drink. Natalie tipped the remains into a mug and took a gulp. She gagged but managed to keep it down. Why did it always end like this? Why was she always the one who lost out? Instinctively she turned to her painting, the crimson slashes looked almost black in the twilight and as always the hollow eyes stared down at her accusingly. Natalie bit her lip. How different would it have been if her witch of a mother hadn't made her do that terrible thing?

'I'm sorry,' she whispered to the painting. The eyes in the painting continued to stare down at her angrily. Natalie picked up her handbag from the counter where she'd left it and took out her purse. With trembling fingers she opened a small zipped compartment in the centre of the purse and pulled out a square of paper. TAYLOR-CASSIDY NATALIE 38878459 OXFORD GENERAL HOSPITAL , the tiny writing at the top of the paper read, above the grainy black and white image. Natalie studied the blurred outline of the huge oval head resting on top of a tiny body and then looked back at her picture, where exactly the same outline had been magnified in angry slashes of black and red.

'I'm sorry,' she cried this time, holding the copy of the scan to her chest. 'I didn't know what to do. She didn't give me a choice.'

Natalie took another swig from her mug of vodka. When she had told her mum she was pregnant, her mum had said two things. The first was 'you must never tell your father,' and the second was 'you're to get rid of it.' By that point the scandal about her and Mr Keller had already got out. He had been suspended from the school and she had been alienated by the entire village. Mrs Keller was the village nurse and as such had Florence Nightingale status. It was all too easy for the do-gooders and the gossip-mongers and the hacks at the local rag to paint Natalie as a wanton teenage temptress, out to seduce school masters and wreck homes. Natalie looked at the picture of the scan and instinctively put a hand to her stomach. At least they never got to add murderer to the list – her mother had seen to that. A quick day trip to a private clinic on Harley Street and the legacy of her shameful behaviour had all been sucked away. Sucked away on a river of blood. Natalie looked back at the picture and the angry dark red streaks. Hot tears began burning at her eyes. She remembered lying on her bed back in the Cotswolds, just before she'd told her mother.

Stroking her stomach and listening to a Whitney Huston CD. And vowing to the tiny person growing inside her that no matter what happened, no matter what shit people threw at her she would always love them. She would always protect them. She would always be their mum. And always, always be there for them. But then she had told the witch and the witch had made her do the most shameful thing of all.

Natalie looked around the kitchen despairingly. Why had she done it? Why had she gone through with it? Why hadn't she just told her mum to get lost and run away and had the baby all by herself? The questions that had been plaguing Natalie for six long months echoed louder and louder in her head. The questions she had tried to drown out with music and men and even drugs. But now there seemed to be no silencing them. She had almost told Gerry that Friday night. When he had asked her about the painting. She had been so close to revealing all, even showing him the scan, the way parents show off pictures of their off-spring. But then he had been in such a rush to get to his son, the moment had been lost. That would teach her for lowering her defences. But she had learnt the hard way, yet again. That the only person you can rely on in this life is yourself. Not parents who are never there for you or teachers who tell you 'you've changed their life' and artistic directors who tell you you're 'fucking amazing' before running back to their wives. Natalie looked at the broken glass on the counter. But what kind of person was she, to have fallen for their crap? What kind of person was she to have listened to her mum and ended up killing her own child? Natalie picked up a jagged shard of glass and yanked up her sleeve. She was stupid, stupid, stupid. A stupid, dumb, idiot. She pressed the edge of the glass into her arm and tore it downwards. At first she felt nothing and then a lovely warm ache. A trickle of blood formed against her snowy white skin. It looked beautiful, sacred almost. Blood, like the blood from her baby. She held her arm up towards her painting as if offering some kind of sacrifice. And finally all the questions and accusations ringing around her head fell silent.

Natalie jumped as her mobile began ringing. Could it be? She grabbed a tea towel and pressed it to her bleeding arm before fumbling in her bag for the phone but when she retrieved it the display read 'private number.' After a moment's pause she clicked on the answer button.

'Hello?'

'Er, all right Natalie, it's Cheddar – from Loose Talk.'

Natalie grimaced. What the fuck was his problem? Stupid fat stalker, hanging around outside her flat, now calling her. Yet another pathetic man – and one who even needed to pay for women he was that desperate. Natalie couldn't help smirking as she remembered the phone call she'd listened in on a few weeks ago at work, when he'd actually rung a hooker and booked a shag. God it had been cringe making.

'What do you want?' she replied sharply.

'Oh - well I was just checking if you were still on for the dinner party on Saturday night?

Natalie leant against the counter, the phone clamped between her shoulder and ear. She cautiously peeled the tea towel from her arm and watched as a new rivulet of blood began snaking down towards her wrist.

'Dinner party?'

'Yes, remember, I asked you and Megan about it at the studio on Sunday?'

'Oh yes.' Natalie licked her arm and her mouth filled with the metallic taste of blood.

'Is Megan still coming?'

'Yes – and me American mate, Danny. Should be a right laugh.'

'Mmm.'

'Good chance for us to get to know each other a bit better, out of work like.'

'Mmm.'

'So – can you still come?'

'Oh yes.' Natalie reached over for her mug of vodka and took a swig.

'Really?'

'Yes. You're quite right. It is about time we all got to know each other better. I think it's a great idea.' And for the first time in days Natalie's mouth twisted into a smile.

Chapter Fifty-One

"Physical exercise is key to our mental well-being. Numerous studies have shown the benefits of keeping fit for sufferers of depression."
Megan Rowe, 'Help Yourself to Happiness.'

It was early Saturday morning and a daffodil yellow sun bathed Hammersmith in a buttery glow. All along King Street café doors were being flung open with a burst of warm cappuccino scented air, tables were being wiped and pastries gently heated in preparation for the first of the day's customers. Glinting cars purred around the Broadway and hummed across the flyover. Florescent clad road sweepers strolled along, bags in hand, clearing away the debris from the night before; the cans and the bottles, the papers and the cigarette butts. Inside the still deserted shops, lights flickered into life and speakers began reverberating with the first of the day's bouncy pop tunes. And down on the bank of the River Thames Cheddar was dying.

Or at least he felt as if he were dying, as his heart pummelled his rib cage and his face spewed sweat in an attempt to keep up with Danny as they ran along the path. Cheddar looked down at his trainers, just visible beneath the bottoms of his baggy jogging pants and attempted to focus on some kind of rhythm. Perhaps if he sang one of those army marching songs in his head? *One, two, three, four, United States Marine Corps.* Cheddar's belly felt as if it were about to drop off as it flopped up and down against his groin. Hmm, perhaps not. He took a huge gasp of warm spring air and tried again. *One, two, three, four, what the hell am I doing this for?*

'You okay?' Danny asked, looking back over his shoulder with a relaxed grin.

Bastard! Cheddar thought, making a conscious effort not to sound like a strangled cat as he struggled for air. How could Danny make this look so effortless? He'd had six pints the night before too. And he was jet-lagged. Jesus! Why on earth had he suggested this? Was he completely insane? Cheddar shook his head, causing sweat to cascade down onto his Metallica t-shirt. It was no good, he was going to have to stop. He was far too fat to run and far too young to die.

'Here, do you think we could just rest up a bit. I can feel that ale from last night coming back up to say hello.'

Danny trotted to a standstill, beneath his crumpled white t-shirt and silhouetted against the sun his shoulders looked firm and toned. 'Sure. You want to sit down?' And he nodded to a bench situated a little way back from the path on a grassy verge.

Cheddar nodded, hauled himself over the verge and collapsed down on to the seat. 'Chuffin'ell! How do you do it, mate? I'm cream-crackered.'

'You're what?' Danny sat down next to him looking puzzled.

'Knackered. I'm knackered and we've only done about a mile.'

'Actually, I'd say it was only about a half mile,' Danny said, running his hand through his sandy hair. He didn't have a single bead of sweat on his forehead, Cheddar noted with disgust before wiping his own face with the back of his hand. It came away absolutely drenched.

'Everyone's got to start somewhere,' Danny continued, bending to adjust the lace on one of his trainers. 'I've been running for years. You wait - a couple of weeks with me as your trainer and you'll be running marathons. They don't call me Mad Dog Nilsson for nothing you know.'

Cheddar stared at him in alarm. 'You what?'

Danny burst out laughing, 'I'm joking, man.' He slapped Cheddar on his knee. 'You'll be fine. So, you want me to bring anything to this dinner party tonight?'

Cheddar shook his head. 'No mate, just yourself.'

Danny smiled and leaned back on the bench. 'How many others have you got coming?'

'Just two.' Cheddar leant back on the bench and shut his eyes, thankfully his breathing was starting to come back under control, he now sounded like a chain-smoking asthmatic rather than a dying animal. 'Megan Rowe, the life coach I told you about the other week, the one whose show I produce, and Natalie. She answers the phones on the show.'

'Oh. Right.'

There was a flatness to Danny's voice that made Cheddar open his eyes and glance at him. He was staring out across the water, his face expressionless.

'You'll like Megan,' Cheddar said, cautiously. 'She's great, a really nice person. I think she's going through a bit of a rough time at the moment though between you and me.'

'Oh really?' Danny turned to look at him. 'So what's this Natalie like then?'

Cheddar frowned and looked away. Down on the river a rowing boat slid past, the oarsmen rigid in concentration as they pulled their way through the sparkling water. 'Yeah, she's all right.'

'You don't sound too convinced.'

'Yeah well she's not really my type.'

'Uh-huh. So are you sweet on this Megan character then?'

Cheddar frowned and shook his head. 'No! Well, I mean, she's a lovely lass and all that but – well we work together and – no. Anyway there's someone else.'

'What? Coming to the dinner party?'

'No. Someone else I like. Actually, I was wondering if I could ask your advice?'

Danny let out a throaty laugh. 'My advice? On women? Oh man. I'm not sure that's such a good idea. It's a bit like asking Tom Cruise for advice on being tall.'

Cheddar stared at Danny in disbelief. How could he not know all about women? He was fit and handsome and funny, plus he had all that messed up cop shit going on. Surely lasses must fall at his feet. 'Well it's either you or Ray,' he replied with a grin.

'Jeez! Okay ask me,' Danny laughed.

'There's this lass.'

'Yeah, there usually is.'

'And I really like her. Well I think I do. It's so bloody weird. I mean I just have this feeling about her. I can't really explain it, like. It just feels as if I've known her forever, that she's my kind of lass. You know what I mean.'

Danny nodded. 'I think so.'

'And the thing is I haven't even met her or owt -'

'What?'

'I haven't met her.'

Danny shook his head in mock dismay. 'Oh hey, you're not going to tell me she's called Jennifer or Angelina are you?'

'Piss off!' They looked at each other and started to laugh. Cheddar began fiddling with the drawstring on his jogging bottoms. 'No, it's nowt like that. It's someone I've met online.'

Danny nodded. 'Oh I see. In a chat room.'

Cheddar shook his head. 'No. Through my blog. I keep this online diary thing. I don't know why I started it really – for bit of a laugh I suppose and I think I needed summat to take me mind off other stuff. I'd just been dumped by me girlfriend and me dad had died and –' he broke off and stared up the path where some kids were fooling around on a skateboard. 'Anyhow. Anyhow, this lass started emailing me. Just jokey stuff at first, but it was like we were on the same weird wavelength, it was great. But now. Well it's got a little bit more serious.'

'Go on,' Danny was staring at him intently.

'Yeah, well, I published this piece, you see, this serious piece. Most of what I put on me blog is a load of nonsense really, but last week I decided to try summat different, summat really personal and she sent me this dead nice email back, saying that I'd changed her life and everything.'

'Wow.'

'I know. And now I just can't stop thinking about her and I really want to meet her but I don't know if there's any point. What if she thinks I'm a nutter or summat? I don't want to lose her friendship.'

Danny shook his head. 'I can't see that happening.'

'Why? She doesn't really know me from Adam. She's not going to agree to meet me is she? It'd be like arranging to meet a stranger.'

'Are you sure about that?'

'What?'

Danny leant forward. 'That she doesn't know you? You said yourself that what you published was really personal and it obviously touched her. I'd say she has a pretty good idea of who you are.'

'Yeah but –'

'But what?' Danny got to his feet and stretched his arms over his head. Cheddar couldn't help glancing at his toned torso enviously.

'You gotta seize the day, man. Or seize the chick. Or whatever. Go for it!' He gave Cheddar a broad grin, his blues eyes sparking in the sun. Cheddar couldn't help smiling back. He'd noticed a change in Danny the moment he saw him in the pub the night before, the way he was laughing with Ray at the bar and now as he stood in the sunshine. He looked relaxed, younger somehow, like a weight had been lifted. He must have been homesick before.

'You reckon?' he asked.

Danny nodded. 'For sure. Life's too short. Why don't you just email her your phone number and leave it up to her. Say you'd like to have a chat. Nothing too heavy.'

Cheddar nodded. 'Yeah. And that way I don't look like a mad stalker.'

'Exactly – let her find that part out later.'

They both laughed.

'And hey,' Danny added, 'If it does come to anything for Christ's sake don't take her to the Prince Albert. One look at Ray and she'll be running for the hills.'

Cheddar grimaced at the thought of Ray slathering all over Bambi / Laura and asking her if she wanted to see his pork scratchings. 'Too right.'

Danny turned and nodded towards the river. 'Look at the way the sun's falling on the water.'

Cheddar got up to stand beside him and followed his gaze. Thin shafts of sunlight were shimmering through the wall of pine trees on the other bank and across the gently lapping river. 'Great isn't it?' he replied. 'About time we got some decent weather after the winter we've had.'

'Man, I wish I had my camera,' Danny sighed.

Cheddar looked at him and grinned. In the pub the previous night Danny had spent about half an hour telling him that his career as a photographer was well and truly over. 'Once a photographer always a photographer, eh?' He said.

Danny laughed. 'I guess.' Then he looked all around him and nodded. 'Yeah.' He slung an arm across Cheddar's shoulders. 'Tell you what, maybe I'll bring my camera tonight. Just in case we get any Kodak moments during dinner.'

Cheddar smiled. 'Yeah, that would be great. Really great.' He started to walk back to the path. 'Come on – lets go and get a celebratory fry-up.'

Danny followed behind him. 'What are we celebrating?'

'Me not having a heart attack,' Cheddar replied with a grin.

chapter Fifty-Two

"Faith is the magic potion that makes dreams come true. When you have faith in yourself and your own abilities anything is possible."
Megan Rowe, 'Help Yourself to Happiness.'

Megan pulled the kaftan over her head and shimmied her arms through the sleeves. As the delicate chiffon folds skimmed down over her, goose bumps fizzed beneath her skin like soda. She smoothed the top down over her new, perfectly cut jeans and smiled. Earlier that afternoon she'd gone back to the boutique off King Street she'd visited a couple of weeks before with Natalie and bought the top she had tried on. The top Natalie had hated. Megan studied the emerald green folds and their swirling pools of embroidered gold. So what if she looked like Robin Hood, she liked the top and that was all that mattered. Over at the bedroom window the setting sun was filtering in between the new lilac drapes and projecting rainbow beams through the crystal hanging in the centre. The crystal was new too, bought along with the top and the drapes on her shopping trip earlier. Suspended from a thin translucent thread, it was shaped like a giant bevelled tear-drop and supposed to bring the owner great spiritual wealth.

Megan watched as a breeze from the window caused the crystal to cast Tinkerbell-like beams all over the pale lilac walls. It had been a lovely day. Laurence had invited her to his cricket match in the morning and as she had sat there on the boundary in the shade of a stooping willow tree, she felt as if her heart might burst with pride. She could hardly believe that the young man bowling the ball at such a terrific pace, the young man hitting the repeated sixes, the young man who seemed so popular with his coach and team-mates was her very own son. And as she sat there, being soothed by the gentle hiss of a distant sprinkler and the hum of a hedge trimmer and the crack of leather on willow, she had the overwhelming sense that everything was going to be all right. That at last she was living the life she was supposed to, like an author who has been blocked for years and finally discovered the magic plot.

After cricket she had taken Laurence and his friend Joe into Hammersmith for some 'well phat' fried chicken before leaving them to an afternoon of virtual sports on the play station while she hit the shops, determined to buy some fitting accessories for her new life. And now, having accessorised herself and her room, she was getting ready to go to Cheddar's dinner party. Megan thought back to all the Saturday nights she had spent in on her own. All the Saturday nights rooted to the sofa, flicking through the television without really watching, skimming through books without really reading, drifting through life without really living. She walked over to the white chest of drawers by the window and picked up her new pair of earrings, two emerald droplets encased in burnished gold. As she hooked them into her ears she glanced out of the window. Down below Turnham Green High Street was getting ready for the night ahead too, decorating itself with glittering lights and twinkling signs to entice hungry eaters and thirsty revellers to its plethora of restaurants and bars. Megan smiled. For the first time in years she felt properly alive. It felt simultaneously terrifying and breath-takingly exciting. She moved over to the wall beside the window, to where she had hung her Grandmother's mirror, took a deep breath and stared into the glass. She studied her gleaming hair and wide eyes, the faint lines on her forehead, the dimples like quotation marks either side of her mouth. If she looked hard enough she could make out the traces of all her previous incarnations. The frightened young girl with the wispy hair and dimples. The determined student with the solemn eyes. The lonely young woman desperate for love. The unhappy wife with the haunted stare. The loving mother and daughter and grand-daughter. Megan brought her hand up to her face and stroked her cheek. They were all there, all those people, like a set of Russian dolls, all slotted away inside of her, making her solid and complete; but now, now she was finally free from fear and disappointment she could start afresh. Continuing to gaze into the mirror, Megan began to smile. She reached out and touched the gnarled frame. 'I'm ready,' she whispered into the oval shaped glass.

*

As Cheddar stood in the doorway between his kitchen and living room he felt a surge of happiness so strong it nearly knocked him off his feet. Behind him in the kitchen a pot of French onion soup was bubbling away on the stove, a carnival of King Edwards, sweet potatoes, parsnips and butternut squash were sizzling in the oven around a huge lemon basted chicken, and a tray of sage and onion stuffing balls were waiting to join them on the counter. The smell of caramelised onions competed with the roasting chicken to send Cheddar's stomach into a frenzy of gurgling and growling so to distract himself he strolled into the living room and proudly surveyed the scene. In front of him his new fold-out table was bedecked in a crimson cloth, Mediterranean style place mats and gleaming cutlery denoting settings for four, and all around the room candles of all shapes and sizes, from whopping great pillars to tiny little tea lights, flickered and glowed in the early evening twilight. It was so warm he had been able to leave the window wide open, allowing a gentle breeze to dance through the flat. Unfortunately the roar from the flyover had waltzed in with it so he'd had to put on a bit of Bonnie Tyler to recreate the right ambience. At the moment Bonnie was singing about 'holding out for a hero' and as Cheddar straightened up one of the placemats on the table he couldn't help feeling slightly heroic himself. Who would have thought that in just a few weeks he could have clambered from the depths of single-bloke-in-bedsit-land-despair to the dizzy heights of the dinner party? He looked around the living room, which had previously been a study in mustard and beige and now, with the help of the crimson tablecloth and a few cushions and throws was a veritable riot of colour. Who would have thought that he could have achieved such a transformation? Cheddar grimaced as he leant over the table to adjust another placemat and felt a twinge of pain shoot up the back of his leg, but almost immediately his scowl transformed to a grin. This post-run twinge must be what all athletic types have to endure. He chuckled. Not only had he transformed his flat but slowly but surely he was beginning to transform himself. His waist was decreasing a belt notch every week and he'd finally started running. Chuffin' 'ell! Cheddar went back into the kitchen and poured himself a celebratory glass of Cabernet Sauvignon. He hadn't thought it possible he could feel this good. He might not be living the dream quite yet, but bloody hell it felt great just trying. He took a sip of the wine and allowed the rich flavour of chocolate and berries to seep down his throat. Not only had he transformed his flat, begun transforming himself and invited some friends round to dinner, but he had also just given his phone number to a lass. He, the man who was usually too shy to even give a lass a nod. He, the man who was so socially inept when it came to women he had actually...

Cheddar frowned. Now was not the time to torture himself with past misdemeanours. The point was all that nonsense was in the past. Things were finally starting to look up, he was staring to change. When he had got back from his post-run fry-up with Danny (in a tremendous feat of will power he had swapped the fried bread for two slices of wholemeal toast and drunk black tea) he had gone online and before any negative voice in his head could talk him out of it he had emailed Bambi his number. 'If you ever want to have a chat,' he had written in the title line. Short and sweet and all he had dared type. Now he gave a heavy sigh and wondered if maybe just maybe one day he would be making dinner for Bambi. He took another sip of wine and went over to check on the soup. It was bubbling away nicely, a rich deep brown. He inhaled deeply before putting the lid back on. Over on the stereo Bonnie Tyler began belting out 'Total Eclipse of the Heart.' Cheddar grabbed a wooden spoon from the counter and began singing along, using the spoon as a microphone. Had there ever been a better, more emotional song, he wondered. "Stairway to Heaven" was unbeatable of course but "Total Eclipse" was definitely coming a close second. Cheddar glanced at the clock. Right, he'd better put the stuffing in and get preparing the cheesy herb bread, his guests would be arriving soon. He put down his spoon microphone and began hacking away at a French loaf and as he cut the bread into thick fluffy white wedges he wondered how his guests would get on. Hopefully Danny and Megan would be fine, but as always he felt a little uncertain about Natalie. Still, it was a dinner party. Once they'd had a drink everyone would be bound to relax. Yes, they were bound to get on like a house on fire. Cheddar frowned and put down the knife. Perhaps he ought to check on the candles?

Chapter Fifty-Three

"Ask yourself, what is perfect? Is it fame or money or power and the illusion of what they bring? Or is it the joy in the everyday? The love and laughter of family and friends, the pleasure of seeing a flower bloom or a sun set? Does perfection already surround us every day?"
Megan Rowe, 'Help Yourself to Happiness.'

Beneath the foremost green turret of Neptune Mansions Natalie sat perched on her kitchen counter, clad in her satin night robe and staring blankly out of the window. The last crimson rays of the setting sun were creating a blood red backdrop to the Broadway Shopping Centre and casting the room in a harsh amber glow. Natalie started from her trance as down below her Megan emerged from the shadow of the underpass and began making her way past the Apollo Theatre. Natalie moved closer to the window and shook her head in disbelief. The bitch was wearing that green top. She must have gone back and bought it despite what Natalie had said. The truth was the top had looked all right, the green had gone pretty well with her hair and eyes, but that wasn't the point. Natalie had said it looked crap so Megan should have listened. She watched as Megan disappeared from view around the back of the shops, followed closely by a sandy haired man. So she wasn't bringing Gerry with her then – that was a shame. In the couple of days since Cheddar had rung, Natalie had gone over various dinner party scenarios in her head. And by far her favourite had been the ones where Gerry had been there too, on the arm of his recently reconciled wife. Oh the look she'd imagined upon his face as she'd waltzed into the room. 'We've already met,' was to have been her opening line upon being introduced. And then she would have waited, bided her time, watching him sweat before revealing all. Still, Natalie could have just as much fun without him there. The amount of dirt she had to dish would cover three courses at least. Yes, this would be a dinner party to remember all right.

Natalie sidled down from the counter and smiled. Finally she had a chance to get her revenge on Gerry Radcliffe and his smug wife and that sleazy fat lump of a producer. But then her heart began to pound as she thought of the reality of what she was about to do. Could she really go through with it? Could she really say those things? She walked over to the breakfast bar and picked up her glass of wine. They had it coming to them, the lot of them. She was so sick of other people treating her like shit. This was her chance to get her own back good and proper. But did she really have the nerve to go through with it? She looked around the kitchen at the newly daubed red paint splattered across the snowy white walls. Of course she did, she could do anything.

The previous day Natalie had gone into town and bought herself some paints. And although she had also bought a sketch pad and easel, as she had sat there in front of them, brush poised but nothing coming, she had felt a wave of anger so strong it had swept her on to her feet and carried her around the flat like a tornado, stabbing and daubing at everything in her path. Now she looked at the red slashes adorning the walls and smiled. It was as if the entire kitchen had become an extension of her painting, an extension of that anger, as it bled out across the walls. She turned to look at the raven black eyes at the centre of the painted storm and sighed. They seemed less intense now, less condemning. Natalie took another swig of wine and tightened her silk gown around her. Perhaps it was starting to realise that it wasn't all her fault. That she had only been doing what her mother had told her, that she had been lonely and scared and assumed her mother knew best.

But look at what had happened. Despite the evening's warmth Natalie couldn't help shivering. She'd done as she'd been told, got rid of her baby and slunk off to London while that bastard teacher had gone grovelling back to his wife. She'd tried to reinvent herself, tried to make a career in acting, only to get trampled on yet again by a bloody man. Shame and humiliation began twisting Natalie's heart like a Chinese burn and her mouth was flooded with a metallic tasting bile. *Pathetic. Pathetic. Pathetic.* She put down her wine, her hands trembling. How had she let this happen to her? Why had she allowed so many people to walk all over her? She was pathetic and stupid and weak. Natalie flung open the drawer in front of her and grabbed her sharpest chopping knife. *Pathetic, weak, bitch.* She pulled up her silk gown and pressed the point of the knife to one of her milky white thighs. As she dragged the blade down towards her knee she felt a rush of warmth and release. As if all the pain inside of her had been allowed to burst out, like a boil being lanced, and now the poison was seeping away, leaving a blood red trail down her leg. Natalie gave a heavy sigh and put the knife down on the counter. Now she was ready. Now she felt strong enough. Now there was to be no more slinking off, tail between her legs. Now she was going to do things her way. She took a large swig of wine in an attempt to get rid of the metallic taste burning the insides of her mouth. She was going to call the shots from now on and never, ever let herself get hurt again. She tore a piece of kitchen towel from the roll and pressed it against her leg. Time to get ready for her big scene.

*

Danny rounded the corner of the Apollo Theatre and began walking down the litter-strewn passageway alongside the parade of shops as Cheddar had directed. Just ahead of him a slim woman with long dark hair made the same turn. He wondered if it could be one of Cheddar's other guests? Perhaps it was the life coaching woman? Danny grimaced, he really wasn't looking forward to having to make small talk with some happy-clappy, self help guru. He was amazed a star player like Cheddar could even give her the time of day, let alone invite her to dinner. Danny couldn't help smiling as he thought back to the night he had called the show, before he had even met Cheddar and how that woman with her honey soft voice and hypnotic commands had made him so mad. It was hard to imagine getting so angry now. Since he had got back from America he had felt strangely disconnected from everything – the grotty flat, the packs of feral kids hanging around the estate, even his photographs – all seemed to belong to a different time and place, a different life, a different person.

Danny followed the woman around to the back of the shops. Her top sparkled in the setting sun, swirls of brilliant gold against a glistening emerald background reminding him of a holiday he had taken in Turkey at the end of the first Gulf war and the way the morning sun had fallen upon the Aegean sea. Since he had returned from America everything looked different somehow. Colours seemed brighter, tones richer, beauty seemed to be lurking everywhere, even in the concrete jungle of Hammersmith. And for the first time since he was a student he felt the burning desire to capture this beauty on film. Danny glanced down at the carrier bag in his hand, housing a bottle of chardonnay and a disposable camera. For some strange reason he hadn't been able to bring himself to use his old camera – perhaps it contained too many bad memories, like a haunted house, forever imprinted with all the blood and gore it had captured over the years.

Danny watched as the woman in front of him started to slow down. He hoped it wasn't the life coach, she looked kind of nice.

The woman came to a stop by one of the tall gates at the back of the shops and looked around. On seeing Danny she began to smile.

'Oh hi. You're not coming to Cheddar Bailey's party are you? I can't seem to work out which gate is his.' Her eyes were a brilliant green, just like her top and her voice was soft and smooth. Smooth as honey.

*

The man stared at Megan for a moment, completely expressionless, and then gave a small grin. 'I sure am,' he replied in a deep southern American drawl. 'It's the flat above the Mexican restaurant.'

Megan looked at him. There was something extremely familiar about him and yet she couldn't place where she had seen him before. And surely she would have remembered, he was lovely. His hair glistened the blonde gold of a sunlit wheat field and his face was chiselled and tanned. She felt her own face beginning to burn. What on earth was wrong with her? She hadn't felt like this since she was a kid. *Get a grip*, her inner voice of coaching reason scolded. *Oh if only I could*, some other, rather giggly school girl voice squealed in response. To hide her embarrassment she turned and began peering through a gap between the gate and the wall. 'I think this is it,' she said, 'I'm pretty sure it's the third one along.'

'Can you see any clues in the back yard?' The man asked, from behind her. For some completely unknown reason Megan's heart began to pound.

'Um, I'm not sure. I can see, no it can't be - well it looks like one of those bucking bronco things!' She heard a crunch of gravel and felt him move right behind her and again her heart performed a tattoo. Slowly she turned to face him. 'What do you think?'

He looked down at her and smiled. His eyes were a piercing blue against his tanned skin. 'I say we give it a go. Well, not the bucking bronco, the flat. Unless you fancy a ride?'

'What?' Megan's face flared even redder and she had to look away.

'On the bucking bronco. Do you fancy a ride?' He leant past her and pushed open the gate. The yard was filled with upturned crates and empty cooking oil drums and battered cardboard boxes and there, right in the middle, a bucking bronco, the brown leather badly scorched and slightly skew whiff. Megan followed the man into the yard. He walked over to the bronco and turned to look at her questioningly. 'Well?'

Megan stared at him. Surely he wasn't serious? 'Oh I don't -' But just as she was about to make a list of excuses why she never rode on broken down bucking broncos in dirty back yards she stopped herself. Clambering on to a broken down bucking bronco in a dirty back yard was something the old her, rigid with years of stress and fear, would never have done. But what about the new her? And what about the other 'old hers' for that matter? When she was a child she had loved riding on the automated rocking horse outside the newsagents. She had regularly begged her mum for two pence for the ride. Megan thought back to earlier that evening when she had looked into her mirror and felt like a set of Russian dolls. That little girl was still in there, still buried deep inside. Perhaps it was time to let her come out to play? 'Oh go on then,' she said with a smile as she walked up to the leather contraption. It was a lot bigger close up and for a second she wasn't sure if she was going to be able to mount it. But as if reading her mind the man grabbed a crate from behind the gate.

'Here you go,' he said positioning it just beside the battered looking beast. He was looking at her with a mixture of shock and amusement.

Fighting to keep a straight face, Megan stepped on to the crate and hoisted one leg over the bronco. She grabbed hold of the leather reins and then felt extremely silly. This was no kids' ride and she was certainly no kid. What on earth was she doing? And what should she do now? Start bucking herself? Fling herself backwards and forwards shouting yee ha? Once again she felt her cheeks begin to smart. But thankfully the man seemed to be finding it highly amusing.

'Ride 'em cowboy,' he yelled and before she could say anything he'd taken a disposable camera from his bag and was taking a picture of her.

'Chuffin' 'ell! Megan is that you?'

Megan looked up to see Cheddar standing at the top of the wrought iron steps running up the back of the building. He was wearing a red and white striped apron over his shirt and jeans and was grinning from ear to ear. In her haste to dismount the pitifully un-bucking bronco Megan slid off the leather and came crashing butt first on to the crate.

'I don't know, getting chucked out of nightclubs, falling off bucking broncos whatever next young lady?' Cheddar let out a booming laugh.

Megan tried to scramble to her feet. 'I'm sorry, I - '

'Here, let me help you.' The American man took hold of her hands and helped her up. His hands were big and strong, and covered in a sprinkling of sandy hair. And ringless, she couldn't help noticing.

'Thank-you.' She looked up and met his gaze and once again was hit by the most powerful sense of déjà vu. He seemed to sense something too as he stared for a little too long into her eyes.

'Well I see you guys have already met,' Cheddar continued from his doorway. 'Come on up and I'll get you a drink,' and he turned and went back into his flat.

Megan dusted down her jeans and picked up her bag. 'I'm Megan by the way,' she said as she followed the man over to the stairs. He turned and gestured for her to go up before him.

'I know,' he replied with a wry smile.

*

'Now are you sure I can trust you with this? You're not going to end up doing "Agadoo" out on the balcony or owt, are you?' Cheddar asked, handing Megan a glass of wine. Megan shook her head, her cheeks flushed. Although she was clearly mortally embarrassed she looked better than she had for ages, Cheddar noted. She seemed to be positively glowing, and not just from the humiliation of having fallen off Raj's clapped out bronco. Cheddar had been gutted when he'd seen Raj dragging it out into the yard earlier that day, following a rather unfortunate explosion in the bronco's starter motor. If only he'd put off playing cowboys and Indians on the seesaw, he could have recreated his childhood in his own back yard, free from embarrassment and the potential placement on any kind of social register. He looked at Megan and smiled. Her hair looked shinier than ever, and her eyes sparkled the same bright green as her top. Perhaps she'd played cowboys and Indians as a kid too. 'You fancy a beer, Danny?' he asked opening the fridge.

'Please,' Danny replied, handing Cheddar a bottle of wine. 'I brought this, to have with dinner.'

'Oh yes and I brought you these,' Megan said pulling a copy of her book and a box of chocolates from her handbag. 'I know you're on a bit of a health kick, but what the hell. You can have the occasional treat, can't you?'

'Absolutely,' Cheddar replied, helping himself to a large swig of his wine. 'Now you guys go through and sit yourselves down. I've put out some of them crude things you like Megan and I've got a bit of Bonnie Tyler on the stereo.' He ushered them through to the living room. Now it had grown darker the candles looked even more magical than before. Cheddar felt another stab of pride. 'I've just got to go and put the bread on. I hope you're hungry, cos I've got enough to feed an army.'

Cheddar sat Megan and Danny down opposite each other at the table and then went back into the kitchen. As he began arranging slices of French bread garnished with grated cheese and herbs on to the grill pan he felt a sudden pang of anxiety. What if the food tasted crap? What if Natalie was late? What if the bread burnt or the chicken was raw? Cheddar took a gulp of wine in a bid to calm himself. From the living room he could hear the soothing murmur of chatter. Megan and Danny had obviously hit it off. Cheddar gave a huge sigh of relief and put the grill pan back in the oven and turned it on. The food would be fine. They were all going to have an ace night. He thought back to his 'perfect day' exercise and the love and laughter he had lavished throughout his description of his perfect dinner party. Well now it was all, or almost all going to come true. Just minus the perfect house and perfect wife and kids. But as Cheddar opened the oven door and checked on the roasting chicken he realised that it really didn't matter. For tonight at least, his life was going to be perfect.

chapter Fifty-Four

"When you realise that you hold all of the answers; that you are the only person who can fix your life, the sense of liberation is over-whelming."
Megan Rowe, 'Help Yourself to Happiness.'

Danny looked across the table at Megan. The flickering light from the wax-spilling candle in the centre was licking at her face and causing her hair and eyes to glimmer as if they had been dusted with gold. Once again Danny felt the urge to reach for his camera. Instead he picked up his glass of beer and took a sip. He smiled as the pale amber liquid erupted in a cool fizz over his tongue.

'So, how do you and Cheddar know each other?' Megan asked before taking a sip of her wine. Man, her voice was smooth as syrup, Danny wanted to close his eyes and let it pour over him. Frowning he sat up straight. Just because the way she said things was saucy as hell, it didn't alter the things she said, and they sucked. He remembered back to the first time he'd heard her on the radio and the smug way she had talked about people not having to be victims. And the pat way she had recommended cutting and pasting as the cure for all of the world's evils. And the hypnotic way in which she had used subliminal commands and almost got him to fall under her spell. Well he mustn't fall prey to her black charms again – combined with the beer and the music and the candlelight that could be fatal. He had to stay on his guard.

'I met him at the pub around the corner, the Prince Albert,' he replied nonchalantly whilst glancing around the room. Cheddar had really done a good job with all the candles, the living room was twinkling and sparkling like an Aladdin's cave.

'Oh, I see.' Megan put her glass of wine down and helped herself to an olive from one of the dishes of appetisers dotted around the table.

'How about you?' Danny asked, deciding to feign ignorance. The last thing he wanted was her knowing he'd heard her show, then she might remember his call. He was beginning to wish he'd changed his accent as well as his name when he'd phoned in.

'We work together at the radio station. He produces a show I – er – I present.'

Danny watched as Megan began fiddling with the olive on her plate, prodding at it with one of the little wooden picks that lay beside the dish. It was kind of strange she didn't seem too eager to talk about the show. He would have imagined she'd be absolutely full of it, recommending motivational exercises and getting him setting life goals before the first course had even been served. As he wondered about Megan's lack of enthusiasm he thought back to what Cheddar had said earlier about her going through a rough time and the last time he'd heard her show and the weird garbled way in which she'd been speaking.

'What kind of show do you do?' he asked before common sense had a chance to intervene.

Megan glanced over at Cheddar's impressive CD collection stacked up in teetering piles next to the stereo. She looked decidedly uncomfortable. 'It's called Help Yourself to Happiness,' she replied. 'I'm a life coach,' she added with about as much enthusiasm as if she'd just confessed to being a sewage inspector.

'A life coach? What's that?' Man, he had to be real careful now, he was straying on to pretty dangerous territory. If she started with all her whooping and motivating he wasn't sure if he could trust himself not to make a wisecrack and then his cover would be blown for sure.

She stared at him for a second with a puzzled frown upon her face. 'That's strange, I would have thought you'd know all about life coaching.'

Danny gulped. He'd been busted, she'd recognised his voice, now there'd be all hell to pay. 'What – what do you mean?' he asked, hardly daring to look at her.

'Being American,' she replied. 'I thought life coaching was huge in the States.'

Danny breathed a sigh of relief and nodded gratefully. 'Yes. I guess so. Truth is I haven't lived in the States for a long time. I have heard the term life coach, but I'm not too sure what it involves.' Jeez, that was close, now play it cool Dan-Dan, look interested and suitably impressed. He cleared his throat and looked at Megan with what he hoped was a genuinely curious and caring expression.

Megan nodded as she resumed prodding at her olive. 'I suppose you could say a life coach helps people to regain control of their destiny and figure out what they want and how they can achieve it. It's a bit like having a fitness trainer for every area of your life.'

Danny took another swig of his beer. 'I see.' He couldn't help noting she'd left out the bit about charging people extortionate amounts of money for this dubious service.

'So what do you do for a living?'

Danny frowned. What should he tell her? What did he do? 'I'm a photographer,' he finally replied.

Megan started to laugh and a pair of dimples sprung up either side of her mouth, making her look even cuter, Danny couldn't help noting. 'Of course,' she exclaimed. He stared at her, puzzled. 'Outside, on the bronco,' she said, 'When you were taking my picture. God, I hope you don't work for any of the tabloids.'

Danny shook his head and smiled. 'No ma'am.' He pressed his thumb into the curved base of his fork and watched as the pronged end rose up off the crimson table cloth. 'No I'm a freelance.'

'Paparazzi?'

He frowned. 'No way! No I mainly work for the broadsheets. I guess you could say covering war zones is – was - my speciality.'

Megan was staring at him quite intently now, her green eyes wide and sparkling in the candlelight. Danny felt bewildered. He wasn't sure whether he enjoyed or hated the contradictory emotions this woman was stirring up in him. 'Anyhow, at the moment I'm writing, or trying to write a book.'

She smiled and once again those killer dimples sprung into life. 'Really? What about?'

'About some of my better known pictures – the story behind them, that kind of thing.'

Megan nodded and looked impressed. 'That's great. So how's it coming along?'

Danny grimaced and looked away. 'Hmm, well I didn't got off to the best of starts, had a bit of trouble with writer's block but it seems to have cleared up now.'

Megan smiled and shook her head. 'Don't talk to me about writer's block. I'm supposed to be writing a book myself. The deadline was six months ago and I still haven't even done the intro.'

'Really? Why not? What's it about?'

Megan looked down at the table. It was impossible to read the expression on her face, Danny wasn't sure if it was embarrassment or shame. 'Oh it's nothing exciting. Just a coaching book about business.'

'Oh. Right. So why are you blocked?'

'I don't know. I suppose my heart isn't really in it.'

Danny watched as she continued to play with the solitary olive upon her plate. Her huge green eyes looked sad now, and had somehow lost their sparkle. Perhaps she wasn't as bad as he'd thought? Perhaps she was human after all? Or perhaps this was all part of the routine? Maybe she was giving him a sob story to hook him in and before he knew it she'd have him standing on the table affirming his love for himself before writing her a big juicy cheque. Danny sighed and picked up his beer.

*

Megan put the olive into her mouth and bit down on the succulent black flesh. A briny burst of liquid shot out on to her tongue and she savoured the taste for a moment before washing it down with a sip of wine. 'The truth is, I'm not sure I really want to help business people become even more cut-throat and ruthless,' she said, looking up at Danny. In the candlelight he looked more handsome than ever, his blonde hair flecked with gold.

Danny looked at her. 'Uh-huh.'

'It's not really what I became a coach to do.'

'Okay. So why did you become a coach?'

Megan gave a small smile. 'To help people feel good about themselves. To help them feel happy.' She took another sip from her wine. It seemed so obvious now looking back. As she'd run from the searching shadows of her mother's depression, it seemed only natural that she'd end up chasing the light of positive thinking. And once

368

she'd caught it, what better way to cling on to it than by making it her life's work. The wine began to work its magic and a warm glow began spreading its tentacles throughout her body. Yet again she felt awash with the feeling that everything was going to be all right.

'And is it as easy as that?'

She looked up at Danny but he was looking away, over at the window where a gentle breeze was toying with the net curtains. 'What do you mean?'

'To make people happy. To make them feel good about themselves? Is it really that easy?'

Megan almost launched into the standard speech about coaching actually being about people making *themselves* feel happy, but something stopped her. She thought back to the countless clients she had seen over the years. All the people who had managed to inject their lives with happiness and hope after a bit of careful nudging and encouragement from her. She thought back to the concertina files full of thank-you letters and cards and printed out emails telling her that she'd changed their lives forever and how the enormity of that fact never failed to blow her mind.

'It isn't always easy, but it is magical.'

'Magical?'

'Yes. Getting people to see that the answer to all of their problems always lies within them. It's magical being able to give them that power.'

Danny stared at her so intently she had to look away. What was it about him that was so familiar? What was it about him that was making her want to tell him everything? That was making her want to grab hold of his big strong hands and look into those clear blue eyes and say, what took you so long? She glanced up at him, her heart pounding and suddenly she was struck by the absolute certainty that this was only the very beginning. That she was going to spend years talking to this man.

Megan looked down at her wine glass. What the hell had got into her? Had Cheddar spiked her drink? This was crazy. She was crazy. She didn't know this man from Adam, why on earth was she thinking such things? But before she could torture herself anymore she heard the living room door open behind her.

'Here we are folks. Our final guest has arrived,' she heard Cheddar announce, and, turning around she saw Natalie standing next to him in the doorway wearing a short black shift dress and thick opaque tights, her hair fanning out around her heart-shaped face like an auburn halo.

Chapter Fifty-Five

"As with the dishes that you serve, the recipe for a good dinner party is to make sure you have the right mix. Invite the perfect blend of people, whose personalities will bring out the best in one another."
Megan Rowe, 'Help Yourself to Happiness.'

'Hello Megan. Hello,' Natalie slid around to the other side of the table and sat down next to the sandy haired man. He was gorgeous. Her mouth curved into a tight little smirk. What a bonus, playing to such an attractive audience, this could be even better than planned. 'Sorry I'm late guys.' She looked at the man and smiled. 'I'm sorry, I don't know your name.'

'Danny,' he replied, smiling back and holding out a hand.

Natalie placed her own tiny hand in his and gave it a squeeze. 'I'm Natalie,' she said. 'Pleased to meet you.'

'You too,' he said.

Natalie smirked and removed her hand. He was going to be a walkover. 'Oh you're American,' she gushed. Danny nodded. 'How exciting.'

'Well, I don't know about that,' he said, looking over at Megan. Megan smiled back at him all gooey eyed.

Natalie frowned. No way! The bitch had only just got back with her husband and here she was making eyes at one of Cheddar's dinner guests. Well she wasn't going to have that.

'How are you feeling, Megan?' she asked, her voice oozing with as much concern as she could squeeze into it.

'Fine thanks,' Megan replied breezily.

God what a phoney bitch. 'Are you sure?' Natalie felt Danny turn to look at her – good.

'Yes, I'm fine,' Megan's voice was a little tighter now, a little more strained.

'I was just thinking what with all that stuff with *your husband*,' Natalie noticed both Megan and Danny palpably flinch, 'And you know, how you were last weekend, in that club.'

'I'm fine,' Megan replied.

'You should have seen her,' Natalie said, turning to Danny. 'Had one too many, didn't you, Megan? The bouncers had to throw her out.'

Danny laughed and looked at Megan. 'Really?'

Natalie noticed Megan's face grow redder in the candlelight, as if it were mirroring the crimson tablecloth.

'I was a little over zealous on the dance floor. I'd just split - '

'I just wish you could have told me,' Natalie interrupted.

'What?' Megan looked at her bewildered.

'When you were leaving. Then I could have come with you and I wouldn't have got hassled by those men.' She turned to Danny, 'I ended up getting a load of grief from these two creeps. It was really scary, especially when they followed me outside. I could have been attacked or anything.'

Megan was visibly squirming now, wringing her hands in her lap. 'I'm really sorry, Natalie. I would have told you if I'd had the chance but it was impossible. The bouncers frog-marched me out.'

Danny laughed and tutted loudly. 'Sounds like you should start drinking in the Prince Albert. You'd fit right in, wouldn't she Cheddar?'

Natalie frowned as Cheddar returned to the room carrying a tray full of steaming bowls.

'What's that?' he asked, placing the tray down on the table and putting small bowls of putrid looking soup in front of each of them.

'Megan here got frog-marched out of a nightclub the other night.'

'Oh yeah, 'Cheddar started to chuckle and Natalie watched in horror as his belly quivered in unison. 'For her crimes on the dance floor. Yes, you ought to come down one night. Ray might even book you as an act.'

Natalie seethed as Megan began to giggle. 'Oh I don't know about that,' she replied, 'Unless he *wants* to get rid of his customers?'

'You can't be any worse than the guy they had down there the other week murdering Elvis.' Danny replied.

Cheddar nodded. 'Oh aye, the Peckham Pelvis. He were dire.'

Again Megan giggled. Natalie picked up her glass of wine and took a huge gulp. How could that bitch be so happy and blasé and flirting with other men when her husband was sitting at home waiting for her? Natalie thought of Gerry and his floppy dark hair and soulful eyes. If he hadn't been such a wanker she might have even felt sorry for him. But he'd made his choice hadn't he? He could have had Natalie but he chose to go crawling back to that scrawny, two-faced bitch.

'I'll just get the bread,' Cheddar said carrying the empty tray back out to the kitchen.

Natalie looked across the table at Megan who was unfolding her napkin into her lap.

'I see you bought that top,' she said.

Megan looked up, her cheeks still flushed. 'Oh. Yes. I went back today and tried it on again and – well I know I might look a bit like Robin Hood but I really like it.'

Danny nodded. 'It looks great,' he said.

Beside him Natalie felt like screaming. What the hell was up with this man? Couldn't he see what Megan was like? Well if not, she would just have to show him.

'Here you go folks, grubs up,' Cheddar called as he returned to the room with a large plate full of bread. Natalie examined it as he put it down in the centre of the table. Each slice was covered in a golden layer of melted cheese flecked green with a sprinkling of herbs. Her stomach lurched. All she'd had to eat all day was half a bowl of soggy cornflakes, but she still wasn't hungry. If anything the rancid smell from the soup steaming away in front of her and the glistening sheen on the cheese was making her feel even more nauseous. She took another swig from her wine as everyone else began to tuck in. As Natalie watched Cheddar stuffing his face opposite her she had to seriously fight the urge to hurl right there and then.

'So, Cheddar. How exactly did you get that name?' she asked.

Cheddar looked up, about to take a bite from the slice of the bread wedged between his lips. Then his eyes darted around the table before looking pointedly at the cheese-covered bread. 'Any guesses?' he asked.

Megan started to laugh. 'Say no more,'

'Apparently I was eating cheese before I'd been brought home from the maternity ward. Or so me mam says. I just love the stuff,' he added before taking a huge bite from the bread and showering the table in crumbs.

Natalie shuddered. 'Oh, so it's nothing to do with the Cheddar Gorge then?' she asked sweetly.

'What? Oh. No,' Cheddar replied, looking down into his soup.

An awkward silence fell upon the table broken only by the clinking of spoons against bowls.

'Man, this is delicious,' Danny finally remarked.

'Mmm,' Megan nodded in agreement.

Cheddar looked up, a stupid grin plastered on his fat face. 'Really?' He turned to look at Natalie. 'Is everything all right with yours, Natalie, you haven't touched it.'

Natalie took a deep breath. This was it, time for the biggie. 'I'm sorry.' She sighed and gazed down into her lap. 'I don't have much of an appetite to be honest. Perhaps I shouldn't have come, but I didn't want to let you down.' She reached into her handbag for a tissue and brought it up to her face. 'I'm so sorry, it's just been a very difficult few weeks.' Around the table she heard the others shuffling awkwardly in their seats and the clink of spoons being put down.

'Are you okay?' Megan asked. Natalie heard her chair moving back.

'Yes, yes, I'm fine,' she said, looking up and gesturing at her to sit back down.

'Here, have a top up,' Cheddar said, refilling her glass.

'Thank-you.' Natalie took the glass and took a large swig. The wine was white and sweet, sickly sweet. Again she felt a wave of nausea slosh through her stomach. 'I've been so stupid,' she said, her voice barely more than a whisper.

'What is it?' Megan asked. 'What's wrong?'

'I've been seeing this guy for the past few weeks and I've just found out that he's been completely using me.'

'But I thought you weren't seeing anyone at the moment,' Megan said.

Natalie bit her top lip to stop from laughing. It was as if she were drunk or on speed or something. Nothing felt real anymore. Everything felt more pronounced, louder, brighter, harsher. And her whole body was pounding. Oh, she was so close now, so close to bringing Mrs Smug Features' world crashing to the ground.

'He told me not to tell anyone. He told me he wanted to keep our love exclusive and that if we told anyone else, it would spoil it.'

Across from her Cheddar started to cough. Natalie looked up and saw his face was twisted into a frown, as if he were constipated. Was he trying not to laugh? Was he finding this funny? Oh just wait till she got started on him.

'So what happened?' Megan asked.

Natalie stared down into her lap in order to create a dramatic pause. What was it Gerry had said to her on the day of the audition? *The real drama in a good play lies in the silences.*

'I fell for the oldest trick in the book,' Natalie replied. Now she wasn't having to act the genuine bitterness seeped from her words. She felt Danny start to shift uncomfortably on his seat next to her. Let him squirm, the bastard, he was probably just like all the rest of them. 'It turns out he's married, and he has a kid.'

'Oh Natalie.' Megan got up from her chair and made her way around the table to crouch down next to her.

Oh Megan, Natalie thought, you stupid, clueless cow. She brought the tissue back up to her face. 'I know. I've been such a fool. And to make it even worse, I fell for the whole casting couch routine too.' She looked up just in time to catch Cheddar shooting Danny a look across the table. The ignorant bastard, oh she couldn't wait to reveal her little titbit about him.

'What do you mean?' Megan asked. Oh, was that a note of concern Natalie detected in her voice? She peered over the top of her tissue. Yes, Megan was definitely looking a little worried now, could it be that something was striking a chord? Natalie pressed the tissue back to her face to keep herself from laughing. Her heart was racing as if she'd just done three lines of coke.

'He's a director. I was auditioning for a part in his new play. That's how we met.' Cue a single, plaintive sob. 'Oh God, I can't believe I fell for his bullshit.'

'I'd better go and check on the chicken,' Cheddar said, starting to collect up the soup bowls.

'Do you need a hand?' Danny asked, pushing his chair back.

'Oh God, I'm so sorry. I'm ruining this for everyone aren't I?' Natalie cried, looking imploringly at the men.

'No, no of course not,' Cheddar replied, sitting back down.

'Not at all,' Danny added, turning to look at her. 'Look, it sounds to me as if you've had a lucky escape.'

'What do you mean?' Natalie asked, looking up at him through lowered lashes.

'Well he's obviously a Grade A asshole. Better to find that out now, before you got too involved.'

Natalie nodded. 'Yes, I suppose it's his wife I should feel really sorry for. She probably hasn't got a clue he's screwing around.'

'That's the spirit,' Cheddar said with a hopeful grin.

'And the thing is, he isn't even that great a director. You should see the size of the theatre he works at, it's like a shoebox. And he's a complete alky.'

'Well what are you crying about? Jeez, you really have had a lucky escape. Let's all have a drink to freedom.' Danny cried, raising his glass. 'Freedom from alcoholic womanisers.'

'With really small theatres,' Cheddar added raising his glass in unison. 'Come on girls, let's drink a toast.'

Megan however, remained rooted to the floor beside Natalie, her face now ashen in the candlelight. 'What theatre does he work at?' she asked in a tight little voice.

Natalie brought her tissue down from her face and smiled at her sweetly. 'Oh I doubt you've heard of it. It's in Shepherd's Bush. The Theatre on the Green.'

chapter Fifty-Six

"A happy marriage should be like two oak trees standing side by side.
Each strong and content in their own space but unseen, underground,
their roots entwining and forming bonds that will last forever."
Megan Rowe, 'Help Yourself to Happiness.'

'The Theatre on the Green.' Natalie's words rang around Megan's head like a taunt as she splashed handfuls of cold water on her face. As soon as Cheddar had gone to check on the dinner she had mumbled her excuses and somehow made it to the bathroom at the end of the draughty hall without completely losing it. Megan pulled herself back upright from bending over the sink and stared blankly at the mildew seamed tiles in front of her. 'The Theatre on the Green.' 'A complete alky.' 'Married with a child.' It had to be Gerry. Natalie had been having an affair with Gerry. The enormity of the revelation left her feeling completely winded. And now she was being bombarded with a flurry of jabbing follow-up questions. How could Gerry have promised her he'd never cheated on her and seem so sincere? How could she have believed him? How could she have fallen for that crap? And all the stuff he had said about them getting back together. How could he have said all that when all along he'd been screwing Natalie? Megan felt a surge of anger rise up inside her as she thought of Natalie and Gerry together. But Natalie had been lied to too. She hadn't known he was married and she hadn't known he was Megan's husband. Megan had made a point of not telling her anything about Gerry.

She sat down on the edge of the bath. Outside at the other end of the hall she could hear the clatter of plates as Cheddar started serving up the dinner. The smell of roasting chicken that had previously smelt so mouth-wateringly delicious was now making her want to throw up, she could barely swallow let alone eat. Why hadn't Natalie told her she was seeing someone when they'd met for coffee? And when she'd broken down in tears in the studio that night why had she told her she was single and just getting over another relationship? It didn't make sense. And all of that stuff about the man – about Gerry - telling her to keep it to herself, to keep their love exclusive. Why would he do that? Megan felt a judder of shock and clasped on to the edge of the sink. Gerry must have known that Natalie worked with her. She must have told him she worked at Loose Talk and he must have carried on seeing her, carried on screwing her, anyway. Perhaps the thought of his mistress working with his wife gave the whole sordid affair extra frisson? She gripped tighter on to the sink. The lying, devious bastard. And to think she had even contemplated getting back together with him. But still something didn't feel right. That night in the bathroom, when she had drunkenly ended up in Nightingale Avenue. He had seemed so genuinely pleased to see her, was he really that good a liar? Could he really be that nasty? Megan thought back to the pair of them standing in the moonlit bathroom and the way a teary eyed Gerry had wrapped the towel around her and the genuine sorrow and tenderness that had seemed to fill the chilled air. And the way he'd practically shouted at her that he wasn't a cheat. What was it he'd said? 'From the day we married till the day you left.' Megan gulped. It had sounded strange at the time, why hadn't he said from the day we married till now, or just I've never ever cheated on you? She thought back to the day she'd left, of telling Gerry and the cool way he'd taken the news. The way he'd gone upstairs and phoned someone – who? Natalie? And then walked out. To go where? To her?

Megan walked over to the small window beside the toilet and flung it open as wide as it could go. She leant her face out and gulped in a breath of air. Although it was now dark outside the air was still warm with the smell of spring. What was she to do? Should she just leave straight away, pretend she wasn't feeling well and go round to Gerry and have it out? But what would be the point in that? They had already split up, without her even knowing this latest development. She couldn't very well dump him all over again. And that was it – the marriage was over. All the hurt and disappointment she was feeling was just a knee-jerk reaction that belonged to her old life. She had already moved on. Megan felt the tiniest prickle of relief as she realised that the only truth she really needed to know was that she no longer loved Gerry. What did it really matter if he'd been having an affair with Natalie? In fact all this did was prove that she had been absolutely right to leave him. All it did was bolster her sense of freedom.

Then she thought of Natalie, and what she had said about falling for the old casting couch routine. What had Gerry cast her in? It must have been his latest play. She thought back to the Saturday night when he hadn't come home from the auditions, the night that had signalled the death knoll for their marriage. Was that when they had met? Had he been with Natalie that night? And if so, why hadn't Natalie told her about the part? Megan shut the window, put the lid down on the toilet and sat down. When they had gone for a coffee in Hammersmith and Natalie had told her all about her acting, why hadn't she told Megan that she had auditioned for a part in Gerry's play? She didn't know Megan was married to Gerry, did she? Megan thought of the way Natalie had behaved when she had first arrived at Cheddar's that night. The way she had seemed intent on embarrassing her in front of Danny and then making that dig about Cheddar's name. There was something so clinical about her at times, despite all the teary outbursts and drama. Megan stood up and walked back over to the sink. She thought back to the way Natalie had looked down at her as she had delivered her killer line about the Theatre on the Green, her overly made-up pale blue eyes as cold as ice. And completely tear free. Megan shook her head. Natalie had been sobbing into her tissue for the previous couple of minutes yet when she had looked at Megan her eyes had been completely dry. Did Natalie know that Gerry was her husband? Megan shivered. No, that was ridiculous.

Just then there was a knock on the door.

'You okay in there?' she heard Danny whisper through the door. Smoothing her hair down she took a deep breath and opened the door. Danny stood in the doorway, a boyish grin on his face. 'I had to get away for a second. It was getting kind of heavy back there.'

Megan nodded. 'I know. I was finding it a little uncomfortable too.'

'Oh yeah?'

'Yeah. The guy she was talking about, well it reminded me of someone – someone from my past.' Megan felt a surge of relief at saying the words out loud and managed a weak smile.

'Really?'

Megan nodded. 'Yes. My ex-husband.'

'Your *ex*-husband?'

'Yes. Well, soon to be.'

They smiled at each other and once again Megan was overcome by the strangest sensation of longing. Part of her wanted to drag him into the bathroom with her and lock the door, sit him down on the floor and ask him to tell her everything. Everything about himself and where he had been and what he had been doing and why he had taken so damned long to find her. She shook her head and sighed, what on earth was happening to her tonight?

Danny stepped a little further into the bathroom and once again Megan's heart began to race.

'You know I -'

'Okey-dokey, grub's up!' Cheddar hollered from the other end of the hall, cutting Danny off. He looked at Megan and smiled.

'Oh well, I guess we'd better get back.'

Megan nodded, but inside her heart sank. How the hell was she going to get through this dinner, knowing what she now knew? But she couldn't leave, not when Cheddar had gone to so much trouble and – she looked at Danny – and she had just met him.

*

Cheddar came through to the living room carrying an earthenware bowl containing a bed of shredded red cabbage cooked in red wine vinegar and dotted with cranberries. As he placed it down amongst all of the other steaming dishes he looked anxiously around the table. Natalie seemed to have composed herself and was sipping away thoughtfully on her wine and both Danny and Megan were back in their seats.

'Okay everyone, tuck in,' Cheddar said, sitting down next to Megan. 'There's a mixture of sweet and normal roast potatoes and I did sage and onion and sausage meat stuffing. That one's the sausagemeat,' he said pointing to a blue and white striped dish next to the potatoes.

One by one everyone started helping themselves to the various dishes until their plates became laden with colourful mounds, apart from Natalie who just added a token piece of potato and a Yorkshire pudding to her solitary slice of chicken.

'Carrots?' Cheddar asked, offering her a bowl.

Natalie shook her head. 'I'm sorry. I don't have much of an appetite. It must be all the stress.' She gave a forced little laugh. 'Relationships eh? Who'd have them?'

Danny grunted and gave a nod in acknowledgement before picking up the large jug of gravy.

'Can I interest any of you ladies in some gravy,' he asked, looking straight over at Megan.

Megan nodded and took the jug. As Cheddar watched her pour out the thick brown liquid he noticed that she'd hardly taken any food either. Chuffin' 'ell, it was like catering for the Anorexics Anonymous Christmas dinner. He'd be living off the leftovers forever. As he piled an extra helping of roast potatoes on to his plate he couldn't help wondering what kind of appetite Bambi had. He hoped she wasn't one of those lasses who just picked at her food like a sparrow. But then what was he even wondering for? It wasn't as if he'd ever get to find out. He thought of the email he'd sent earlier and smarted. What on earth had he been thinking? He'd been way too presumptuous. After all she'd been through lately the last thing she needed was some strange bloke hassling her. He'd probably never hear from her again now.

'You're single, aren't you Cheddar?' Natalie trilled as if reading his mind. Christ, there was something dead spooky about that girl.

He looked up at her and nodded. 'Fraid so.'

'Hmm.'

Cheddar glanced back at her. What did she mean by that?

'The worst thing about being single is the frustration, you know, sexually, don't you think?'

Danny spluttered and took a hasty sip of beer.

Cheddar looked at him and then back to Natalie, who was still staring at him intently. Beside him he felt Megan shift in her chair.

'How long have you been single for, Cheddar?' Natalie asked, her voice sickly sweet.

Cheddar felt his cheeks start to flush and he reached out for his glass of wine. 'Oh I don't know, about a year or so.' He took a much needed drink.

'Wow! A year. How do you do it?'

'Do what?'

'You know, keep from getting frustrated?'

Was she being serious? Cheddar looked at Natalie who was continuing to stare at him. What did she want him to do? Announce to the table that he had a wank every morning over *Big Jugs Monthly?*

'Erm, I - '

'It's all right,' Natalie continued. 'I know all about the call girl.' She put down her fork and looked at him earnestly. 'I'm so sorry, I accidentally picked up the studio phone line at work one night and I heard you booking her. But I think it's really admirable. Don't you?' And she turned to look at Megan and Danny. 'I mean, he's a single guy, he's obviously frustrated, if he wants to go with a hooker, well, that's his prerogative isn't it?'

Cheddar felt all the blood drain from his face as quickly as it had rushed into it. What was she doing? Why was she saying all this? How had she heard him? Oh God, she had heard him. He thought back to his desperate fumbling phone call and how it had taken him about five minutes just to give his name. He had been so desperate that night – not for sex, just for female company, he had seriously thought it was the only way he could have got to spend some time with a woman. But he couldn't explain that now, to his surely horrified guests. He didn't dare look up.

'I mean, someone has to keep those poor girls in business, and anyway, better that you satisfy your urges with them than, well, you know,' she continued.

After a silence that seemed to last an eternity, Cheddar somehow managed to get to his feet. 'I've just got to check on the desert,' he mumbled, before stumbling from the room.

*

Danny sat back in his chair and shook his head in disbelief. Man, these English dinner parties sure were intense. As he watched Cheddar make his clumsy exit from the room Danny thought back to the women who used to hang around outside The Palestine Hotel in Baghdad in their high heels and tight fitting business attire. At first he'd thought they were disgruntled ex-employees of the hotel, but then Mike had told him they were hookers. After that he'd spotted them several times disappearing off into bombed out buildings with off duty American soldiers. Although Danny had never been tempted to go with a prostitute on any of his travels, he could certainly understand the frustration and loneliness that could lead to it.

'I'm just going to give Cheddar a hand,' he said getting up from the table. Megan nodded at him, her green eyes solemn. Danny sighed. Despite all of his initial misgivings he'd been kind of hoping to get to know her a little better this evening. Things, however, weren't exactly going as he'd anticipated.

'Hey, how you doing?' Danny asked walking into the kitchen. Cheddar was staring out of the window with his back to him and didn't reply.

'Cheddar? You okay?' Danny walked up behind him and placed a hand on his back.

'I was lonely,' Cheddar eventually replied, his voice just a whisper. 'I just wanted to be with someone, you know?' he turned and looked at Danny, his eyes filled with concern. 'It was only a couple of times and it was crap, but I thought I'd never -'

'Hey. It's okay,' Danny replied, patting him between the shoulders.

'No it's not,' Cheddar replied, almost shouting now. 'I should never have done it. I feel terrible. I felt terrible the minute it was over. Oh God, what will Megan think? She'll think I'm a pervert. She won't want to work with me anymore.'

'That's not true,' Danny replied, 'She isn't like that.' He stopped dead – how did he know what Megan was like and what she'd think? Until this evening he'd had her down as a complete charlatan, but he hadn't met her then. He thought of her huge green eyes and her mesmerising voice and the way she lit up the room when she laughed. There was a softness about her too, a gentleness – he just knew she wouldn't condemn Cheddar for what he'd done, he couldn't really see her condemning anyone.

Cheddar shook his head. 'Of course she will, any lass would.' He looked despairingly about the kitchen at all the dirty pots and pans lining the counter and stacked up in the sink. 'This was all a big mistake. This whole dinner party thing. I should never have done it. It's been a disaster.'

Danny shook his head. 'That is absolute crap, man. It's a great night. The food is awesome and the flat looks fantastic. Look, I don't want to bad mouth one of your friends but I think Natalie was way out of line in there. She shouldn't have said what she did, especially not in front of all of us. I don't know what she's playing at but I think the best thing you can do is get back in there and pretend like it never happened.'

Cheddar looked at him and sighed, before walking over to the fridge and taking out a can of beer. 'But that's just it, Danny, it did happen.'

*

Natalie twisted her napkin into a tight little roll, her heart pounding from a mixture of adrenalin and excitement. It was all going exactly as she'd planned, in fact it couldn't be going any better. She'd burst Mrs Smug's bubble and completely humiliated the northern lard arse all in one evening. She held on to the napkin and took a deep breath before continuing.

'Oh I hope he's okay,' she said looking over at Megan, 'I didn't mean to embarrass him. To be honest I thought he was the kind of guy who'd be quite upfront about that kind of thing. Still, it is pretty gross isn't it? Sleeping with a prostitute. I mean, you don't know what you might catch.'

Megan sat motionless just staring at her for a moment. Probably still in shock, pathetic cow. 'No, no you really don't, do you?' Then she leant forward and picked up the bottle of wine. Natalie noticed that her hands were shaking. Ha, she couldn't fool her with her super cool exterior. Inside she must be in absolute pieces over her revelation about Gerry. It was a shame she hadn't actually broken down yet – and run from the place crying and screaming like she had in Natalie's dreams. But oh to be a fly on the wall when she went home to Gerry tonight.

'I mean, we have to work with him. I thought you ought to know what he was like,' Natalie said, leaning across the table conspiratorially, 'What with the risk of infection and all that.'

Megan filled her glass and offered the bottle to Natalie. 'Oh God I know exactly what you mean,' she replied.

Natalie nodded for Megan to top up her glass. 'Really? Oh I'm so glad you understand. I didn't mean to be a bitch but still - '

'No you absolutely did the right thing.' Megan leant forward too. 'To be honest, I've had more than enough to worry about on that front.'

'What do you mean?' Natalie sat back in her chair and took a sip from her wine.

'Well,' Megan turned round to check behind her and dropped her voice to a whisper. 'My ex-husband slept around an awful lot.'

Natalie nearly choked on her drink. 'Your *ex-* husband, but I thought - '

'What?' Megan was staring at her a little too intently for Natalie's liking.

'Oh nothing.' What the hell was Megan playing at, calling him her ex? Natalie frowned. Of course, it was because she had her eye on that American, Danny. Bloody hell, what a tart. She pulled her face into a concerned expression. 'Oh God, poor you.'

Megan nodded and took a swig from her wine. 'Yes – and it wasn't just with women either.'

'What?' Natalie put her glass down on the table.

'He liked to sleep around with men too, used to spend half the weekend in gay bars. That's probably where he caught it.'

'Caught what?'

Megan smiled at her. 'Oh it's okay. I stopped sleeping with him years ago and I was tested as a precaution when he found out he had it, but still, it is worrying isn't it. I'm just so glad I'm not with him any more'

'Caught what? What did he catch?' It took all of Natalie's will power not to scream at her.

'That's the trouble with sleeping with people you don't really know, isn't it? You could end up with all kinds of nasty side effects.' Megan's voice was colder than Natalie had ever heard it before and she leaned even further towards her. 'If only you'd told me sooner, I might have been able to warn you,' she continued, staring at her menacingly.

Natalie sat back in her chair. She wasn't going to be intimidated by this two-faced slut. How dare she try and turn the tables on her.

'What do you mean? Warn me about what?' she asked, for some annoying reason her voice rising to a squeak.

'About the kind of person you were sleeping with,' Megan replied.

'But I – I really don't know what you're talking about. What are you trying to say?'

'Oh I'm not *trying* to say anything.'

'But I don't understand.' Bollocks, this was all going wrong. Her revelation was meant to have left Megan devastated, not on the war path.

'Oh I think you understand perfectly,' Megan said, getting to her feet.

Natalie watched her, suddenly panic stricken.

'You know, don't you?' Megan asked, slowly walking around the table towards her. 'You've known all along.'

'Known what?'

'Who I'm married to.'

'No I - of course I don't, how could I? Gerry never told me -'

Megan stared at her. 'Gerry never told you what?'

Natalie looked down into her lap. 'That he was married to you,' she muttered. What did it matter anyway? She'd done what she'd come to do. But what did Megan mean about catching something? What did Gerry have? Was he really bisexual? She thought of his long floppy hair and the way he called everyone darling, men and women alike. She'd put it down to artistic temperament not being a bloody poof! And what about the times he hadn't been able to get it up? She'd put that down to the drink, not the fact that she didn't have a penis. Out of the corner of her eye Natalie saw a rush of movement from Megan's direction and felt something warm and slimy hit her head and begin trickling down her face.

'What the hell?' she screamed, leaping to her feet. Megan was standing directly in front of her, brandishing the now empty jug of gravy.

'You poisonous little bitch,' Megan hissed.

'What? But I -'

'You knew all along didn't you? That day when we went for coffee and when we went clubbing. You knew you were sleeping with my husband.'

Natalie couldn't help smirking. Finally, the naïve cow had worked it out. 'So,' she spat back at her.

'So?' Megan put the jug back on the table and shook her head. 'So?'

'Right, how are you ladies getting on in here?'

Natalie and Megan both turned to see Danny standing in the doorway. 'Jeez!' he exclaimed upon seeing Natalie.

'Natalie wanted some gravy,' Megan explained, picking up her glass of wine from the table and taking a large gulp.

'Yes, er, so I see,' Danny replied, scratching his head.

Natalie picked up her rolled up napkin and began dabbing at her face. The gravy was thick and gooey and reeked of onions. She fought the urge to gag.

'Well, I really would love to stay for dessert but I have a more pressing engagement,' she hissed between gritted teeth. Stay cool, stay cool, she urged herself as she began making her way around the table. To her shock Megan moved in front of her to block her way.

'How could you do - ' she began but then stopped mid sentence and looked away.

'Can I go now, please?' Natalie asked in a deliberately sarcastic voice.

'Oh yes, absolutely,' Megan replied, standing aside.

Natalie took a deep breath and headed for the door, but just as she got there Cheddar arrived.

'Oh,' was all he could say, staring at her gravy-splattered hair.

'I'm leaving,' Natalie muttered.

'Oh – right,' Cheddar replied, moving to one side to let her past.

'And don't even think about showing your face at Loose Talk tomorrow,' Megan shouted behind her.

Natalie froze in the doorway. As if she wanted to go back to answering phones for that pathetic bitch and her pervert producer. Bile burnt at the back of her throat. 'Oh don't worry, I won't,' she spat back, before racing from the flat.

Outside the air felt warm and muggy as Natalie tripped and stumbled her way down the steps from Cheddar's flat and along the passageway behind the shops. In her dreams it hadn't been like this, it hadn't been her fleeing the flat - and with gravy all over her too. Natalie stopped and leant against the wall. Great juddering tremors began coursing through her body and she went to be sick but nothing came, just a mouthful of foamy, metallic tasting bile. What had gone wrong? Why had she ended up the one being ridiculed? How dare that cow throw the gravy over her? Slowly she began making her way back around to the concourse in front of The Apollo. To her right the lights of Hammersmith twinkled away in the darkness and overhead a stream of traffic roared its way into town. And there in front of her loomed Neptune Mansions. As Natalie stood there shivering in the shadow of the underpass she had never felt so alone. She thought of her kitchen nestled beneath the green turret. She thought of her picture with its accusing eyes and the slashes of red everywhere she looked and she began to sob. She couldn't bear the thought of going back to that flat, anger and hopelessness ricocheting like squash balls around the paint splattered walls as she sat all alone. Natalie wiped her face and took a deep breath. The air was like a thick soup of stale cigarette smoke and petrol fumes. Once again she fought the urge to gag. What was wrong with her tonight? Why was everything making her feel so sick? Natalie caught her breath. Surely it couldn't be? Her mind started doing fevered calculations. Was she late? She was late. Surely not? But she was. Her period was about a week late. She gulped and thought back to the last time she had got that horrible metallic taste, the last time just the mere smell of cigarettes or food had made her want to hurl. A kaleidoscope of memories tumbled before her eyes. Julie-Ann Rogers making coffee in the sixth form common room and Natalie having to race to the toilets. Mr Keller waiting for her in the carpark behind Waitrose as she did the test in the customer toilets, her hand trembling so violently it got covered in warm pee. That awful day when Mr Keller had taken her into Oxford and told her that he couldn't leave his wife and how the smell of the candy floss drifting on the hot air from the nearby fair had seemed to have lodged itself into her nostrils, sticky and sickly sweet. Natalie clasped her hands together. Could she be – again? She bit her lip as hot tears the size of pearls began rolling out on to her cheeks. She hardly dared think it, but if it were true, if she were – pregnant. Well how different everything would be. She wouldn't be all alone for a start. Natalie's heart pounded faster and faster as she slowly placed a hand on her stomach and felt a tug of longing so strong it nearly caused her legs to buckle from under her. She was five days late. Five whole days. In the morning she would go to the chemist and get a test. And if it came back positive? She thought of Megan and Gerry and her mum and Mr Keller and Danny and Cheddar and the men from the club. Smug, arrogant, tossers the lot of them. Well this time it would be different. This time she was going to do things her way and everyone else could go to hell. Skin prickling with a mixture of fear and excitement, Natalie stepped out from the shadow of the underpass and began making her way home.

chapter Fifty-seven

"Buddhists have a saying, 'when the student is ready the teacher shall appear. It is only when you are truly ready to learn that you will be given the tools to do so. It is only when you are ready for love that you will meet your soul mate."
Megan Rowe, 'When the Student is Ready…'
sequel to 'Help Yourself to Happiness.'

'I'm so sorry, Cheddar, I don't know what came over me, she just - ' Megan looked across at Cheddar standing in the doorway, his face etched with confusion. How on earth was she going to explain this one? On top of the nightclub debacle and the bucking bronco, he was going to think her a complete lunatic for sure. And she daren't even look at Danny. 'She just really pissed me off,' Megan offered lamely before going to pick her handbag up off the floor. 'Perhaps I ought to go.'

'No!' Cheddar exclaimed. 'No – not unless you really want to. But I'd like you to stay.'

Megan looked at him and smiled cautiously. 'Are you sure?'

'Of course I'm sure,' Cheddar came into the room and stood next to Megan by the table. Then he looked down at the floor. 'Listen, about what she said, about the you know – the prostitute?'

Megan nodded.

'It was a mistake. I was feeling lonely and I just wanted someone to be with. It was only once – well twice but I only, you know did it once and it were a total disaster. I don't know what I was thinking, I was just lonely and I missed being with a woman. You know, being with a woman not you know, *being* with a woman. Although I did end up *being* with her the second time, but I wish I hadn't and I'd never ever - '

Megan reached out and touched Cheddar on the arm. 'It's okay. You really don't have to explain. It's nothing to do with me, or anyone else, is it?' And she glanced at Danny who was seated behind her at the table. He nodded and smiled.

'That's exactly what I said,' Danny stood up and reached across the table to Cheddar. 'Forget about it, man. It really doesn't matter. She was bang out of line saying what she did. Sit down and have a drink.'

Cheddar and Megan both sat back down at the table. Megan looked at the dinner in front of her. Like the rest of the evening it seemed to have lost it's sheen, the potatoes and other vegetables seemed soggy and limp and the gravy had congealed into a thick brown skin. 'Anyone for gravy?' she offered lamely. Danny gave a throaty chuckle.

'I don't think so,' he replied, 'Not if you're serving.'

'What the heck happened?' Cheddar asked, toying with one of his roast potatoes.

'I – er - ' Megan paused. What should she say? Somehow she didn't think they'd believe her if she said she slipped whilst pouring the gravy on to Natalie's plate. She sighed. 'Well, you know the man she was talking about. The married man, with the child?'

'The one with the small theatre?' Cheddar added.

Megan nodded. 'Well, it turns out he was my husband.'

'What?' Both Cheddar and Danny uttered in unison.

Megan swallowed hard.

'Your *ex*-husband – right?' Danny asked.

Megan looked at him and gave a watery smile. 'Yes, we'd already split up. So really it shouldn't matter, but still.'

'So hold on a minute, let me get this straight,' Cheddar stared at Megan. 'Natalie has been having it away with your old man?'

'*Ex* – old man,' Megan corrected, trying not to look at Danny.

'And you just found out tonight?' Cheddar went on.

'Yes, when she told us where he worked.'

'Shit! But surely she can't have known that he was your - ' Cheddar shook his head. 'I mean, all that stuff she said about him, with you sat there. She wouldn't have - ' he broke off mid sentence looking bewildered.

'I didn't think so at first, but there was something so weird about her tonight. And there were certain things she'd said to me in the past. It just didn't all add up. I think she deliberately wanted to let me know.'

Cheddar nodded and sighed. 'Chuffin' 'ell, it seems like madam had quite an agenda going on tonight.'

Danny nodded. 'I told you she was up to something.' He looked at Megan, his face full of concern. 'Are you all right? It must have been one hell of a shock.'

Megan reached out for her glass of wine but realised her hands were trembling. She put them back in her lap. 'Yes. Yes I'm fine.' But she wasn't fine at all. All of the tension of the evening seemed to have reached boiling point and was simmering over into her eyes in big hot tears. 'It's just been a bit weird that's all. I thought she was my friend. I thought he - ' she searched in her handbag for a tissue. 'Oh what does it matter anyway? I'd already left him.' She pressed the tissue to her eyes and wiped away her tears.

'Oh, here, don't get upset,' Megan felt Cheddar's arm around her shoulders, warm and soft.

'Yeah, it sounds as if they deserve each other. She's quite a piece of work,' Danny said.

'Yeah, and he's only got a small theatre.' Cheddar added.

They all laughed.

'How about I make us all an Irish coffee?' Cheddar asked, getting to his feet.

'Sure,' Danny replied.

Megan nodded and smiled. 'That would be lovely.'

Megan and Danny watched as Cheddar left the room.

'So,' Danny said, looking back at her, 'You okay, coach?'

Megan nodded. 'What a night,' she said with a sigh.

'Uh-huh.'

'It's just so confusing. Finding out about her and my husband, *ex*-husband, I don't know, it feels as if my life is one of those snow storm toys and she's come and shaken it all up so I can't see anything clearly any more. I mean I work with her, I went out with her and all the time she was – and he said that -'

Danny looked at her and smiled. 'Someone once told me that the answer to all your problems always lies within yourself.'

Megan looked at him and again was hit with the most overwhelming sense of déjà vu. Had she really only just met him? She must have known him in a previous life or something, it really was uncanny. 'Is that so?' she said with a smile. Then she thought about how she'd felt when she'd got ready to come out that night. About looking into her Grandma's mirror and feeling like a set of Russian dolls. Feeling solid and complete. If she thought back to that, focused on the woman she really was, free from all the pain and fear of the past, everything did seem clearer again. She looked at Danny and really smiled. 'Thank you,' she whispered, bowing her head.

'No problem,' he replied.

Just then the phone started ringing, causing them to both jump.

Cheddar came clattering back in through the door. 'Sorry about this folks,' he said with an apologetic smile.

Megan looked at him and felt warm inside. At least she had one decent new friend. She glanced across at Danny, hopefully even two?

'Hello,' Cheddar said into the receiver. 'Yes, speaking.'

Megan watched as his face flushed as crimson as the stripes on his apron.

'Laura? Chuffin' - I mean – how are you?'

Across the table from her, Danny started to grin. 'I think it's the chick he's sweet on,' he whispered conspiratorially to Megan.

'It's so nice to hear your voice,' Cheddar continued, 'I wasn't sure if you'd call to be honest.'

'Do you think we ought to give him a bit of privacy?' Megan whispered across to Danny.

Danny nodded. 'Good thinking. Let's go get some fresh air.'

They both stood up and began creeping towards the door.

'Just popping out for a sec,' Danny whispered to Cheddar. Cheddar grinned and gave them both the thumbs up sign before turning back to the phone.

'I'm so glad it made a difference. Your email really made my day,' he said into the receiver, grinning from ear to ear.

Megan stared out from Cheddar's balcony into the inky darkness. There across the way loomed the first block of flats in the Queen Caroline Estate, random windows lit up like the lights on a switchboard. And beyond that lay the Loose Talk studios and beyond that the river. She took a deep breath and sighed. What a night. Danny placed his hands beside hers on the wrought iron railings.

'I only live over there,' he said, nodding to the block of flats on the other side of the road.

'Really?' Megan turned and looked up at him. Even in the dark his eyes seemed to twinkle.

'Uh-huh. Well for now, anyways.'

They fell silent and listened to the sound of the cars humming by in the distance and the very faintest of siren wails.

Megan raised her head and looked up into the sky. As always it was tinged with the orangey glow from the city beneath but she could still make out some stars, tiny silver pinpricks in the blanket of amber black. As she stood there gazing out into the night she wanted so badly to tell Danny how she was feeling; to tell him that she had the *strangest* feeling, but then he would think her insane for sure.

Megan thought back to the nights when she was a child and she would lie in her cold scratchy bed and will her father to come back home. And the nights she would spend hatching plans to make her mother smile. And the nights she would spend watching the teenagers on the estate entwined behind the bins and wishing it was her caught up in that passionate embrace. And the nights she'd spent wondering where Gerry was and longing for him to come home and tell her he'd changed for good. She shook her head and sighed. For as long as she could remember it seemed she had lived her life in some kind of reflex to the actions of others – her father's absence, her mother's depression, Gerry's philandering – but what about her? What about what she really wanted? She thought about the Buddhist saying *show me the face you wore before you were born*. If none of those things had happened – if her mother hadn't been depressed, if her father hadn't left, if Gerry hadn't drunk – what kind of person would she be today? If she had just been free from everyone else's baggage. She thought back to Danny's advice, her own advice, about the answer always coming from within, and smiled. That person would still be in there. That essence of her, the person she was before she was born, the littlest, most flawless Russian doll of all. She just had to dig deep, that was all.

Megan glanced up at Danny. 'I was thinking,' she said, heart pounding. 'After this is over - the dinner party I mean.' She took a deep breath and somewhere in the distance a car beeped. 'Well, I'd really like to see you again.'

There – she'd done it. Megan gripped on tighter to the railings. She suddenly felt so light she felt certain if she let go she'd go spinning out into the darkness. She saw Danny's hand slowly moving closer to hers along the railing until they were just touching. Pulses of electricity began charging around Megan's body like a million shooting stars.

'I'd like that too,' he replied in the voice that seemed so uncannily familiar. The voice that made her certain she'd finally found the right path; the path that led to true happiness.

The Beginning.

Behind the Scenes of 'Finding the Plot.'

Journalist Daisy Thornton talks to Siobhan Curham.

What was the inspiration behind 'Finding the Plot?'

While I was training to become a life coach I was fascinated to discover that we all have the power to change our lives for the better simply by changing the way we think about the world. I have also always been really interested in the ways in which people's lives can cross in the most seemingly random ways and yet have such a powerful effect. Originally the book was just going to be the story of Megan and Danny and how his random phone call to her show at the start goes on to trigger a seismic change in both of them.

How did the characters of Cheddar and Natalie evolve then?

They were always going to feature but as so often happens when I write a novel, the secondary characters seemed to take on a life of their own and they were such fun to write. It was also good to explore through them other takes on self-help and the pursuit of happiness. Hopefully it has made the novel richer for the contrast and I know Cheddar goes down extremely well when I read his chapters at events – I haven't dared read any of Natalie's yet!

Which of the characters can you most relate to?

All of them to a greater or lesser degree. On paper I guess it would appear to be Megan – a fellow life coach and author and mother of a budding cricketer. But I am not and never have been married to an alcoholic theatre director, with a 'small theatre!' I think with the character of Megan I was testing out some of the theories I had been learning on my life coaching course and asking the question, is it really possible to help yourself to happiness, as Megan so firmly believes? It was also a very good 'what if' as the starting point for the novel – what if you had a renowned expert on happiness who was actually as miserable as sin? A lot of my own feelings and doubts and fears came out when I was writing Cheddar – and my love of food and wine! Natalie was a great channel for thinking evil thoughts and being really, really angry! And Danny was very loosely based on someone I once met who had given up on love and hope following a personal tragedy. I guess I wanted to write him a happy ending.

How much of 'Finding the Plot' was plotted out – did you know the characters' outcomes before you started writing?

No. I had a rough idea, but once I started writing, the characters really took over. I had planned for Danny and Megan talking once at the beginning of the book and then not meeting up until the end, when they were ready to meet. But apart from that I had no idea how it was all going to end up. Even when I started writing the dinner party scene and I finally brought the four of them all together I had no idea what would happen.

What do you mean by Danny and Megan being 'ready' to meet?

It's from the saying, 'when the student is ready, the teacher shall appear.' I am fascinated by the way some people only come into our lives when we are ready for whatever it is they have to teach us.

What do you think Megan and Danny will be able to teach each other?

How to love unconditionally I hope. And maybe Megan could teach him to stop wearing his University of Texas sweatshirt!

Why did you make Danny an American?

I love America and all things American and writing him brought back a lot of happy family and holiday memories. Also right from the start I saw him as being American and again I hope it made for an interesting contrast.

Why did you decide to use quotes from Megan's book 'Help Yourself to Happiness' at the start of every chapter?

To ram home the irony of her situation. Here is a woman who has worked so hard at achieving the 'perfect' life and yet so much of it is a sham. At the start of her chapters in particular I would make sure to write a really ironic quote, like one about the sanctity of marriage right before the disclosure of her husband's infidelity.

Are the conclusions about life that the characters reach based upon your own personal conclusions?

This book did end up containing a lot of my own theories about life but I always intended for it to make people stop and think about their own lives too, as well as hopefully give them an entertaining read. I hope that by reading about Cheddar and Megan and Danny people are inspired to take control of their lives and destinies and become authors of their own life stories.

Why did you choose to self-publish this novel?

As a literature events manager I get to meet a lot of other authors, editors and agents and there is such a sense of disillusionment about the state of the publishing industry at the moment. It seems that unless you fall neatly into a pigeon-hole or are a 'celebrity' the publishers are no longer interested. Given that one of the strongest themes of *Finding the Plot* is the importance of living a life that is true to yourself, self publishing seemed the natural choice. At least this way I have full creative control and won't be wrongly marketed as I have in the past. I'm really looking forward to the challenge. I want to prove to myself and other writers that you don't have to have a big publisher behind you; that's why I set myself the target of beating the sales figures I achieved last time with Hodder & Stoughton. Maybe I'm crazy, but it's really exciting!

What advice would you give to other aspiring writers?

Don't give up. Accept that rejection is part and parcel of being a writer. Don't try to edit your work as you write. Let the creative side of your brain have full control first – you can tidy it up later. Write about the ideas or characters you feel most passionately about and write from the heart.

Printed in the United Kingdom
by Lightning Source UK Ltd.
123303UK00001B/49-135/A